TOWER OF RUIN

By William A. Kooiker

Cover Art by Arco den Haan
To see more Artwork by Arco, visit **http://www.visualmatter.net**

This is a work of fiction. The names, characters, places, and incidents are fictitious or are used fictitiously. Any resemblance to any person or persons living or dead is purely coincidental.

Advanced Praise for *Tower of Ruin*

"Kooiker's *Tower of Ruin* engages you from the very first few pages. Full of mystery and suspense, the book creates a rich world populated with fantastic characters that readers will eagerly immerse themselves within. Fans will appreciate the plot elements brought to life in vivid, living color."

— Luke Hodgson, author of *The Gates of Omin*

"This tale hooks you early with a captivating mystery and engaging characters. It gets better and better as the story continues. Action and intrigue, *Tower of Ruin* delivers plenty of both!"

— Flames Rising

"Mr. Kooiker's first foray into the world of fiction most decidedly won't be his last. Tower of Ruin is a finely woven tale of fantasy made all too believable by his compelling characters. A fast moving and entertaining read for all. One turns the last page with disappointment there is no more — yet."

— Eastern Shore Post

"*Tower of Ruin* is a worthy addition to the world of fantasy fiction. Kooiker's characters jump off the page, swords at the ready! An adventure sure to please. Read it! William A. Kooiker will have you hooked!"

— Shawn P. Cormier, author of *Nomadin*

"The character development twists are nice and juicy . . . I'd recommend Kooiker."

— GameWyrd

For Heather and Aubrie. I love you both with everything I am.

Acknowledgements

My heartfelt thanks go to Mom, Dad, Carol and Pip for the time they gave to me and their endless support. Also, a special thanks to Steven Manchester for his guidance and assistance and to Ed Cha for a great many things. Additional gratitude goes to Robert Denson and anyone else who helped make this book a reality.

The Lands of Northeastern Calas

PROLOGUE

From the Journal of the Wiseman Welnor,
– advisor to Baron Vernest of Oester

Year 1153 of the Second Age

Damn you, Welnor! My affairs are my own!

Those were Baron Vernest's last words to me before throwing the door in my face. Alas, for the past several weeks our conversations have ended in just such a manner. Yet, never before have I seen him so angry as tonight. His words were uncaring, distant, his eyes like daggers piercing my heart.

How can it be? There was a time Baron Vernest was my closest friend – a friend to all who knew him. I recall the nights he would entertain us under the night stars, philosophizing life or exaggerating heroic deeds of the past. Vernest was once a great storyteller and could hold an entire room captive with tales of quest and adventure. In those days, I would have sworn he was invincible. In full armor, his massive greatsword sheathed at his waist, he would lumber through the halls of the tower jovially greeting all who crossed his path. I still reminisce fondly over such memories.

Sadly, those days are no more.

This once great man is now avoided like a plague. He is young, only in his thirties, but a sudden callous demeanor taints his handsome features. He shows no interest in casual conversation and has become brutally impatient. Those who anger him find his temper severe and unyielding. Because I have known him for half his life, this newfound transformation over the past year seems utterly implausible. What could corrupt him so quickly? I have my suspicions, but he spurns my every attempt to discuss the matter.

Along with the changing of his disposition, the lord of this tower, Baron Vernest, has been performing strange tasks. He has been delving through my books most curiously, voraciously reading through scriptures that I myself have never touched. I would never dabble with the dark invocations that Vernest has been seen needling through. What mysteries does he seek in that basement laboratory? I know not what has prompted his interest in these scriptures, or what experiments he performs, but I fear it has something to do with the recent changes of his character. Why have I not stopped this earlier? Now, I fear I have allowed it to carry far too long.

What pains me worse is the scorn he holds for his wife, Baroness Anisa. Poor Anisa! Of all people, she has weathered the baron's abrupt change most of all. He is especially cold to her, giving her attention only when he must. My heart yearns for her. It is obvious what Vernest once saw in the mistress. Beautiful enough to make the gods themselves jealous, her long black hair falls down a face so pure and enchanting that one would think they were staring at a painting. I have always felt uncomfortable in her presence, as her angelic beauty makes me uneasy of my own ungainly appearance. Yet, in her caring nature, when she speaks to me it is as if I am the only one who exists.

Vernest's callousness has even extended to his own six-year old daughter, Clorisa. Sometimes, I wonder if I am the only father figure the child has left. The baron has not given her a moment of his time in weeks, and I cannot overlook a girl who is such a strong reflection of her mother that it grieves me. Never should a child as sweet as Clorisa be ignored by her own father.

To add to our troubles, one of our scouts has reported that the Hellar barbarians have blanketed the northeastern shore, working their way inland and overtaking Aeslington and Tergen. They now persist south, heading in our direction, slaughtering those who oppose them. Mordan, the captain of the tower guard, has already made preparations for a defense. Mordan is a good soldier, but his men are too few in number to repel a full-scale attack.

It is fortunate that I have convinced Baron Vernest to request assistance from the Crown. With the king's army coming to our aid, we can be assured of our safety and I am free to contemplate my next course of action in dealing with the baron.

Perhaps the sight of the Calas army arriving for our protection will boost my disheartened spirit and tear the baron free of his enigmatic state. By the gods, I hope it is not too late.

*   *   *

Our tower is under attack.

Three nights ago, the Hellar emerged from the darkness under the midnight sky and charged from the hills into our village. By sheer numbers, they quickly cut down the outer defenses. The parameter was severed and the remaining guards, along with some peasant militia, fled to the safety of the tower. Others were able to escape the village by fleeing south. Hopefully, they have found refuge in Mullikin, or perhaps Calas.

Sadly, many have been captured. And for those unfortunate souls, there has been little mercy. Their screams resonate ruefully through the sorrowful air, and there is little we can do to stop it while we remain trapped within our own construct.

The Hellar are now using Oester as a base, attempting to overtake the baron's tower. Thick greystone walls provide us momentary shelter, but they have also become our prison. Confined, escape is not an option. We continue to maintain faith for the arrival of reinforcements from the south, but the Crown has yet to respond to our request for aid. Thus, we must persist in our defense until they arrive. Alone, we cannot defeat these savages, but we must hold them off as long as possible.

Even as they stare down an opponent with numbers so superior they should have been routed the first night, Mordan and his troops have fought like champions, giving not an inch. Even Baron Vernest has immersed himself fully in battle, single-handedly scoring many deaths. After all these years of knowing the man, it is still awe-inspiring to watch him wield that giant sword and cut through his adversaries.

Though I am no warrior myself, I have done my part in the conflict, exercising nearly every battle-ready conjuration I have memorized. To my own shame, I must admit I found amusement watching a handful of barbarians abruptly flee in terror from the skirmish, to the utter bewilderment of their comrades, after I used my powers to strike an unnatural fear into their hearts. Sadly, my knowledge of the arcane is far from strong enough to change the tide of this battle. We are now holding refuge within this stone haven, uneasy of our impending fate.

Though he has fought hard during the hours of the sun, the baron still spends his nights down below in the basement laboratory, locked away with my ancient tomes of scripture. I have not unearthed what he aims to accomplish, but I have heard rumors from the servants that he is searching for some way to cheat death. How this is possible, I cannot say. My suspicions are too grave to even broach upon.

Though such tales seem more credible than ever before, I still find them hard to accept. I can only believe, and pray, that it is mere gossip. Yet, somewhere within the recesses of my thoughts, the baron's anomalous change in personality does not rest well. If he indeed seeks eternal life, he will only achieve to damn himself to some veneer of inner hell. Such things are to be left alone! Vernest is not knowledgeable enough in the arcane to manage the dark paths that necromancy bears.

Because of the battle, I have had little time to speak to the baroness. I have been informed that the servants have done well in caring for her. Anisa appears calm, but I know she deeply fears the outcome. She, as well as everyone else who takes cover within these damnable walls, can only hope that reinforcements from the Crown will arrive within the next day or two.

Otherwise, I suspect we shall not survive.

*　　*　　*

A horrible, horrible tragedy has befallen us! Even as I think of it, I am filled with an anguish that overwhelms every fiber of my essence.

The baron's daughter, Clorisa, is dead; shot by a stray arrow that flew through her window at night. Vernest had ordered all the openings to the tower shuttered, but poor Clorisa always loved looking at the stars. She must have opened her window to do so. No one heard her scream or had known what transpired until the next morning when a servant found her, the projectile lodged in her neck. Such a doom is undeserving for an innocent like Clorisa. What cruelty does fate play with us?

When Vernest discovered this, he became wholly incensed and a dreadful shouting match ensued between the baron and his wife, Anisa. Even now, I cringe as I recall the utter rage that came forth from the baron . . . and the words he said; knives would have been less hurtful. He blames Anisa for Clorisa's death, though even he knows the allegation is entirely unreasonable. Fate alone is to blame. Sadly, it seems their relationship has been ruptured to the point of never being mended.

Anisa is devastated and has not left her quarters since the fight with her husband. If only her tears could wash away reality.

For a tenday, we have defended the tower and still there has been no aid from the king. Has he forsaken us? It seems so. Vernest feels betrayed by his wife and the king, and it torments him. He no longer thinks clearly and his presence is unbearable. I, his own advisor, have not spoken with him in almost two nights. What purpose is there? What advice can I give? We have lost Clorisa and the rest of us will soon follow in her path.

Vernest now spends almost every waking hour down below. Though he locks the basement to prevent entry by others, I swear I hear screams coming for the bowls of that dungeon hell. These screams are not short-lived cries, but elongated howls of pure terror that make every hair on my body stand on end. Even after they cease, those hideous sounds have remained burned in my memory. What is making them? Surely not the baron himself! Yet, the idea that he is causing something, or someone, to emit such a horrifying clatter makes me physically ill. I have resigned myself to the belief that whatever he is doing will have dire consequences. I only wish I could do something to cease his studies. Alas, if I tried, I fear I would only be the object of his wrath.

Only Mordan gives me a morsel of hope. The man is relentless. He rarely sleeps and is constantly heard barking orders to his remaining troops. Apparently, he refuses to succumb to the dread that has overtaken the rest of us. Can we endure through his courage alone?

Perhaps . . .

*   *   *

I am dying.

Everything is lost. My lone companion is the constant trembling of my body and warmth has become foreign to my weary bones. Though I have no true way of conveying time, it must be days since I have last eaten or had drink. It is through every ounce of my strength, or what remains, that I hold this pen and record my final thoughts. No longer shall I grieve, for it matters little. Everything I once knew, once cherished, has vanished. My world is over and death is my only escape.

Only to maintain what little sanity I have left, I shall return to the beginning, or shall I say the end, of this grisly tale.

On the 14th night of the siege, the Hellar finally breeched the tower walls. The skirmish was brutal, as the beasts flooded within. Most of our troops, though bravely they fought, were cut down by brute force. Mordan threw himself before the flood and slew many, but he could only persist for so long before drowning within a sea of those savages. He died far more honorably than I will.

Along with a few remaining warriors, Vernest rushed the rest of us down to the dungeons below. Just before we locked the heavy steel trap door to keep out the hoard, he ordered the tower set afire. He had hoped the flames would overwhelm our enemies above, but the greystone walls did not burn as he anticipated. Only one small portion of the tower was damaged. Even in our underground sanctuary, we could hear and feel the small section collapse above us.

The ruin did nothing to stem the aggression of our enemies. Earsplitting rattles bounded off the walls of our haven as they furiously pounded against the trap door. We could hear their harrowing shouts above as they strove to get beneath; but the door held. We were safe, if only momentarily.

The baron still clung to the unfounded optimism that the king would send troops to our rescue. The rest of us did not share such hope. Indeed, the king had forsaken us. To appease the baron, we hid below for two more days, hoping for what could no longer be hoped for.

That is when doom extended its gruesome hand and encompassed us.

Though the steel trap door protected us from the intruders, it could do nothing for our hunger. Our supplies dwindled and we weakened, body and mind. By now, Vernest had succumbed to madness. Continuous were his rants and raves about nothing significant, and he spent more time in his laboratory, not allowing the rest of us entry. We pleaded with the baron to release the lock on the trap door and die bravely, with honor, rather than as cowards wasting away. He refused. His twisted mind was no longer focused on reality.

Then Anisa died; not from hunger as one might think, but from suicide.

Evidently, as her personal servant frantically attempted to explain, she caught a glimpse of the future, perhaps through a dream. What she saw must have been bleak, indeed. She had already lost her beloved daughter and the mind of her husband, and wished to suffer no longer.

Poison was her freedom.

To me, her death was demoralizing; like a blade in my spine. The final, thinning strand that connected me to this world was severed. Until then, I had persevered solely for her. I cared so much for her. She was an angel among mortals. With Anisa gone, there was nothing left for me.

Vernest seemed indifferent to her passing. The man had lost his mind and true terror ensued. Through trickery or force, he began to lock us in the cells. His own men! By the time we discovered what he was doing, it was too late. There were too few of us left to overtake him. I was one of the last ones imprisoned, but I never offered a struggle. I no longer cared. Fortunately, I had my journal and pen hidden within my robes, allowing me this final entry.

Then, the screams began. The same screams I had heard from before. Now, they were as clear as the light of the sun. These cries were hideous; shrieks of pain and horror that were so grueling to my ears that I passed out several times. Day after day, through my prison bars, I could see him force potions down the throats of his captives. They would shudder horribly for hours, even days, before dying. Then he would cut them open to view their entrails. Never before have I witnessed something so evil, so wicked. I realized my days were near an end. Eventually only a handful of us remained.

An hour ago, I watched the last be led away by the thing that was once Vernest. The prisoner, once a loyal follower, bellowed and sobbed for mercy. Mercy would not be granted and his screams halted just minutes ago.

I am next and will suffer this same torture as the others. No longer do I fear it, though. I am so near death already, I shan't last long in his hands. What truly pains me is that, to this day, I know not what he seeks. Why has he done this?

I will never know.

After this, I will lay down my pen for the last time. Perhaps, through some grace of the gods, I can care for Anisa in the afterlife. It is this that I hold, for I have left everything from this world behind.

Death is my only escape.

- Welnor, advisor to Baron Vernest (Vassal to King Anuron of Calas)

I

Year 1313 of the Second Age

He awoke to discover himself sitting upright, his naked torso and chin length brown hair dripping with cold beads of sweat. Lifting an arm, he wiped moisture from his sodden forehead and breathed slowly while reality reappeared in stages. Gradually, he drew his eyes across the small room of the inn and realized it was scarcely past midnight. He was still shaking.

He tried to concentrate, tried to remember. For a fleeting moment, he thought this time might be different, he might actually grasp hold of his demons. But as each time before, he could only muster vague, indistinct recollections of the nightmare that had stirred him awake; the very same nightmares that had plagued him consistently for over a year.

There were many hours of darkness remaining before dawn, but Kyligan knew he would achieve no more sleep as long as the flickering, obscure images lingered in his mind. The nightmares had deprived him of another restful nights slumber and he shivered unwillingly. The dreams were terrifying, horrific premonitions. He didn't need to specifically remember them to recognize their misery. Every time one consumed him, he was enveloped by dread for hours, sometimes days on end.

And yet, something else drew his curiosity, something compelling and seductive.

Why? What has drawn these distorted visions my way? Why, after I awake, do they stay cloaked in darkness, lurking in the back of my mind; there, but unwilling to reveal themselves? These were the questions Kyligan asked himself recurrently.

There would be no answers.

He found such a quandary disconcerting, but what frightened him most was how he might one day learn the truth of them.

Though he had nothing to base his beliefs upon, he held a hidden suspicion that they professed a future for the Kingdom of Calas; something that did not bode well. As a man of the woods, of nature, this deeply unsettled Kyligan. His greatest fears overcame him; seeing the great forests destroyed, hordes of monsters overflowing within to infect them with their foul presence.

Ridiculous, he chided himself roughly. *Why must I punish myself with these senseless notions? This land is strong and the people can defend it against such threats.* Yet Kyligan knew of other threats, as well; threats hidden from even the most observant of eyes. The worst enemy is often unseen until it is far too late. Perhaps these dreams are a warning of a different peril?

"Curse it!" he yelled. As always, he found himself succumbing to his dreams, obsessing over issues that he hadn't control over. Hastily he altered his thoughts and soon concluded that a walk on such a tranquil night would perhaps amend his dark musings. Rising groggily from the noisy cot, he slipped into a pair of loose cloth breeches and a shirt. After fitting his boots, he took two lazy steps toward the door before prudence stopped him short. Rarely was he in the great city of Calas, and thus, he was unfamiliar with its surroundings, particularly the slums in which the dilapidated inn was located. It made sound logic to carry protection. Though he neglected to wear his chainmail, he felt it wise to at least carry a weapon. Thieves and cutthroats were a constant threat in cities, especially during the nighttime hours, and added protection would provide him reassurance if nothing else. Seizing a loose leather strap which hung off a stilted peg on the wall, he latched his sword belt tightly around his waist and departed the room, securing the bolt of the door firmly as he left.

The staircase that descended into the main foyer of the inn was wooden and rickety. He took careful, purposeful steps, hoping not to alarm other sleeping patrons in the middle of the night with the stairs' pitiful creaking. He soon discovered it mattered very little. As he reached the bottom and proceeded into the foyer, Kyligan was surprised to witness several people still milling about, drinking and chatting freely. He was in no mood for discussion, but sneaking by these freebooters unnoticed would be tricky. Every occupant seemed to be probing for new entertainment and Kyligan suspected they might employ him as a way to curb their constant pursuit of amusement. Quietly and slowly, he passed through the crowds, keeping his eyes on the floor so as not to invite company. To his surprise, the vagrants had apparently not distinguished him as someone of interest. He went disregarded, as he shuffled past and reached the door that would lead him outdoors. As soon as he stepped beyond the front door, he sucked in a lengthy gulp of fresh open air.

For all purposes, it was the perfect night. The moon was full and it speckled a glossy golden hue over the dimly lit city. Along with the cool breeze that sifted lazily through the air and the resplendent stars that surrounded the full moon like an accompanying concerto of bards, the atmosphere had set a mood that could soothe even the most hardened soul. Even the broken decanters and bottles that littered the roughly paved streets could do little to offset the serenity the night brought forth. Yet, despite these delights, Kyligan felt uneasy. He was a man of the woods, a ranger, and had lived his entire life in the wooded cover of the Great Forest. The wide cobblestone streets of the city were foreign and uncomfortable.

At least, he mused, they're empty for the moment. He shuddered at the thought that in a few hours the roads would be crammed with people. Such bustle was not for Kyligan, whose quiet, introverted nature didn't mix with the intense activity of the urban community.

His anxiety over the surroundings was doubled by the nightmares that continued to stab at him mentally. He was forced to make a concentrated effort to shove them aside. He wished, even prayed, it were already noon, the designated time he would be meeting his friends. Anything to take his mind off such dark omens was welcome, and his comrades would surely help in that matter. Though noon was a mere half-day away, he had no doubts it would seem an eternity.

For over a year, Kyligan had not seen Cadwan and the others, when together they had helped a small hamlet of halflings defeat a pack of kobolds that had been terrorizing the citizens. Kyligan found himself anticipating the upcoming meeting. The group had proved to be good company, and Kyligan didn't have many friends. Actually, to be more specific, he had *no* other friends. It was a drawback he wished he could say wasn't his fault, but there were few truths to such a statement. Although he was commonly pleasant and courteous, his problem was that he was too quiet, too difficult to openly read. It took much effort to befriend him and wrench him from his shell. Kyligan knew of his problem, yet he found himself unable to remedy it. The barrier he had built over the years was simply too sizeable to break overnight. The steps would have to be small and Cadwan's group had helped. Somehow, they had slipped past his introversive shell and, ever since, Kyligan had missed their camaraderie. Though their gathering would be nothing more than a few drinks and some far fetched tales, he smiled at the thought.

Unfortunately, some hours had to pass before such revelry could occur. Following the open street, Kyligan stretched out his arms and turned upward his neck, gazing at the effervescent moon. Even in the dank slums the sky was beautiful. He started to actually believe the soothing night would help pass the time more quickly.

The scream that pierced the night nearly caused Kyligan to leave his feet in surprise. It was not drawn out and elongated, but rather a short, high-pitched shriek. The ranger nearly dismissed it as a stray animal, a dog perhaps, when a second rang out, louder this time. Now, he was certain. It was a person, most likely in peril. Feeling some unheeded sense of duty and perhaps a tinge of curiosity, he slid closer to the buildings, using the dark shadows as cover, and pursued the noise.

His sharp ears led him to a dark, enclosed alleyway. Ducking behind some old abandoned crates at the entrance, he cautiously peered within and gaped at what he saw. Three men with shadowed faces had cornered a family; mother, father, and three small children.

What in the hells is a family doing outdoors in the middle of the night, in the slums no less? Kyligan would have liked to ask that very question, but as he examined them further he succumbed to empathy. They looked worse for wear, as if they had traveled a long distance and eaten little. The children were slouched and dirty, appearing tired and weak. Kyligan crouched lower and listened.

"We haven't all night!" one of the shadowed men was saying. Kyligan instantly recognized them as common thugs, ruffians.

The father, a short portly fellow, pleaded his case. "Please! I beg you! This is all the money we have. Have mercy for our children!"

One of the thugs, apparently the leader, nodded to a comrade. In the blink of an eye, a swift arm shot forward and wrested one of the children, a boy of maybe seven winters, away from his mother's grasp. He placed the thin blade of his rapier to the flailing child's throat. The leader, his ears and cheeks jingling with several piercings, spoke again. "Your purse, or the little one dies. Quickly now!"

Had the boy's mouth not been covered by a hand, the child would have fabricated a noise that could have awakened every soul in the near vicinity. As it was, he could only struggle to produce a muffled whimper behind the dirty grasp of his subjugator. The father turned to look at his wife, saw her screeching frantically for her child, and knew there was but one decision to make. Dropping his head, he reached into a pocket and withdrew a small leather bag. The lead bandit moved forward and snatched the purse away.

Kyligan witnessed the exchange, infuriated that these men could so callously take advantage of people who already had almost nothing to give, nor any way to defend themselves. He took one large, deep breath before stepping away and scanning the adjoining street. Unfortunately, there was no sign of guards on night patrol. Either he took action himself, or there would be nothing done for the helpless family. The ranger irritably swore under his breath. He knew he shouldn't get involved, shouldn't risk his own life for a family of strangers. After all, there were *three* rogues. Could he defeat them all?

Then again, like all complicated choices there was an accompanying moral dilemma, one that Kyligan always strictly adhered to. If he walked away, his conscience would forever haunt him. He suddenly wished he hadn't elected to take a walk. Only one action would allow him to retain his honor, and the ranger briefly wondered why the right decision always seemed the most difficult to make.

Scolding himself for his irrational choice of heroism, he evaluated his strategy. Three enemies. The leader wielding a short blade, the other two holding rapiers. His initial instinct was to reach for his bow, but regrettably he had left it in his room at the inn. All he carried was his sword. To prevent himself from reneging on his certitude, he leapt recklessly from cover and into plain view. Unsheathing his blade, he called out, "Return the purse!"

Every head in the alley turned his direction. The ruffian leader, whose creased and leather hardened face Kyligan could now see clearly, laughed with jovial intensity. "What do we have here? Some lone warrior of justice and righteousness? A man of the night who helps those in need? I admire your courage friend, but I fear your attempt to thwart our foul dealings will come to an unexpected, painful end." He smiled, his mouth showing only a couple yellowed teeth and several black gaps in the moonlight. After a moment, he added, "I also wonder what your own purse holds?" He gestured to his cohorts. The two men lifted their rapiers and slowly approached Kyligan, while their leader held back and watched with amusement.

Kyligan sized up his opponents. Both were of average height and build, though one was considerably older. He knew that if he allowed his aggressors to press too far in, too close simultaneously, he would be unable to defend himself, so he swung his sword wildly to keep them at a distance. As the flashing blade whirled before them, one of the skirmishers stepped backward. With the man's weight rearing, Kyligan instantly drove in with a giant overhead slash, hoping for a quick kill. The man brought up his rapier to parry the blow, but his thin blade gave ground under the breadth of the ranger's sword and the man reeled backward before falling. Kyligan readied to pounce on the man and finish him off, but the other thug attacked from his left side. The ranger veered his hips and scarcely avoided the point of the man's weapon from piercing through his ribs. Instead, it grazed his back, tearing thin threads of his shirt and leaving him with a small cut.

Kyligan instinctively backed away, giving himself time to resituate. Unfortunately, it also gave his enemies a chance to reassemble themselves for another assault. Risking a quick glace sideward, he was surprised to find the leader still not engaged in the battle. The man was watching, obviously enjoying the duel and confident of its outcome.

Again, his foes moved into formation. Kyligan made the abrupt decision to alter his stratagem, opting to play the defensive and allow his adversaries the opportunity to make a critical mistake of their own. As they attempted to flank him, he patiently waited; a wait that was short-lived.

Quick as a cat, one of the rogues darted in, the sharp tip of his weapon aimed for Kyligan's throat. Though he expected the strike, Kyligan was startled by the speed at which it was delivered. He moved his torso just enough to evade certain death. The blade missed by inches, but the thug's wild thrust had carried his body close enough for Kyligan to drive the point of his own sword deep into the gut of his attacker. The man screamed and released hold of his weapon. He dropped to his knees and felt his stomach, ineffectively covering the wound that would soon drain away his life.

As Kyligan pulled loose his sword, he felt a sharp, stinging pain in his upper thigh. Swinging his neck, his observed the other man's rapier protruding from the upper portion of his right leg. The gash was profound and his white pants were quickly overwhelmed by the dark crimson of blood. His foe withdrew the thin blade and cocked his arm, reaching back for another strike, but Kyligan was able to lean in and push the man away with his free arm.

Trying to reposition himself, the ranger quickly found that any pressure he put on his right leg pained him. He also understood, with regret, that defeating a second enemy in his wounded state would be a challenge, indeed. His foe, the younger of the two, was jumping and feigning back and forth, obviously taking advantage of his own mobility. Kyligan waited, knowing it would do him no good to pursue the man. The rogue seemed primed for attack when his body went suddenly crashing to the ground, his head landing face first. Kyligan blinked a moment, then realized that the body of the family's father was included in the tangled mess. He had tackled the ruffian from behind.

Kyligan wasted no time. He drove his sword into the skirmisher's throat, killing him instantly. Then, just as quickly, he scanned the alley in search of the leader. The man with the piercings had vanished. In true bandit form, when the tide of the duel had turned cowardice won over and he fled. Kyligan spat at the thought, wishing he was given at least one chance to kill the scum. As it was, he was thankful he'd survived.

"Friend, you are hurt badly. Sit down, while I bandage you," the husband was saying the words, raising himself awkwardly off the dead bandit.

Kyligan looked down at his leg. The cloth of his pants, now stained red, matted the limb uncomfortably. Reaching down, he peeled the clammy material from his thigh and mouthed, "I am fine."

The other man was already forcing him to sit. "I insist. It is the least I can do for your valiant assistance. Few in this world are willing to put their own life on the line for total strangers, especially with no reward at stake." While Kyligan seated himself, the man removed his own shirt, revealing a corpulent physique, and wrapped the ragged fabric tightly around the ranger's wound. "I am sorry I do not have something better to dress your wounds," he muttered apologetically.

"Did the other man escape with your money?" Kyligan asked, his mind still on the bandits.

The man's face grew sad. He nodded, solemnly. "I am Ragnall. And this . . ." he pointed to his family, who had crept closer to Kyligan since the battle. "is my wife Fitga. My three children, Hamo, Sigrid, and Odda, are there. Although our money is gone, we owe you our lives."

Kyligan nodded and made a small motion with his hand. "Well met. I am Kyligan." Taking a few deep breaths, he continued. "I fear I did not help you much. Your money has still been stolen."

Ragnall smiled. "Even so, your bravery is commendable."

Poking at the wound with his finger, Kyligan found it quite painful, but he withheld any air of discomfort around Ragnall and his family, so as not to guilt them. A former question arose. "I mean not to query your judgment, but why are you out at this time of night? Surely you should have expected something of this nature to happen."

The visage on Ragnall's face suddenly transformed from that of a grateful, appreciative man to an agonizing, tortured soul. Kyligan also saw similar looks on the wife and children.

The ranger remained quiet, waiting, and eventually Ragnall answered. "We hadn't a choice. We come from Oester, but the town is . . ." Ragnall threw glances at his wife and children, then somberly shook his head as if no words could fill the blank. "We had to leave. Our lives were doomed had we stayed."

"Doomed?" Kyligan questioned the derivative word.

"Horrors," Ragnall mouthed. "Mere words cannot describe it."

Kyligan stared at the man a moment longer. He found Ragnall's words excessively curious and wanted to know more, but as he peered into their faces, he could not bring himself to cause additional mental suffering. *Perhaps later I can revive the discussion,* he decided. Changing the subject, he asked, "What will you do now, without your coffers?"

Ragnall shrugged. "I do not know. That was all we had and even it was paltry. I presume we will have find a good hidden place on the streets to sleep for the remainder of the night and then beg passerby's in the morning."

Thinking it was a joke, Kyligan had nearly scoffed before realizing Ragnall was in complete earnest. The ranger was beset with pity and knew he could not consciously allow such a thing to happen. "An inn rests not far from here, just down the street. I have rented a room you can use. It is small, but we should all be able to fit within. At least you shall have a roof over your heads for the night."

"No. We have troubled you enough already." Ragnall was shaking his head, but his defiance was weak and ill-gotten.

"This time it is I who insist. I cannot, in good conscious, allow your family, your children, to sleep on these perilous streets."

Ragnall turned to his wife, to his children. Their sad, withered, exhausted faces answered for him. "You are most gracious, milord."

II

"Cadwan, do you ever miss the army?"

Atop a spotted white gelding, Cadwan turned his neck to regard the dwarf riding slightly behind him. "Only the friends I had," he muttered. He ran his fingers through his short hair. "The service itself was tedious. My travels since," he swung his arm to include both the other horses, "have been far more interesting." The soldier took a moment to view his companions and allowed himself a smile.

Slightly behind him on a well-muscled horse strode the dwarf and a female halfling, her short arms wrapped as far as possible around the stout upper body of her armored escort. Cadwan chuckled inwardly. Dwarves were not common in these parts and were often greeted with nothing short of raw skepticism. This particular dwarf had no trouble gaining attention, wanted or otherwise, for he sported a large, fiery red beard, and the small halfling fixed to his back removed any hopes of discretion.

Beyond the dwarf rode yet another figure.

"Yes, interesting indeed," the man in the back sarcastically muttered. He was an odd looking fellow, with rust colored skin and a long, copious black beard that fell from an overhanging cowl. Over his body draped dull, tattered gray robes, and his thick, bushy eyebrows hung over eyes that darted constantly in every direction. His mannerisms seemed to mirror that of the chameleon which sat calmly on his shoulder. It was obvious that the small lizard had been his pet for some time, for it seemed well contented. "I was certain that spiked pit you encountered was your doom. It is fortunate I was there to rescue you."

"Your memory fails you, Alazar," the halfling chimed in. "It was Darin," she gestured to the dwarf, "and I who rescued the both of you."

The robed man suddenly appeared disinterested in the conversation, turning his vision away from the others and slipping his face deeper into his hood. The halfling giggled, her petite waist and pretty face bouncing in unison with her shoulders.

In the earliest hours of daylight, the road was already being traversed. Only minutes ago, the orange sun had peeked over the cloudless scope, spraying glistening beams of infant light across the multicolored sky. The ground still held a thin layer of moisture left from the previous night, bestowing the late spring morning a sense of freshness. Among the untimely risers was the party of four, trekking eastbound on their way to the city. As a rule, those who took the time to lay eyes on the group had to blink once, often twice, to insure they were seeing properly. It was a common reaction and one that the four friends had grown accustomed to. They were well aware that their grouping was an odd assortment. Humans were seldom seen riding with dwarves; or halflings, for that matter.

The road from Houghton to the city-state of Calas was wide, its girth covered with dirt that was packed firm from years of constant travel. Nary a passageway in the entire kingdom was found which contained more activity, more bustle than this one. Farmers and merchants alike hauled their goods back and forth, depending on their destination. Imperial patrols were ever present, maintaining the safety of a route vital to the financial success of the great city. Just south flowed the River Hem. It bristled majestically, giving the travelers eye candy, as the swift current carried its waters east, towards the Nardûn Sea.

"Thank the gods Darin had rope, or I fear we would still be trapped in that crevice," Cadwan, the soldier, added. He wore common chain armor and a bow over his shoulder. A mace dangled loosely from his hip, as he galloped steadily ahead. There was little extraordinary about him; simple brown eyes, a light stubble over an even jaw line and brown hair that hung loosely to the top of his ear.

"Yes," the dwarf declared, his voice calm and stately, "and nary in good shape."

Cora, the halfling, turned toward Alazar and sneered at the man mischievously. Alazar only grinned at her playful jest. Although the two of them were as different as day and night, they enjoyed one very similar quality; they enjoyed poking fun at others when the opportunity arose. Since the very beginning of their travels together, they had commenced an unwritten contest to see who could slight the other more.

Darin scratched the top of his massive dome, which incidentally lacked hair on top, then reached under his flaming beard and grasped a pendant that hung from a silver chain around his neck. The polished chaplet bore the image of a double-sided warhammer smashing rock beneath it; the standard of the dwarven god of war, Grimgar Frundin. The dwarf spoke with fondness. "Once again, great Frundin had blessed us with good fortune." Though the religious words meant little to him, Cadwan acknowledged the cleric with a nod.

The sun was unrelenting as it rose higher, and soon the party was but a few hours from Calas. Every passing minute the path grew busier and maneuverability visibly worsened.

"Damn these crowds!" Alazar mumbled impatiently, attempting to induce a stray ox to leave his mare's path.

Cadwan ignored his friend's irritation. "It will be good to see Kyligan again," he stated, diverting everyone's focus from the swarm of travelers.

Cora's face brightened instantly. She was quite fond of the soft-spoken ranger. "I cannot wait. I often wonder how the last year has been for him."

"The same as always, no doubt, spending all his time deep in the trees, terrified he might actually be forced to speak with someone." Alazar smirked. "It is still a wonder how he ever mustered the courage to approach us a year ago."

Cora snapped a retort. "It is unfortunate you are not as quiet as he."

Ever the diplomat, Darin maneuvered his horse between the two quarrelers. With his dwarven accent, he spoke as if he hadn't heard their verbal sparring. "Yes, Kyligan will be a welcome sight for sore eyes. I wonder if he already waits for us. If the road is not overly busy, we should arrive by noon, as promised."

The dwarf's words proved prophetic. By the time they witnessed the fortified walls of Calas ascending to meet the azure sky, the morning was drawing to a close. As the residing home of King Anuron and several other high-ranking officials, the city of Calas was clearly the political heart of the kingdom. Beyond the walls and past the hovels and shops, other grand structures of various craftsmanship and magnificence could be seen, including the palace which loomed majestically over the city, as if it were regally watching the other structures with a vigilant eye.

Either atop the ramparts or down below on the now cobbled streets, several guards eyed the party warily as they bypassed the entrance. The group hesitated momentarily, wondering if they would be inspected. When no guardsmen neared them, they shrugged and spurred their mounts onward. Abruptly, a sentry wearing the livery of the Calas army and carrying a halberd hailed the group from the other side of the avenue and hustled across to Darin's horse. "Name and business," the sentry declared, matter-of-factly.

The dwarf looked down at the man and smiled, congenially. "Darin, son of Farin, and emissary of the kingdom of Ludun. This," he gestured to the soldier, "is Cadwan Ceres, formally of the Calas army. Behind us are Cora Hobshollow of Thumble and Alazar of Asharria."

The guard looked at Cadwan, curiously. "Formerly of the Calas army? I do not recognize you. Which regiment?"

"Started with the sixth," said Cadwan, "but was moved to the fifteenth after a few weeks. I mostly patrolled Grembel Forest before leaving."

The sentry grunted in apathy and glanced over the others, pausing when his eyes fell upon the halfling. After a brief period of wrinkled scrutiny, he shook his head in a gesture of bafflement and muttered, "You look harmless enough. Enjoy your stay." The footman scurried off to other duties.

"Remarkable." Alazar commented, rounding his horse to avoid a thick pile of animal dung lying on the ground. "He finds you harmless, Cora. Will wonders ever cease?"

Cora turned her cobalt eyes to Alazar. "Do you think up those clever insults on your own, or does your lizard whisper them into your ear?"

*   *   *

Only a few lanterns illuminated the Broken Jug and the dim confines of the tavern were complimented by a scant amount of conversation that was nothing more than mere whispers amid a leaden silence. Today was no anomaly, for the establishment was never especially crowded. It was for that very reason that Cadwan, who had frequented the tavern during his duty in the city, had elected it as the meeting place. The drinking hole sat well off a main road, residing conspicuously in a quiet alleyway, its business coming primarily from locals who had been regular patrons for years. There were plenty of taverns in Calas if one wanted an exciting night with lots of commotion. But if one merely wished for a quiet time of relaxation and a savory drink, there was no better place than the Broken Jug.

It was shortly after noon and the confines of the establishment were occupied by just two other customers in addition to Cadwan's party. The four had arrived only moments before and were seated near a window, so Cora could keep a watchful eye on the entrance for Kyligan's approach.

In what could be observed as a rare occasion, silence hung over the foursome as they greedily nursed their beverages. They were all relieved to have an opportunity to unwind after the long journey. Even Darin, who had to wedge his way uncomfortably into a chair that was clearly not made for a dwarven physique, was all but dozing off when Cora's voice interrupted the peace. "That is him! Look! Here he comes!"

Everyone peered through the glass. Sure enough, a man who resembled Kyligan was ambling his way toward the front doors. A second man followed behind him.

"He appears to be limping," Cadwan said, "and it looks as if someone is with him. Perhaps our reticent comrade has befriended another?"

Stranger in tow, Kyligan stepped into the tavern and immediately paused, giving his eyes a moment to adjust to the faintly lit interior after exiting the bright expanse of high noon.

Cadwan swiftly moved over to welcome him. "Kyligan, well met!"

Now dressed fully in his chainmail armor, Kyligan reached up to give Cadwan a hearty slap of the shoulder. "Good to see you, Cadwan."

A remark or two of idle greeting ensued before Cadwan suddenly noticed the dark rings around Kyligan's eyes. He knew he should have said nothing of it, but regrettably his mouth moved quicker than his mind. "Friend, you look tired." He scolded himself silently as soon as the words left his mouth.

Kyligan nodded slowly, forlornly.

Cadwan raised his hand in apology. "I am sorry, my friend. I had forgotten. The nightmares. Do they still plague you?" he asked with compassion.

The ranger nodded as before, but added, "The same. Alas, I still have not discovered their purpose."

Cadwan sighed heavily, empathy written on his face. The conversation had swiftly become uncomfortable, but he felt compelled to give an encouraging word. "One day you will know, but for now, let go your troubles and enjoy your time here. I am certain we can help you forget such sorrows."

Something struck Kyligan from behind. "Kyl, how are you? I missed you!" It was Cora, who had leapt upon his back.

"Hello, Cora." A smile grew across his face. If one person could help him dispense his troubles, it would naturally be Cora. Her endless cheer would no doubt keep him from dwelling too much on negatives.

As Kyligan greeted the others, the man who had accompanied him stood a few steps away, remaining respectfully silent. He almost went completely unnoticed until Darin spotted him.

"Who is your friend, Kyligan?" the dwarf gruffly mouthed.

Every head swung toward the short, round stranger. In response, the man took another step backward and timidly dropped his eyes.

"I apologize for my discourtesy." Kyligan moved beside the man. "This is Ragnall. He hails from Oester. His family was beset and robbed by thugs last night."

In unison, the party muttered simple condolences, but their faces betrayed their inquisitiveness. An awkward moment of silence followed where the group eyed each other, foreheads wrinkled, wondering why Kyligan had taken the man with him.

Ever bold with words, Alazar spoke. "If I may ask, Kyligan, what does this man's unfortunate plight have to do with us?"

"There is a reason I have brought him here." Kyligan looked at Ragnall and then back to the party. "He has a story I think you might be interested in hearing."

III

King Anuron of Calas diligently studied the round, polished wooden panel that rested on the table before him. Embedded in the oak board were triangles of various colors, and atop many of the triangles were figurines of every type of military personnel, figurines that had been placed with a meticulous hand and purpose. He stroked his thick graying beard with a smile.

Anuron already knew he would win. The king was widely considered the best war-stone player in the palace, if not the city, and this particular occasion would be no different. In fact, the game was already well in hand. Still, the head monarch never went placid, never relaxed until he had routed his opponent thoroughly. Reaching over, he calmly slid a figurine from one triangle to another and smiled. "There, Calien, let us see how the one day king-to-be handles that."

Prince Calien frowned, mostly due to his opponent's confidence rather than the move itself. He hated losing, but when the victor was his father it was far worse. As a child, he could handle the frequent thrashings with more dignity. But he was now twenty-four winters old and well-educated, so his expectations were far greater. Impatiently, he viewed the board, scanning for any sign of weakness in his father's offensive. There were none. As was typical, his father's strategy was flawless. Head swimming, Calien abruptly stood and mumbled, "Important military decisions must not be made in haste, correct Father?"

Anuron raised an eyebrow. "That is correct, son, but I am inclined to believe that you are merely stalling."

Calien smiled. His handsomely chiseled facial features and cropped blonde hair complemented his muscular build. In every sense, he portrayed nobility. "Perhaps, but is stalling not also a viable ploy of warfare?"

The king erupted into laughter. "Hah! My son has certainly learned the delicate tongue of politics. Has he not, Geran?"

A third man, wearing the stylish lavender robes of the king's personal advisor, sat in the far corner of the oblong shaped room, his nose buried in the pages of a thick book. At the mention of his name, he turned toward the king, the crest of his forehead deeply creased. "It would seem so. Truly, much like his father. How often have you escaped penitent affairs with mere words alone?"

"More times than I would like to remember." The king shrugged. "Alas, such is the plight of a king. One day, Calien, you will know."

Calien knew all too well. He had reverently observed the head monarch with a keen eye ever since the prince was nothing more than a small child. He envisioned his father as perfect, a king that would be remembered for his justice and might. Anuron was Calien's one true hero and he aspired to one day be as commendable a leader as the king. "If only my words flew from my lips as yours do, Father."

"They will, son," the king reassured him. "You are young and I am not near my death bed, yet. There is ample time to perfect your skills."

"And remember, Prince, there is always advice hidden in the shadows of the background." Geran, the king's advisor, stood and closed the tome, placing it in the chair. Walking to a window, he removed the wooden shutters covering the glass and peered out. The room was in one of the highest towers of the palace, offering a marvelous view of the bustling city below. Geran watched guards, freebooters, sailors, merchants, along with every other type of civilian mentionable, crowd the streets as they went about their personal business. In the heart of daytime, the city was a virtual whirlwind of activity.

The king grinned. "Sometimes more advice than you would like."

Geran made no reply, but the wrinkles on his face tightened ever so slightly.

"Shall we continue our rousing game, or are you still deliberating your defense?" Anuron asked, returning his attention to his son.

There was no hope of winning and Calien knew it. Still, pride forced him back into his chair. He had nearly reached forward to transfer a section of his army in a futile attempt to guard his flank when a steady rap came from outside the room.

Anuron frowned at the interruption. "Enter," the king declared.

A servant swung open the door and immediately bowed as he strode in and found himself within the presence of the king.

"What is it, Osric?" Anuron asked.

"Your majesty, two men have come to the palace and requested your audience for a matter they deem of utmost importance."

Anuron glowered and scratched his well maintained beard. "Were they not made aware of the proper means to seek my consultation? There are others they must speak with first."

The servant swallowed and absentmindedly twisted his foot on the tiled floor. "They were told of the appropriate channels, my King, but they refused to confer with any but the king himself."

The head monarch shook his head and looked to his advisor. "Quite bold of them to demand a direct audience with the king, would you not say?"

"Indeed," replied Geran, his deep set eyes and slanted eyebrows heavy on the servant.

"Well," the king pronounced, "who are these men who are apparently significant enough to bypass all the officials?"

A spindly fellow with a crooked nose, the servant reached into the folds of his trousers and pulled loose a thin piece of parchment. Unfolding it before his face, he loudly cleared his throat before speaking. "Darin, son of Farin, emissary of the dwarven kingdom Ludun, and Cadwan Ceres, former member of the Calas army. Both were insistent that you knew of them and would freely welcome their company."

"Darin of Farin." Anuron muttered. "I know him. Was he the dwarven emissary who helped handle the crisis with the halfling village?" The king's question was directed to his advisor.

Geran took a long, deliberate sigh, then slowly shook his head. "Perhaps. I confess I cannot remember."

Still seated, the king languorously fingered one of the war-stone pieces within his generously adorned hand. "Well, it is a simple matter. Either I accept this man's request, or I refuse. Geran?"

The purple robed advisor looked at the king, then restored his gaze upon the servant. "I do not like it. These men show no respect with their blatant disregard for proper policy. If you allow them an immediate audience, what next? When word spreads, soon every lowly commoner will want to speak with you." Geran opened his hands in a gesture of helplessness. "Would you take them all in?"

"And if the matter *is* urgent enough?" the king asked.

"Urgency is not the issue, my liege. If it were truly urgent, they would have already spoken their mind. They simply think they are important enough to speak to you directly, which they are not. This is purely a matter of upholding guidelines." The advisor closed his eyes for a moment, then offered, "We should refuse."

Anuron gazed thoughtfully at nothing. "Yes, I should have guessed. You always were a martinet for rules. Still, I must admit that the issue has pricked my curiosity." He turned to Calien, who had remained silent throughout the conversation. "What say you, my son?"

For Calien, the decision was shamefully easy. Anything to divert his father's attention away from their game, and thus escape defeat, was welcome. For the shortest of moments, he suffered a twinge of guilt for basing his decision on a simple game of war-stone, but it quickly subsided. With an level voice, he replied, "Like you Father, I am curious. My impression is to accept."

"Well then, in the true spirit of diplomacy, by a vote of two to one we will grant this brash request." A smile of amusement caressed the king's face. "Osric."

"Yes, my King?"

"Prepare one of the meeting chambers and escort them in. I will attend shortly. Go."

The servant rushed from the room without another word. Calien watched the spindly steward depart before returning to his father once the door was firmly closed. "Will I be allowed to attend?"

Anuron appeared taken aback by the question. "You voted, did you not? Of course you will attend, as will Geran. Together, we will discover if our quarry was indeed worthy of our immediate audience." The king chortled before adding, "Not often do I find this much amusement from my duties."

"I am glad you are enjoying yourself," Geran muttered, tritely.

"It is either that, or slaughter my son in yet another game of war-stone. And that routine has grown all too commonplace."

*   *   *

In lavishness, the meeting room chosen did little to represent the opulence that much of the palace offered. The modest chamber was paneled with wooden walls that shown bare save for a pair of decorative swords that hung crossed above the door. A single oil lamp was suspended from the ceiling, scarcely presenting adequate light for the full room. The square table positioned in the middle was surrounded by ordinary chairs that held the same lack of décor as the remainder of the chamber. For all purposes, the hall could have been suited for any house in all of Calas.

At first, Cadwan found the lack of ornamentation strange, but then it made him realize how unimportant they were being viewed as. Obviously, the soldier mused, this particular assembly room was not utilized for important conferences. Perhaps it was designed for commoners in hopes they would not feel overwhelmed by excessive extravagance. He almost expressed his feelings to Darin when the door latch suddenly released and three gentlemen proceeded forth.

The bright clothing and golden crown of the king was a direct contrast to the dull interior of the room. When he brought his eyes upon the individuals within, he paused for a brief moment, taken aback. He had anticipated two men, but instead there were three. Almost before it had shown, Anuron wiped the surprise from his face, though he remained irritated at being caught off guard. Rarely did such things happen. Inwardly he noted that he would have to inquire as to how a duo had inexplicably evolved into a trio. Putting the notion aside, he coolly led himself and the two men at his side into chairs.

When he found his companions and himself comfortable, he offered the first words. "You must excuse my entrance. I had expected only two men."

"We apologize, yourHighness." It was Darin who spoke. "We determined we could not give an effective portrayal of the circumstance unless we brought along the witness to explain it for himself. We pleaded with your hard working couriers. Ultimately, they allowed a third party."

Anuron sat silently for a moment, threw quick glances at his two cohorts, then muttered, "Very well. I'll admit that as a king I see a lot of faces and forget many. But now, seeing you before me I indeed recognize two of you. Was it not you," the king pointed to Cadwan and Darin, "who aided the halflings and removed the threat of the kobolds in Thumble?"

"It was, your Highness. The others are here, as well. They wait outside the palace," Darin answered.

Anuron smiled, remembering the kobolds that beleaguered Thumble a year ago. "Yes, that situation was a nuisance and your services were quite appreciated. But I hope you have not come for hand-outs. If my aging mind remembers correctly, you were plentifully paid."

"No, King, we seek no charity. Our reward was more than enough." The dwarf fiddled his thumbs as he spoke.

The king nodded. "It is no wonder you were made an emissary. You are far more courteous than most dwarves I have met." He allowed the dwarf no chance to respond before continuing. "Anyway, before we go any further I believe introductions for the others are in order. To my right is my first-born son and king-to-be, Prince Calien, and to my left is my advisor, Geran."

The prince graciously smiled. Geran, however, made no change to his scrutinizing glare.

The three guests nodded to each before the dwarf spoke for them once again. "We are honored and humbled to be given this chance to speak before your royalness. This is Cadwan Ceres," he pointed to the soldier. "I am Darin and this is Ragnall from Oester. He is the one whom bears news you must hear."

Anuron regarded the small, chubby man who was scarcely taller than the dwarf. "Oester?" He paused a moment, as if a thought struck him. The king glanced at Darin, then Cadwan, before reverting his interest to Ragnall. "Well, there is no sense wasting time. What is this important news that I must hear so hastily?"

Ragnall opened his mouth to speak, but his eyes, and his resolve, weakened. He lowered his head and said nothing.

"What is this? Speak, man!" the king demanded.

"Please forgive him, your Highness. He has been through great hardship," Cadwan interposed.

Anuron sighed hard and fixed his vision solidly on Ragnall. He lowered his voice slightly, but the influence of his words had no less impact. "Gather yourself swiftly. You have been granted a rare opportunity to speak openly to the king. If you wish to address me, now is your chance. Rest assured, you will not receive another. Do you understand?"

Ragnall nodded, but his countenance did nothing to convince Anuron.

"Listen, friend," Prince Calien said, "your eyes speak of pain. What has caused this? What must we know?"

"It is Oester." Ragnall whispered.

"What of it? Has something happened there?" Anuron asked.

As before, Ragnall nodded. "Horrors."

Geran, who had stayed motionless throughout, suddenly banged a fist on the table, startling the entire procession. "Do you not find this irritating, your Highness? The man has been given a generous opportunity and yet he can hardly speak."

Anuron threw his advisor a stern glance. "Calm yourself, Geran. I will ask for your opinion when I desire it. You need not interrupt us."

Geran glowered at the king, but did not reply. Instead, he shifted his darkened brow onto Ragnall, as if he were trying to see through the small man's head.

The king returned his attention to his guest. "Now tell us, what has happened in Oester?"

As if granted some unseen encouragement, Ragnall suddenly stammered, "It was awful, my King. Something began happening to the people. Some kind of sickness . . . or madness." He drew a shuddering breath. "They were dying and being killed. Everyone is either dead, or has fled the town."

"Killed? What is killing them?" Anuron asked.

"I . . . I do not know. Perhaps the madness. They were killing each other."

Killing each other? For the king, who by all rights was a sensible man, the tale seemed far too bizarre to be accepted. He wondered if he had mistakenly granted audience to a raving lunatic, but for the sake of his own pride he shoved these notions away and asked, "Why? Why were they killing each other?"

"We had to flee." Ragnall's speech had regressed to simple rambling. Tears streamed down his round cheeks as the unspecified memories returned. "My family and I would have died horribly. Others escaped, too. We left everything behind. Our money, our possessions, our . . . ."

"Stop!" the king roared, impetuously. "You are not making sense. Other than this *madness* you speak of, I haven't an idea what actually happened."

Ragnall went silent. As before, he quietly lowered his head, but the tears had not ceased their gradual decent.

"Your Highness," Darin said, "What you have heard is the full extent of what our party could extract from him, as well. I do not believe he can elaborate further. For what reason, I do not know. I suspect the trauma has distorted his memory of the entire event in some way." The dwarf patted the back of Ragnall, but the comforting gesture had little effect.

The king deliberately leaned back in his chair and pitched glances at his

18

son and his advisor. A strange air, complemented by a discomforting silence, had overtaken the room. Pairs of eyes exchanged fleeting looks and many found themselves involuntarily readjusting in their chairs.

Ultimately, Anuron broke the silence. "What am I to make of this? The man does not speak sanely. Can I truly believe any of it?"

"Father, look." Prince Calien pointed a finger at Ragnall. "His eyes cannot lie. Obviously he suffered through some considerable tragedy."

The king silently admitted that indeed, the man looked traumatized. There was no denying the obvious. Yet, something about the situation bothered him, as if a dark cloud hung over every word spoken by the stranger from Oester. Persistent intuition told him he would be far better off never knowing the enigmatic secrets hidden inside the man's head.

Unfortunately, he was the king. As such, he was obligated to take action of some sort. "What is your opinion, Geran?" the king asked, directing his words to his advisor.

Geran turned his head sideways. "My King, in this instance I abstain from counsel."

With a consternated face, Anuron sneered. "What in the hells has your tongue? The one time I actually want your bedamned advice and all of the sudden you have none to offer?"

"I know nothing more of the situation than you," Geran answered. "This is a decision you alone can make."

"If I may, your Highness?" Darin asked.

"Please, go ahead." The king waved an exasperated hand.

"There is another reason we have brought this knowledge to your attention."

"Yes?" Anuron prodded, edgily.

The dwarf looked over to Cadwan, who merely nodded his encouragement. With a firm, deep reverberation, Darin cleared his throat. He stroked his long beard once and proceeded. "Your Highness, we are here to offer our services. Because Ragnall's story is so vague, it would be risky to send official soldiers to investigate. News of such a mission would travel quickly. If the tale proves untrue, or even heavily exaggerated, it would only waste time and resources. Not to mention you might look foolish in the process. However, we have already accomplished a similar task for your Highness before. You know we are fully trustworthy and faithful."

Anuron considered the dwarf's proposal. "What would I gain from sending anyone? Why waste contract money on you? Oester is far to the north on the border of the kingdom. Why should I care for a village that contributes little, if anything, to Calas?"

"Think of it this way, King," Cadwan interjected. "If a real danger exists, then you will want to know about it for fear it might present a threat further south. If you send us, you have the capability to keep the process quiet and you do not risk wasting your own men. The reasoning is sound. If the tale proves false, we simply return. If not, then we are your first report, and your first line of defense, if need be."

The king grinned. "And why would you risk your lives for this? What exorbitant payment are you expecting?"

"Only a modest amount, if anything," Darin answered. "It is not money that motivates us, your grace. We are merely in search of work. This proposal would benefit us both."

"Would it?" Anuron responded. "I consider myself fairly reasonable, but do none of you find this strange in the least? Why have I not heard something about this from anyone else?" The king swept his eyes to Ragnall. "You mentioned others that escaped, as well. Where are they? Have they not also arrived in Calas?"

Ragnall shook his head. "I do not know."

The head monarch said nothing, but continued to stare at Ragnall, sifting over the man with a dissecting gaze.

"Your Highness, some could have stayed in Mullikin or Houghton. It's a long journey here from Oester. I'm sure many did not have the strength for it," Cadwan commented.

"True," Anuron granted. "Yet, I cannot help but feel circumspect. The details of this tale are indeed vague, and as so, I cannot make a decision without fully considering the implications. I have much to ponder." Abruptly, the king arose from his chair. Reaching into his velvet robes, he withdrew a small ornate bell and rang it with the twist of his wrist. Instantaneously, two armed guards burst through the austere door. "My guards will show you to the waiting hall. In two hours time, I will present my verdict. If your proposal is accepted, we can talk payment. Is this suitable?"

"Of course, your Highness," the dwarf answered, also standing. "Though I urge you to accept."

Anuron waved the dwarf's words away. "You have demonstrated your position. I need hear no more."

"Certainly, your Highness. My apologies," Darin said, as he, Cadwan, and Ragnall were swiftly escorted from the room.

As they left, the king followed them with his eyes. When the door closed, he turned his attention to Calien and Geran. "I guess our deliberation is not yet over. Let us leave this dreary room and confer the matter in more appropriate surroundings."

IV

"Have you lost your mind? I will not allow it!" King Anuron bellowed, as he paced the confines of his quarters. The three men were inside Anuron's personal chamber. The highly festooned décor of the room was a far cry from the bare furnishings of the meeting room they were in only minutes before. Immaculately crafted tapestries hung lavishly from the deep russet fernwood walls and the floors were covered with comely shag rugs.

Geran rested comfortably in a padded chair, with stylishly bejeweled trim. He watched the king and his son banter between themselves, happy that he was not directly involved.

Prince Calien sat on the edge of his father's bed, pleading his case. "There will never be a more opportune time to prove my worth. Too long I have protected myself within the excessive walls of this palace. Do you wish for me to never know what waits for me outside this shell of a world?"

"Of course you should experience what lies beyond the gates of this city," the king retorted, "but it should be in safer circumstance, with safer company."

"Safer company?" Calien unknowingly fidgeted with his finely embroidered vest as he argued. "These men are proven fighters who have faithfully served you prior. Surely, you are confident in their abilities?"

"Their abilities are not the issue. You must realize, my son, that they are but a handful of mercenaries, *not* a legion of soldiers as is fitting for the escorting of a prince."

The prince shot up from the bed and clenched his fists. His face turned blood red as his frustration escalated. "I am no longer a small child who plays with wooden swords. I am not to be coddled, Father! I should be allowed to travel with whom I please!"

Anuron turned a painful gaze toward his son. His eyes were earnest and filled with concern. "But, son, none of us know what even happened in Oester. What if, gods forbid, something horrible awaits there?"

Calien saw the worry in his father's eyes and felt a pang of guilt for triggering it. Intentionally, he allowed his anger to subside, if only slightly. "My whole life I have been heavily trained in combat. With your own eyes, you have seen me best your most skilled soldiers in sparring duels. Do you not believe I can handle myself?"

"Believe me, son, nobody takes pride in your ability to handle a sword more than I," The king slowly pivoted away, choosing to stare at one of the delicate tapestries on the wall, though his mind did not follow his vision, "but pride cannot mask my fear of losing you. The mere thought rips away at my very soul. You are wise, honorable, and a skilled fighter. *And*, you are my son. I loathe to see it all thrown away by some unwarranted sense of heroism and adventure."

"Can you truly say this is unwarranted? Did you not see the man, his face, his eyes?" The prince sighed, letting the rest of his anger escape. He lowered his voice and spoke with rational intent. "Father, I wish to do this for two reasons. The first is for myself. I must know if I am capable of the fortitude it takes to be a king for the people. But even more so, I do this for *you*, Father. I long to prove myself. All of my life, I have looked up to you as faultless."

Anuron shook his and snickered. "No man is without fault, my son. Especially me."

"But in my mind you are! You are the greatest man I know, and the idea of one day taking your place makes me feel," Calien lowered his head and shrugged, solemnly, "inferior."

The king swung his body and looked directly at his son. "You have never been inferior."

Calien gradually lifted his eyes to meet his father's. "I want to show you that I am worthy to be a king and that I care for the people as you do, even the people on the far northern border. Oester is still within our great kingdom's boundaries. Thus, it is my burden to turn my ear toward its cries."

King Anuron smiled, admiringly. "Son, if my heart encompassed half the honor of yours, strife would never infest Calas with its ugly claw. You are far more fitting to be king than I ever was. There is nothing you need to prove to me."

"Your words fill me with pride, my King." The prince resumed his position on the end of the bed and somberly nodded. "Even so, I feel called to this journey. I cannot refuse."

"Is there no other way?"

The prince shook his head. "No."

Anuron sauntered over to a window. Throwing back the silk curtains, he peered down to the city below. "All the riches of this world put together, *all of them*," he emphasized, "are but a mere grain of sand to how much you mean to me." He breathed deeply and, after another few moments, shrugged in a motion of helplessness. "I guess there is nothing more I can do but wish you safe passage and ask permission to endlessly worry for your safety."

Calien grinned only slightly. "It is natural to worry. But Father, I give you a promise. I will return just the same as I leave."

22

"Yes, we shall see." Anuron nodded and brushed his hand outward. "Go forth and deliver the news to the others. I even grant you consent to elect the appropriate compensation for their efforts. Depart whenever you choose to do so, but for the sake of the god, you had better return, or I will never forgive myself."

The prince walked over and embraced his father warmly. "Do not fear. I will return."

*   *   *

With a determined pace, King Anuron ambled down the ornate palace hallway, the conversation with his son, finished only minutes ago and still fresh in his mind. His destination could have been reached much quicker had he employed the main hallways, but the king was in no mood to cross paths with the other nobles and vagrants who dwelled within the palace walls. Tedious conversation was the furthest thing from his mind. To avoid such unpleasantries, Anuron weaved his way through several indirect passages that contained far less traffic.

Eventually, he reached a thin-walled stairwell and guided himself downward, beyond several stories. Upon reaching the level of his choosing, he dropped unto the rough stone landing and drew himself forward through a dimly lit hall, eventually reaching a door constructed of heavy, sienna timber. The metal hinges whined in protest as Anuron released the latch and pulled back the door. The king paid little attention to the noise of the portal, or the interior of his new surroundings. Instead, he strode assertively onward until he reached a second door of the same make as the previous. This time, however, he stopped.

Fumbling in the pockets of his robes, he withdrew a small iron key and forced it into the lock. After a sharp click, he returned the key to his pocket, undid the latch, and swung open the door.

Excluding the think layer of dust that coated the furnishings, the scenery changed dramatically from the previous room. The new chamber was lined with sturdy bookshelves on three of the four walls and a large desk rested in a corner with a lone candle atop. The room was a study, though it was rarely used. Spider webs clung to the corners and niches. Anuron's own study was high in the palace near his sleeping quarters. This particular room was employed to house old tomes and documents that were rarely, if ever, researched.

Anuron withdrew a tiny box from the same pocket that had held the key. Reaching inside the small container with his index and middle finger, he removed a small stick of timber and slashed it along the edge of the container. Instantly, a tiny spark erupted and matured, igniting the dim interior of the old study with moving shadows of flame. He lit the candle on the desk, then guided himself to a sconce that hung above the entrance, lighting it as well. Although the illumination was not overpowering, it was sufficient for his needs. The shelves were crammed tight with bound manuscripts, but Anuron knew exactly what he was searching for and where to find it. Extending himself to his fullest capacity, he reached up and pulled loose a medium-sized volume before shuffling quickly over to the desk. Easing himself into the chair, he drew the candle close and delved within the tome.

The pages flipped swiftly. Anuron's eyes darted with rapid succession as he scanned each thin sheet for a single objective, his face contorted in contemplation. When he found what he was searching for, he froze and gazed meticulously at the yellowed parchment. Intently, he read . . .

. . . envoy from Oester arrived at the palace today bringing a request from Baron Vernest. The pompous ass demands that I send troops to Oester to aid them in their defense of the Hellar barbarians that have been invading the northern lands of late. Does he have no tact? Naturally, I will not comply. What would I gain from defending Oester? Vernest is consistently overdue with his taxes and has done nothing to facilitate the construction of a prosperous kingdom for the rest of us further south. In fact, it is almost as if he has purposefully separated Oester from Calas. Yet now, in his time of need, he begs for support. He has been a thorn in my weathered crown for long enough and his death shall be more of a reprieve than tragedy. The gumption he has; demanding assistance. Hah! Sending valuable troops to Oester would only be an excessive waste of our resources.

As an alternative, I have decided to prepare a counter offensive in Mullikin, lest these Hellar choose to invade further into Calas. Their siege on Oester will be a sensible way to gauge their numbers and tactics, and it will allow us to respond accordingly. I am willing to sacrifice a small village, if it will help to insure victory on a grander scale. Within the . . .

Anuron closed the journal of his grandfather, the former king, but continued to stare ruefully at the leather-bound cover. He already knew the story, had read it several times prior. But now, as his son prepared to journey to the very same location, the tale took significance anew. Could there be a connection? King Lodan's betrayal of Oester was 150 years ago. Any kind of reprisal would have happened long before now. Whatever phenomenon is happening there cannot possibly be related.

Despite his own reassurances, his anxiety grew with each passing notion. Something wasn't right. The man's face . . . Ragnall, his eyes reflected visions that should only appear in nightmares. Even his words were fouled by something. Anuron shuddered involuntarily as he pictured the broken man.

And now, despite his fears, he was allowing his son, the future king of Calas, to travel there with but a mere handful of shabby adventurers.

Suddenly, the king wanted to take desperate action, to run back up the stairs and prevent his son from leaving. Alas, even he realized the that time for convincing the prince had past. He had committed permission to Calien and there was no chance of swaying his willful son now.

As repose, he was left with one other entity; hope. But would the hope of one simple king overcome the many sins of his fore-father long past away?

As expected, the King's palace was, without question, the most opulent, lavishly constructed and adorned building in Calas. The endless rooms were elaborately designed, each having its own style and uniqueness. Even the waiting hall, which saw more commoners than perhaps any chamber in the palace, bore textiles, murals and paintings that would make the poorest man wealthy beyond credence. And like any other area not shrouded by the dense cover of the woodlands, Kyligan was uncomfortable.

The ranger, seated in a cushioned chair far too snug for his own liking, gazed at the others seated around him, waiting for the very same news. In attendance was Cadwan, Darin, Alazar, Cora, and all of Ragnall's family. Two hours ago, Cadwan, Darin, and Ragnall had returned from their conference with the king, bearing the details of the meeting. Now they waited; the others eager for a new commission and Kyligan merely hoping for an excuse to travel with his old companions. Ever since seeing them at the Broken Jug, he immediately felt the longing to journey again, a craving that continued to build with each passing moment he spent near Cadwan and the others.

Indifferently, the ranger looked down at the injury he'd sustained the previous night from the ruffians. It was still painful, but nothing he couldn't bear. Later, after they had left the palace, he planned on having a healer tend the wound further.

Kyligan's attention fell on Ragnall's family. They were clumped together closely and he found it odd that they rarely spoke. Even the children, *especially* the children, said nothing. Only a couple of whispers between Ragnall and his wife from time to time gave the indication that they were even alive, much less aware of what was happening. By now, it was more than obvious that something terrible had occurred at their home. Few happenings could make children remote and solitary. And still, none of them would, or *could*, explain what this frightful occurrence was.

"How long do they plan to make us wait? There has been plenty of time to discuss the matter," Alazar complained, breaking the momentary silence of his lounging cohorts.

"Patience, Alazar," Darin chided. "The king must be somewhat skeptical, being that our tale was not the utmost convincing."

Frowning, Alazar shook his head. "But what would he lose by sending us? There would be no risk."

The paunchy dwarf lifted his shoulders. "His pride. If the story proves false, he might appear unwise taking action after the only report he received of the event came from a group of simple mercenaries."

Cadwan, who was casually listening, learned toward Darin. "Perhaps, but it would seem more foolish and costly to take no action at all. My grandfather used to say 'A wise man takes heed to every warning.' He lived to an old age."

His thick red beard hanging in uninhibited knots beneath his chin, Darin nodded slowly. "I agree, Cadwan, but regrettably we cannot make the decision for him. Although, he did see Ragnall in person," the dwarf paused to throw a glance at the huddled family, "and few could ignore a face as ravaged with dread as his has been."

The others nodded gravely and more silence ensued, as neither Cadwan nor Alazar felt obliged to respond to the obvious.

"Ah, there awaits the group I seek," a voice spoke very near them.

Every member of the party jumped to their feet, turning to see Prince Calien standing a mere five steps away. A warm smile bred across the prince's face. Kyligan briefly wondered how he was able to approach unnoticed, especially by Darin and Cadwan who had already met him and would have recognized him drawing near.

The prince continued, his voice friendly and cordial. "If you are suspicious as to why I rather than the king am conveying the verdict, fear not. King Anuron did not send me as a bearer of bad news. He simply had others matters to attend."

"Prince Calien," Darin spoke loudly and clearly, as if representing everyone, "we are honored by your presence." Those who had not already met the prince, save for Cora, were instantly self-conscious in the presence of nobility. Kyligan and Alazar fidgeted restlessly, suddenly wishing to be elsewhere. In contrast, Cora's face lit up excitedly. She drew as near to the prince as possible.

Prince Calien waved a muscular arm outward. "I am grateful for your compliment, but there is no need for flattery. Our decision will be a surprise to you, I think."

"Oh?" Cadwan mouthed with suspicion. "Tell us."

Calien cleared his throat and announced, "As per your request, the king has partially agreed to your proposal. He . . ."

"Partially?" Alazar interrupted.

The others simultaneously cast Alazar irate glances. "Alazar! Let the man speak!" Cadwan scolded.

Alazar made an apologetic face and said nothing. Darin stepped toward

Alazar and stated, "I apologize, Prince Calien, for the interruption, and for not introducing the others." The dwarf pointed at each person in turn. "This is Alazar of Asharria, a land across the Great Divide and very far to the south. The halfling is Cora of Thumble. That is Kyligan, the ranger, from the Great Forest. And over there is Ragnall's family. Uh . ." Darin stopped, realizing he had never learned their names.

"My wife is Fitga, and my three children, Hamo, Sigrid, and Odda," Ragnall added quietly.

"A privilege," Calien said, tilting his face forward. "As I was saying, the king has agreed to send you to Oester. However, I have been appointed to accompany you on your journey."

For an instant, everyone stared at the prince. Speechless and immobile, they could not hide their surprise over his startling announcement. In contrast, it was all Calien could do to keep from smiling over their reaction. He had fully expected such astonishment.

"Really? You are coming with us?" Cora cried, clasping her hands with elation. Her enthusiasm, however, was not reflected by the others, who were casting about glances filled with skepticism.

"I am," the prince answered. "and I am eager to travel with such a fine group of warriors."

As the unofficial speaker of the party, Darin was the first to reveal his uncertainties. With his deep, stately voice, he questioned, "With all respect, my Prince, are you aware of the dangers we might face along the way? The assignment will be arduous enough without having to protect such an important noble as yourself."

Calien grinned with amusement, though the others found the expression curiously naïve. "I can assure you," he said, "I will not need protecting. I have been trained in warfare by the very best the Calas army has to offer. I am a well-skilled swordsman and strategist. On our journey, I wish not to be thought of as the king's son, but rather as a companion who will fight by your side, if the need arises."

"Have you traveled outside the city before?" Cadwan probed, staring at the prince's smooth, silky hands which had clearly never seen a day of labor in all of Calien's twenty-four years of life.

"I have hunted in the Grembel Forest." The prince smirked, his expression pure honesty. "I will admit, this journey will take me places I would otherwise never go, but never have I fervently awaited something so eagerly. This is a tremendous opportunity for me to see the kingdom I will one day rule over."

"Are you certain of this, Prince? Life outside the assistants and servants of the palace will be a drastic change," Darin argued. The dwarf's comments were silently mirrored by the others, who were not convinced of Calien's readiness for the harsh realism of the world beyond. "This task can be accomplished without you. There is no need for you to needlessly risk injury, or *worse*." He added extra emphasis to the last word.

Calien calmly listened to the dwarf. When he finished, the prince answered, cordially. "Your concern is understandable, but our decision has already been made. I am looking forward to the challenge."

Darin looked at Cadwan, then Alazar, then Kyligan. Every face displayed identical concern.

"Why not let him come, Darin?" Cora pleaded, already beside herself with the thought of traveling with a prince. "How many people can say they have journeyed with a real prince? It will be fascinating!"

Cadwan, oblivious to Cora's chatter, was struck with a sudden notion. "And what happens if you do get hurt? Are we held responsible? Do we suffer the consequences of allowing the prince of Calas to come to harm?"

"Certainly not," Calien retorted. "You have a task to attend to and I am merely offering my aid. As I said earlier, I need no protection."

Everyone stared at the prince, unsure what to say. Realization began to take hold that the actual prince of Calas was to join them in their expedition. Finally, Darin mumbled, "Well, I presume there is little else to be said." Looking up at Calien, he announced, "Despite our reservations, we accept your company and look forward to our journey together."

The prince nodded. "Thank you. I am certain I will gain your confidence. Now, I must momentarily take my leave, for I have much to prepare and other matters to handle before our departure. Tomorrow morning, on the seventh hour, we will meet at the palace stables. Is this acceptable?"

"Of course, Prince Calien."

"Excellent. I will see you then." The prince turned to leave when a voice startled him.

"Wait!"

Calien, and everyone else, whirled to gaze upon Kyligan who had spoken for the first time since his arrival within the palace.

"Yes?" Calien asked.

"What of Ragnall and his family? Will you not help them?" Even Kyligan was surprised with his boldness.

Calien turned his handsome features upon Ragnall and regarded the man thoughtfully. "What is your line of work?" he asked.

Ragnall nervously fiddled his thumbs under the prince's gaze. "Uh, I am, was, a tanner."

"Sir Ragnall, I will find you work and a place for your family to stay. Meet with the rest of us at the stables tomorrow morning and I will give you details."

Ragnall fell to his knees in tears. "Thank you, my Prince, thank you!"

"That is enough," Calien stopped him. "You needn't thank me. It is the least I can do for a man who has undertaken such tragedy, and yet maintained the strength to embark on a long trip to Calas all the way from Oester. You deserve it." The prince brought his eyes across the party. "I shall see you in the morn." With those words, he trotted off.

The group silently watched him go until he had disappeared around a large decorative pillar that rose to the ceiling. Alazar suddenly laughed, startling everyone. Reaching into the folds of his dull azure robes, he withdrew his chameleon. The small lizard's tongue flicked, rapidly matching the movements of it's eyes. "Disfrazal is uncertain of our new companion."

Cadwan sighed. "Disfrazal is not the only one."

*   *   *

The two stone walls that flanked the palace rose up like guardians, presenting themselves judgmentally for any passerby who was even vaguely tempted with the notion of sneaking inside the great citadel uninvited. Several guards paced the battlements atop the thick walls, warily scanning the streets below for any indicator of wrongful intentions or doings, ready to take appropriate action.

Among these guards, though not dressed in the same livery as the others, was a young man in his early twenties. Instead of the heavy plate mail, emblazoned with the official Calas royal insignia, he wore only bland leather garments and carried no weapons on his body. He leaned back in a rickety wooden chair, with his feet propped on a small stone bier, idly chatting with another guard. His thick, uncombed brown hair swayed in disheveled strings across his forehead, though the back was much longer and fell well beyond his shoulder blades.

"You should have seen her, Rhet," the man said, with a voice that reeked of confidence. "Hanging on my every word, she was. I could have been speaking rubbish and it would have mattered little. Besotted she was. Although," he hesitated a moment before adding more slyly, "I believe her wit left much to be desired."

The guard laughed. "Since when are you concerned about a woman's wit?"

"Not often," the man confessed, with a smile, "but even I have some standards."

"Ha! I've seen your *standards* before!" the guard scoffed. "You had better hope your father never finds out about your little nightly escapades."

"Since when has my father given a goat's shaft what I do?" He paused, as if considering something, then finished, "Regardless, he has discovered nothing."

"Prince Hetnar."

Both the guard and the man were on their feet before they even knew they were standing, their eyes on a man with stately posture and flowing, deep lavender robes.

Scowling, the leather-clothed man asked, "What is it, Geran?"

"I have some interesting news for you," the king's advisor proclaimed.

"Can it not wait?"

Geran shrugged. "It is quite important, but if you are busy then so be it. I will not disturb you further." He slowly turned on his heel to walk away.

Prince Hetnar looked at the guard, then to the departing Geran. With an annoyed sigh, he called, "Hold up, Geran." Shifting his gaze to the guard, Hetnar said, regretfully, "We will have to finish our discussion later, Rhet."

The guard nodded. "Of course, Prince Hetnar. I look forward to it." With those words, the guard ambled off, as if he suddenly had important duties to attend to.

When the footman was gone, Prince Hetnar returned his irritated eyes to the king's advisor. "Damnit, Geran, what is so important?"

"I am afraid this is not the most appropriate setting to discuss it. We must find a more . . . private setting."

Hetnar narrowed his eyes, understanding Geran's undertone. "Indeed? Let us go then."

The two walked silently down the precipitous stone stairs of the battlement wall, reaching the eastern terrace of the palace. Across the well-maintained lawn, several servants were tending to the grounds, while commoners and nobles alike crossed paths, going about whatever weighty or menial task they were set upon. Every day, barring certain holidays, the palace was a nucleus of commotion. Geran and Hetnar sought to evade the flurry of activity. They strode past the terrace, continuing along the edge of the courtyard until they had reached a bailey that looped around a small building used for garden and lawn tools.

As they proceeded, Geran viewed Hetnar with interest. Though both princes had identical parents, their physical features varied greatly between them. Where Calien's face exuded nobility, striking and pronounced, Hetnar's appearance was more stylish, like that of a cunning knave. His devilish smile complemented a pair of narrow, shrewd looking eyes and a perfect nose. There was a certain roguish look about him, which, Geran mused with a slight grin, matched his personality. He had always been looked upon as the 'other' son of King Anuron, not only in birthright, but also in the amount of attention and praise he garnered. Geran could only guess at how much that affliction had affected the young man's personality through the years.

With the crowds blocked from view, Prince Hetnar stopped and cast Geran a dubious look. "Speak, Geran. What news do you bring that I should find so interesting?"

"Prince Calien is traveling to Oester," Geran said, matter-of-factly.

Hetnar jeered loudly and followed it with morose laughter. "He has found the audacity to leave the shadow of his father? I am surprised he is even allowed to go. I presume Father is sending the entire army to escort him?"

Geran's lips curled at the last statement. "That is why this news is so interesting, my Prince. He travels not with an army, but with a handful of mercenaries."

Hetnar stared at the king's advisor, mouth open. After a moment, his composure was regained. "What is in Oester? What has possessed him to journey to the northern border of the kingdom?"

"Some incident of minor importance that needs looking into. Strangely, Calien decided it was time to prove himself to the king. He finally persuaded the old man to be allowed to accompany this group of mercenaries to Oester."

"When do they leave?" Hetnar asked.

"Tomorrow morning," Geran replied, watching Hetnar's face closely and taking note of every minute expression his visage portrayed.

"So sudden?" Hetnar shook his head. "So, my brother has an inkling of courage after all. I would have never guessed."

Geran had waited long enough. It was obvious he would be forced to plant the seed himself. Apparently, Hetnar would not recognize the potential if it crawled right up his leg. Darkening his demeanor, Geran lowered his voice ever so slightly and spoke slowly. "Do you glimpse the opportunity, my Prince?"

Hetnar froze and gave the king's advisor a wary look. "What are you getting at, Geran?"

Geran returned the prince's gaze, his face devoid of an expression that would betray his guile. He was a man of perception and he possessed a keen ability to see the weaknesses, and strengths, of others. His goal now was to manipulate a particular weakness of Hetnar, a weakness for which he had waited years to exploit. His patience was finally going to pay off. The right time, perhaps the only time, had come. He did not discern his task to be especially challenging. All that was needed was to plant the germ within the rogue prince. Hetnar would handle the rest. Speaking calmly and even, Geran asked, "Honestly, have you never dreamed of being king?"

Hetnar had never considered himself a genius, but he was a clever man. He had studied under the same handpicked tutors as his brother and even managed to do well despite his lack of interest or effort. When he heard Geran's words, realization flooded him all at once. Though his love for his brother left much to be desired, the idea of actually *killing* him had never seriously crossed his mind. He found himself at a loss for words and was only able to stare in a state of stupor at the king's advisor. Yet, even in his staggered condition, the notion swirled ever more enticingly within the back recesses of his mind.

"My Prince," Geran added, observing with pleasure as the concept blossomed ever so slowly before his eyes. "I have watched you grow just as I have your brother, and it is with no ill-gotten notion that I say you are far more suited to be the successor than he. Believe me, Prince, my concerns are for this great kingdom and I cannot bear the image of it shattering before my eyes as Calien sits like a cold stone upon the throne."

Hetnar remained silent, not yet daring to make a verbal move until he was certain the king's advisor was not jesting. He listened as Geran proved his case, hungrily sucking in every bit of reason the robed man threw forth.

"You are a man of the world," Geran continued. "A man who knows what life entails beyond the safety of the palace. You would understand the cries of the people, for you, yourself, have undergone such neglect. I believe the people would no longer suffer under your reign."

"You speak as if they suffer now? It is my understanding that Calas seems quite content with my father as king. Never has there been a political charge to dethrone him." Hetnar knelt and plucked a blade of green grass from the ground. "Even the farming has been fruitful."

"Anuron has done an acceptable job and I would never dream of harming him, but there are many things that lay hidden behind a veil of secrecy. By appearances, King Anuron may seem all-knowing, but I can assure you that that is not always the case."

By now, Hetnar was certain of Geran's intent, but he still felt it safer to continue testing the waters. "What makes you believe I wish to be king? I have never spoken of outward envy for my brother. Truthfully, I have never held much loyalty, or regard for Calas. Why would I want to live my life with such heavy responsibilities weighing me down?"

Geran smiled, inwardly. Although Hetnar rebuffed him, he knew his bait was snared. All that was left was to carefully reel him in. "Nary a man alive has not dreamt of becoming a king. Surely, you are no different."

"And why not?" Hetnar balked.

"Because nothing in life would bring you more prestige, more admiration than that of a king. Prince Hetnar," Geran lowered his voice and grew stern in demeanor. "Most men of this world are forgotten, disappearing in minds like the sun at dusk. A king is remembered forever."

Hetnar stood and paced the ground. Geran certainly had a way with persuasion and Hetnar was already envisioning himself upon the throne. The idea was not as dreadful as he might have once thought. Many of his life ambitions could be carried out with the riches he would have as a king. Stepping away, he stole a glace back at Geran. For some unexplainable reason, the man unsettled him. He had no true motive to fear the robed wiseman, but something about his guise kept Hetnar alert. Turning to face Geran, he asked guardedly, "Why should I trust you?"

Geran shrugged. "For years, I have kept a secret of your nightly exploits –

exploits that would certainly have you disowned, or at times, even jailed. You know I am trustworthy. Prince Hetnar, my goal is to make you king. There is no other scheme I could have."

The prince didn't remove his eyes from the king's advisor. "You say they leave tomorrow morning?"

"They do." Geran gazed upward. The sun had almost fully withdrawn for the day. All that remained of its earlier reign were vague threads of purple across the darkening sky. "On the seventh hour."

"Well then, how do you propose we accomplish this?"

Geran lifted his hands in a gesture of refusal. "I am afraid you are on your own for that, my Prince."

"Ha, I should have guessed!" the prince sneered and threw up his arms. "Propose the action and leave me with the responsibility. If something goes wrong, it traces back to me and you are left no worse for wear. Quite clever, but I'll not be your puppet for this, Geran!"

"No, you misunderstand me," Geran implored. "I will do whatever I can to back you. However, you are the one with the contacts, or should I say *associates*, who can carry out a task of this nature."

Hetnar scratched the thin stubble of his chin. It was true; he was acquainted with several individuals that would gladly take part in an enterprise that required dubious morals. His father would most likely keel over and die of shame, if he knew his son was associated in any way with characters of such disreputable quality. But, his father did not know, just like he did not know a great deal of other things about Hetnar. *Neglect can have its benefits*, he mused, glumly. "If they leave on the seventh hour, I must get started now. There are people to speak to. I will undoubtedly be out most of the night. If Father calls for me, I can assume you will cover?"

"Of course, my Prince."

Hetnar nodded. He still had not fully realized what he had just agreed to. It would take much of the night for the full effect to overwhelm him. "I will speak with you early tomorrow, Geran."

"Certainly." Geran smiled, shrewdly. It was a smile Hetnar noticed but decided was due to the nature of the task ahead. The king's advisor reached out and clasped the elbow of the prince. "Worry not, Prince. I have a feeling things will go well and that soon you will be the heir to the throne. Soon enough, I will no longer be allowed to call you a prince, but a king."

Hetnar turned away without reply and walked back toward the courtyard, leaving the privacy of their quarter behind. For the briefest of moments, he stopped and looked back at Geran, but he quickly resumed his departure. *A king*, he thought as a nervous smile emerged on his face. *A king*.

Geran watched him leave. When the young man had disappeared around a corner, he allowed himself an expression of satisfaction. As he had expected, the proposition was successful. Though strong-willed, Hetnar could be easily manipulated. He had never fully understood his role as the second son of the king and had spent his life searching for that very thing. Now, Geran was handing the prince a future, one that was impossible to refuse. With Hetnar as the heir, Geran's scheme would pan out perfectly, as would his influence over Calas.

"I'll not be your puppet," Hetnar had said to him.

The statement made Geran grin with wicked pleasure. *I guess, my dear Prince Hetnar, we will find out soon enough.*

VI

"So tell me, Prince Calien, what military training did you undertake as the heir of King Anuron?"

Calien straddled an extravagantly groomed stallion and trotted side-by-side with Cadwan at the front of the moving party. They had departed only minutes ago and were maneuvering their way through the teeming streets of the city. Like the previous two days, the heavens had again bequeathed the lands a pure blue expanse, leaving nothing to obscure the clear vastness above. The clouds were merely thin wisps of poetry among the shimmering cobalt skies. Calien hoped the weather was an auspicious prophecy for their journey ahead, though he admitted that his buoyant eagerness for adventure would lend itself to an encouraging premonition regardless of the weather. After hearing the question directed his way, the prince gazed at Cadwan with interest. "You are a former member of the Calas army, are you not? I am certain my training was similar to yours, though I probably received more individual attention. I practiced swordsmanship under the tutelage of Naráno, a master swordsman and the best the army has to offer."

Cadwan knew of Naráno and had briefly met the man once during his own service. In a duel, Naráno was highly regarded as unbeatable by most in the servitude of the Calas military. "Indeed? Then I am anxious to see you in action." He regarded the prince curiously. Visually, there were few similarities between the company and their new companion. Calien's unblemished platemail, embroidered with intricate silver and gold designs, was the highest of quality and made a stark contrast to the scuffed, drab chain armor and shabby torn robes worn by the others. A bright red mantle fell elegantly from Calien's shoulders and down his back, shifting gently to the movements of the stallion. His sword was likewise flawless. The instrument, encased in its jeweled scabbard, displayed a decorative hilt and blade that was etched with inlayed patterns. Though it was doubtlessly a fine weapon, the blade's opulence seemed more fitting as a decorative wall ornament rather than being subjected to the gruesomeness of battle. Such equipment, Cadwan reflected sardonically, could alone bring the party a fortune.

Soon, the city gates emerged ahead. Prince Calien raked over the city's exit with fervent anticipation, his stomach rising to his throat. Finally! His time to venture on his own had come and he was more than ready; ready to escape the haven that had been his home, perhaps his prison, for twenty-four years.

As a student growing up, he had excelled in his studies of geography. From an academic aspect, few could name landmarks and locations of the kingdom better than he. But to experience it, to see it with his own eyes without the constant protection of sentries would bring a new realism to a world he had only learned about through the thin ashen pages of books.

"Are we ready?" Cadwan's voice broke the prince's internal musings as they approached the gate.

A chorus of subdued mutterings followed Cadwan's call. Prince Calien peered back at the others, who were all engrossed in their own conversation. Returning to Cadwan, the prince asked, coolly, "How is it that you ride in the front of the others? Do you lead us?"

Cadwan smiled and shrugged. "Not intentionally. I am no more deserving than any of the others, but someone must do it. I have always felt Darin more fitting, as he is the one who speaks for us, but he has always insisted on following my lead."

Prince Calien glanced back at the dwarf, who was a good horse-length behind. Darin was watching them casually, but Calien wasn't certain he had heard their discussion. He then swept his eyes over the rest of the party, who were riding further behind Darin. Returning to Cadwan, the prince mouthed, "I must admit, you certainly lead an odd collection of troops."

Cadwan considered the comment. Truthfully, he was the least enigmatic member of the party. He possessed a straightforward, even manner that left little hidden from view. With Cadwan, what you initially perceived was exactly what you got; an honest face, a level demeanor, a common humor, and little else. Those same qualities, he knew, were not particularly true of the others. Eyes remaining on the road ahead, Cadwan answered, "Perhaps, but they are effective nonetheless. Even Cora," Cadwan chuckled, as he pitched a glace back at the halfling who was now riding with Kyligan and effortlessly chatting away, "will surprise you if you take her too lightly. Riding with them has been the greatest joy of my life."

"I admire your courage to leave the security of a paying job behind to pursue a life that is unrestricted by the bonds of common society. If I had lived another life, perhaps." The prince stopped, letting the words drift away.

Cadwan gave the prince a curious look, but quickly gave a motion of indifference. "Our journey might provide enough adventure to curb any such desires."

Prince Calien smiled, genuinely. "Perhaps."

Midday arrived quicker than the party had anticipated. Soon the afternoon hours were upon them. They had ventured well down the road heading west to

Houghton, and the crowds had thinned as they drew further from the city. They had taken no wagons along. What supplies and provisions they carried, such as food, weapons, an extra set of clothing, and some tools, had to be fitted into each individual's rucksack. Despite being accustomed to the added weight the horses groaned sporadically as they carried their masters onward.

So far, their trip had consisted of nothing more than idle banter, with only modest talk of what might possibly await them in Oester. Considering it would be a four or five day trip, each rider knew there was plenty of time for speculation of that sort. Still full of fervent optimism, Calien had used the early hours to get acquainted with the others. He hoped to put their minds at ease regarding his intentions and was determined to win their trust. Yet, the prince was unaware that while he had proved himself sincere and knowledgeable of history, his life as a coddled prince was obvious to the others. Although it was appropriate for the political banter between nobles within the lavish boundaries of the citadel, the regal cadence of which the prince spoke was not well suited to the world of commoners. Cadwan made a mental note that either he or Darin would have to dissuade the prince from speaking often, especially when the circumstance was crucial. The common world did not take fondly to the haughty, over-the-top bearing of nobles, and Cadwan certainly did not want their company perceived in such a way.

Though the going was slow at times, their trip thus far had gone uninhibited. Cadwan found himself enjoying the ride. Despite his reservations of traveling with a prince, the future king of Calas no less, he felt curious to how the journey would play out. Calien was not difficult to get along with, only untried in the outside world and filled with naïveté. Cadwan deemed it was their job to help him adjust, and befriending a future king could only be beneficial.

As if intentionally interrupting Cadwan's thoughts, a group of men emerging from the thick woods north of the road began to wave and shout loudly to the riders.

"We are being hailed," Darin muttered, looking over to Cadwan.

Without a verbal retort, Cadwan steered his gelding toward the men, the others following in his wake. There were three men total, dressed in the garments of simple woodsman. Cadwan examined them closely upon their approach and noted that two of the men were holding hatchets, while the third man's hands were empty.

Darin rode up next to Cadwan. Leaning over to the soldier, the dwarf whispered, "Bandits, perhaps? In the guise of woodsman? There could be more waiting in the trees."

"If so, they have seamlessly perfected the look of true woodsman," Cadwan answered. "I do not believe they are, but your dubiety is noted. It is wise to be on guard." Looking back at the others, Cadwan gave a nod. The remaining members of the party, save Calien, understood his meaning and gripped their weapons in response.

As they steered their horses closer, one of the woodsman, a broad-shouldered man with an overhanging brown mustache and a checkered woolen shirt, called out, "Friends, thank ye for answering our time of need!"

"How can we be of servitude?" Darin asked cheerily, though his slanted eyes belied his jovialness.

The man pointed his finger north into the dense thicket of trees. "For over a week, we have been working to clear a small section of trees just north of here in efforts to develop a permanent encampment. Our progress had gone well until a pair of worgs took residency in the clearing. They do not chase us, but they refuse to allow us to return to our work." The woodsman looked at his two companions. "We cannot handle the beasts ourselves, for surely we would be killed."

"So you ask us to eliminate these worgs, so you can continue your work?" Darin asked as he turned to Cadwan, who smirked in response to his dwarven friend.

"Only if you are up to it," the man replied. "Worgs are nasty beasts and we do not wish to send you to your deaths, if you are ill prepared."

Darin drew his horse closer to the head woodsman, his large, balding head tilted down on the man with heavy scrutiny. "And how can we be sure this is not some trap, that there are not more of you waiting in those trees to ambush us as we enter the wood?"

The man shook his head. "There is no way I can prove such a thing. But I ask you, do we truly look like brigands?"

Darin admitted it was unlikely these men were cutthroats. As Cadwan had stated, they looked like true woodsman, not only in attire but in their facial features and mannerisms. He looked at Cadwan. "Two worgs shan't prove difficult for the six of us," the dwarf commented.

"Hopefully not," the soldier retorted, as he allowed himself a glimpse back at the others. Each member returned his look with vigor and he was fully certain they were spirited enough to rid the world of a couple worgs.

Abruptly, Kyligan sauntered his horse forward from the back, bringing it sidelong with Darin's. Gazing down at the woodsman, the ranger withdrew his bow and began to string the weapon. "You are certain they are worgs?" he asked.

The man nodded, vigorously. "I have not a doubt. No wolf I know is that size, or has those ghastly red, blood lusting eyes."

Kyligan sighed, as if he already knew what the man's answer would be. Regarding Cadwan grimly, the ranger verbally spat, "Worgs! They are an abomination and their evil has no place in the forest."

The lead woodsman reached into a pocket and withdrew a single silver coin. "We have little money, but we can pay you a silver for each member of your party."

"That is unnecessary." Cadwan waved his hand, declining the offer. "We will help. What is your name, woodsman?"

"Ornan. This is Tamlynon and Wes." The other two men nodded.

Cadwan reached up to scratch his chin. "Well then, Ornan, show us the way."

With the woodsmen at the fore, the party plunged ahead, leading their mounts slowly through the thick underwood of the Grembel Forest. Packed tight, the trees left little room for the horses to maneuver, but the troop pushed onward as hanging branches and leaves brushed across their faces. Although it made a difficult going, Kyligan was pleased to see the greenery looking healthy and thriving. Plants and other types of flora concealed the ground, greedily weaving their way upwards in search of light. The tops of the trees blocked much of the lighted sky. Only the occasional stray sunbeam reached the tangled foliage below. For almost a half-hour, the party followed their escorts north.

Without prior notice, a heavy dose of light shone up ahead; an opening in the trees that was most certainly the camp of the woodsman. Ornan halted the group and pointed a stubby finger forward to the clearing. "The worgs are up there. They will not let you get very close."

"Tie up the horses," Cadwan called out. "I'll not risk losing one. We will enter on foot."

Dismounting, each individual secured the appropriate weapons from their saddles and straightened out their armor. Calien unsheathed his flawless blade and walked over to Cadwan who was slinging a quiver of arrows over his shoulder. The prince leaned close to the soldier, whispering in his ear, "I have never fought worgs before. What shall I expect?"

Cadwan cast the prince a furtive glance. "Expect an overly large wolf, with uncommon intelligence and a ceaseless lust to kill." Cadwan walked away leaving the prince to stare at the back of his head.

"Will you need our help?" Ornan asked, while the group gathered in efforts of making strategy.

"No," Darin said. "Stay with our horses. We will return shortly."

The sunlight grew brighter as the six snaked through the shrubbery toward the opening. While Cora appeared to effortlessly make her way though the dense thicket, hopping and lurching along random cavities of open ground, Darin did not have similar success. His short, stubby legs lacked the agility of his halfling companion and he stumbled along, often tripping on the vines and plants below. Several times, Kyligan grasped hold of his dwarven friend before he plunged headlong into the leafy earth.

It was to Darin's pleasure above all else when they reached the fringe of the future campsite Ornan had described. It was as if a large circle had been burned into the forest, leaving the space open to the mercy of the sky above.

Though the trees had mostly been cut down within the area, much of the vegetation beneath had yet to be removed before a suitable camp could be completed.

"There are the fiends," Cadwan pointed to a spot where two excessively big wolves were on their feet, growling in the party's direction. "And they seem wise to our presence."

Kyligan noticed Calien staring at the creatures, with a sickened expression. The ranger was certain the noble had never before laid eyes of such a monster, so he placed a reassuring hand on the prince's shoulder. The prince looked back at Kyligan and gravely shook his head. "I have read of worgs before in books, but I have never seen one until now. The sight of one consumes me with an odd shiver."

"Fear not, Prince," Kyligan comforted. "Though filled with unnatural evil, they are but mere animals. They bleed, and they die. There are six of us, and two of them. We will make short work of them, I am certain."

Calien nodded in response, but he was no more assured.

Cadwan called everyone together, whispering quietly, while the guttural moan of the worgs carried threats in their direction. "We must be careful. Worgs do not die easily. Cora, you and Darin will remain here. Kyligan and I will circle around to the back side. Alazar," Cadwan threw the hooded man a stern look. "take Calien halfway across the perimeter. When you see the first arrow fly from my bow, attack. Cora, use your crossbow and for Orithen's sake keep your distance. One bite from those jaws will tear you in half. Do not get foolish on me!"

Though she said nothing, Cora furrowed her brow at Cadwan, then swung her eyes to the others in an expression that conveyed a sense of unfound blame.

Satisfied that everyone understood the plan, Cadwan continued. "Prince Calien, can you handle yourself?"

The prince guffawed at the question. "How many times must I exclaim that I am an expert swordsman? You needn't worry about me."

Cadwan nodded, but he thought he noticed a hint of fear in the prince's eyes. Understandable, he reflected, as this was surely the first time he would be dueling with his own life on the line. "Let us finish this quickly then. I am anxious to be back on the road."

Darin grasped the pendant around his neck and murmured a quick blessing. "May Frundin grant us victory." Following the dwarf's prayer, Cadwan moved off into the wood, with Kyligan trailing.

"Come, my Prince." Alazar mouthed to Calien. "We must find our position and be ready."

Calien followed Alazar around the fringe, the opposite way of Cadwan and Kyligan. As they proceeded, Calien eyed the robed man curiously. He found Cadwan's choice of pairing as odd considering Alazar was probably the one member of the group he had conversed with the least of anyone. His outfit, nothing but unkempt loose fitting robes, did not seem appropriate attire for combat. And yet, the man seemed completely placid and unconcerned, a characteristic echoed by the lizard that sat calmly on his shoulder. "What will you fight with?" the prince asked the bearded man, while they maneuvered through the bush.

Alazar smirked only for an instant. "Though I haven't a sword, my approach in battle is no less daunting. You will see."

Calien's eyes fell on the man's hands, and then to the long staff that he carried. The wooden rod was finely crafted, but was no more imposing than other objects of similar fashion he had seen before. Is this what he means? Is he so extraordinarily skilled with a staff as to equal the ability of others with more destructive weapons? Calien found the man exceedingly odd. Alazar could have been more forward and explained how he fights, but he was obviously reveling in the notion of surprising Calien during the battle. Shaking his head, the prince raised his own blade to eye level, peering at its razor-sharp edges. One thing he was certain of; he'd take his sword over a wooden pole anytime and be thankful of it.

"And what of your lizard?" the prince furthered. "In taking him along, do you not worry he will be hurt?"

"Ha!" Alazar grasped the chameleon in his russet colored hand and kissed its scaly back before returning the writhing lizard to his shoulder. "I am not worried. Disfrazal takes care of himself."

The prince waited for an explanation, but quickly realized he would receive none. Apparently, Alazar had few words for the prince. It was well enough, as the robed man stopped suddenly, motioning that they were in a sufficient location. Calien peeked past the single tree that blocked their way into the clearing. Unexpectedly, the pit of his stomach began to ache.

The worgs were in a state of unrestrained alarm, fully conscious they were being surrounded. Each of them were pivoting on their paws, swinging in every direction so as to keep a keen eye on each of their foes. With their reedy, thinning fur standing rigid, backs hunched, and ears that rotated to match every sound, their disposition was nothing short of hostile. Their mouths were in a perpetual grimace and curled upward to display every inch of their fearsome sharp teeth, growling angrily. Large droplets of drool fell from their gaping maws onto the leafy ground.

Calien felt apprehensive, almost numb. Certainly, he did not dread the coming fight, did he? After all, this is what he had begged his father to partake in. But this was unlike sparring in the barracks, honing his skills against friends and acquaintances. Back then, death was not an option. Now, death was the solution. It suddenly occurred to him how that one variable entirely changed the outlook. This time, he would be fighting for his life.

His dour ponderings were cut short when an arrow whistled through the air, planting itself into the hide of a worg. The animal howled in pain as another arrow screamed past, this one from Kyligan. Had the animal not moved just as he released the string, the projectile would have hit the same worg square between the eyes. Instead, it missed its target by mere inches. The ranger dropped his bow and took up his sword, rushing into the heat of the fray. Calien also noticed Darin on the opposite side, wielding a large dwarven waraxe and hefting a steel shield, stumble his way past the last tree toward the worgs.

With a deep breath, Calien gripped his sword more firmly and jumped forward. Kyligan was already engaged in close combat with one the beasts, while Darin was harrying the other to come his way. From the very corner of his eye, he thought he saw Cora firing bolts from her crossbow, but he had yet to see any physical evidence on the adversaries as a result of her assault. The prince could hear nothing but the pounding of his own heart as he moved closer. He raised his blade high, ready to strike the oversized wolf in which Darin was also closing in on.

His vision went red.

As Calien blinked, a crimson flash flew past him. It was a ball of flame, and it had narrowly missed him as it shot forward into the unwary worg; the very same beast that still had Cadwan's arrow lodged in its side. On contact, the fire sphere exploded into the animal, scorching it terribly. Even then, the beast did not fall, though clearly the monster was wounded badly. Its skin and thin fur were smoldered black, and in some places tiny pockles of fire still burned. Its legs appeared weakened, as its steps slowed considerably. But still, the beast fought on. Calien looked back to see the source of the flame, only to find Alazar standing several feet behind him. The hooded man merely grinned when the prince looked his way. Calien decided it was one mystery he would have to decipher later and he swiveled back around, returning his attention to the scuffle.

Darin had his shield before him and the injured worg was leaping against it, clawing at the steel buffer in efforts to get past the dwarf's protection. Darin held his ground, putting his weight forward. Unseen from behind, Calien sliced his sword downward into the back of the animal. The worgs howl was hellish. It slid off the shield and groggily twisted around, legs hobbling, to face the new opponent. All the while, a stream of crimson ichor ran freely from its cracked spine. Calien stepped away to put space between himself and the savage jaws of his foe, waving his sword hypnotically to keep the creature baffled. Seeing the wolf's attention diverted, Darin lowered his shield and raised his massive waraxe, driving it with ruthless strength into the back skull of the crippled worg, splitting its head in two. The greenery below the animal turned red with the dead beast's blood.

In a moment of dream-like shock, Calien observed the bloodied heap, taking in every detail of the death he'd helped manufacture, noting the grisly carnage that resulted. He realized his initiation into real combat was completed, but before he could dwell on the spectacle any longer the sounds of more combat yanked him from his internal ponderings. Kyligan was still dueling solo with the other worg. Thin streams of blood ran leisurely down the hide of the animal, the result of several arrows and crossbow bolts Cora and Cadwan had fired its way. Kyligan stayed on the move, jabbing in with his sword and then backing away quickly, preventing the beast from getting a clean path to his throat. He had successfully slashed off the end of one paw, but the furious creature stayed on him nonetheless. Alazar came into view, snapping his staff hard into the posterior of the worg. The beast yelped, taking note of its new attacker. Indecision filled its mind as it deliberated which foe to strike at.

The momentary hesitation proved fatal. By now, Cadwan had given up his bow in favor of his mace and was moving toward Kyligan for support. Additionally, Calien and Darin also drew near. Together, the party converged on the overmatched worg. A shrill bellow chimed loudly. Moments later, the second worg looked much like the first, a gruesome mess of torn flesh, entrails, and blood.

With the battle concluded, Cadwan wiped sweat from his brow and looked over the group. "Any injuries?"

Save for a small claw mark on Kyligan's forearm, there were none. Although the ranger said nothing, Cadwan noticed the wound and tossed him a bandage to wrap around the cut.

Prince Calien gazed at the remnants of the mêlée. Adrenaline still coursed through him. It seemed strange that the two bloodied masses on the ground were once active, living beings. Thankfully, he didn't feel the dreaded pang of remorse. His first real combat experience and he had survived unscathed, mentally and physically. A sense of satisfaction permeated his confidence and he grew ever more excited for what must lie ahead.

The prince noticed Alazar sitting on a chopped tree stump, calmly readjusting his robes. Something else entered the prince's mind.

Alazar heard the prince approach, but he did not gaze upward until the prince spoke. "You . . . what *are* you, some kind of *wizard?*"

Pulling his hood farther over his head, Alazar gave Calien an odd expression. "In truth, I am uncertain. All my life, I have had the strange ability to wield fire and flame from my fingers. I am devoted to discovering the purpose for this gift and mastering its power."

The bearded man looked away, ignoring Calien, as if he no longer stood there. The prince could not help but stare at the man a minute longer. Alazar was indeed eccentric and Calien had the feeling there was much yet to learn of his fire-throwing companion.

Viewing the battle scene, the prince brought the blade of his sword to eye level. Blood, from the grossly overlarge wolves, remained on the weapon and was already beginning to dry. Never before had his sword been soiled by the blood of others, but he had an ominous feeling it would not be the last.

"Not in the palace anymore, are you, Prince?"

Calien turned back to see Alazar grinning at him.

*   *   *

Prince Hetnar, second son of King Anuron, peered through slits of narrowed eyes at the four riders in his company. Two of them he knew, if not particularly well. One was a female, a lithe figure who, though not shatteringly attractive, was by no means a blight to the eye. Her sandy brown hair was cut shorter than most women, falling only to her ear, and her unblemished face bore an endless scowl that delivered a stern message to anyone who mistook her for a common harlot. Hetnar knew her by the name of Ayna, though there was no way of knowing whether that was indeed her true name. As with most of his acquaintances that hailed from the slums of Calas, false names and concealed identities were as common as the rising sun. Hetnar had only met Ayna briefly on two previous occasions, but he wholly understood she was no one to be trifled with.

It was Endias, riding beside him, who Hetnar had spoken with the same night Geran had presented him the notion of murdering his own brother and subsequently attaining the throne when his father passed on. Hetnar grazed his eyes over the rogue only briefly before returning them to the road. Endias was a man in which appearances meant little. His cleanly shaven face was even and placid looking, preserving no outlandish features that might convey his dark facade and even darker objectives. Even the man's clothing, which was nothing more than thick leather garments, gave away little. Only the short sword hanging from his belt and the crossbow strapped to his steed's back hinted at something greater.

Although Endias was nearly ten years Hetnar's elder, the prince had instantly taken a liking to the man from the first night he'd encountered him in one of the ramshackle pubs that dwelled in the shadowy side of the city. Since that night, Hetnar had spent many hours listening keenly to Endias's tales of stealth and bounty. Soon, Endias was one of the very few people in the slums in which the prince had granted his real identity to. The assassin had kept the truth a secret, for with any man of wisdom, such knowledge would one day become quite profitable for a man in his line of business. Endias was Hetnar's first choice for the job and the prince was pleased the scoundrel was available. He knew no other who could efficiently and callously succeed in such a dicey undertaking. He was a ruthless cutthroat who, given the right price, would carry out the most vile task, with no conscience and even less remorse.

The other two riders Hetnar had never seen before, but Endias had insisted that they were of the finest mettle, the perfect men for the assignment. Even so, the prince felt uncertain of them. He was a man who trusted none, yet he had no other option but to rely on Endias's judgment, for he was certainly an expert cutthroat of his own accord and likewise would do well discerning similar abilities in others. What didn't sit well with the prince was that Endias had informed the others of Hetnar's true identity. Although it took away the burden of having to hide it throughout the mission, he worried that such knowledge would haunt him in the future. Ultimately, he shrugged it off. Besides, the prince mused, they could always be removed afterward if need be.

The company's departure was later than Hetnar had hoped for and he guessed they were several hours behind Calien. Not that he was worried. He knew they would most certainly make stops in both Houghton and Mullikin before they reached their goal north in Oester, and Hetnar had the option of intercepting them in either place.

The prince brought his black mare alongside Endias. Silence had engulfed them for almost an hour and he was itching to break it. "When do you propose we strike?"

The assassin cast sapphire pupils on Hetnar, his expression remaining unchanged as he did so. "At this point, there is no way of knowing. Of all people, my dear Prince, you should know that the best opportunities often come unexpectedly. I can only presume we will successfully locate where they take lodging each night and from there determine if a suitable opportunity presents itself. We are fortunate that we can be patient to some extent. If we prematurely rush toward our goal, the consequences of failure would be dire indeed. In that regard, let us hope for a quick death, as I can only imagine the harsh penalty for attempting to murder the future king of Calas."

Hetnar grunted. "I can assure you, I have no intention of allowing such an outcome to occur."

"Nor I, Prince," Endias said, sardonically. "But who can accurately predict the future?"

"Your pessimism makes me question your abilities," Hetnar said.

To the prince's surprise, Endias allowed himself a brief chuckle. "You need not worry for my abilities. They are as sharp as ever, and my focus the equivalent. I only speak in such a way to point out the importance of how precise we must be in our endeavor."

Hetnar nodded, slowly. "That is something we can agree upon."

Ayna, the female who had apparently heard parts of their conversation, drew her own mount near and spoke. Her voice was deceptively soft and tender. "I would think Mullikin would be a better commune for our ends. It is a haven for travelers and passing merchants. Our presence will be ignored, as long as our profile is kept low. When the sun sets, we will become just one of many threats the city holds at night. The guards will have other concerns and with any luck, we should go unnoticed."

"Agreed," Endias added. "though it will do no harm to find where our friends stay in Houghton. We shan't pass up any opportunities."

Hetnar gazed at the two cutthroats and smiled. His comrades were all business, cold and pitiless in their plotting. There was a saying that great men surround themselves with great company. He didn't know if he considered himself great, not yet anyway, but there was no question in his mind that his company held that status.

For the first time ever, Hetnar began to truly wonder what it would be like to be king.

VII

There was only darkness.

Then something moved within the black shroud. Emerging like a butterfly escaping the confinement of its cocoon, the tendril slowly appeared. Dripping a fetid liquid, the green worm-like vine reached forward, searching for its prey. A vile stench wafted upon the air, corrupting whatever purity the night had held before its arrival. Though small, the tentacle was imposing nonetheless, inching into full view toward the man that could only stare helplessly, his face frozen in utter repulsion and ghastly horror.

Breaking free of his stupor, Kyligan shakily regained his bearings. He was encircled by the cover of trees, but he dolefully realized that this was not his home in the Great Forest. The trees of this place were warped, twisted; the green of the leaves, the brown hue of the bark altered just enough to give the copse a misshapen, almost perverse look. Even the moon was fouled, bestowing but a fraction of its normal light. A thin film of mist hung languidly in the air, further hindering his vision. Kyligan shivered, feeling a sense of evil unnaturalness. As he listened intently, he could hear no animals, no wildlife, no whisper of the wind about him. The only sound to combat the eerie silence was his own beating heart.

Though Kyligan had momentarily turned away to view his unfamiliar surroundings, the tendril, still writhing upon the undergrowth, would not be ignored. It surged forward, the fallen leaves and flora rustling as it squirmed across the ground. The ranger again fixed his eyes on the abomination. Though it was not long, perhaps the length of his leg in full extension, he was consumed with fear.

Searching frantically through the darkened woods, Kyligan spotted a tiny path through the underbrush leading away from the object of his terror. He ran. With no sense of direction, Kyligan simply hoped to escape the horrid atrocity. He moved his legs with great haste, plunging into the shadows of the wood and leaving the thrashing limb behind. Overhanging braches scraped his face and tore his clothing as he flew past, but they were barely noticed in his desperation to flee. A noise, much like the squealing of a pig, caused him turn back. *Gods, it was chasing him! And it had grown larger!* The tentacle was now at least equal to Kyligan in size and was easily keeping pace with the fleeing ranger. It scuttled through the trees at remarkable speed, the sound of breaking twigs and crumbing leaves left in its wake.

Kyligan pushed himself harder. The path weaved back and forth, never straightening. He found it difficult to maintain adequate speed as he repeatedly altered his direction to remain on the narrow trail. The reverberation of his pursuer was still coming from behind and he could feel its unabated determination to seek him out. He felt as though a target had been painted on his back, and sooner or later, the arrow would reach him and strike true.

Fear still urging him, he intensified his speed. His legs ached in defiance, yet he had no desire to heed their call. Kyligan was well conditioned and an adept runner, especially in wooded surroundings. He was sure he could outrun whatever this monstrosity was. As he scurried onward, the trees and plants whipping past his peripheral vision, he wondered if there would be an end to the path, or if it would continue on, forever twisting through the thick brush and leading him in circles.

Ultimately, the noises from behind abated, and Kyligan, breathing heavily, slowed for a moment to see whether he had successfully escaped his tormentor. A cautious glace backward revealed only the eerie wooded path. What lie beyond the dark veil of his vision he could not determine, but it seemed as though his pursuer had given up the chase. He could hear nothing, and no movement was discernable to his eyes.

Kyligan's breathing slowed as he came to a stop. He rubbed his aching legs and pondered where he might be.

It appeared again.

Bursting from the black wall of night, the hideous shape was larger still, nearly three times its previous size. It plowed through the forest, uprooting unfortunate trees that happened to get in its way, as it zeroed in on the ranger. The skin of the giant tendril, a green-brown hue, continued to ooze some type of putrid liquid. The tip narrowed to a point where it wriggled discordantly with the rest of its body.

Mercy's sake, what demon-possessed fiend do I face? Now, as it bore down on him, Kyligan realized there was no possibility of outrunning the giant vine. Slinging his bow from over his shoulder, he readied it and reached for an arrow. His hand grasped only air. His quiver was empty! For an instant, he wondered how that was possible. He always kept it well-stocked with arrows. It seemed implausible that now, in his time of need, it would be utterly void of them. Unfortunately, he had no time to reflect on the oddity, for the colossal form, which seemed to be ever growing, had reached him.

Thankfully, his sword was still in its scabbard. Kyligan freed the blade and held it before him, defensively. The tendril, now twenty feet higher than the ranger, towered over him, swaying back and forth menacingly. Kyligan nearly keeled over and retched from the rancid smell that invaded his nostrils.

"What do you want?" the ranger screamed.

There was no answer. The shape continued to shift before him, as though sizing up its prey. Kyligan swung his blade and the edge of the weapon cut deeply into the sinewy form. A stream of black fluid erupted from the wound. The tentacle spasmed once, then flung the tip of its body forward, thrashing the ranger across the face.

The force of the blow was great and Kyligan's neck snapped back fiercely. His body followed and soon he was crumpled on the dirt ground. He lost grip of his sword and heard it thud against a malformed tree, too far from his reach. When he opened his eyes, his blood was staining the rough earth as it poured from a gash across his jaw line. The tentacle hovered above him threateningly.

Kyligan tried to reposition his body so he could regain his feet, but the massive form dropped its midsection square onto his shoulders, pinning him down. The tip of the monstrosity then wheeled around and directed itself at his stomach. *It's going to impale me!* Kyligan screamed and kicked his legs, attempting to either scoot out from under the object, or at least keep away from the pointed tip. His efforts were in vain.

The point, far sharper than Kyligan would have guessed, moved gradually down into his gut, skewering him slowly. His own cries of pain were the last thing he heard, as he died.

*   *   *

"Stop him, Alazar!" Cora shouted.

"What do you think I am trying to do," Alazar snapped back. "Kyligan!" The robed man shook the ranger by the shoulders.

Beside the bed within the modest room, Kyligan was standing upright on his own power, yet he was completely unaware. His body trembled with eyes that gazed forward into nothing, as the other two occupants attempted to bring him to consciousness.

"His screaming is horrific! I can hardly bear it," Cora cried out, near to tears from panic.

"Kyligan! Gods man, wake!" Alazar looked at the halfling, helplessly. "Perhaps I should hit him?"

Cora shook her head. "How should I know?" She peered frightfully up into the face of the ranger, who was expending every ounce of his vocal strength, as he screamed. "Just do something to stop it!"

All at once, as if by Cora's command, Kyligan went silent and his eyes gained focus.

A man not easily shaken, Alazar quivered unwillingly when he glimpsed the mixture of horror, bewilderment, and utter submission within the ranger's eyes. Kyligan's knees buckled and Alazar grabbed him to prevent the ranger from collapsing to the ground. "You are safe now, friend," he mouthed calmly, as he helped sit him down on the bed. "Just relax. You have had a nightmare. Cora, get him some water."

The halfling rushed to a large pot and dipped a tin cup inside. The three were inside one of the few rooms the scanty inn had had available. Cadwan, Darin, and Calien were in a separate room down the hall. Earlier in the night, when the party had reached the village of Houghton, they had elected the meager inn over more luxurious alternatives due to its cheaper price. At first, the prince had argued the selection. Then, abruptly, and with much shame, Calien realized he had neglected to bring along money of his own, and he promptly withdrew his objection.

Moments later, Cora returned with a full cup of water. Alazar took the cup and handed it to Kyligan. "Here, drink."

Still trembling, Kyligan took the water and greedily swigged the fluid. After emptying the contents, he returned the cup to Cora and sighed heavily. "I am fine now."

Alazar snickered. "Hardly. Even now you shake."

"Oh, Kyligan, your dream must have been awful," Cora added, hugging his shoulder.

Kyligan looked into Cora's eyes for a brief moment before turning away and rubbing his sweaty face. "I can remember it," he muttered, sullenly.

"What?" Alazar's eyes widened. "You remember? Is this the first time?"

Kyligan nodded.

"Ah, we have our first breakthrough in the matter of your plaguing dreams. Perhaps we should wake Cadwan and the others?"

"No," the ranger answered, his body slowly calming itself. "Let them sleep. There is no reason to wake them in the middle of the night. We can tell them in the morning. Besides, there was little that revealed itself to me."

"Well, go on. Tell us!" Cora demanded, still clinging to Kyligan's side.

Alazar studied the ranger's face intently. In a manner rare for the outspoken sage, he chose his words carefully. "I know it must be painful to retell the experience, Kyligan, but perhaps we can help in some way? I am very interested in hearing of this frightening dream."

Kyligan shrugged feebly. "There is little to tell, really. I was chased and murdered by a giant vine."

Frowning, Alazar walked over to a small desk and lifted Disfrazal. The lizard had been lounging contentedly after devouring a meal of small insects that Alazar had set out prior to Kyligan's outburst. "Dreaming of one's own demise is never good omen." He tapped Disfrazal's head, causing the reptiles eyes to dart upward. "A giant vine? Indeed, that is unclear. Are there no other details you can offer?"

The ranger stood up from the bed and sauntered over to the water pot to dip himself another cup. "I was surrounded by trees." He paused to take a sip. The liquid glistened on his lips. "But they were like no wood I have ever encountered. Everything was distorted, poisoned."

Kyligan stopped to wait for a reply from the others, but when none was offered he continued, "It was in this place that I was attacked."

"By this . . . giant vine?" Alazar asked.

"More like a tentacle. It was hard to distinguish exactly what the thing was in the unnatural darkness." Kyligan closed his eyes, trying to remember. "When I first saw it, it was tiny, the size of a small snake. But it grew, and soon it was easily thirty feet in length, with girth to match. It chased me through the woods and eventually caught up. I tried to fight, but it held me down and . . ." He stopped, letting the others imagine what had happened next.

Cora looked ruefully at Alazar, whose face was in deep contemplation. Once again, the halfling went to Kyligan's side and clasped his midsection. "I am glad you are not harmed, Kyl. I have never seen any man, or woman, scream like that."

Kyligan couldn't help but feel warmth from Cora's concern. She was affectionate and caring. He felt fortunate to be in her company. Patting her head, he whispered, "I am fine. Thank you both for your aid."

Alazar had hardly acknowledged the comment. He was deep in thought over Kyligan's story. Ultimately, he shook his head. "I am afraid your story is too unclear to infer anything specific. I do wonder, however, what it was that made you remember this time after you awoke. For a year, these visions have escaped you. Now, all of the sudden, you remember it clearly. Perplexing, would you not say?"

Returning to the bed, Kyligan gazed at the bearded man. "I wish I had an answer, Alazar. Unfortunately, answers seem hard to come by."

The comment made Alazar chuckle. "Is that not always the way? Forever too many questions, never enough answers."

"What now, Kyl?" Cora asked. "Can you sleep yet tonight?"

"I am afraid sleep is impossible. My thoughts are consumed by what I have unconsciously witnessed."

"I will keep you company," the halfling stated, a small hint of glee in her voice.

Alazar glanced at Cora, then over to Kyligan. With an elongated sigh, he muttered, "Well, I presume I am left with little choice but to stay up, as well. I dare not leave you to Cora's mercy. You will end up in more trouble than you could ever wish for."

Kyligan smirked and wiped the hair out of his face. I am lucky to have such faithful friends, he told himself. For years, he had lived the life of a recluse. Now, he realized why he had missed them so much over the past year. To be able to share one's burdens was a priceless quality and he knew that Cora and Alazar, as well as the others, would gladly share his.

Breaking the momentary silence, Kyligan suddenly asked, "What do you think awaits us in Oester?" His question was not particularly directed at either individual.

"I do not know." Cora answered with a frown, a serious intonation abruptly overcoming her normal upbeat timbre. "But the horror in the eyes of that man was equal to the horror in your eyes just now. What lies ahead must be formidable, indeed. I believe Cadwan and Darin underestimate the danger."

Though he had witnessed it before, Kyligan always found it exceedingly strange when Cora altered from her normally cheerful and often childish behavior to the subtle, grim bearer of wisdom. With each instance, it intrigued him more. "Perhaps," Kyligan spoke softly. "But neither are fools. I trust them fully."

"As we all do," Alazar added. "But life is fragile. We must prepare as if death awaits in eager anticipation."

"Such is our life, yes?" Kyligan gently laughed. "We have chosen this path."

"Yes we have," Cora furthered, "but we yet hold influence over where the path leads us."

VIII

Though a light sprinkle had reemerged from above for the first time in a week, the next day of travel had left the party with unexpectedly few obstacles. Early on, Cadwan, Darin, and Calien had listened intently to Kyligan retell the grim tale of his nightmare. Like Alazar and Cora, they were equally puzzled, offering few answers, though they each agreed that Kyligan's sudden remembrance of previously veiled dreams was hopefully a change in a positive direction.

The riders had turned north from Houghton and now jaunted onward, pushing past the overhanging braches of the Great Forest to the west and the Grembel to the east. The woods pressed firmly against the road, thinning the path that stretched beyond the suspended leaves and out of sight. Even so, throughout the lighted hours the roads had proved less crowded than they had feared. By late afternoon, they had made excellent progress and were rapidly approaching their objective for the day, the fortress town of Mullikin. With the improved travel, the overall mood of everyone had also taken a turn for the better. The overcast skies did little to dampen their newly charged disposition and with an extra day to grow acquainted, they had generally accepted Prince Calien as a viable member of the group, though admittedly he would remain the *other* member.

"How did a dwarf come upon your company?" Prince Calien asked aloud, seeking conversation more than answers. He shifted uncomfortably within his saddle.

"Largely by accident." Cadwan answered, inwardly amused at the prince's aching of his tired frame. It was clear that Calien was not accustomed to riding a full day, much less two days continuous. "When King Anuron granted me an assignment to examine the unknown problem in Thumble, Darin was present."

"Aye," the dwarf furthered, "I was an emissary of the dwarven kingdom Ludun, endeavoring to build better relations between the two lands. When I became aware of Thumble's situation, there was nary a better opportunity to exhibit Ludun's goodwill. I was approached by Geran, the king's advisor, to accompany Cadwan in his investigation." Darin itched his forehead and wiped his rain weathered dome. "Since, our friendship has grown strong and I have found myself unable to abscond from the party. I now find myself eagerly anticipating the exploits that will follow."

Calien's eyes swept across the entire party, visually taking in each individual before pausing on the dwarf. "So you have renounced your position as emissary in order to adventure freely?"

The dwarf shook his head. "Not so. Officially, I still act as an envoy. As with the assignment ahead, each task I take proves Ludun is willing to give aid to Calas and promote amity."

"Do you ever plan on returning to Ludun?"

"One can never foretell the future, but I have no burning desire to go back anytime soon." Darin gripped his battleaxe sturdily and grinned broadly. "I am enjoying myself too much."

The prince squinted to view the ornament around the dwarf's neck. "Your pendant, it looks religious."

Darin clasped the symbol in his large hand. "I am a priest of the great Grimgar Frundin, dwarven god of battle."

Calien had another question in the ready when he was suddenly interrupted by Cadwan. "Ah, here we are," the soldier proclaimed, looking ahead.

Turning a bend in the road, the party witnessed a circular walled stronghold beyond the wood. Pressed against a hill, the settlement sat under gray clouds that cloaked the sky. The surrounding land was relatively barren. Only the dark protrusion of the Barren Hills beyond covered the distant horizon. The group silently observed a merchant caravan approach the fortress gates where several guards methodically examined it before approving its entrance.

Mullikin was located directly on the crossroads of an important trade route and though its population barely surpassed a thousand, its daily activity rivaled that of any city. Its close vicinity to the roaming orc tribes of the Barren Hills to the north caused it to be a harsh, no-nonsense kind of settlement that was heavily patrolled. The guards kept a sharp eye on the visiting merchants and travelers, as well as looking out for orc raiders. The raw, durable feel of Mullikin was a stark contrast to the opulence of Calas, as most of the buildings and outer walls were constructed of rough stone and granite. Its overall appearance gave the town a frontier feel, and in doing so attracted individuals of all ilk.

Mullikin had already been the site of more than one battle and the locals prided themselves on their resiliency and toughness. Apart from certain exceptions, they greeted visitors uncaringly and viewed them only as a means to profit the local economy.

Three guards approached the company as they neared the main gate, the only way in or out of the walled interior.

"Greetings!" Darin called out, cheerfully.

Two of the guards stopped before the horses, while the third continued to flank Cadwan's lead horse. Cadwan strained his eyes in the fading light to examine the man, but the silhouette from the jagged stone walls looming above darkened the man's features.

"What is your business in Mullikin?" the guard inquired in a straightforward, unemotional tone.

"Just passing through on our way to Oester. We are simply looking for a comfortable place to stay for the night," Darin answered. "Would you happen to know of any?"

"A comfortable place? There be the Mullikin Inn, but I dare say the rocks at our feet be just as comfortable." The guard snickered and turned back to his comrades, who promptly took their cue and chuckled with him. When his laughter had run its full course, the man resumed his interest on the party. With a tip of his head, he announced, "I am Brisdan, Lieutenant of the Mullikin militia. Give me a moment to inspect your belongings and take your names, and then you can be on your way."

Lieutenant Brisdan promptly removed the cover of Cadwan's pack and proceeded to casually dig though his possessions.

"Do you have the proper authority to so freely view our personal effects? I find this disconcerting."

With a face of annoyance, Brisdan pulled his eyes away from his task and over to the speaker that had questioned him, Prince Calien. "Well, you certainly seem out of place, like a drowning eagle." The watchman waved a hand toward Calien's outfit. "Might I ask who, with such textbook knowledge of guard protocol and a grand outfit that hardly matches that of his comrades, graces my presence?"

Prince Calien scowled at the guard's audacity. "I am Prin . . ."

"He is Peredan." With the verbal swiftness rivaling that of any bard, Darin interrupted the prince, his voice reaching a volume rarely used. "He is a noble of the Daire House of Calas. We are escorting him to Oester. Please forgive his rashness, Lieutenant Brisdan, for he is unaccustomed to many of the common worldly ways."

Throughout the dwarf's comments, Brisdan had remained calm, visibly showing no affects of Calien's brash inquiry. When Darin had finished, Brisdan approached the prince and smiled cordially. "Noble Peredan," he explained with the smallest hint of cynicism. "my job is to keep Mullikin safe from any foreseeable circumstances that might jeopardize the lives of our residents. That includes protecting it from solitary bandits and scheming organizations, alike."

Calien only stared back. When he did finally open his mouth to answer, Brisdan cut him off.

"Men of such ill intent rarely volunteer their true intentions willingly. It is not words that prove identity, *nobleman*," the lieutenant emphasized the word

56

with dripping sarcasm, "for words are fickle at best." Brisdan could see the red pocks of discomfiture and humiliation form on the blond man's face, but he continued unheedingly. "And just for future reference, Noble Peredan, most folk are not fond of being told how to do their job. Just as we tell the children; you worry for your own skin and let everyone else worry for theirs."

"You have clearly made your point, Lieutenant Brisdan," Darin interceded. "There is no need to further it." In the back, Alazar covered his mouth to keep his laughter from escaping his lips. His shoulders bobbed up and down, and Cora threw him an angry glare. Like most people she met, she had taken a liking to the prince.

Straight-faced, Brisdan nodded in satisfaction and continued his inspection. After finishing up and then recording the names of each member, he looked curiously at the dwarf. "You say you are making your way to Oester?"

"We are."

Brisdan ran a gauntleted hand over the hilt of his sheathed sword and looked to the distant horizon, as if viewing the far off village. "I advise you to be cautious on your way. Several folk from that place have arrived recently, all of them looking for shelter."

Darin shot a glance at Cadwan, and then the others of the party. The incident with the prince was quickly forgotten, as their minds immediately focused upon the words of the lieutenant. For several seconds, the party stared silently at Brisdan, who only returned their gaze with apparent confusion.

Taking his horse a step forward, Cadwan spoke with grim interest. "Have these people spoken of anything that occurred there?"

The lieutenant shrugged. "That is what I found the curious. They would hardly speak at all, and they acted scared, as if something terrible had frightened them."

"Are they still inside the town?"

Brisdan looked back at the other two guards, who in turn shook their heads. Returning to Cadwan, Brisdan showed a face of uncertainty. "I cannot be sure. We pay more attention to who enters rather than who leaves. Now that I think of it ,though, I seem to remember a few on their way out." When the lieutenant noticed everyone hanging on his every word, he narrowed his eyes suspiciously. "Why such concern over a few people?"

"We are merely protecting our own interests," Darin quickly replied. "Obviously, if danger lurks ahead, we wish to know about it."

Brisdan chuckled at the dwarf. "Well, I have spoken everything I know of it. Perhaps some of the refugees are still within these walls? Ask them if you wish."

"Of course," Cadwan said, reining his mount forward and motioned for the others to follow.

"Hold it!" Brisdan yelled, stepping up to Cadwan's saddlebags. "For taxation purposes, I must ask the following: Do you carry any goods which you intend to sell within the walls of Mullikin? If so, you will need proper paperwork."

Cadwan shook his head. "We have nothing to sell. We only seek lodging before we move on."

Brisdan waved his hands toward the gate. "Then you are free to enter. Understand though, there will be strict consequences for disorderly behavior."

"You can be assured we will cause no such thing. Thank you for your time." Again, Cadwan spurred his ride ahead towards the entrance, nodding at the other two guards as he past them by.

As soon as they reached the interior, Darin pulled his horse alongside Cadwan. "Do you think we will find anyone from Oester here?"

Cadwan peered into the eyes of his dwarven friend. Ultimately, he shook his head. "We can always try, but even *if* they are here somewhere they will not be easy to locate."

With a terse grunt, Darin leered at the streets ahead. "Well, the night is far from over. Where do you propose we start?"

*   *   *

The Iron Hill Tavern was a busy place, especially at night. Patrons of all sorts; travelers, merchants, soldiers, even a thief or two, crammed every nook and cranny of an operation that seemed far too small for the large crowds that attended it each evening. The constant resonance of chatter filled the pub like buzzing from a hive, while the heavy stench of alcohol pervaded strongly enough to be noticed by those outside who had yet to enter the building.

For Elessa, the comely establishment had virtually been her home for the last ten years. Often, she found herself wondering how the years had whisked by so quickly and with so little memories to fill them. In the beginning, when Gully had offered her the part-time job as barmaid when she was but a mere twenty-one winters, she would have scorned the notion that ten years later she would still be in the same exact place. Yet, here she was, still tending tables, while everyone else she knew had moved on and pursued their ambitions, whatever those may have been. She could hardly remember her youthful dreams anymore. It seemed reality had bolted her feet firmly on the ground, preventing her imagination from obscuring the heartlessness that life had by now fully implemented.

But how could she leave? Gully would do anything, *give* her anything, to keep her. He had seen too many servers leave over the years, and truthfully, he knew full well that Elessa was the probably the biggest reason the Iron Hill Tavern was so popular. In one respect, she knew she shouldn't complain. Gully was a good friend and protected her well from the ruffians that would occasionally harass her, not to mention that he paid her generously. Her job, though painfully demanding, gave her financial solidity and allowed her to exercise her sociable nature. She felt pulled in opposite directions; her loyalty to Gully one way and her desire to rekindle long lost dreams the other.

"Come, lass, there be tables to tend." Gully's voice startled her from her momentary lapse. "Six and nine wait to give orders."

Elessa looked at Gully, who stood at the door of the kitchen. He was only a few years her elder, but the gruff nature of his job had taken a heavy toll. He looked older than his years. His brown hair was thinning at a remarkable pace atop the crown of his head and small wrinkles had begun to take shape around his eyes and forehead. He was a diligent worker and ran the tavern with uncompromising efficiency, but Elessa wondered if he was truly content with life. *Does he share the same sense of regret as I?*

"Coming," she answered, scooping up two platters of food and lofting both overhead. Exiting the kitchen, she entered the main room and immediately weaved her way through the tight spaces between tables. The platters were heavy, but the years had conditioned her well and she rarely buckled under the weight, or experienced sore muscles when closing time arrived.

As she maneuvered through the crowd, she could feel the eyes of the patrons following her. At least the catcalls have been kept to a minimum this night, she thought. Although an occasional compliment was flattering, there were nights when the jeering would get agonizingly out of control and she would be forced to call upon Gully to physically remove the guilty party. Though her appearance was often harried by the demands of her job, few could deny her attractiveness. Her youthful face and well-formed figure were almost impossible to ignore in a tavern full of drunken males. Her loose-fitting barmaid uniform only accentuated her lovely extremities.

Six tired looking travelers slumped in their chairs, as Elessa approached a table. One of the men, a hooded fellow with a drooping black beard, was mumbling something irritably. Though she couldn't quite make out what bothered him, she guessed it might have something to do with one of the corner legs of the rickety wooden table. It was shorter than the others and caused the table to slightly bob up and down, depending on how one put weight upon it.

Gazing at the party, Elessa found them an exceedingly odd combination. One of them wore extravagant armor that belied his presence in a pub filled with commoners, and the inclusion of a dwarf and a halfling in the same grouping was nothing short of extraordinary. Quickly, however, she dismissed her musings and smiled broadly as she threw out her usual greeting. "Hello there! I am Elessa, your server for the night. What can I get ya? If ya like ale, we make a mighty fine good ale here at the Iron Hill."

A soldier with brown hair that fell down his forehead in uneven strands mirrored her smile. "We have just spent the full day traveling from Houghton and would like nothing more than a giant platter of mutton and ale."

Elessa nodded playfully, her tousled black locks bouncing off her naked shoulders. "That is a reasonable demand, friends. I have no doubt the six of ya can eat more than your share. I'll get that order out to ya right away." She left the party, but before they could restart their own conversation she reappeared bearing mugs brimming with drink. "Here ya are. I'll bring your mutton when it is ready."

The server watched arms reach across the table greedily. At once, the surly mood lessened while each person happily threw back the fluid, settling their fatigue if nothing else. After several giant swallows, the dwarf grunted and slammed the mug down heartily. "Fine ale indeed, m'lady. Far better than the rancid horse-spit we had in Houghton."

"I am good to my word. You'll not find a better meal and drink anywhere in Calas." Elessa grinned at the contented party, the tiniest of dimples dotting the corners of her mouth. "So, ya have names?"

As if surprised by the question, the same solider that had spoken first looked at her momentarily with squinted eyes. Shortly thereafter, he recovered his demeanor enough to answer, "Indeed, each of us has a name." Smirking, he focused back on his drink without saying another word.

Elessa glared at the man, aware that she was being toyed with. She was about to respond in kind when the dwarf interceded.

"Excuse my friend, m'lady. He is Cadwan, I am Darin, and this," he pointed to the man with the exquisite livery, "is Calien. Over here we have Alazar, Kyligan, and the halfling is Cora."

Elessa's eyes paused on Kyligan. The man had lowered his head, intentionally using his hair as a shield to hide his face. Her intrigue was peaked immediately, as if he were some cryptic message she was determined to decipher. "Sir Kyligan, are you okay? Are you sick?"

"He is fine," answered the man with the hood, the one the dwarf had called Alazar. "He is nervous around people and has a deathly fear of them, especially astonishingly attractive woman."

"Alazar!" Cora, the halfling, scowled at him, pounding her small fist into Alazar's shoulder. Following four adequate jabs, she turned to Elessa and added, "Kyl is fine. It just takes some time for him to open up. He is never comfortable with crowds."

"I see," Elessa replied, her eyes lingering on the man a few moments longer before pulling them loose. Though she would not pursue her inquiries of Kyligan now, her curiosity of the withdrawn soldier would not leave so easily. Perhaps later, she decided, I might learn more of him. Casually allowing her vision to wander, she asked the group, offhandedly, "Whereabouts ya from?"

"Just about everywhere," Cadwan answered. "Calien and I are from Calas, but that is where the similarities end."

60

"I am from Thumble." Cora announced, as though Elessa cared of nothing else.

Elessa nodded. "Really, I . . ."

"Wench! Me mug is empty!" From a table across the aisle, a large man with a bellowing voice had yelled over to Elessa. When she didn't immediately respond, he banged his mug on the table and repeated himself even more loudly.

Elessa pulled a black curl from her eyes and sighed. "Be right there." Turning back to the party, she spoke apologetically. "I am sorry, but I've work to do. Perhaps later we can continue our conversation?"

Cadwan and the others watched Elessa whisk to the adjoining table where the cow of a man was still complaining to his comrades concerning her slow service. Cadwan fought the urge to approach him and teach the man appropriate manners, but dismissed the idea soon after, knowing it would achieve little and bring them much unwelcome attention.

The remainder of the night passed quickly. After the party had eaten their fill and sufficiently rested, they elected to return to their rooms at the Mullikin Inn.

"We will have to find another time to ask the barmaid of the refugees from Oester," Darin mentioned, pointing out that Elessa had been too busy to return to their table and resume their discussion.

Cadwan sighed an affirmation. "Yes, perhaps tomorrow. But it has been a long day and I can hardly keep my eyes open." They exited the establishment into the concealment of night and a starless sky. The cloud cover had thickened in the waning hours of day and now enveloped the town with a dreariness that only daylight could do away with. Rain spattered heavily on citizens and streets alike, indifferent to whom or what lay beneath its falling ire. The inn was only a street block from the tavern and the tired company trundled the short distance in no time. When they reached the front door, Kyligan scooted near Cadwan.

"Do not turn around." The ranger leaned close, whispering slow and deliberately so as to make sure his tone was taken in full seriousness. "We have been followed from the tavern. The man crouches across the street, hiding in the shadows of the tiny alley behind us."

Cadwan involuntarily froze, as any man would do after hearing such news. He knew Kyligan spoke the truth. He never questioned the ranger's competence in matters of this nature, for as quiet as he was, few were more observant. Though obviously startled, Cadwan tried to appear normal as he reached for the outside handle of the door. "Can you make out his appearance?" he whispered from the corner of his mouth.

"Nay. I can guess it is a man, for his build is slightly larger than a typical woman. But he wears a hood to hide his face."

"What is the matter?" Darin had heard the men whisper and was instantly alarmed.

With a subtle gesture of his hand, Cadwan motioned him quiet. Darin instantly obeyed, though his sentiment of alarm only amplified. Cadwan pulled the door open and everyone followed him into the lobby of the Mullikin Inn. By now, all six were conscious that something was awry, though only Kyligan and Cadwan knew the true nature of the predicament. The others could only nervously grip their weapons, as the atmosphere around them intensified uneasily.

As though he were discussing the day's weather, Cadwan mumbled, "All of you leave for your rooms, except Kyligan. I will explain later."

They hesitated, each staring back at their leader with a pang of doubt. Finally, Darin grunted irritably, "Whatever is going on, you had better not be getting yourself into something dangerous without us."

Cadwan gave the dwarf a furtive look. Darin had been around the soldier long enough to understand that the expression was meant to imply something like '*trust me*'. He didn't like it, but he obviously had little choice but to do that very thing. With a shake of his large head, Darin grabbed the front of Alazar's robes and pulled him toward the stairs on left side of the room. Cora and Calien followed. Soon, only Kyligan and Cadwan remained in the lobby.

Resisting the urge to look out the window for their stalker, the two moved toward the clerk's desk. Heaney, the innkeeper whom they had met when they initially purchased their rooms, looked up from a stack of gold coins he was counting and smiled at their approach. "Well 'allo again. What can I do fer ya?"

"Is there a side entrance to the building?" Cadwan asked with seriousness.

The older man squinted and appeared taken aback. "What? What do ya need to know that fer?"

"We have our reasons. Do you, or not?"

"There be a door in the back we use fer trash, but I keep it locked, otherwise."

Cadwan's stare had not varied from the innkeeper. "We need the key."

Heaney scoffed at the two men. "Ha, I do not think so. That door ain't fer customers. Ya think I need thieves sneakin' in the back at night?"

"We will bring it right back to you. Certainly, you can allow us use of the door this one time?"

The innkeeper shook his head. "I told ya, that door ain't fer customers. The front door works jus' as good."

Cadwan cast a fleeting look at Kyligan and the ranger shrugged. Accidentally, Cadwan caught glimpse of the stack of gold coins sitting on the man's desk and it spurred a rather simplistic idea. Reaching into his pocket, he removed a gold coin of his own and dropped it on the desk. "We will bring the key right back to you," he repeated.

The old innkeeper gazed at Cadwan grimly, the wrinkles on his gnarled face deepening. Opening a drawer, he removed a small iron object and held it before Cadwan. "Look, I do not know what ya are using it fer and I do not want ya to tell me, but ya damn well better bring it back!"

Heaney handed the key to Cadwan.

Cadwan smiled politely. "You are most gracious." Taking the small object, he placed it in Kyligan's hand. "You can find him better than I. I will stay in front of the window in full view. If you need me, just yell."

Kyligan said nothing, but instead swept to the left, as if he were heading for the stairs. When the ranger deemed he was out of view, he ducked past the stairwell toward the backroom of the inn. For a few moments, Cadwan watched him go before turning and casually leaving the desk. He moved closer toward the window and left himself in full view of those outside. His boot suddenly demanded his attention, and he knelt as if working to fix some unseen problem while he fought the impulse to peek outside.

The latch on the back door gave Kyligan little trouble. Soon, he was once more within the black cloak of night and the rain above. Heaps of trash filled two barrels alongside the swinging portal, and some littered the surrounding cobble. The ranger wasted no time as he veered his way down the tiny pathway behind the cold limestone of the inn. He was pleased to note that moving quietly posed little dilemma. The pebbled ground was far quieter than the leafy underbrush of the forest in which he was accustomed to. He stayed along the cramped path for an extra building, a small structure which judging from the various gear and paraphernalia choking the path looked to be a trading post. Rounding the corner, he returned to the road that the party had used to enter the inn.

Peering across the street through the darkness, he found himself unable to see any figure hiding in the shadows. The thick drizzle from above only facilitated his difficulties in spotting anything substantial. However, from his current vantage point he could only perceive a small portion of the alley where he had last seen the man. As he crept across the road, he wondered if the poorly lighted streets were a blessing or a curse. Certainly, it would help him sneak up on his stalker, but it also hindered his ability to locate the man.

Now, on the opposite side, he leaned in close to the shadowed buildings for cover and covertly made his way to where he hoped the man would still be surveying Cadwan. Kyligan ventured a glance back to the window of the inn. Sure enough, Cadwan could still be seen working on his boot, which had apparently proved to be quite the setback for the soldier. Kyligan smirked and wondered how foolish he must feel wrestling with his boot in full view of everyone outside. Nevertheless, he prayed the ruse would work long enough for him to overcome whoever it was that had taken an interest in their standing.

As the ranger neared the alley, he could still see no sign of his quarry. He must have slipped further back within the small opening of the alleyway,

Kyligan decided. Standing at the edge of the alcove, he took a single breath, listened a moment to the dull drumming of the rain, then leapt within and prepared to tackle whoever might be inside.

The alley was empty.

The ranger swore under his breath and ran deeper, probing for signs that the figure was still hiding, or had fled only moments ago. After surveying the entire area he perceived no indications that anyone had recently been there.

"You did well to spot me. There have been few that have done so."

Kyligan whirled to face the speaker as his hand fell immediately to the pommel of his blade. He felt his heart increase in rhythm and his energy multiply. The threat had completely revived his adrenaline. Only minutes before, the ranger was dead tired and ready for slumber. Now, he was vigilant and fully prepared to defend himself. Kyligan quickly examined a man who now stood in full view within the alleyway. There was little to see. A large cowl, dripping wet, covered most of the man's facial features and the dark gray mantle draped over his body, revealing nothing of significance. However, two long daggers gripped in each on the man's gloved hands were far from discreet, the steel of the thin blades glinting ever so slightly in the pale light. Kyligan's eyes fell to the weapons attentively.

"Relax. I have no quarrel with you," The figure, obviously a man from the resonance of his voice, said placidly. "Let us not make this more than it needs to be."

"Who are you?" Kyligan had not moved. His eyes remained on the knives held casually by his foe. "Why have you followed us?"

A malicious grin flashed from under the hood. "Had I wanted such questions answered, I would not have trailed you in the manner I did. Do not worry, though. My interest lies not with you."

"My worry would undoubtedly be lessened if you would tell me your name and your intent." Kyligan took one step closer to his foe. In sequence, the man backed a step.

"You will discover my intent soon enough. Rest assured, when the time comes, if you do not interfere you will be spared."

Kyligan examined the man intently. If only he could see his face, read his eyes. On normal occasions, the ranger was deft in attaining a strong intuitive sense of the sort of man he dealt with merely by speaking with him and studying his face. Yet now, he could gather nothing and it bothered him to no end. He felt as though he were speaking through a haze that was conjured by an invisible enemy. Taking a half-breath to regain his resilience, Kyligan boldly proclaimed, "Unfortunately, I have no reason to trust you. Whatever your plans are, they do not bode well for me or my companions. I will not let you leave until you thoroughly explain your intentions."

The large hood weaved back and forth. "Your courage is commendable, but that is not for you to decide. There is no incentive for us to fight. I am leaving now. I have no desire to hurt you, but you will leave me no recourse if you impede my departure." The figure turned on his heel and commenced walking away slowly.

For a fleeting second, Kyligan nearly allowed him to go. To overcome his cowardice, he abruptly rushed ahead to seize the man from behind. Though the ranger was stealthy, on this occasion his footsteps were louder than he hoped and the hooded figure spun around before Kyligan reached him.

"Fool! Do you wish for death so freely?" The daggers flashed, as the man flung them upward, ready for combat.

Kyligan's own sword was fully drawn as he came in, but he was forced to halt before getting impaled on the sharp blades held by his adversary. "Neither of us needs to die. Why have you followed us?"

The question went unanswered. The two daggers came forward. Kyligan stepped away to avoid the attack, then slashed his own sword in retaliation. The swipe was easily avoided and the skirmisher quickly moved out of range of the longer weapon, remaining unharmed. For the next minute, the two combatants sized each other with cool purpose.

The rogue took slow, deliberate side steps, as he circled the ranger. "Your skills are not on my level. You cannot best me." Kyligan felt as though the figure was grinning beneath his hood. "Alas, I am not a hateful man, merely one of business, and I gain nothing from your death. So, I give you one more chance to live. Sheath your sword and walk away."

"How can I walk away if it places my friends in danger?"

The barest trace of impatience graced the man's voice, as he spoke. "I am not here to discuss your moral dilemmas. Your death at my hands will mean little to me, yet I am certain you shall not feel the same. Such imprudence will make a waste of your life."

Kyligan moved closer to his foe. "An imprudent man would have little trouble forsaking his companions. I am not such a man." He swung his sword in a low arc, attempting to debilitate the man's leg.

With remarkable speed, the skirmisher jumped upward and sideways, flinging his body out of harms way. Upon landing, he instantly threw his body toward Kyligan with daggers poised, the steel flickering ever so slightly in the dark. The rogue's quickness made it impossible for Kyligan to parry the attack, so he simply attempted to step away. Unfortunately, the ranger lost his footing on the wet, slippery pavement and staggered backward, body flailing, into a pair of trashcans. A loud clanging echoed through the alley.

As Kyligan's body came still in a heap of trash, the first action he took was to insure he had maintained a grip of his sword. Luckily, he had, and the ranger quickly lashed the weapon out in the direction of his opponent while he attempted to stand.

The hooded figure watched Kyligan stumble to his feet and attempt to reassemble his body while regaining his whereabouts. Just as the ranger appeared sufficiently organized, the rogue leapt again. He used one of his knives to hold Kyligan's focus, while the other was poised to plunge through his neck. The attacker thought his aim would strike true, but at the last moment the ranger elevated his free arm to bat away the fatal blow. The rogue still maintained the advantage and he kicked Kyligan's knee, sending him back down to cobbled ground. The ranger hissed in pain and grabbed hold of his injured leg. This time, the rogue mused darkly, there would be no blocking his death thrust.

"Hey!"

Both combatants swiveled their heads to perceive yet another man enter the dark confines of the alley. When the man drew near enough to be recognized, Kyligan nearly hollered for joy. "Cadwan!" he answered in a raspy voice still affected from the pain in his leg.

The skirmisher required no more prompting. Confident in his abilities but not wishing to battle a second foe, his mind was hastily made. With quickness that would make a panther envious, he darted down the other end of the alley, disappearing into the shelter of night. Spotting Kyligan on the ground, Cadwan made no move to follow the fleeing suspect and instead elected to check on his friend.

"Kyligan, are you wounded?" The soldier clamored up to Kyligan's side.

The ranger gingerly moved his leg. It already seemed less painful than only seconds before. "No." Kyligan lifted his emerald eyes upwards. "You showed up just soon enough, friend. I have never been so happy to witness your face." The ranger paused for a second before adding, "How *did* you know when to come?"

"I heard some rattling coming from the alley. No one drums noise like that intentionally, especially if their whole objective is silence."

"Ah, the trashcans." Kyligan nodded. "Thank the gods for your common sense."

Cadwan lowered an arm and helped the ranger to his feet. "Well, are you going to tell me what happened?"

Kyligan brushed off his vestments and carefully replaced his sword into its scabbard. "I will, but not until we return to the inn. I have had enough prying eyes for one night."

*   *   *

Elessa had the kind of headache only a long night's sleep could cure. It was already well past midnight and she wished for nothing else but to curl in a warm bed and plunge into a deep slumber. Because the streets of Mullikin were occasionally dangerous come nightfall, after she got off work in the late hours she would normally have either Gully or a town guard escort her home. Tonight, however, she was tired and in no mood for conversation. As soon as the Iron Hill closed, she intrepidly whisked off alone.

Moving into the slums of the residential area, the falling rain, the absence of noises, and the scarce amount of street lamps only succeeded in making her surroundings darker. In nervous haste, she refused to divert her eyes from the road ahead. Though she knew it impossible, the faint silhouettes of the buildings and signposts on her flanks seemed to inch ever closer, as if intending to consume her in their leaching shadows. *Ridiculous*, she thought, scolding herself for her unfounded trepidation and knowing that her fears were merely stemming from a mind prone to exaggeration. Even so, she upped her pace to coincide with the repeated beating of her heart and the pounding in her head. The barmaid was never more thankful to see her ramshackle home only a block away. By the time she reached the door, her adrenaline was at its peak. She had to pause a moment to calm her wits.

When the lock released from the latch on her door, she nearly wept in relief and inwardly promised she would never again leave for home in the midnight hours unescorted. Still, her guardedness did not fully dissipate when she cracked open the door and noticed something strange.

Her oil lamp was lighted.

Thoughts reeling, she slowly peeked inside and caught sight of a figure sitting in the divan of the front room. Stopping herself in mid-swallow, she scratched out meekly. "Finney?"

Arms folded, the figure lifted its head toward the door. In a high male voice, it said, "It is me, Elessa."

Elessa recognized the voice instantly and exhaled a giant breath of air before raising her voice. "Blessed Orithen's mercy! I nearly died of fright! You said you would be at Hermoc's festivity the whole night."

Finney leapt off the divan and extended his halfling body to its full three feet in length. He had lived with Elessa for the past several years. Although he was pushing forty years of age, and had lost a hint of his physical luster and gained some inches at the belly, Elessa still found his blue eyes and clever demeanor attractive, if not alluring. He waddled over to her and took her hand in his own. "I did go to Hermoc's party, but I left early. I," he paused and averted his vision, as if he were hesitant to verbalize what was on the tip of his tongue. Ultimately, his resolve won over. He fumbled into his pocket and withdrew a small gold coin. "I found this little trinket. It is . . . special."

Pulling the black locks from her face, Elessa's brow furrowed. "What do you mean?"

"Come and look!" Finney pulled Elessa over to a featureless wooden table. He held out the coin and flipped it over in his hand, showing an eagle's head on one side and a lion's tail the opposite. "Call it, heads or tails?"

Elessa frowned. "This is silly, Finney. I've a headache."

"Please! Indulge me this once. Heads or tails?"

"Heads." Elessa muttered with little interest, rubbing her throbbing temples.

Finney tossed the coin high into the air and closed his eyes. The coin twirled before falling onto the table, pinging several times and eventually coming to rest; the eagle's head shining golden before the two onlookers. "You see! Heads!" the halfling proclaimed with excitement.

The barmaid shrugged her delicate shoulders. "Simple luck. A one in two chance."

"Let us do it again, then. Heads or tails?"

"Tails."

Finney repeated the process, and this time the lion's tail showed upwards toward Elessa. Finney laughed with elation. "Tails!"

Elessa narrowed her eyes, skeptically. "Throw it again, Finney. Tails."

The halfling abided and again the gold piece shown the lion's tail. They continued and Finney flipped the coin nearly twenty times. Each time, the coin complied with Elessa's command.

"Finney! That coin is not special, it is *magical*!"

Finney held the gold piece high in the air and gleefully jumped. "Yes! A magic coin." He grasped Elessa's arms and vigorously shook each one. "Do you not understand? This tiny piece of gold will bring us more riches than we ever imagined! It is our ticket to a wealthy life." The halfling began to dance around the table joyously, his voice hooting an old tavern ditty, albeit off-key.

For nearly a full minute, Elessa watched the halfling celebrate, all-the-while taking in the significance of the event in slow amounts.

When Finney grew winded from leaping, he paused and took several lengthy breaths. "We can leave now. Go south to Dunmar perhaps." Finney winked, cunningly. "Imagine how much gold I can win using this coin."

"We will finally have enough money to settle and get married." The barmaid's comment was deliberate, testing, but also in pleading earnest.

"Yes, well . . . perhaps." The halfling drew his eyes to the floor uneasily, obviously not interested in pursuing this particular route of conversation. "We will have time to discuss such things afterward."

Elessa glowered in disappointment, though she did her best to conceal it from Finney. It was no secret that the halfling had little interest in settling down from his life as a vagabond, despite Elessa using every opportunity available to demonstrate her stance on the delicate issue. One day, she hoped, he'll realize that he is no longer the spring stallion he views himself as, and then he'll entertain the idea of marriage more willingly. And perhaps this coin is the first step towards such aspirations.

As if the last segment of the conversation never existed, Finney clapped loudly once and announced, "Excellent! It is settled then. Pack only what you can carry and let us leave this place."

"What?" Elessa stared at the halfling. "You mean now? In the middle of the night?"

"Of course!" Finney pocketed the magic piece and began digging through some of his junk possessions that had been crammed into a cracked wooden chest in the living room's corner. Gadgets and utensils of all makes and kinds went flipping out of the box. "The sooner we leave, the quicker we can forget about this forsaken town. A better, nay, a *new* life awaits!"

Elessa ran to the halfling and grabbed hold of him. "Why must we leave right now? I can hardly stand, I am so exhausted."

Finney batted the woman's arms from his own and continued to delve into the chest. "A better question is why must we wait? I have no inclination to stay one more minute in Mullikin."

"I cannot just leave Gully with no warning. He would," she paused, then froze entirely as an unwelcome thought dawned on her. All at once, she could feel her throat dry up, her body wither into numbness. "Finney, where did you get that coin?"

"I found it," the halfling muttered, examining a large wooden fork that was missing two of its four prongs. He grunted and threw the item into the scrap pile.

An awful realization hammered down upon Elessa. All her excitement and enthusiasm from only seconds prior exploded into a painful awareness of shattered hopes and broken dreams. "Finney, you stole the coin, didn't you?"

Finney suddenly appeared too absorbed in his efforts to notice her question, but the barmaid knew better. She reached over and snatched a rusty piece of steel from his hand, then grasped his face and forced it to look her way.

"Damn you, Finney! Answer me! Did you steal that coin?"

In spite of his best efforts to pull his head loose from her grasp, the barmaid's grip held firm. "I, uh . . ."

"You did!"

"Elessa, I . . ." The halfling went quiet, as if his silence would better explain his tomfoolery more subtly than had he spoken.

The woman released her hold on Finney and covered her own face to hide her tears. "Oh, Finney! Who owns the coin?"

Finney exhaled a heavy, elongated sigh and began to show signs of guilt on his well-traveled face. In the many years Elessa had known the wily rogue, she had never seen him display guilt of any sort and she found herself momentarily taken aback. Unable to look his companion in the eyes, Finney muttered softly, "It is Hermoc's. He was showing it to others during the festivities and when no one was looking, I grabbed it and snuck off. That is why

I left the party early."

"Hermoc? Oh gods, Finney! Does he know who took it?"

The halfling dolefully bowed his head. "I am afraid it will not take him long to figure out, being that I disappeared around the same time the coin did."

"He is going to kill you, Finney!" Although Elessa had only talked to Hermoc once, his reputation preceded him well. He was deemed the wealthiest, most successful gambler in Mullikin. And he was also the most short tempered and vengeful. He had heavy influence in the underground and enough contacts to get what he wanted.

"I know," Finney blubbered. "That is why we have to leave right now."

"Finney, I told you," Elessa was close to hysteria. "I cannot just leave Gully so suddenly. He has been too kind to me over the years for me to just abandon him." She took several loud, heavy breaths and then screamed, "Why are you so damned stupid? Of all people, stealing from Hermoc?"

"Please calm down, Dear," Finney pleaded.

"Why should I calm down?" Elessa fumed. "You are as good as dead and if I am caught with you, I am as good as dead, too!"

The halfling buried his head in his hands and cried out loudly. "I am sorry! I could not help myself. I never wanted to put you in danger."

"Well, it is too late now!" The barmaid stepped into a separate room, leaving the halfling to brood alone.

Several minutes passed with verbal silence. Elessa had ultimately peaked in her rage and was now slowing coming down, while Finney's hands still covered his miserable face. When Elessa felt grounded enough to speak again, she returned to find that the halfling was in the same position as when she'd left him minutes ago. Though she couldn't see his face, she could hear him weeping softly beneath his hands. She was shocked. Never in her life had she seen the scoundrel cry. The image before her was surreal.

"Look," she cursed herself for the pity she felt, "you need to hide somewhere else until I can figure out how to handle this. You know his thugs will come here first. If they find you, then we are both dead. But if you are not here, I feel confident I can play ignorant and fool them."

"What if they try to hurt you?"

"Thanks to you," Elessa glared at him, "that is a risk we will have to take." When she saw the lines of worry deepen in Finney's face, she managed a weak smile. "Do not worry. I will be fine. You should be more concerned about yourself. Do you know a good place you can hide?"

Finney nodded. "I have several places, but the best is the crawlspace under the abandoned hovel near Felton's. Hermoc should not find me there."

"Then you need to get over there now. Stay hidden until I come for you." Elessa began to press him toward the door. "There is no telling when Hermoc's cronies will show up. Oh, and take the damnable coin with you."

70

Finney opened the outside door and stepped into the night. Before he left, he looked back and whimpered, "I only wanted to make you happy."

The barmaid gave him a sad smile, then whisked him off and shut the door, all-the-while shaking her head and swearing beneath her breath. Finney was conundrum in every way; sometimes conniving, sometimes delightful, and always challenging. Did he really want to make her happy? Or did he want to make himself happy? That was the question she posed to herself almost daily. Truthfully, she had trouble answering it.

One thing was for certain; she needed to straighten herself out, and quick. Her womanly charm had to be at its fullest echelon tonight, if she was to thwart Hermoc's henchmen. Hustling to a mirror to fix her hair, she caught herself wondering if staying with Finney was worth the price she had to pay.

IX

Hate is an entity in itself.

For the figure gaiting within the confines of the solemn chamber, hate had consumed it well beyond its own fading memories, the burning embers long ago erupting into a blazing inferno of untainted abhorrence. Each thought, each reflection, only invigorated the burning lust that had been nothing short of an obsession in a world where little else mattered.

A negligible amount of illumination emanated within the chamber, but that suited the shadowed figure just fine. It had little use for the light. Not that it mattered, really, for its vision was unaffected either way. The pervading darkness seemed to suit the melancholy atmosphere of the room far better.

With heavy steps across the stone rostrum, its plan was to retrace the same path it had taken day after day, year after year, since the ill-fated moment it realized what it was destined to become. Yet, after only a few strides, it stopped. Or rather, something stopped it. For the first time in its vanishing, enfolded quintessence, the aura surrounding the figure distorted and its senses instantly heightened. Initially, it had trouble grasping the meaning of the change. Then, suddenly, as if clutching an object long sought after, it understood.

Something, or someone, was coming.

The interlopers were still a great distance away, but they were coming nonetheless. Although most common emotions, other than the single passionate hatred it felt every passing moment, had long withered away, the figure sensed what must have been a small pang of anticipation.

It feared nothing. Life, love, pain, death; mere words and nothing more, for the sensations they conveyed were long forgotten. In essence, these newcomers would bring with them something the dark figure hadn't possessed since it could remember; an instrument of release for the anger suspended within its pitiless shell of a body.

A sinister gaze drew to the door of the enclosed room. It would have to be patient, but patience was not a problem. It had already waited innumerable years.

Undoubtedly, it could wait a little longer.

X

The balled fist slammed hard into the paneled wall. "Incompetence! How could you allow them to spot you? The entire plan has now been placed in jeopardy!" Hetnar was fuming, betrayed by his blood-red face and aggravated scowl. From unsullied frustration, he delivered yet a second blow to the innocent wall, then quickly regretted it afterwards, as his hand began to throb painfully from the contact.

"Fear not, oh Prince." Endias muttered the last two words, with a tone dripping of sarcasm. The assassin rested calmly in a wooden chair, the front two legs off the ground as he leaned backwards leisurely. His facade was a complete contrast to that of Hetnar. He appeared relaxed and unconcerned toward any misgivings of the previous encounter. His right hand held a long dagger and he absently fingered the cold steel of the blade, as he spoke. "The man had no inkling who I was, nor what my true intentions were."

"What does it matter?" the prince shot back. "They now know someone has taken an interest in them and they will be far more alert of their surroundings. Your imbecilic blunder has cost us the element of surprise. Moreover, you did not even kill the man. He lives to warn the others."

"And how would that have been beneficial, Hetnar?" Endias placidly drawled. "If I had killed him, authorities would be crawling all over the place, with your brother right in the thick of it. Any chance of killing him afterwards would be impossible. As it stands now, they are wary, but unaware of what they are up against. Nothing has changed."

Hetnar opened his mouth to refute the assassin, but bit his tongue. What good would it do? The damage had already been done. Endias, at least outwardly, was obviously unconcerned in the slightest regarding the consequences. Hetnar ruefully shook his head, the prevailing confidence from only a day earlier now replaced with apprehensive concern. Was failure a possibility? Truthfully, he had never pondered such an improbable avenue before now. Yet, a measure of doubt had trickled its way into his thoughts and he found it extremely unpleasant. Being a relative loner his entire life, he had never placed so much faith in others. He suddenly found it difficult not having full control. What would happen to him if he was discovered?

The female, Ayna, who had been leaning against the opposite wall of Hetnar, unexpectedly approached him. As she moved, her hair bounced slightly and Hetnar studied her attractive physique. As with many men, she held for the prince a certain fascination. But even then he dared not dream of bedding her, knowing she'd most certainly knife him in his sleep. The woman paused only a step away from the prince and when she spoke her voice held no particular sense of sentiment. "Understand, we want the payout, as badly as you want the task completed. To that end, you can be assured we will deal with your brother cleanly. A mistake from Endias is rare." The woman cast the composed assassin a brief glace. "You can be certain there will not be a second."

Hetnar shook his head. As he replied, he surprised himself with his resolve to look the female rogue directly in the eyes. "And you need to understand, if we fail and I am discovered then my life is in ruin. I have every right to feel anxiety over the outcome, especially if my own life is at stake."

The woman narrowed her eyes, making them appear darker than before. This time she slowed her speech, accentuating the meaning of each and every word. "Do you take us for amateurs? Is not every client we work for under the same pressure you suffer?" Her lips curled backward, making a face of repugnance. "We are successful for a reason, the very same reason you chose us. You may be a prince to some, but to us you are merely another client and our business is to fulfill our end of the agreement. You just worry about fulfilling your end."

Endias watched Ayna intimidate the prince and for a short time he reveled in it. Hetnar was moderately tough, impressive considering he was of noble birth, but few could hold up to Ayna when she drew forth her devilish womanly deportment, including Endias himself. The assassin couldn't withhold his grin as he interrupted the two. "Hetnar, you know me well. And now, as we are on the verge of finishing this you decide to question my skill?"

Hetnar brought his eyes away from Ayna, and was happy to do so. Looking at Endias, he briefly pondered the question. Did he question the man's skill, or was he simply letting his trepidation control his mood? In length, he answered, "No, but we need to end this quickly. This ragged party he rides with will not stay in Mullikin forever, delaying their mission until we succeed."

Endias nodded. "It has already been worked out. Garevus!" On being called, one of the other assassins came forward. The man was slightly shorter than average, with a fiercely angular face and no hair visible anywhere upon his body. When the man smiled, only a few yellowed teeth shown to contrast the several black gaps. "Garevus will be the bait tomorrow. He will lure them to us. After that, it is simply a matter of killing them swiftly and quietly so as not to draw notice."

Hetnar frowned. "That explains nothing to me."

"Let us gain a few hours sleep and we can discuss it fully in the morning."

The assassin rose from his chair and commenced preparing his bed. As he straightened out the sheets, he mumbled nonchalantly to the prince behind him, "It shocks me you are not more joyful, Hetnar. By midday tomorrow, your brother will be dead and you will be heir to the throne."

*   *   *

"You have no idea who it was?" Darin asked with a gruff, crusty voice typical of most dwarves.

"Should I have?" Kyligan answered. "Have we enemies in Mullikin I am not aware of?"

The dwarf lifted his palms. "I do not think so."

Though the party had used two separate rooms for the night, they now convened in one. Outside, daybreak was just revealing its countenance upon the sleepy settlement. The vivid shine of the waking sun assaulted the room, as rays of light forged their way past the window. Each individual relaxed within the small quarters while listening to the conversation between Kyligan and Darin. The previous night, Kyligan had explained in detail his encounter with the hooded figure, but they had discussed it only briefly before electing to rest their tired minds and continue the discussion the following morning.

"He insisted that if I did not interfere, I would be spared," the ranger explained.

"Interfere in what?" Darin inquired.

"Obviously, that is the quandary presented us." Cadwan had only listened, while the two had bantered between themselves for the last minute or two, but he finally decided to add his own worth. "Unfortunately, we have no way of knowing the answer."

"Perhaps," the dwarf delved, "the man was merely a common thief and was only trying to scare you with false words?"

"No, I do not believe so." Kyligan retorted. "He had nothing to gain by lying. Also, he seemed quite hesitant to fight me, as if the ensuing commotion would be unwelcome."

Cadwan listened to Kyligan intently. When the ranger finished, he concluded, "Then we must assume the threat is real, whatever it may be."

"Why do we not we just leave town and continue north. I doubt anyone would follow us," Prince Calien said sleepily, rubbing weary eyes. In their few days of adventure, he still had not grown accustomed to waking so early. In the palace, the sun was well within the sky before he would arise and start his day. He guessed it would be some time before his body would adjust to the lack of sleep.

Cadwan shook his head. "As of yet, we have not acquired the information we need. We have already learned that villagers from Oester came here and I want to know if they are still here, or if they spoke of what happened. Such knowledge is vital if we plan to succeed," the soldier paused a moment, then added glumly, "or survive, for that matter."

"And how do you propose we get this information?" Darin asked, while he aggressively scratched his bushy red beard. To Cadwan's discernment, the dwarf seemed grumpier than was the norm for the usually gracious emissary, but he guessed that was a direct result of being uninvited to partake in the previous night's scuffle.

Cadwan grinned at the stout dwarf. "Well, my friend, after you purge yourself of that sour mood you and I are going to give Baron Guthram a visit. Surely, as the vassal he has heard something about Oester."

Prince Calien's face brightened. "I should come along. I know Guthram well. He might be more willing to help in my presence."

"I am sorry, Prince, but that is exactly why you cannot come," Cadwan said. "Can you imagine the buzz that would ensue, if the town discovered that the future king of Calas was strolling about?"

"Agreed," Darin echoed. "Some, in their misguided vigor, would probably follow us north to Oester. I have no desire for such attention."

A single shot of laughter resounded in the room and every head rotated to find its source, Alazar. "This is all fine, but what are we supposed to do, while you two are sharing recipes with the baron?" the robed man mouthed, derisively. He was sitting on a sofa next to Cora.

Cadwan viewed the man coolly. He had expected such a comment and was well prepared for it. "Relax and enjoy your time on Mullikin. I have no idea how long this meeting with Guthram will take, or how long he will make us wait, so let us plan on convening back here at the inn tonight. We can leave for Oester tomorrow morning."

"Hmph," Alazar grunted. "Just what I feared, more time spent with her holy stubbiness!" He playfully thrust his elbow into the side of the halfling.

Cora gave Alazar a look that, had the bearded man not known her better, would have given him the impression of horrendously evil intent. As it was, he took great pleasure in her irritation.

"It would be wise, however," Cadwan mentioned, ignoring the spout between Cora and Alazar, "not to enjoy yourselves too much. It would be useful to keep an eye out for anyone who might be following you." The soldier glanced momentarily at Kyligan, knowing that he was the obvious candidate for the task. The ranger nodded in turn. "Also, some civilians might know something about Oester, so it never hurts to ask. You might even take the time to stock up on supplies. It could be our last chance and I could use some additional arrows. There is no telling what we might need later on, or if the shops in Oester are even in business."

"Are you going to tell the baron what happened last night?" Cora asked.

"No," Cadwan swiftly replied. "What good would it do? Even if Guthram cared, it would only bring about more pointless attention. That is a problem which is ours alone." The others nodded in response and silence followed. Eventually, Cadwan finished. "That seems to be it then. I recommend you wear your armor and carry your arms, just to be on the safe side, especially after what happened last night. Are we all in agreement?"

The rest muttered identical responses. Within a few minutes the room was empty as each member left the inn and ventured off to what they deemed would be an uneventful day.

*   *   *

Cora had lived twenty-three of her twenty-four winters in the tiny hamlet of Thumble. The quaint village was the dwelling place of halflings and she spent most of her youthful days tending to the gardens with her mother. The monotony of such a life and the innate curious spirit Cora boasted led the halfling to sneak into the nearby forest whenever she had the opportunity. It was these youthful days in the forest that Cora learned how to avoid traps and set animals free from them, which then spurred her interest in other such contraptions. She always prided herself on looking for new ways to solve old problems, but such a mischievous nature often found her in hot water with her loveable neighbors. Cora longed to know more of what lay beyond the confines of Thumble and she would often harry travelers in hopes that they would tell her stories of their adventures. Even as she would hang on their every word, she seemed destined to live her life growing old in the peaceful hamlet.

And then the kobolds, or as the villagers called them, 'yappies,' began raiding the settlement from a nearby cave, and everything in her life changed.

Arriving in Thumble was a group of men commissioned by King Anuron himself to investigate the problem. Ever ready for exploits beyond the mundane, Cora took it upon herself to show the men around and eventually helped them find the cave where the kobolds were located. Despite the danger, she had never enjoyed herself more. When the kobolds were eliminated soon afterwards, the halfling made a brash decision. She wished to remain with these new travelers.

Initially, her parents begged their only child to stay, but in the end they abated their pleas when they realized Cora would never be happy, otherwise. After Cora promised she would visit as often as possible, she departed with her four new companions amid a score of tears. These new companions were Cadwan, Darin, Alazar, and Kyligan.

Thumble had no marketplace, but the halfling had traveled enough in the last year to come across several places which did. Now, as she ambled though the Mullikin marketplace, it appeared no different than any other she had seen.

Alazar and Kyligan seemed as indifferent to the setting as she, but Calien was mystified by the commotion. Cora guessed that the prince had never really taken the time to visit the marketplaces in Calas, considering he had servants who would obtain everything he required. Calien watched the activity with keen interest and even a little excitement.

The fresh morning air and cheerful sun brought with it the conclusion of the previous night's downpour, along with a sense of newfound energy.

The four of them leisurely walked about the makeshift tents and huts that made up the pavilion. Hawkers and patrons hustled between the tiny structures. The shouts of traders could be heard brazenly claiming their merchandise was of the finest quality and their prices the cheapest. Bargain hunters would banter back and forth with the merchants, sometimes leaving for a different tent when unsatisfied. If one looked hard enough, almost anything could be found at the marketplace, though the value of such goods were often questionable.

Kyligan led the group to a weapon stand. Behind the counter, a sullied-looking merchant with an eye patch over his left eyes and a scar falling to his cheekbone glared at the ranger. Cora found herself wondering if the eye patch was really needed, or if the man simply chose to wear it in a vain attempt to appear battle proven.

"How much for the arrows?" Kyligan asked, pointing toward a barrel stacked full of wooden arrows.

"Ten for one gold," the man ungraciously answered.

Kyligan seemed to ponder the charge for a moment. Cora leapt forward and answered just as the ranger was about to speak. "We will give you one gold for twenty." The halfling found the process of haggling for merchandise exceedingly amusing and she never hesitated to jump in on a dispute, especially if Darin was not present to scold her afterwards.

The trader shook his large head back and forth and looked away, as if completely uninterested in bargaining. "No, no. Ten only."

Cora shrugged innocently and pivoted to leave, pulling the arm of Kyligan with her. They had taken only a few steps before the merchant's hoarse voice was heard behind them.

"Fine, twenty arrows."

Cora stopped and smiled up at Kyligan, who briefly chuckled before turning back toward the roughneck man. "Excellent," he said, "I will purchase sixty arrows."

The merchant frowned. Though he said nothing, the creases in his forehead showed displeasure. Reaching into the barrel, he pulled forth six tied stacks of ten arrows each and placed them on the counter before greedily snatching the three gold pieces Kyligan had already dropped there. The ranger inspected the stacks and quickly approved their quality.

Cora noticed that Calien had watched the entire process with fascination.

With his well-combed blond hair and handsomely pronounced features, the prince's sky blue eyes observed the transition with ardent curiosity. When the deal was over, he eagerly approached the young halfling. "That was remarkable! How did you know he would concede?"

Cora found Calien's compliment humorous. Of the people in their company, she would have ranked herself second behind Darin when it came to haggling with merchants, but such a sight was commonplace in market-squares. Was the prince really so isolated? If so, she guessed such experiences were good for him. She patted Calien's arm. "Bartering is a common practice in marketplaces, Prince. If you think that was impressive, you should see Darin at work. He probably would have gotten the arrows for free."

Calien's worldly inexperience was very familiar to Cora, as she was in a similar state only one year ago. Just as he rarely left the palace, she had never left her village. The thought made her smile. In a way, it was like looking into a mirror. Yet, something made her nervous. Calien's naïveté proved him to be uncorrupted by the world's evil; innocence that few his age still retained. But sadly, she could foresee little chance that he would remain so after his travels with the party. Surely, evil would show itself in one form or another, and his innocence would drain like blood from a wound. She quickly brushed the grim thought away and realized the group was just wandering about the marketplace with no particular destination.

"So, what do we do now?" the halfling asked.

The others looked at her, then each other. Truthfully, they didn't know. The whole idea was to kill time, while Cadwan and Darin met with the baron. As Alazar opened his mouth with the intent to say something derisive, he was interrupted by a man walking their way.

"Excuse me," the man said, as he came near. He was heavily favoring one leg, limping his way along. His face was pointed and raw-boned, his head and face clean shaven. He wore tattered brown garments that dragged behind him on the ground.

"Speak your mind, friend." Alazar examined the man suspiciously.

"I . . ." the crippled man wavered, as if determining the decency of the group. "I need your help."

"Go on," Alazar prodded.

The man looked at each person, pausing slightly longer when his eyes reached Prince Calien. "My daughter is hurt badly. She needs a healer, but I . . ." He looked down at his leg. "I cannot carry her. You seem friendly folk. Please help me. She is but a short distance from here."

Alazar studied the man's lame physical prowess. He pitched a glance at Kyligan, who returned the look by slanting his head, uncertainly. Both men felt something wasn't right. Cora's visage revealed she was feeling identical skepticism.

"For the sake of Calas, let us help the man." Calien urged the others. "A child needs our help!"

"What is your name, friend?" Alazar asked.

"Beornis. Please hurry. She bleeds badly!" Cora thought the man had hesitated a moment when he answered, as if the question startled him, but she wasn't entirely sure.

His ornate platemail shining bright, Calien stepped forward. "Lead the way, good Beornis. We will help."

"Oh, gods bless you! Follow me." The man hobbled away as fast as his crippled leg would carry him. Calien was right on his heels. Kyligan and Alazar exchanged glum faces, but neither said a word. Soon, they, along with Cora, were also trailing Beornis.

The four were led west, away from the marketplace and down a narrow street where the crowds quickly thinned out. Cora's eyes were darting in every direction. Though she saw nothing, her inner sense of alarm only increased with each step. The buildings along the road grew older and more dilapidated. Occasionally, piles of trash would flank the sides of the street.

"She is just around this corner." Beornis huffed between breaths. "Hang on, my child, I am coming!"

They turned down an empty avenue, with nothing but a cracked wooden fence along one side and the backside of worn buildings on the other.

"Here she is!" the man said, triumphantly.

Prince Calien peered about for a moment, wondering that perhaps he was missing something obvious. After realizing such a miscue was impossible, he cried out, "I see no child! What is this about?"

Cursing, Kyligan drew his blade. Just as he and the others had suspected, they had been duped. He quickly glanced at Alazar and Cora, noting with satisfaction that their weapons were also readied. He looked to Beornis, intending to gain an explanation of the man's deception when a high-pitched whistle broke the stunned silence.

He was too late.

An arrow streaked through the air, plunging with force into Calien.

Baron Guthram's estate was situated in the northern part of town, built solidly along a large hill. While the building lacked the grand beauty most nobles would deem necessary for a residence, it made up for such minor deficiencies with practical durability. The sturdy greystone structure was a veritable fortress in itself. Several towers and armed fortifications lined the stronghold, and it was elevated by an earthen tor. Below, a wide man-made canal, filled with water, protectively surrounded the manor and blocked any false entrances. Only a single drawbridge gave access to the estate. The baron, once a warrior himself, took great measures to ensure that it suited his standards of defense.

As Cadwan and Darin neared the drawbridge, several footman eyed their approach with attentive discernment. One of the sentries stepped directly in their path. "Halt! You approach the residence of Baron Guthram, Vassal to the Crown. Please be forthwith with your intentions."

"We seek an audience with the baron," Darin answered, smoothly. "It should not take long."

The guard stared back at them. He was broad shouldered and muscular, wearing armor embroidered with the Mullikin insignia and a steel cap. The straight shaft of a spear jutted upwards from his right hand. "What are your reasons to seek an audience with Baron Guthram? He has no patience for solicitors."

"I assure you, we are not seeking a petition, nor are we traders. We only require information in which the good baron might possibly have knowledge of."

The guard raised an eyebrow. "Information, eh? What sort of information?"

Cadwan turned to Darin and tipped his head ever-so-slightly. The dwarf frowned. Clearing his throat, he squared his eyes on the guard and spoke calmly. "We are wondering if he has heard from Oester as of late. We have reason to believe something tragic has happened there."

"Oester?" The guard seemed startled at the mentioning of the northern village. "What makes you think something has happened there?"

"Only three days ago some refugees arrived in Calas, fleeing some unspoken horror. We are on our way to investigate," Cadwan answered.

The guard did not immediately respond. In methodical fashion, he looked back at his fellow footman, staring toward each one as if sending messages telepathically. Cadwan attempted to read their faces, but he could discern little from their expressionless features. The guard returned his attention to Cadwan and Darin. When he spoke again, he lowered his voice in peculiar fashion, as if hiding his words from eavesdropping spirits. "Other guards have mentioned refugees arriving here, as well," the sentry said. "I have not seen any myself, but a friend has said he met a couple who had just arrived from Oester. They acted strange, hardly speaking, as if their souls had been stolen. It had visibly given him the shivers."

A glimmer of hope rose up in Cadwan. "Are any of these exiles still here? We would like to speak with them."

"I cannot say," the guard said. "And truthfully, I wish not to know. If they be bringing a curse with them, I want none of it."

Darin drew forth a large smile across his lips. "Afraid of the arcane, are we?"

"If I cannot see it, I want no part of it. An enemy that cannot be killed with my spear is an enemy to stay far away from."

The dwarf laughed. "Sound reason, friend. I cannot blame ye for it."

The sentry nodded and moved his vision toward the large manor past the drawbridge. "Well, the baron is not fond of unexpected visitors, but if you are persistent enough he will concede. Marwan here," he pointed to another guard, and the man quickly stepped forward, "will escort you to the front gates. Oh, and one more thing, make certain you address the baron as 'Your Excellency'. He can be a real orc's ass about that."

"Advice taken, thank you," Cadwan said with a tilted head, as he and Darin rambled forward with their new escort. "Your assistance has been helpful."

In response, the guard simply waved away the complement with his armored hand.

The drawbridge was constructed of solid lumber, sloping subtly upwards across the artificial gulch until it reached the prominence above. Their escort, a young foot soldier wearing the exact same livery as the previous guard, was affable but said very little. He led the two men across the overpass, through the fortified gates and into a large enclosed courtyard. The open space was nothing more than an oversized lawn consisting of well-maintained durn-grass, with little in the way of flowers or other types of exquisite flora. Like the rest of the manor, it was designed to be efficient and low maintenance. The guard leisurely directed them across the grass and before the entrance to the manor. Lifting the heavy knocker, he dropped it once to a resounding *boom*.

Seconds later, a stiff looking man wearing the garments of a servant unlatched the heavy door and peered through the small crack of an opening.

"These men wish to see Baron Guthram," the guard stated with an obvious lack of enthusiasm. "They have no appointment."

The servant scowled, but pulled open the door further. After a scrutinizing look, he waved Cadwan and Darin forward. "Come in." Once both had fully emerged from the natural lighting of the sun into the simulated light of the mansions interior, the servant asked, "And what is this regarding?"

Cadwan cleared his throat. "The village of Oester."

The servant waited, expecting more. When Cadwan offered nothing else, he asked, "What of Oester?"

"Any further information, we prefer to discuss solely with the baron," Darin interceded, as genial as possible.

The servant's brow furrowed in bewilderment, absently scratching his pointy elbow. A brief time later, he shrugged. "Very well. Guthram is present in the manor today, but I cannot guarantee his willingness to meet with unexpected guests. Please seat yourselves within the lobby and I will bring him your request." The servant showed no hesitation scooting off and leaving the men behind.

The lobby of the manor was massive. The spacious room was unquestionably the centerpiece of the building, sporting all the excesses the baron deemed allowable. Overhead, a thick bronze lamp hung from the ceiling, its rugged, sturdy shine symbolic and preferred over the fragility of a chandelier. To Cadwan, the full interior seemed more fitting of a fortified castle, not a nobles estate. In one corner, a broad, curved stairway descended regally into the foyer. Sconces paralleled the bowed railing and each one boasted a single lighted candle, giving each individual step an imperial glow. It was this stairway that the servant had ascended moments earlier.

Cadwan and Darin seated themselves in two of the several chairs placed in a circular pattern in the center of the room. Ten minutes later, the servant returned. "Baron Guthram has agreed to see you, though he is currently engaged in other matters. He is uncertain when he will become available. Are you inclined to wait?"

"Of course," Cadwan responded, glancing at Darin who nodded in affirmation.

"Very well. Remain here and Guthram will join you when time permits."

Again, the servant departed. Cadwan and Darin spent the next hour and a half rehashing the previous day's events. They touched on many subjects, but a substantial amount of their conversation was devoted to predicting what they would find when they reached Oester.

"Perhaps a horde of monsters besieged the village?" Cadwan conjectured. "A tribe of orcs from the Barren Hills."

The dwarf grunted. "A possibility, no doubt. But what kind of monster is so brutal that it forces those who flee into utter silence? Certainly not orcs. That man Ragnall would not speak out of some kind of fear or horror," he massaged his bald head with wide fingers and ruefully added, "or blight. His family had fled to safety and yet even then, it was like they were already damned. Such a bane suggests a foe of a different power."

Cadwan sucked in air and released it slowly, thoughtfully. "Friend, we may not be equipped to handle such a foe."

Darin merely nodded. "Your fears echo my own. And still, neither of us consider turning back, for we know that fear alone cannot be our undoing. If it were, we could never be successful in the lifestyle we partake in."

Cadwan remained silent for long moments, and then whispered, "Even if we master our fears, does not death remain as potent?"

"Of course," the dwarf preached. "But folks succumb to the reaper's scythe in the safety of their own home, as well, do they not? Death is death, no more, no less. Even if we fear it, it will never change. Do I welcome it? No. But I'll not let it control me, not while I walk the earth as a living soul. Frundin has granted me the will to control my fears."

Cadwan couldn't help but smile. His dwarven friend always had the right answers, at least for himself. It was plainly evident that Darin's faith in Frundin helped him push aside his doubts. Cadwan had never been much of a religious man, but he found himself wondering how his life might be different had he worshiped a deity. The soldier almost asked Darin a question regarding Frundin when he caught sight of a regal looking man descending the stairs, eyeing them.

Baron Guthram.

Once a great warrior of his own merit, Guthram had since traded in the tribulations of battle after elevating to the higher circles of the noble hierarchy. Approaching fifty years of age, he could still wield a sword, if necessary, but preferred to spend his days commanding his charge, the town of Mullikin. Cold and distant by nature, the baron had developed into a viable aristocrat and had become adept at turning on the charm when the situation arose.

Cadwan had never met the baron in person and he studied the noble with interest. Despite his high position, the man still wore his full armored regalia, with a sword sheathed at the waist. His attire, as well as the baron himself, were spotless and well primped. The weapon was obviously battle proven, evidenced by the nicks and scrapes on the protruding hilt. His hair grayed and receded, but his face remained strong and vital. Deep set eyes returned Cadwan's stare with unflinching intensity. As Guthram reached the landing he made his way directly to the two men, who had stood from their chairs at the noble's approach.

"Your Excellency," Cadwan proffered, and both men bowed before the baron.

With nothing more than a diminutive nod, Guthram shifted his eyes away from Cadwan and placed them upon the dwarf. He waited coolly, as if expecting something.

Darin stared back with no expression, unsure what to make of the prurient gaze.

"My friend," Cadwan whispered for Darin's benefit, though Guthram could plainly hear just as well, "please address the baron."

Darin bit his lip and bowed slowly. "Your Excellency." While his days as an emissary had familiarized the dwarf with aristocrats and nobles of similar ilk and manner, he still had no use for such vanity. Self-righteousness was a sign of weakness in his home kingdom of Ludun and it was often used to over-compensate for self-doubt. The dwarf felt his blood boil, and wished he could address the baron with a balled fist instead.

Guthram appeared satisfied. He lifted his arms toward the chairs and insisted they sit. The two obliged, while the baron procured his own chair and settled himself in. "Now," Guthram spoke with a voice that defined confidence, "what is it you wish to speak of?"

"First off, Baron Guthram, thank you for your willingness to meet with us," Cadwan said. "Your information could be critical in our quest."

"You have my ear," Guthram responded.

Cadwan quickly glanced at Darin, silently asking if the dwarf would rather speak. Obviously, Darin needed a few moments to cool down after his indignation. He merely gestured with his hand, prompting Cadwan to continue. "We have been commissioned to investigate some events that might have taken place recently in Oester. As we travel north, we are seeking any information others might possess. This is why we have come to you."

Before Guthram could reply, Darin added, "Surely, *Your Excellency*, you must have heard something about the village."

Guthram apparently didn't notice the sarcasm in the dwarf's voice. He examined both men simultaneously. Within his countenance, it became plainly evident to both that he was hesitant on the subject. He even drew his eyes to the floor for an instant before returning them. In time, the baron asked, "Have you brought your query to the guards?"

"We have, Your Excellency," Cadwan affirmed. "They made known to us that some refugees from Oester had entered the town, but these exiles spoke very little and some have already left to unknown destinations."

Guthram leaned back in his chair, lowering his face again. The overpowering demeanor from only moments ago seemed to evaporate, replaced by a moment of docile frailty, as he searched for just the right words. Gathering himself, he raised his attention to the men, though his voice remained unsteady. "I had expected such a meeting would eventually occur. What I am to tell you, I have yet to tell another soul. Listen carefully, for it is all I can offer."

The expression the baron portrayed seemed to heighten the air of apprehension around them. Cadwan absently lowered his hand to the handle of his mace, though there was no real reason to do so. He noticed Darin shuffling his feet ever so slightly.

"A few days past," Guthram continued, "Oester occurred to me in a . . . vision of sorts."

"A dream?" Darin asked.

"No, not a dream. I was not asleep. It was sometime around noon. I was simply mulling over some inconsequential documents in my office when I had a kind of foresight," the baron paused, then corrected, "or aftersight, I suppose. I really do not know which."

Cadwan intently listened. "And what was revealed to you in this vision?"

"It was exceedingly odd. As I weighed a particular local matter, I suddenly thought about Oester. I imagine most people would have considered it a simple random thought. I knew better. It had coerced itself into my mind, forcing me to think of nothing else." Guthram stopped to mentally gather more of the story. Cadwan and Darin had fallen jarringly quiet, offering no words of their own to interrupt the baron's thoughts. When he was ready, he resumed the telling. "While the mental imagery was blurry, indistinct, it was carved within my memory and I have been unable to shake it away. For that reason, I am more than happy to speak of it, if only to release a small portion of the burden it has left."

"By Frundin's great beard! Tell us what you saw." The tension had made Darin anxious and he blurted the words before he could stop himself. After realizing that he had shouted, the diplomatic side of him quickly made amends. "I am sorry, Your Excellency. I must admit that your tale causes me unease."

Baron Guthram only looked at Darin for a second or two, then acted as if he never heard him at all. "First, my mind raked over the entire village as a whole. I have visited Oester a time or two and knew instantly that it was the place I was seeing. It was daylight and the people walked leisurely about their business, with no worries. Everything appeared normal until the sky turned black in a matter of seconds. The populace stopped in place, gazing about in confusion. Then, an odd blue glow shown, yet I could not immediately discern its source." Guthram shuddered. "The people began to fall down, dying as quickly as they landed. Not all at once, but one-by-one, many seeing their friends die right before their eyes, only to die themselves seconds later. It was a horrific sight.

"Soon the village was nothing but a graveyard. Only the azure glow lived on, growing brighter and stronger. I could feel its lawlessness, its disorder consume me. For many seconds, I could only see blue and I was filled with revulsion. Then, just as suddenly as it had come to me, the dark revelation vanished." The baron looked relieved, showing the signs of a man who had just unloaded a great weight off his shoulders. Now he fell silent, drawing his vision between the two listeners, awaiting comment.

Long moments ensued, as the three men simply stood and stared at each other, speechless. Darin, deep in reflection, leaned toward Guthram and calmly asked, "Do you have any idea what prompted such a vision? Or possibly what it means?"

Guthram shook his head, his smile exuded irony. "I wish I could tell your more, but I have nothing else and am consequently at a loss, the same as you. I find it strange that adventurers would come asking about Oester only days after, but on the same token it seems fitting. I now feel there was a reason for such grim musings. Tell me, what has happened to make you believe foul events have occurred there?"

"Refugees have shown in Calas, the same as here," Cadwan said.

"Then it can only be presumed that a tragedy has indeed taken place. If you plan to continue north, be especially attentive and expect the worse. Regrettably, I cannot spare any of my own men. You must understand, you are on your own." Abruptly, Guthram stood from the chair. "I have said all I can. Now that we are finished, I have other matters to attend."

The others stood with the baron. Cadwan reached up and clasped the man's shoulder. "Your Excellency, your time has been much appreciated. We will keep you no longer."

Guthram nodded. "Very well. May fortune smile upon your quest." With those words, the baron moved toward the stairwell and began a slow ascension.

Both men silently watched the baron leave. When he had disappeared into the upper level, Cadwan looked at his dwarven friend. "Will you still control your fear?"

Darin slowly looked to Cadwan, his round face offering nothing more than a grim stare.

*   *   *

Up until this point in their journey together, Calien had done nothing to merit respect from Alazar as a laudable companion. He asked too many questions, was far too naïve, and stuck out from the others like a sore thumb.

Now, as he watched the prince, his entire outlook changed.

The arrow that had been aimed for Calien struck true, yet there was evidence that it missed its intended mark fully. The projectile had grazed off the prince's breastplate and lodged itself into the side of his neck. The wound was still fierce and a crimson stream poured forth. Yet, as evidenced by Calien's subsequent actions the strike was not fatal, at least not immediately. While everyone else stood frozen in place, utterly shocked by what had happened, only Calien kept his immediate wits.

Beornis, the man with the crippled leg, appeared miraculously healed and from his loose garments pulled forth a sword with the intent of finishing up what the arrow had started. He drove the blade forward, but Calien, with no time to free his own sword, ducked the thrust and leaned his shoulder inwards, hitting and knocking back his assailant a few paces. Reeling away, the man quickly regained his footing and prepared a second assault.

"Kyligan!" The words were from Alazar who screamed at his companion to intercept the attacker. The ranger was closest to both men. Before the assassin could extend his blade toward the prince a second time, Kyligan engaged him.

Prince Calien dropped unsteadily to a knee, wincing as he felt the arrow burrowed deep within his flesh. To the naked eye, few would believe a man could remain conscious after such a blow, but apparently the wound appeared worse than it actually was. Still, his hand grew sticky from the torrent of blood rolling unrestrained from his neck down into his torso. He speculated he wouldn't be conscious for long, and contemplated whether to pull the arrow loose. Ultimately, he elected to leave it be, thinking it was better to keep the injury plugged as much as possible. Ignoring as best he could the throbbing pain, he cast about. Alazar and Cora were still behind him, but both were on pins and needles seeking the guilty party who had loosed the original arrow.

Cora had a bolt cocked in her crossbow and she hastily scanned the area. Fifty feet further down, a figure stood behind an opening in the wooden fence along the street. The figure had bow in hand, the drawstring pulled taut and aimed at Calien. "There he is!" Cora yelled, as she pulled the trigger on her crossbow. Her shot was too hurried. The bolt took flight and drove into the wooden fence, missing its mark by a foot just as the figure released another arrow.

Fortunately, her errant shot provided enough distraction for the figure's aim to alter ever so slightly. The shot was long, streaking above the head of Calien by mere inches. Cora loaded another bolt into her crossbow, but her opponent had evidently had enough of ranged combat. He dropped his bow and dashed with remarkable speed toward the prince. Cora fired again, but her moving target seemed to sense her intent and hesitated at just the right moment to cause the bolt to fly harmlessly past.

"No!" Cora watched the figure move closer to Calien, who remained on his knee recovering from his wound. "Calien!" she screamed. "Watch out!" She let go her crossbow and it thudded onto the stone ground. Reaching to her belt, she unveiled her only melee weapon, a short spear, and prepared to rush to the prince's aid.

Then she heard the footstep behind her.

She blinked and swung her shoulders just soon enough to see the silver glint of a sword, as it sliced through the air toward her chest. There was little time for reaction, but Cora did manage to twist enough so that the blade pierced her side instead of her heart. She cried out painfully, as the weapon bit through skin, flesh, and tissue.

Alazar had been preparing to send fire at the figure advancing on Calien, but the shrill scream interrupted his focus. When he turned, he witnessed the halfling crumpled to the ground, the cobble below her budding red. A strange sentiment gripped him, welling up from his gut and rising until it burst forth with a forcefulness he could never have predicted.

Fiery rage consumed the robed man.

The vagabond who had struck Cora down was standing over her with his weapon poised for the killing blow. Before he could lower his weapon, a scorching ray of pure intensity hammered him, exploding as it made contact with his body. The flaming ray sent the man flying backward in a jumbled heap of body parts. Still furious, Alazar was not finished. He stepped purposefully toward the attacker, who was now laying alongside the street moaning in agony, his flesh charred and smoldered. It took one more blast to finish him off. The flame emerged from his hands, and the man died. Alazar observed his own wrath with little emotion, save for acrimony. His death could not erase the past thirty seconds or undue the wound to Cora. Distraught and cringing, he peered downward at the halfling, fearful of what he might discover. Before he could fully examine her, another foe appeared, seemingly from the air itself.

The newest enemy was female. She possessed passionate, sharp eyes, ear length hair, and held a long rod with a curved blade at one end. Gazing at Alazar with interest, she articulated calmly, "What do we have here, some kind of dark sorcerer? You are quite the rarity, my friend."

Alazar would have liked to blast her to oblivion right then, but his previous eruption, a mixture of overwhelming emotion and inherent ability, had left him mentally weakened. He didn't feel the usual alacrity of his skills. Unable to put Cora out of his mind, he risked a glance her way. The halfling was laying in the same place as before, but her arms shown slight movement.

"There is time to help the halfling," the woman said, "but you must act quickly. Help me kill the other two," she pointed to Calien and Kyligan, "and I give you my word I will help you save her."

"I do not deal with murderers," Alazar spat, readjusting his grip on his staff. "A warrior never strikes a deal with his opponent unless he feels threatened. Obviously, you are threatened."

The woman laughed, confidently. "Ha! Save your false wisdom for another. Do I appear threatened to you? It is an exceptional day indeed to be given the opportunity to kill a user of the arcane. I will revel in this!" The woman swung her rod at Alazar, the curved blade veering forward with dark intent.

*   *   *

The man's fingers tingled in anticipation. His mark was only steps away, still kneeling on the paved street holding his neck. He was pleased with his decision to rid his bow in favor of melee. The halfling with the crossbow would have proven a nuisance and he dared not risk allowing her to attain a lucky shot. If he moved in close to the prince, she would cease shooting for fear of accidentally hitting the wrong man. His skill with his long daggers would be an unfailing way to finish the prince off once and for all.

Through his dizziness, Prince Calien could hear the hushed footsteps of a figure approach with blatant speed. He wanted to take up his sword, to fight, but his body resisted. *Come on*, he chided himself, *ignore the pain!* The light tapping of boots upon stone continued to carry toward him. The figure was close. He could even hear the man's short breaths now. If he did not stand, he would die. Squeezing his eyes shut, he lowered a shaking hand to the silver and gold pommel of his blade. But could he pull it from its sheath?

The aggressor raised his daggers high, convinced of a victory close at hand. Yet, one step before his triumph the prince rose up with stunning abruptness. His blade was drawn and the polished steel shined vibrantly, as he waved it before his body. The attacker faltered and fell back several steps to size up his reinvigorated opponent. The injury to his neck looked no better than before. Clotting blood had soiled the right side of his body, yet he stood nonetheless. In addition, he was prepared to do battle! Resolutely, the assassin gripped his daggers tighter and refused to let his confidence wane. Let the prince fight if he must, he ruminated darkly. He is no match for my skill.

"Be careful, Prince. That is the same opponent I faced last night. He is skillful indeed." It was Kyligan who had yelled. The ranger was still dueling his own opponent, but he had taken a moment to look Calien's way and recognized the daggers the man held.

Calien heeded the ranger's words, but he kept his attention on his attacker. The two circled slowly. "Who are you?" the prince questioned.

"If you wish to know the man who has paid for your murder, I cannot help," the assassin mocked, with supercilious pride. "However, if you wish to know the name of your murderer, it is I, Endias."

Calien stared at the man. "Someone has paid to have me killed? For what reason?"

"Too many questions," Endias scolded, weaving the daggers menacingly before the prince. "Your death has brought me a fortune." He lunged with the weapons, slashing simultaneously with both.

Calien dodged the attack and lashed his blade out to keep Endias at swords length. Although he had trained relentlessly in the skill of dueling back home in Calas, he was not accustomed to battling a foe with the fighting style, nor the weapon choice, in which Endias preferred. Though the daggers were longer than most he'd seen, they were still just daggers. Only someone with extraordinary speed and stealth could be effective with weapons of such short range. Calien knew he needed to keep the man at a distance with his sword.

Again, Endias darted in, swinging his two knives at the prince. Calien successfully parried the attack, but discovered something of more concern in the process. His leg had buckled for just a moment. His blood loss was weakening him. The prince then knew that he couldn't extend the fight. He had to end it quickly before his body could no longer hold him up.

To the assassin's surprise, Calien suddenly went on the offensive. While Endias had not figured on the prince's aggressiveness, he was utterly shocked by his skill with a sword. Calien was a whirling menace, lunging and slashing his blade with untamed fury. Endias was able to parry most attacks, but he was being pushed backwards, reeling on his heels. The sharp ringing of metal on metal echoed down the street, as the combat spilled from one side of the road to the other.

Calien could see that his opponent's face had changed. Where once there was unabashed arrogance, there was now creases and wrinkles of doubt. The prince ached all over, but his confidence and determination grew with each parry. Every time Endias attempted to slip past Calien's guard, the prince forced him away with staggering proficiency. Soon, it was evident where the tide of the duel was progressing. Endias found himself backed against the wooden fence, with few options at his disposal against an unyielding foe.

"May the hells take you!" the assassin sneered.

Calien answered with his blade. He feigned an attack to the legs, then raised the sword and drove it through the brigand's stomach. The steel penetrated the body with ease, carrying past the spine and into the fencepost behind. Endias let out only the faintest of gasps before his mouth filled with blood. Eyes bulging, he stared at Calien with a look of shock before his head lolled and he went motionless. He was still impaled upon the fence.

The prince let go of his weapon and stepped backwards. He gazed upon his handiwork with a mixture of grim satisfaction and utter revulsion. His body twitched and he suddenly remembered the arrow. Reaching up, he felt the wooden shaft still protruding from his neck. Then his legs gave way beneath him and he collapsed.

*   *   *

Kyligan and his opponent seemed at a standstill. The ranger had a nasty gash across his bicep, but he had repaid Beornis, or whatever the man's real name was, with a painful slash across his ribs. Both men seemed of similar skill, their blades singing, as they swept them back in forth in the eternal dance of battle.

Earlier, Kyligan had risked a glance at the prince and found him engaged with the same assassin from the night before. He hoped Calien was faring well, for he had problems of his own and had no time to come to the prince's rescue. The ranger was focused entirely on the man who had previously faked a lame leg. There was no lameness in him now. He was nimbly hopping about with his weapon, in full health save for the wound Kyligan had inflicted upon him. The ranger briefly wondered what had happened to Alazar and Cora and guessed there must be more enemies in the area, or they would have certainly made their presence known by now.

Bringing up his sword, he blocked an overhead attack and countered with a lunge of his own. His foe knocked away the strike and lurched backward. Kyligan pursued him, stepping forward and slashing his blade sideways, aimed at the shoulder of his enemy. Again, the blow was parried and the force of the two weapons connecting rang loudly, carrying them askew.

Like a sudden prophecy of total clarity, Kyligan recognized his opening. With both men's weapons at their sides, the ranger lowered his head and drove it into the face of the assassin. A *crack* was heard and the skirmisher grunted in pain. He fell to his backside, his face a mess of crimson from his shattered nose. Kyligan primed his sword and steered it with all his might into his enemy's neck. The man never had a chance to scream.

"Kyligan! A little help!"

The ranger turned to find his friend at arms with a woman. It was evident that the woman was far more adept at close combat than Alazar, as she kept the robed man consistently on the defensive. Alazar was using his staff to block her advances, but there was no telling how long he could last before succumbing. Disfrazal was loose on the ground, scurrying in circles and doing his best to distract the woman – whether by biting her ankles or simply getting in the way just when it seemed she would overcome his master.

From an unnoticeable distance, Kyligan deftly circled to the woman's backside, out of her vision, and then rushed her from behind. The woman, however, must have heard his approach because she rotated her body to see both men. Stepping backwards, she regarded each foe with equal disdain and then scanned the area searching for her comrades. When she spotted each of them, dead, she coolly returned her focus to her nearest opposition.

"Explain yourself," Kyligan demanded.

The woman did not immediately answer. She probed her opponents, mentally seeking a weakness or a conduit to defeat them, all-the-while she twirling her bladed rod before her body.

Now, with help and extra time to deliberate, Alazar reached internally, seeking the power of flame he had wielded minutes just before. Nothing. Evidently, something about his startling emotional outburst had left him temporarily spent of his inner powers. He positioned his staff with the knowledge that for now, it was his only weapon.

With proficient quickness, the woman reached down to her boot and pulled loose a throwing dagger. She reached back and flung the knife at the ranger. Kyligan ducked the spiraling blade and looked back up, only to see the woman fleeing rapidly. He nearly chased after when a hand firmly grabbed his shoulder.

"Let her go. We have other concerns," Alazar said, pointing to the injured Cora and Calien. Despite her pain, the halfling was sitting upright and gazing at the two men. Her forearm was pressed heavily against her side, as she winced. Her leather garments were wet and sticky from blood loss. Alazar went to her immediately.

Calien was not as fortunate. As Kyligan reached him, he instantly noticed the complete absence of movement. The man was unconscious and laying on his stomach, face down. Gingerly checking, Kyligan detected a hint of a pulse. "He lives, but barely!" the ranger yelled to Alazar.

"Can you carry him?" the robed man asked.

"I think so." Kyligan procured the prince's sword from the fence and then scooped up the limp body with much effort.

Alazar pulled Cora's arm away and viewed the wound. There was little to see. The whole of the halfling's side was blotted scarlet. He commenced sliding his arms beneath the woman to lift her.

"You saved my life," Cora mouthed through anemic breaths.

Alazar acted as if he hadn't heard, though the words had in fact engraved themselves deeply. But what could he say? His actions had been a mystery even to himself. Saving her life did not bother him, for that was required of comrades. It was the way he achieved it. *Why the sudden rush of sentiment?* He had never regarded Cora as anything more than a friend and companion, and still felt that way even now. What had happened to inflame such fury? Alazar shook his head glumly and sighed. This was a mystery he wanted no part of.

"Are you ready?" Kyligan inquired, standing near Alazar with the prince in his arms. "Calien is not far from death. We must get him healed."

Hoisting the halfling skyward, Alazar followed the ranger toward the center of town.

XII

"By all that is holy! What has happened?"

Darin could not contain his astonishment, as he and Cadwan returned to their room at the inn following their visit with the baron. What they witnessed was Calien sprawled unconscious on one bed and a grousing Cora upon the other. Alazar and Kyligan were tending to each.

"Can you invoke the powers of your god to heal him?" Alazar asked.

The dwarf scuttled over to the side of Calien, examining the deep lesion in his throat. The arrow was still present, the wooden shaft jutting from a red mouth. The skin and tissue around the wound were inflamed and swollen. Darin angrily grunted. "This man dances on the throes of death! How long has he been like this?"

"An hour or so," Kyligan answered.

"And you have not sought a healer?" Darin snapped, furiously.

Kyligan had rarely seen the dwarf this mad and it caught him by surprise. "We thought it was better not to draw such attention. Alazar visited a local apothecary and acquired some healing herbs and potions. They have kept him stable, but I fear not for long. We need use of your priestly talents."

Darin gazed at the halfling, who was awake and listening. "And what of her?" the dwarf asked.

"Just heal the prince first." Cora retorted. "I can hold on far longer than he."

His bushy red beard and chiseled face in consternation, Darin simply shrugged. "Very well, but afterwards I want a damn good explanation how this all happened." The dwarf prodded the area around the abrasion. "First, we need to get this arrow out of there. I'll need some water to clean around the wound before I can remove it."

Kyligan disappeared from the room and reemerged moments later with a bucket of fresh water. Dipping a towel in the bucket, Darin dabbed around the wound, as he spoke. "Fortunately, the arrow appears not to have punctured a vein or artery. Unfortunately, I cannot push it through without doing just that. I'll need to pull it, and arrows are not made to be pulled out easily. I'll have to open the wound larger to free it. Kyligan, hand me your dagger."

The ranger obliged and Darin carefully slid the knife in a circular pattern around the injured area, repeating the same pattern several times more. The dwarf was thankful that Calien was unconscious. Had he been awake, he would most certainly be howling in agony and writhing about, no doubt impeding the dwarf's delicate work. When Darin felt he had cut deeply enough, he slowly drew out the jagged arrow, with loose strands of red tissue and tendon trailing the bloodied tip. A gush of blood, held within by the wedged arrow, hastily escaped to the freedom of air. Darin cast the culpable projectile on the ground and covered the wound to stop the crimson flow, as he examined it. Somehow, the arrow had spared all the vital appendages, but his blood loss was severe, and the dwarf knew he had to heal the man now.

Although Darin's deity, Frundin, was a god of war and battle, he granted his clerics certain healing abilities. The dwarf was not a healer by nature, but he had experience dealing with minor, sometimes moderate wounds. Alas, this wound was far from minor and Darin knew he was taxing the extent of his curative skills.

Kneeling beside the flaccid body of the prince, he gently adjusted his hands upon the red opening. He commenced a prayer under his breath. The others waited in absolute silence. For many seconds, the only sound was a temperate murmur coming from the dwarf. The wound suddenly tightened and closed in, but only to an extent. Darin paused and opened his eyes to view his workmanship. The flesh surrounding the gash had improved, drawing back some natural color, but the injury remained clearly visible. Sighing from exertion, Darin gazed at the others.

"I have done everything I can. We need to bind the wound tightly and let him rest. Perhaps tomorrow morning I can call upon Frundin again. As it stands, I am confident of his recovery, though we should all feel fortunate."

Afterwards, Cora's injury proved less troublesome for the dwarf. When she was tended to and bandaged firmly, Kyligan, Alazar, and Cora proceeded to retell the story of how she and Calien found themselves in their current state. Cadwan and Darin listened without interrupting.

After the tale concluded the dwarf, threw up his arms in exasperation. "Must I forego every battle we stumble upon?"

Cadwan clasped the dwarf's large shoulder. "Calm yourself, friend. If what the baron says is any indication, you will have many more chances to exploit the worth of your waraxe."

The words did little to ease Darin's misgivings, though he went momentarily quiet. Cadwan refocused on the others and resumed his deliberation on the story they had imparted. "You are all exceedingly fortunate to have lived. Any guesses as to why they attacked you?"

Kyligan nodded. "It seems their objective was Calien. He was the target of the arrows. The lame man first assaulted him before I interfered."

"And the prince was able to fight? Even after being struck with an arrow in his neck?" A noticeable inclination of shock invaded Cadwan's tone.

Kyligan gave an affirmative half-smile. "More so, Cadwan. He slew the man with the daggers. The very same man that had bested me the previous night." The ranger paused to gaze at the unconscious prince. "One thing is certain, I will no longer question his ability to employ a sword."

Cadwan considered Kyligan's words. In one way, he was relieved to know that Calien could handle himself in battle. Now, he wouldn't have to keep a close eye on the prince every time they happened upon a scuffle. Yet, he was not keen on having a marked man travel with the group. It put the others in greater danger and offered less than desirable attention. "What of the woman who fled? Do we have reason to be cautious of her?"

The ranger looked at Alazar, but the robed man only shrugged. "There is no way to tell. I suppose if she has more associates, she is still a valid threat. But if we have already killed them, it is more than likely she will not bother with us again."

Within the small interior of the room, Cadwan commenced the slow steps of contemplation, pacing before the others. From the very beginning, he hadn't felt comfortable taking the prince along. Though friendly enough, Calien added a completely different slant to the cohesion of the group. From the moment they departed Calas, he felt as if he were constantly looking over his shoulder to insure the future king was safe from danger. There was no telling how King Anuron would react, if Calien were to fall to harm. With the latest episode, he wondered if he could convince the prince that they were better off, and him safer, without each other. He glimpsed at the limp body of the prince upon the bed and knew it would be at least morning before they could discuss the idea.

Lowering himself into a chair, Cadwan pronounced, "It appears that there is little else we can do until tomorrow morning and a half-day still remains. We should use the remainder to relax and regain some lost sleep."

"A brilliant concept," Alazar contributed, with a mocking smile.

"You are in no condition to be leaving the inn today, Cora," Darin interluded, scolding the halfling. Despite her acute silence, he apparently had figured where her mind was already wandering. "Rest up, so you can be in sufficient condition tomorrow."

Cora made an expression of being unduly wronged. "But . . ."

"This is not a point that is up for discussion, halfling child." Darin grumbled, his tone in full seriousness. "You are staying here. Perhaps your good friend Alazar will keep you company?"

The last comment was made in jest, but seeing Alazar's eyes open like saucers gave the dwarf a curious impression.

*   *   *

A myriad of emotions, doubts and fears siphoned outward from Hetnar, as he sped his mare north, headlong into a rigid wind. He had observed the attack on his brother in its entirety and his mind still staggered from the shock of its outcome. Impossibly, Endias had failed, thwarted completely by Calien and his companions. His anger had yet to subside and his thoughts would not deter from rehashing the event over and over. Never had he hated his brother so much as now. Although he observed Calien led away in a state of unconsciousness from a gruesome wound, deep down he knew his brother would survive, if only to spite him. *How is this possible? Curse him!* Hetnar felt insulted, astounded by Calien's gall to ruin his scheme.

Ayna had escaped, but it did him no good. The woman showed no penchant for prolonging the contract. Perhaps she decided that, without Endias at her side, the danger was more than she wanted. Hetnar never even had a chance to speak to her. She had hurriedly left town before he could convince her to stay. Yet, in her wake an ominous question remained; during the battle, had she told them who her benefactor was? Hetnar feared the worst. If indeed Calien knew his own brother had hired assassins to kill him, then he had no choice but to finish the job, one way or the other, and quickly. He was fortunate to have more than a few acquaintances in these parts. As he rode at breakneck speed through the Barren Hills in the dead of night, he realized those contacts would come more handy than he ever imagined.

The Barren Hills were one of the most dangerous parts of the region and treks through the ill-famed land only invited trouble. Even the roads that paralleled the hills demanded great caution. The rolling mounds and rises were infested with orcs, berserkers and creatures of worse renown, almost all of the unfriendly sort. The murky lake adjoining the territory to the south, aptly named 'The Mull,' held rumors of a great monster amid its watery depths, though there had never been evidence to prove or disprove the myth.

Had Hetnar not carried a particular banner over his head, even he would have considered himself categorically insane. It was an hour past midnight and only a short time ago he had reached the southern outskirts of the hostile territory. The stars and moon shone perfectly in the otherwise torrent darkness, giving minimal light. But Hetnar's rabid urgency caused him to overlook obvious dangers that could occur, such as stumbling into a hidden pit or hurling over the side of a crag. With a shout, he kicked the sides of his mare, spurring the mount relentlessly onward with the knowledge that he could ill-afford to waste time.

Few trees ascended from the pitiable soil of the Barren Hills, but when Hetnar neared a group of oaks growing next to each other in the formation of a crescent he realized he was nearer his goal than he had presumed. Slowing his pace to the unambiguous delight of his mount, he trotted past the trees and cast about expectantly. He caught glimpses of a moving shape just at the edge of the bordering darkness. A moment later, the shape moved away and disappeared behind the black cloak. Hetnar observed with little reaction, his face frozen in a state of expectancy.

It will not be long now, he mused.

Distant grunts escalated from beyond his vision, but shortly the sounds grew louder, more prominent. Hetnar could discern language amid the primordial mumbles, simplistic words of communication that were no doubt aimed at his presence. He pulled his mare to a lingering toddle, approaching the noises in an unthreatening manner. Emerging from the wall of night appeared figures, at first only a few, then many more. The figures panned out and surrounded his mount on all sides, all-the-while grunting and speaking in the same crude language. When all of Hetnar's escape routes had been cut off, he pulled his steed to a complete halt.

Rising his voice to insure clarity, he called with an ambiance of self-assurance. "Respects to Farnok, Chieftain of the Tribe of the Skull."

A large figure separated himself from the outer-ring and neared Hetnar. When he came close enough, Hetnar could clearly see the upturned nose, the overlarge pointed ears and the prominent teeth. Each feature was a dead giveaway of the characters identity; an orc. The beast carried a large mace and strutted with poise and bravado. Its voice was guttural and abrasive, as it attempted to speak the common language rather than the orc language which would have come far easier for the humanoid. "Garn come back? Farnok not expect you for long time."

Hetnar repressed a smile at the mention of the name Garn, one of his many aliases. He regarded the orc chieftain closely. His characteristics were nothing short of common for his ilk, the grayish pigmentation, sloping forehead and large eye, the piggish snout. This particular orc was well battle-scarred, his hairy torso and face carrying the marks of tribal pride in large quantity. One eye socket stared with a black emptiness that clearly sported the greatest of Farnok's battle wounds. Speaking with confidence that was necessary when dealing with orcs, Hetnar nodded coolly. "Dire circumstances have brought me to you. I come bearing gold, and a request."

Farnok's one eye widened. "Request? You bring request to Farnok?" He wheeled his square-shaped head back to gaze at his tribe warriors. They all returned his stare with respect and ready obedience. Grunting tersely, he looked at Hetnar. "Garn been good to Skull. Farnok listen."

Of course you will, you damn stupid orc. Hetnar spat the words silently in his mind, with antipathy. Gods above, he loathed orcs! Their lack of intelligence and their straightforward, simpleton initiative made him curse himself for stooping to such a level. Even so, he realized the usefulness of having such beasts at his disposal and the current dilemma was certainly one of those times.

While he took no pleasure being among the fetid ranks of orcs, he forced himself a stoic, hearty expression. Straightening his back and clearing his throat, he spoke directly. "A group of adventurers will be heading north on the road that is just to the east. There should be six of them, five wearing common warrior garb and one wearing expensive, shiny armor. I would be quite pleased if you would do me the favor of killing them – all of them."

The orc chief nodded, unevenly. Though the beast did not speak with fluidness, his mind worked like any other brigand of similar nature. "Farnok not question Garn, but Farnok wonder what payment to get for killing?"

"Trust me, Farnok, you will be paid handsomely." Hetnar gave a charming smile and tossed up a single gold piece into the air, as if proving he had more in abundance. The coin fell unperturbed back into his calloused hand. "You have never failed me before and I honor your assistance. A thousand gold now and twice that after you have fulfilled the bargain."

Such wealth for one task, a task that sounded simple to Farnok was unheard of in the Tribe of the Skull. It took the orc little time to contemplate a response. "Farnok agree. Men die for Garn. Skull get thirty gold now and twice after."

Hetnar brushed a lock of hair from his face and waved his hand in a gesture of gratitude. "You are truly a great chieftain. There is one more minor detail. I trust you, Farnok, but I humbly ask something else, as well."

The orc tilted his head at an odd angle. Hetnar was aware that most orcs could not make the same distinctive facial expressions as humans and other races of similar birthright. Their animalistic nature and unsophisticated minds did not typically allow looks that were easily readable. However, the prince figured that Farnok's crooked head was a sort of circumspect gesture, as if he were suspicious of being tricked. "Speak to Farnok."

"I would like to enlist some giants in this task, as well." Hetnar watched the eyebrows of Farnok drop low over his one good eye and the empty abyss of his other socket, but the prince showed no concern. He made sure his voice was calm and unassuming. "I am aware of a small clan of such giants not far to the west. If you could persuade a few to join you, I will pay an additional thousand gold to the Skull and the giants a thousand gold for helping."

"Farnok know of giants which you speak, but Farnok not need them. Tribe of Skull will kill men alone."

Hetnar had expected such a response. Orcs were full of pride and distrustful of any other species, whether they be humanoid or otherwise. It had taken him years to gain the Skulls trust. Allying with giants was another matter entirely. "I understand your position, Farnok. I have faith in the Skull, but surely, mighty Farnok, in your great wisdom you must understand the importance of success. Please remember, you will get an extra thousand gold for getting the giants to help. This alone is a fortune for you."

Gold was always enticing, but Farnok was not sold yet. Slamming his mace into the dry earth, he complained, "Why Garn want giant help to kill men so badly?"

"It is better you do not know, Chief Farnok." There was no reason to confuse the chieftain, but to any person with a scrap of intelligence the answer was simple; giants would almost certainly ensure a quick victory. Hetnar knew the Skull were strong and unyielding, but for reasons he could not verbally express he didn't quite trust them to the task alone. "Will you gain the giants help?"

The prince waited calmly for an answer. Farnok would not turn him down, that was assured. The sheer amount of gold Hetnar offered would make certain that Farnok put aside his pride to agree to an uneasy alliance. To his credit, the chieftain waited longer than necessary before responding. It was probably just for show, Hetnar ruminated, but the pause proved his loyalty to the Skull and would increase the respect he received from his peers. Only after sufficient time had passed did the chief proclaim his answer. "Farnok agree and promise to Garn that men die."

Showing appreciation, Hetnar offered his thanks, but insisted they go over all the minor details more than a few times. For nearly an hour, the Chieftain of the Tribe of the Skull and the second son of King Anuron deliberated every detail of the attack. Hetnar was adamant that they attack no other travelers, asserting that it would only prevent them from surprising the real targets. He placated them by claiming they could keep any spoils the adventurers kept after they were killed. Once the prince felt as confident as one could be when trusting orcs, he made his farewells and thankfully departed their company, turning his mount south.

The idea of seeing his brother die with his own eyes was provoking, but Hetnar had decided not to follow the group of six any longer. He had drawn his last hand and now was returning home to the city-state of Calas. It would be beyond miraculous if Calien survived an ambush of orcs and giants and Hetnar expected that news of his death at the hands of such beasts would reach the palace soon enough. He only needed to wait for it. Calien had foiled him once, but defeating a legion of orcs and giants was far different than defeating four assassins.

With night still in bloom, Hetnar streaked across the southern hills, homeward bound. He felt positive, but not certain. Never certain. The next few days would be long ones, indeed.

XIII

Darin knew all too well the pressures and expectations a father can project on one's son. His own father was a warrior of great renown back home in the kingdom of Ludun, holding much esteem for it. One swing of his great warhammer could shatter rock, so it was said. He also put a great deal of pride in his two sons, though that would change later on. Darin was the older of the two and his father had anticipated his own footsteps to be followed with the vigor expected of a first-born. When Darin told his father that he wished to become a priest, his father was furious. "How can my son choose religion over might?" his father had screamed that day. For his father, religion was an afterthought, for it was the hammer itself which was worshiped above all else. It was difficult for Darin to explain that Frundin was a god of battle and that he himself would still wield a weapon on the bloodied fields of war. The only difference was that his priestly duties to Frundin would always come first.

Since those early disputes, his father had come to terms with his son's ways, yet their ideals remained dissimilar. For Darin, you defeated your opponents not for the sake of the kill itself, as his father would have it, but because it served a greater good.

Glumly watching Calien's motionless form on the bed, Darin guessed that the prince's own father, King Anuron, was likely not accepting of his own son's foray into adventure. A similar dispute, different circumstances. Anuron is eager for a son ready to rule, and Calien is eager to venture forth and test his mettle not as a prince, but as a warrior of virtue. Both sides had solid arguments, a quarrel which Darin wanted no part of. Regrettably, he and the rest of his companions had been thrust directly and unwillingly in the middle.

It was morning in Mullikin, if only in theory, for the sun had yet to cast its light and draw color back to a grayed world. Darin had slept uneasily and after the last of many waking moments, he decided it was no longer worth the effort. Calien had still not woken from his healing sleep. The other in the room, Cadwan, was sprawled awkwardly on a cushioned pallet and breathing loudly, as he dozed. Wishing not to wake either, he quietly slipped into his armor, took up his weapon and exited the room. The stairway to the first floor of the inn was just down the hall. Though dwarves were not celebrated for their stealthy movements, Darin guided himself as best he could without waking other patrons.

The stairs descended into the lobby. Darin climbed down, endeavoring to lighten his heavy footfalls. The door to the outside world lay just ahead.

"And where are you off to this night?"

The dwarf turned to find Alazar lounging tranquilly atop a stone bier within the lobby. The bearded man returned the dwarf's look without altering his expression. Disfrazal sat upon the man's shoulder.

Darin had always found Alazar peculiar. Even though it was the dwarf who had initially convinced Cadwan, through much effort, to allow Alazar to join them, he had always found the bronze-skinned man an enigma. He hailed from Asharria, a desert land far to the southeast, and he continually found clever ways to avoid any questions that dealt with his past or background. The modest information he did offer usually centered on his reasons for coming to Calas, which in his own words were 'to seek one called the The Dragon.' Yet, Alazar would comment little about the man, other than he had seen this 'Dragon' in his dreams and was compelled to find him. Such cryptic expressions gave the bearded man a mysterious air and made him an uncertain companion, though Darin had never regretted his decision to invite the man to journey along. The dwarf could sense a heart of good intent and his arcane skills with the elements of fire had already proven useful.

"Alazar," the dwarf muttered, "I would not have expected you to be awake at this hour. Kyligan perhaps, but not you."

Alazar curled thin lips upward. "Kyligan sleeps peacefully for once, or at least he appears to. It is refreshing to see him in such a way. It is rare these days."

The mention of Kyligan's nightmares filled the dwarf with momentary despair. In some strange way, as a priest he felt responsible for not having a cure for the tortured ranger. Despite all his efforts, he was rendered helpless in aid, just as Kyligan was rendered helpless to the whim of his dreams. With swiftness, the dwarf altered the discouraging subject. "What has brought you awake? You are commonly the last of us to rise each morn."

The enigma shrugged. "If you wish a definite answer, I fear I will disappoint for I am not fully certain what forced me to stir. However," Alazar's thick eyebrows furrowed, "I have guesses. But perhaps you already know the answer, for the sun has yet to rise and you are also awake, yes?"

Darin nodded. "I woke several times tonight and sleep came in small fragments."

"Ahh, then you feel it, as well. I should not be surprised, knowing you are a man of religion and have connections with such," Alazar hesitated momentarily, searching for the precise adage, "otherworldly sensations."

Darin might have been a priest, but his patience was short when it came to abstruse language. He fixed Alazar with a serious glare. "What are you talking about? Otherworldly sensations? I have no time for your esoteric nonsense."

"You do not feel it then?" The enigma shook his head, unconvinced. "Surely, that is untrue. You have only to place the puzzle together. I have felt it myself since we arrived in Mullikin two days prior, but only a few hours ago did I understand."

The dwarf was silent, staring motionless at his counterpart. His stoic face belied his thoughts. Inside, the wheels were turning. Words dabbled on the tip of his tongue, but he held them back, hesitant to express his feelings immediately.

"Shall we take a walk?" Alazar said, pointing to the door. "It is quite a peaceful morning, even if the sun has yet to rise."

With a nod from Darin, the two exited the inn and emerged outside. The dwarf took in a gulp of air. Alazar was correct, the mood of the early hours was indeed peaceful and calm. Stragglers had yet to intrude the empty streets and the path seemed open only for them. The soft droning and buzzing of insects radiated about. Otherwise, no sounds infected their privacy. The two men stepped softly down a street, at first saying nothing as the apex of the fiery orb peeked over the eastern horizon and cast the opening beams of light arching above the town walls. A symbol of rugged austerity, Mullikin spread openly before them and they strolled leisurely though its heart, passing several businesses along the way. Though every shop had yet to open its doors, in one window a baker could already be seen cooking his goods for the day. The walk proved soothing, but neither man could ignore the tension that built within them. When the dwarf could no longer handle the silence, he spoke gruffly through averted eyes. "Something waits for us."

The enigma stopped and tapped his oaken staff on the cobble. "Then you do feel it. I thought so." Alazar nodded, retrospectively. "It is ominous, is it not? My senses tremor uncontrollably."

Again, the dwarf had no retort. His proud nature suppressed expression, though internally he nodded.

"I am surprised you have not said anything," Alazar continued. "When did this revelation occur to you?"

"Since we began traveling north," Darin answered. "It is strongest here, in Mullikin, but I suspect as we continue farther toward Oester it will only intensify. It looms over me, threateningly, yet alluring all the same."

In the distance, a dog's bark was heard. As if in reply, several blackbirds flew overhead, darting to unknown destinations. The two men gazed at each other, barely aware that luminance continued to spread across Mullikin, bringing the colors of the world with it. Alazar tapped his staff with his fingertips and asked, "Your perception furthers my own. Why have you not said something before?"

The dwarf lifted his heavy shoulders. "What good would come of me bringing words of ill fortune to the others. This is no time to cast more fear. It seems we will need every ounce of bravery our hearts can retain. Whatever awaits in Oester anticipates our coming."

"Yes," Alazar agreed, "your wisdom holds much truth, priest. It makes me wonder why we would willingly seek out such a foreboding gloom."

Darin grinned and patted the shoulder of the spindly man. "When one seeks heroics, often times one gets more than formerly expected. Such is the life we have chosen, Alazar, and such is the commitment we made to King Anuron. It is true that our group is an odd blend," the priest motioned at the robed man's lizard still perched on his shoulder, "but collectively, we possess strength, cunning and ingenuity. I remain hopeful in our success."

Alazar took in the dwarf's insight with pensive eyes of contemplation. For long moments, he stood in thoughtful silence. When he did reply, his words were wistful, brooding. "I find your choice of words intriguing. You claimed to be 'hopeful.' Are you no longer *confident*?"

*　　　*　　　*

To a man of normal size, the crawl space under the abandoned shack would have been completely unusable, as one would have to lay sprawled flat on his back just to fit beneath. For Finney, a halfling, the space was merely unbearable.

There was just enough room for him to sit upright without his head scraping the top, but the muck and grime that lay exposed below was neither comfortable or appeasing. Finney was accustomed to hiding, but he took no pleasure in being dirtied or waiting helplessly while another person, in this case Elessa, handled his problems. He had sunken to the furthest depths of shame and was overcome with a forlorn depression.

As morning sunrays reached the outer portion of the opening, Finney scooted his seat over to feel what little warmth he could. Today was the beginning of his second day in seclusion. The previous day, Elessa had stopped by once for a brief visit, bringing him food and drink. She had told him that Hermoc was scouring the town in search of his thief and had even informed, and paid, the guards at the gate to insure the impossibility of escape. When he had asked her how long he must stay hidden under the forsaken hovel, she only shrugged glumly and said she was "working on it." *Working on what?* Truthfully, he saw no way out of the situation, unless of course they were able to somehow scale the stone walls to freedom. Finney had spent his remaining time endlessly flipping the magic coin, testing its abilities and morosing sadly over its limitless potential.

The halfling didn't know when Elessa would visit today. For him, the lack of knowing was the worse part. He was sure he wouldn't last much longer wedged below the building, but what else was there for him to do? The fresh daylight of morning brought him hope and misery at the same time.

When he heard the footsteps scraping along the path next to the hovel, he instantly caught his breath. When he discerned it was only one person, he exhaled slowly. It was doubtful that Hermoc's thugs would travel alone, so he assumed it was the one person he wished to see. His suspicions were proven true when the person spoke. "Finney?"

"I am here," the halfling answered.

Along with several black curls of hair, Elessa's head dropped below into the opening and she peered within. "I have brought you some ham and water." She slid a covered dish into the gap, along with a wooden cup.

Finney snatched the plate and greedily gorged himself with the bland slab of meat. He was not fond of ham or water, preferring wine and foods of more delicacy, but he was starving and anything was fit for consumption now. "Has the situation improved?" he inquired between mouthfuls.

"How can it?" she hissed. "As long as that coin is missing, you will never be able to show your face in Mullikin again. Escape is impossible because you will be arrested by the guards." Elessa hesitated a moment. What she planned to say next had to be offered with care. "Listen, Finney, I know you do not want to hear this, but I think the only way is to return the coin."

"But . . ."

"Let me finish!" Elessa screamed. She was stunned, as was Finney, by her sudden forthrightness. "You must give me the coin. I will return it to Hermoc and plead for his forgiveness. Surely, with his coin restored he will listen."

Her words struck Finney's ears painfully. "I do not want you pleading to anyone!" he said, with conviction. "I have brought you to a situation I deeply regret and I will not have you on your knees begging on my account. Elessa," the halfling hesitated, "go home. You have no more responsibility. I will handle this folly on my own."

"Finney," Elessa whispered, "stop."

"I mean it! None of this is your doing and I never should have allowed you to partake in it. This is my . . ."

"Would you listen to me. Someone is coming. Stop talking!" Elessa snapped. "Wait a moment." Finney watched the woman's feet disappear to one side.

A long silence followed. He could see little through the small opening of the crawlspace, and he wondered were she had gone, or if she was coming back. Was someone truly coming? Finney realized he was holding his breath again, broken only by a sudden shout.

"Hold there, Miss! May I have a word?" Finney heard several footsteps break into a run and then saw them scuttle past in a flash. At least three or four men, he guessed.

"What do you want?" Elessa said from some distance away.

Finney knew the men had reached Elessa. Their hurried footsteps had ceased. "You are Elessa, correct?" a man said.

"I have told you, I do not know where Finney is."

Someone guffawed. "Oh, I think you do. You see, we followed you this morning."

Finney's blood went ice cold. Were they bluffing? His mind began to spin relentlessly in desperation. Should he crawl out and run? The answer was simple. He no longer had the speed of ten years ago and would be caught in no time. His only hope was to remain still and hope Elessa could keep them away.

"Your harassment has no affect on me," Elessa combated. "I am a barmaid, remember? I get harassed every day of my life. Go pester someone else and leave me be."

Finney listened from his hole. He had never before heard Elessa handle ruffians so confidently, and had never been more proud of her. Again, the pang of guilt flooded him. Gods, why had he involved her?

"Your resilience is impressive, m'lady," one of the men said. "but we know that our query sits under that crawlspace, as we speak. We ask you to urge him out, for if we attempt so it will be much less," he paused, "cordial."

Elessa went quiet.

All remnants of hope dolefully seeped from the halfling. He was found. *Heaven's fury, what will they do to me?* Finney began to tremble, but then something forced him to hold resolute. Elessa had done everything she could and now it was his turn. Leaning forward, he crawled out from his hiding space and into the open sunlight for the first time in a day and a half. His clothes were haggard, wrinkled and covered in filth. Brushing his garments, he stood and called out, "I am here."

There were four men, each of them whirling to view the halfling with grim pleasure. Elessa had her face in her hands, sobbing. "Oh, Finney!" she cried sorrowfully, though it was barely audible beneath her hands.

The leader of the ruffians stepped two paces forward and bowed. "Finny, finally we have the pleasure of meeting."

The halfling regarded the man warily and with some surprise. He was a far cry from the brutish common thug Finney was used to. The man was a handsome rake, with flawless blond hair, intelligent eyes and well-maintained vestments. A beautiful rapier hung from his hip and his cloak hadn't a wrinkle. On his face was a smile of duel purpose; flirtatious for the woman, assertive for the men. He was sly and silver-tongued, the perfect combination for extracting information in whatever manner required. Finney knew the type. Although he hadn't the dashing looks of the man, the halfling could still charm almost anyone with a few words.

When Finney did not reply, the confident leader continued. "I am Rendan. As I am sure you are aware, Hermoc has hired me to seek you out. My associates," Rendan motioned toward the other three men, all of whom garnered the appearance more appropriate of the type of thug Finney was used to, "and I have sought you out since two nights ago. We are pleased to finally find you."

Again, Finney made no response. The halfling had made a living off of his roguish ways. As such, he had always had an 'out' of sorts, a way to escape whatever trouble he found himself in. Yet, there was no 'out' this time. He had taken his thieving too far and was left with nothing to say, no recourse to erase what had happened.

Rendan looked at Elessa, who was still sobbing softly, and then refocused on Finney. When he spoke, it was not harsh, but there was no hint of remorse. "Your silence is understandable and you no doubt know why we are here. Let us deal with the most pressing issue first. You have Hermoc's Coin of Chance and he wishes it returned."

Finney reached into his pocket and tapped the coin with his fingertips. All he had to do was grip it, pull it out and hand it to them. Strangely, he couldn't. The gold piece's potential still lured his inner greed and forced him motionless.

Rendan frowned. "My halfling friend, do not be foolish. My cohorts will take little pity on you and I fear things are bad enough without you making them worse."

Amidst a grin, one of the men behind Rendan withdrew his sword, the scraping sound echoing ominously in the early morning. Elessa couldn't stifle her scream.

A single droplet of sweat fell down Finney's forehead and across the bridge of his nose. He eyed the men behind Rendan, all of whom seemed eager and hopeful that Finney would not oblige. He grasped the coin hard, feeling its edges in his palm.

"What is happening here?"

Every head in the path swiveled to find two newcomers, a tall, bearded man with tanned skin and tattered robes, and a balding dwarf. An odd looking lizard was perched on the robed man's shoulder and the dwarf was wearing solid half-plate armor and wielding a menacing waraxe. Finney didn't recognize either of them, but he held a sense of hope at their abrupt appearance. They obviously heard Elessa's scream and presumed it was a cry for help.

"Your bravery is most extraordinary," Rendan said to the newcomers, "but the situation is under control. I urge you to leave before you get caught up in something you wish you hadn't."

The bearded man raised a finger to Elessa. "You are the barmaid at the Iron Hill, correct?"

Elessa's eyes widened like saucers. She suddenly broke into a run toward the man and the dwarf. "Yes, yes! I remember you! You were with the quiet one a couple nights ago." She reached the bearded man's side and grabbed his arm. "These men are going to hurt Finney!"

The robed man gave the dwarf a questioning look. The dwarf's gaze rotated from the four men, to the halfling, then back to the men. With a trained diplomatic tone, he inquired, "Is this true? Are you planning to hurt the halfling? He appears defenseless."

"This *defenseless* halfling has thieved an object of great worth from my client. Now, he refuses to return it." Rendan stared through tapered, cunning eyes at the dwarf. "Do not involve yourself. There are four of us and only two of you."

The dwarf appeared to ignore the last statement, calmly focusing his interest on Finney. "Give your recourse. Have you stolen from this man's client?"

Finney wanted to lie, but the dwarf's eyes were intelligent, wise. They would no doubt discern any lies he might shed, which would only worsen his circumstance. Instead, Finney simply nodded in confirmation. Something about the dwarf's dignified manner and empathetic expression made him honest.

The brash dwarf contorted his face only slightly, as if displeased with the halfling. "Do you have the object with you?"

Again, Finney nodded wordlessly.

"Give it to me." The dwarf reached out a pudgy hand and waited expectantly. He seemed fully certain Finney would comply without question, like a father would a son. Finney withdrew the coin and walked slowly to where the dwarf stood. With minor hesitation, he dropped the shiny object into the dwarf's hand. Rendan and the others watched the sequence play out, fully enthralled.

The dwarf brought the gold piece to his face, turning it over in his fingers and examining it. When he finished, he looked over to Rendan and held the coin upward. "Is this the object your client seeks?"

"It is," Rendan stated, simply.

Reaching back with his thick, muscular arm, Darin flung the gold piece forward. It arched through the air toward Rendan who casually reached forward and clasped it in his right arm.

"There, you have what you seek. You may leave the halfling be and go about your business," the dwarf boldly proclaimed.

Finney watched Rendan briefly inspect the coin to insure it was indeed the Coin of Chance. When satisfied, he stored it away in a pocket and looked at the dwarf. "I do not think it will be that easy. Yes, we have the coin, but there are consequences for stealing from Hermoc. He was quite distraught over losing his valuable coin and he would like to see the halfling first-hand. It is our duty to escort Finney to Hermoc."

"The halfling goes nowhere with you," the dwarf said. Finney could not believe his audacity. He surely had no idea who it was he was dealing with. "Perhaps another time he can visit this 'Hermoc.' For now, he stays in my care."

The ruffian's face flushed and for the first time he showed signs of frustration. "This is not your matter, dwarf. Finney is our problem and you are unwise to stick your nose is someone else's business. Must I remind you that you are outnumbered?"

The dwarf smiled, assertively. "I am aware of your numbers, but as you can see I am unconcerned. My friend here," the dwarf motioned to the robed man beside him, "is a master of the arcane arts and could kill you without so much as raising his staff." Darin lightly slid his finger across the steel of his waraxe. "The four of you would pose no problem for us."

Rendan laughed. "Ha! Master of the arcane arts? Your words reek of false gallantry. Does not every liar claim to be a wizard with extraordinary powers? Your bluff is ineffective, my dwarven friend."

Finney was breathlessly watching, fully engrossed with the knowledge that perhaps his fate rested on the words of these two combatants. He noticed that although Rendan endeavored to remain poised, the seeds of uncertainty had been planted. He wondered how the dwarf would handle the latest accusation from his antagonist.

The statement was answered with nothing more than an indifferent shrug from broad shoulders. "If that suits you," the dwarf mumbled with slight tone. "But know this, I give you one final warning. My companion and I have no desire to kill this morning, but if you force the issue, rest assured you will soon be dead, and for no reason. It rests on your shoulders." The dwarf withdrew his waraxe and held it apathetically before him.

The conflictive mood of the surrounding area had reached a climax. For several seconds, everyone involved did nothing but cast furtive glances back and forth, their eyes saying all that was necessary. Rendan's hand lingered around his rapier, but then he pulled it away. Pointing a thin finger and glaring at Finney, the man spoke with intentional malice. "Hermoc is not finished with you, halfling!" Intentionally averting his focus from the dwarf, he spun on his heels and stalked off, the ruffians following his steps.

When the men had fully disappeared, those who remained seemed to collectively exhale at once. Elessa heartily thanked the dwarf repeatedly while Finney viewed the dwarf curiously. "Are you really so powerful?"

The tall man with the robes allowed a sardonic smile to cross his face.

The halfling noticed the look and it dawned on him. The dwarf had been bluffing! Finney leapt into the air. "That is marvelous! How did you know he would not fight, regardless of your boasts?"

The dwarf merely scratched his bald head. "He did not wish to die wantonly. I've no doubt he still suspected I was overstating our might, but he had already attained the coin and further risk was unnecessary." He paused, adding, "I am certain you will see more of him, on his terms."

Finney smiled, gleefully. "Yes, well, that is a worry for another time. You have my heartfelt thanks, both of you, but now Elessa and I must be on our way. Perhaps one day we can repay you?" He spun around, taking one step before something snatched his upper arm.

The halfling gingerly looked back to see the dwarf's strong hand holding him firmly. "Hardly. I am not yet finished with you, little one."

*   *   *

"We must leave today. Our welcome in Mullikin has been overstayed." Cadwan reclined in a padded chair, his words singular and unhurried, though meaningful nonetheless.

Sitting along the foot of the bed, Kyligan absorbed the scene before him. The small room of the Mullikin Inn had been crammed past its serviceable limit. The six adventurers had been joined by the barmaid Elessa and a halfling that Darin introduced as Finney. The dwarf recounted the events that took place only a half-hour ago, exclaiming that Finney and Elessa might hold useful information. From Kyligan's perception, Finney appeared discontented and edgy, like his time was being thoroughly wasted conferring with a bunch of soldiers he knew nothing about. The ranger could perceive the halfling as the cunning sort, the kind to persevere in unwelcome circumstances, if it benefited him over time.

It had been only two nights ago when Kyligan first met Elessa at the Iron Hill Tavern, but after the encounter with the assassins the previous day it was already a distant memory. He found Elessa attractive, but at the same time she made him uncomfortable. He frequently caught her staring at him since she'd arrived in the room with Finney. She hadn't spoken to him yet, but he knew enough of female ways to understand the curiosity that lay behind her eyes. How could this be good? With his mind set firmly on their task at hand, he wasn't certain it was sensible to involve himself in womanly interests. Still, her alluring stare was difficult to ignore.

"Agreed," Darin articulated, as he wedged his way between the crowds. "There is nothing more to gain in our dawdling."

"How do you feel, Calien?" Cadwan asked, turning to the prince, who still rested on his back. Earlier, Darin had laid healing hands on the injury again and much of the natural color on his face had been restored. The wound was bandaged tight, but Calien was moving his head and neck far better than expected. "Perhaps we should go on without you? You could return to Calas knowing of your bravery and without risk of further harm."

110

Cadwan's comment was more a subtle prodding than a suggestion, but either Calien did not pick up on the implication, or he wanted no part of it. "I shall not leave a task unfinished. I am well enough to continue."

"My Prince," Cadwan continued, leaning up in his chair, "you almost died. Do you understand that? As you now realize, this is no game and you might not be so lucky next time. We are not even certain if these assassins are still hunting you."

Prince Calien shook his head demurely, his blond locks shifting in a lazy pattern. "I never believed this to be a game. This is not some bedtime tale that I wish to live out. From the first day we left Calas, I knew of the dangers ahead and I am a better man for my experiences. If my assassins are still out there, they'll not catch any of us unawares again." Calien stopped to insure that the others were fully listening. When he was contented with their focus, he added decisively, "This is not a matter of debate."

An awkward silence lingered after Calien's irrevocable statement. Kyligan noticed Cadwan and Darin throw fleeting looks at each other, but the ranger could only guess what they were meant to articulate. Inwardly, Kyligan admired the prince's fortitude. True, he was brash and green, but there was something to be said for his persistence and fearless outlook. He was unlike the others. Kyligan had left behind very little when he chose to travel with Cadwan and the others. His isolated life had brought him nothing in relationships or assets, and his decision had not been one of difficulty. Calien lived in an elegant palace with roomfuls of wealth and riches, destined to become the ruler of an entire kingdom. Nevertheless, here he was, residing in rundown inns and fighting for his life in alleys, alongside three people he barely knew, but was forced to trust. Kyligan wondered if he would do the same had he been in Calien's position.

For several minutes after the prince's avowal, Cadwan seemed on the threshold of a retort, but at last leaned back in his chair and was silent.

Darin waited until the quarrel was entirely past before focusing on Finney and Elessa. "Have you heard anything about the events in Oester of late?"

Creases of disbelief formed around Finney's eyes and forehead. "Oester? You mean that tiny village up north? What interest have you there?"

"Just answer the question, halfling," Darin barked. He had saved Finney from unknown suffering earlier at the hands of Hermoc, but the dwarf had little use for rulebreakers and Finney's thievery had still rubbed him the wrong way.

Finney huffed loudly at his rebuker, but when he caught Darin's penetrating stare he quickly found words to answer. "I have heard nothing of Oester, other than the usual; a tiresome little hole with little appeal."

"Wait!"

It was the barmaid who had shouted in revelation, shocking everyone. They anxiously looked on, as she stepped to the dwarf.

"A few nights ago," she continued, "some families from Oester had eaten at the Iron Hill. They hardly spoke and seemed distant and aloof. Simply being near them filled me with a strange sadness. I did not pursue conversation with them, for it was an unbearable feeling."

"Did they say *anything* of what happened to them?" Cadwan chimed in.

Elessa shook her head and absently twirled a lock of hair with her finger. "They spurned the few questions I did ask. I've seen many a person come through town and never have I seen the likes of what I saw in their faces." The barmaid stopped, but everyone remained on edge, tense in their anticipation, waiting for more. When it was evident she had no more to offer, it felt as if the air left the room.

Darin grumbled something under his breath, then rose his voice for everyone. "We have received a sufficient amount of portentous warnings. Let us prepare to leave this place and move north."

It took little time for the party to pack their meager belongings. Each one had been granted enough adventure within Mullikin and all were anxious, though still apprehensive, to move on. For safety reasons, each dressed for combat and carried their weapons on them. Before they departed, Darin regarded Finney. "You understand that you cannot stay here, in Mullikin. You have thwarted, to an extent, a man of obvious influence."

"But the guards at the gate will stop me. There is still no way for me to leave," Finney replied.

Darin swung his head to observe Cora, as she adjusted the bandages on her side. "I guess," he said, still speaking to Finney, "we have two halflings in our party until we are past the gates. Then, my little thief, you are on your own."

"But," a sudden realization hammered the halfling, "but that means I must leave Elessa. Or will you come with me?" he asked the barmaid, traces of hope brimming on his face.

Tears began to well-up in Elessa's eyes. "Finney, I have already told you, I cannot leave Gully so suddenly. He needs me at the Iron Hill."

"But you have always wanted to leave Mullikin," Finney pleaded, his own tears falling with surprising suddenness. "Now you have your chance!"

Elessa shook her head and covered her face with her hands. "I . . . I cannot."

"Please! Please!" Finney cried, letting emotion overtake his being. "I need you! I am nothing without you!"

Elessa's head sagged, her watery eyes falling to the floor. "I am sorry, Finney."

"Then I will come back for you!" he shouted, as if trying to convince himself. "When Hermoc has forgotten, I will come back!"

"I will be here waiting," Elessa whispered, her tone dripping with sadness. Both of them knew Hermoc never forgot.

The procession for departure went no more smoothly than the parting of Elessa and Finney. A small pony was purchased and the thieving halfling was covered in large clothes, cloaks and hoods to hide his appearance from the guards at the gate. All were eager to leave the town behind, but they still traveled slowly toward to exit. Elessa escorted the party on foot, saying nothing to Finney along the way.

When the gates shown themselves ahead, Kyligan was startled to find Elessa standing directly next to his horse, peering up at him. Her mouth was open like she were about to say something. The ranger waited a moment, returning her stare with revealing eyes, then suddenly spurred his horse forward, away from the woman. He cursed himself, as he gazed straight ahead, refusing to look back. He would not risk losing focus now. His life depended on his readiness. Perhaps he could visit the Iron Hill Tavern on his return trip from Oester? If there was to be a return trip.

XIV

Following a full day of riding, camp was made shortly after dusk. Soon after leaving the outer gates of Mullikin, Finney had parted ways with the others, proceeding south atop his miniature mount. Though he hadn't announced his destination, it was perceived by the rest that he was bound for Calas where ample purses would be available to liberate from their owners.

Those that the halfling thief left behind trekked northward with solemn determination. Oester was a full two days worth of travel from Mullikin on horseback. After the first uneventful day, they set up camp near the road, alongside an outcropping of trees from the nearby Grembel Forest that partially concealed their presence. With a fire burning lazily amid a circle of small stones, five of the members found themselves lounging around the blaze, warming themselves and cooking small bits of meat on wooden pokers. Only Cadwan was alone, leaning on a nearby tree, fast asleep. The stars had appeared, blurred by a hazy sky that produced drifting clouds of black amongst the vast firmament. The clear air and the soothing sounds of the crackling fire proved therapeutic and peaceful. Even Calien, unaccustomed to sleeping outdoors, appeared relaxed and comfortable in the gentle company of his companions.

With Darin's clerical help, both Calien and Cora had healed amazingly well from their injuries. Neither mentioned them, as they rested.

"Your god, this Frundin, is the god of what aspect?" the prince asked the dwarf, who was chewing a piece of squirrel that Kyligan has arrowed shortly before.

Pausing from his snack, the dwarf turned to regard Calien, while wiping bits of scrap from his red beard. "Frundin is more than a god, he is a legend. It is said that he once walked on the hard soil as we do, slaying evil with his mighty axe, as he forever wandered the world. A stronger, more powerful dwarf there has never been, and fearless, as well. Now," Darin lifted his eyes to the heavens, "he reigns in the sky, overseeing all battles, all wars."

"So Frundin is your people's god of battle?"

Darin took one last large bite before tossing the poker to the ground beside him. "Of course! He is the only god of battle we serve. In comparison, others pale to his might and justice."

Calien nodded. He took a minute to rub his hands beside the flames, then leaned over onto his side and rested on his elbow. When it seemed he was finished with the discussion, he abruptly rejuvenated it with surprising vigor. "Battle is not always justifiable. Does Frundin also revel in the conquering of a righteous army at the hands of evil, or the merciless slaughter of innocents?"

The dwarf glowered at the question and grunted, roughly. "Frundin revels in nothing that furthers the spread of evil or wanton destruction. Clearly, you do not understand. War is a crucial reproach in stemming the foul tide of wickedness. Frundin celebrates such necessities, and wallows in the triumph of justice and the routing of impiety! With Frundin, we prevail. Without him, we are conquered." Darin gave the prince a staid expression. "That is why he is worshipped."

"Why do you not ask Frundin to strike down our foe in Oester?" Alazar cynically intervened. "Or is he too busy 'reveling' in past victories."

The dwarf shot Alazar an unpleasant look. "One day, Alazar, your tongue will regret its sarcasm when it is lying on the ground, several feet from your mouth."

The bearded man only smiled back, the flickering light from the flames giving him an indistinct appearance.

"In any case," Darin added, "Frundin has been with us the entire time. He has even shown himself with Calien's healing and with the lessening of our fears. But it is our responsibility to carry out his will. He is merely the subtle hand that guides the keys. We are the music that plays forth."

No retort was made from the others. Eventually, everyone found that the silence was preferable, while their bodies tentatively, then more stubbornly, yearned for sleep. Slowly, the fire withered, the ginger locks of flame becoming shorter and less fierce as the repetitive droning of insects lulled the travelers into a weary trance. When Cora announced she could no longer sit upright and that she needed sleep, the others followed her example. Only Darin remained awake. The dwarf had volunteered to take the first watch, with Cadwan filling in after a few hours.

Kyligan, who had hardly said a word around the campfire, was the last to depart the gathering, not leaving until the final spark disappeared when Darin killed the fire. He was also the last to unfurl his bedroll, the last to lie down, and the last to close his eyes. On his back, the ranger stared up into the bleak sky until his eyelids would no longer hold their position.

When consciousness flickered away, a dream came to him with uncompromising vivacity. Unlike the nightmares that had plagued him unremittingly for over a year, Kyligan found himself fully aware, still cognizant of himself. He knew he was dreaming and though he could not control where the dream wandered, he was willful in its knowledge and bearing its memories clearly.

This time, Kyligan was not within his body. Rather, he was drifting impalpably above the ground over what appeared to be some kind of swamp. Sickly green vegetation and decaying trees moved beneath him, pulling him nearer, yet revolting him all the same. He swept downward, falling beneath the trees and into the undergrowth below. The view was no better and the repugnant stench invaded not just his sense of smell, but every pore of his body. It was then that he realized he was in the same location as his previous dream; a forest fallen under the vehemence of some horrid blight.

Steering aimlessly amid the afflicted plants and greenish-brown pools of water, whispers suddenly echoed around him. The many voices were distant and vague, like the far off cries of children playing. As he continued, the voices drew nearer, merging with each other until ultimately one remained, strong and alluring. It was a female voice that called to him now, a tone that was outwardly kind and tender. Inwardly, however, it held sinister intonations that made him shudder. Against his urgings, Kyligan felt himself pulled onward, as the words called to him louder and louder until he was certain they were directly in his ear.

Then, they stopped.

A silence, no less dreadful than the previous voice, fell upon him like a blanket. For a moment, he wondered if he were waking, but then a vision formed before him, one he had not expected. A girl, young and small, stood near a wide brook staring down into the muddy waters. Kyligan could not decipher her face, as her long hair fell past it, covering her features from the side. Unable to stem his movements, he surrendered to them and suddenly found himself looking into the same rivulet as the girl. A strand of long hair fell past his eye before understanding grasped him. He wasn't looking into the water *with* the girl. He was looking into the water *through* the girl. He had slipped inside her head; was seeing through her eyes.

The dark fluid sloshed listlessly. Try as he might, he could not see his reflection, or the girl's rather, within its depths. The water was eerie and he wished to step away from it and leave it be, but his eyes remained fixed. He couldn't tear them away.

And then he fell.

The splash was inaudible, but he felt himself struggle against an invisible current that towed him relentlessly further downward. As he plunged deeper, the air above grew dimmer, more obscure. He saw his long hair get tossed about by the water before his eyes and he thrashed frantically, hoping to break free of the tide and resurface. His efforts were useless. Something pulled at his leg. Looking down, he witnessed a tentacle wrap around his petite ankle, holding it firmly. He could not escape.

He was overcome with a sense of frightful admission; he would drown. As he neared death's looming gate, his eyes, his acuity, faltered.

Kyligan awoke with a single, heavy gasp. He still lay on his back, the night hanging above him, gazing downward at his body, mourning his saddening plight.

Or, perhaps it was laughing at him?

*　　　*　　　*

When the sun cheerfully greeted the travelers the following morning, only Cadwan and Calien were up and about. Expectantly, the prince had not found his bedroll particularly comfortable and had woken more than once during the night. He finally gave up altogether, and when he arose he discovered Cadwan on watch, whittling a piece of wood with a dagger. Cadwan was pleased to see Calien awake and greeted the prince with a hearty slap across his shoulders. Another waking soul gave the soldier a chance to catch breakfast. Momentarily, he left Calien on watch and disappeared into the woods. A half-hour later, the skilled bowman reemerged with a brace of rabbits and a real trophy, an overlarge ringbird. By the time the others began to stir, a fire had been erected and the meat nearly cooked.

Kyligan was the first to join his two other comrades in the initial daylight meal. Not long after, Alazar and Cora also joined, with only Darin still sleeping over his previous late night. The food was well complemented, especially the ringbird, which was considered a delicacy saved only for nobles. Ringbird's were uncommon, small, and fidgety, making them a difficult catch. Their meat, however, was delicate and flavorsome, and Cadwan received more verbal accolades for this particular accomplishment than he had in quite some time. When Darin was finally woken by Kyligan, he had to settle for rabbit. There was nothing left of the bird.

As they set off, the mood of the company was high, save for Kyligan who could not shake the dream from the night before. He hadn't told the others. He felt it would only distract them from the daunting task that loomed ahead. They were too close to Oester to worry of other matters. For now, Kyligan felt it best to bear the troublesome burden alone.

Like the previous day, travel showed itself to be uneventful, if not lonesome. The weather was compliant, sunny and warm but not intolerable. Strangely, not a single traveler passed them going south, and Alazar brought this to the others attention more than once. Cadwan and Darin gave such comments little attention, as they needed no more ominous warnings. It was already apparent that they faced an arduous task ahead of them and they wished to enjoy what little serenity they could grasp beforehand.

"Do you hear that?" Calien remarked, turning to Cadwan, who had only moments ago proclaimed that they were about three hours removed from the village of Oester. They had passed the Grembel Forest hours ago and now the eastern side of them was mostly level grassland.

"I heard nothing but the hooves of our mounts upon the gravel," the soldier replied. "What is it you hear?"

The prince frowned. "I do not hear it now. It sounded like shouting in the distance. Perhaps I was imagining it?"

The debate was cut short when the shouts rang out again, this time for all of them to hear. Six heads whirled to the left, where they observed a small collection of figures descending a nearby hill toward the party. Kyligan counted eleven total. With arms raised, holding objects, the figures rushed in at breakneck speed.

"Orcs!" Cadwan shouted, slinging his bow off his shoulder and readying it. Nocking an arrow a moment later, he loosed it towards the incomers. The projectile found the chest of one of the attackers and the orc fell hard and rolled, eventually coming to a stop and laying still. Cadwan already had another arrow ready.

Kyligan followed suit, launching arrows of his own before the assailants were too near to fight with ranged weapons. He and Cadwan had downed four of them, but seven remained. All involved drew steel for hand-to-hand combat.

The skirmish was so sudden and unexpected that there was no semblance of strategy or joint effort. It was merely chaos among the flailing of weapons. Cora had finally managed to pull her crossbow loose from her pack and had wisely scurried away from the scuffle, taking clear shots at the enemy. The rest had also left their mounts in favor of more maneuverability.

Screams resounded, bodies fell, and seconds later it was over. The blood of two orcs soiling his ornate blade, Prince Calien quickly examined the others. Everyone still stood. The worst injury seemed to be a minor gash over Alazar's forearm, one that would take little healing. Satisfied, he returned his attention to the lifeless bodies of the orcs. Although he knew well their reputation and stature, never before had he seen one firsthand and the sight disgusted him. It was no wonder that few accepted their kind.

"They killed our horses!"

Darin, the one who shouted, scrambled over to his mount which lay on its side. A massive wound was opened in its belly, reddish bowels and fluid coating the small area. The horse was not dead. It neighed and kicked its feet weakly, eyeing its master. The dwarf hugged the animal once around the neck, then wasted no time putting the animal out of its misery. He did so with a saddened heart, as the horse had been his riding companion ever since he arrived in Calas over a year ago. Alazar's mount was also down. The beasts throat had been cleanly skewered with a sword. It had died instantly.

"They were attacking our horses!" Calien said, with wonderment. "Why would they do that?"

Alazar shook his head. "Who can say? Orcs are dumb enough that they probably did not realize that . . . ."

"No," Darin interrupted. "it was intentional. I cannot say for sure why, but we best get on the move."

Calien scoffed. "But we only have three horses."

"We will have to double up. Cora does so already, so that only leaves myself and Alazar. Do you have a better idea, my Prince?" the dwarf replied.

Calien offered no response, nor did anyone else object. Darin began untying his pack from the corpse of his mount and motioned for Alazar to do the same. Glumly wondering which of the men he would have to haul along, the prince began to adjust his own belongings to make room for a second passenger when his thoughts were interrupted by a myriad of cries and shouts resonating from beyond the same hill the orcs had attacked from. This time, the roar sounded not like a handful, but like hundreds.

Every man froze, as the cries grew in scale, sweeping over the skies and surrounding them like a plague of locusts. With a certain trepidation, they viewed the hill, waiting for what they realized was imminent.

From the crest of the hill, the next group of orcs appeared, running in the same manner as their predecessors. More emerged behind them, scurrying forth with weapons raised. They were being urged on by a handful of mounted orcs.

"There are far too many!" Cadwan yelled above the noise of the stampede. "Hurry! We must flee now!"

The solider turned to Darin, but the dwarf stopped, planted his feet, and slung his pack over his shoulder. "We cannot outrun them, not two to a horse. I will stay and fend them off."

"Foolish dwarf!" Alazar yelled. "Do not waste your life!"

"Did you not hear me?" Darin snapped. "The horses would ride too slow and tire too fast."

Cadwan moved his gelding near the dwarf and fixed him with a cold stare. "I'll not leave you to die."

"Better I die than all of us," Darin said mulishly, not moving from his spot.

"We must hurry!" Cora screamed, watching the horde draw near. She had climbed up on Kyligan's mount and was unknowingly digging her nails into the ranger's shoulders. The pounding of the stampede was overwhelming, a thundering wail that echoed from all sides.

Suddenly Kyligan, leapt from his horse, leaving the halfling by herself. Snatching a handful of supplies from his rucksack, he ran to Darin. "Alazar, take my horse!" The ranger pointed to a small grove of trees that rested in the middle of a flat, grassy plain, on the opposite side of the rushing force. "Darin and I can hide within those trees. Cadwan, you will have to lead them away from us, perhaps back toward the Barren Hills until you have lost them."

Cadwan could find nothing to say in response to the startling take-charge manner of Kyligan.

"We have no time to discuss this," Kyligan continued. "We can meet up on the fringes of Oester after we have escaped. It is walking distance from here. Go now!" The ranger grabbed Darin by the arm, but the dwarf pulled away.

"Let me get my shield." Darin shuffled over to his downed horse and began unlatching his shield from the dead animal's back.

Kyligan scolded the dwarf. "Leave your bedamned shield! It will only slow you down! We've no time to waste!"

With an angry grunt, Darin gave up on his shield and followed Kyligan away from the others. The trees were a good two hundred yards from their current position and Kyligan impelled Darin to make every use of his stubby, round legs. Together the two sprinted. After a short jaunt, they heard the sounds of battle behind them. Kyligan looked back and witnessed the others buying them additional time, hounding the orcs upon their horses. Still, some had run past and were pointing infuriated fingers toward the dwarf and himself.

"As fast as you can, Darin. They are right on us!" Kyligan urged.

"I move as fast as I can! Could this little jog have been any longer?" The dwarf was huffing loudly and not pleased with his predicament. He pushed onward, nonetheless, his rotund body bobbing up and down over the grass below.

Kyligan slowed himself to allow the dwarf a second to catch up. They were two-thirds the way, but the orcs were gaining. "We are almost there. A little father and then we can fight them amid the wood."

"This tiny copse is not large enough to hide in. They will easily find us inside and surround us." Darin panted hopelessly, as he pressed ahead, making the best speed possible.

"It is our only hope now."

A javelin flew past them, missing by a good ten feet. It was enough to give Darin one last surge of endurance, and a few seconds afterward, they reached the first tree.

A small ways within the narrow orchard, Kyligan grabbed the dwarf's shoulder. "Hold here a moment behind this tree." Bow unslung, the ranger cocked an arrow and sent it flying just as an orc came into view. The missile dropped its target, and Kyligan did likewise to a second. "That should hold them, if only for a few seconds. Come, further in."

Once more the two ran, plunging deeper within the tall trees. They could still hear the shouts of their pursuers, but the battle sounds of their comrades had gone to the wayside. Kyligan hoped they had escaped. Presently, he had more pressing matters; getting Darin and himself to safety. The dwarf was slowing as he maneuvered his hefty physique past bushes and dried pine needles, exhausted but refusing to show it. Kyligan knew he couldn't force Darin much further.

Several minutes passed. Listening with a keen ear, Kyligan could now hear only faint noises of the orcs that were hunting them. Oddly, the woods had grown considerably thicker, the pressing trees blocking out the sunlight. With the distinct impression that the orcs had scurried the wrong direction, it suddenly seemed doubtful that they would be found. Kyligan pulled their excursion to a halt.

"Let us catch our breath," the ranger respired. Darin was only too happy to oblige, falling against a tree in heavy panting, his barrel-shaped chest moving inward and outward inches at a time. "We might not have to run again," Kyligan furthered. "Somehow, it looks as if we have lost them."

Darin only acknowledged his friend with a slight motion of his hand. He closed his eyes and slid down the tree, the reddish-brown pine needles shifting as his rump hit the ground. When he regained his breath, he muttered, "How did we lose them so easily? This grove is not large."

Kyligan shrugged. "Perhaps they were called off? Whatever the reason, I'll not complain."

Moisture dripping from his nose and chin, Darin dropped his axe and felt his face with both hands. "I must persuade myself I am still alive, for I had already resigned myself to death." Darin looked up at the ranger. "Tell me, what made you leave your horse and force me to run like a damned animal?"

"We live, do we not?" Kyligan answered.

Darin finally smiled and nodded. "Aye, we do. I must admit that I have not run that hard," he paused before including, "*ever.*"

Kyligan chuckled. "Yes, it shows, friend. But do not worry, I'll not judge your style."

The two rested, remaining in the same location as the noises faded away. Soon, all that could be heard was the wildlife around them. Kyligan unstrung his bow and withdrew a waterskin, drinking ravenously before passing it to Darin. The dwarf drank his share and returned it to the ranger.

"You are a man of the forest. Where do we go now?" Darin queried.

Kyligan considered the matter carefully. "We dare not return the way we came. They might be waiting. We should move to the edge of these woods a different direction, perhaps the northern way."

"And if all is clear, on to Oester?" Darin asked, although it was not particularly a question. The answer was obvious.

"Apparently so. Let us hope our friends still live."

*   *   *

Cadwan had held his crew in place longer than he should have, attempting to give the fleeing dwarf and ranger a few precious seconds extra. Just before they were overwhelmed, Cadwan commanded a retreat, sending them northwest away from the copse that Kyligan and Darin had disappeared within. The three horses emerged among a plague of orcs, riding down any who stepped in the way. Rolling hills lay ahead, granting few obstacles but a difficult riding terrain.

"Cadwan, giants!" Alazar yelled, pointing up ahead.

Coming into view before them was four absolutely massive figures standing almost seventeen feet tall. Two bore spiked clubs that nearly equaled the size of his own horse, while the others shuffled several boulders in their enormous hands. Cadwan cursed under his breath. There was no riding down a giant and one boulder or swing from a club was all it took to knock one senseless, or far worse. His steed's hooves kicked up dirt and dust, as he veered the animal to the right and motioned for the others to follow.

A large stone flew past them, thrown by one of the giants. It barely missed bashing Cadwan in the shoulder and he tensed, anxiously. He couldn't afford to let many more of those come their way. Grasping his bow, he pulled an arrow from his quiver. "Alazar!" he rasped.

The dark skinned man took his prompt and raised a hand, sending an orb of fire toward the newest threat. The fiery sphere battered a giant, knocking it several paces backward. Cadwan let go of the pommel of his saddle and took aim with his bow. He was well practiced and accomplished using the weapon atop a horse, and he made no hesitation firing several arrows, as he balanced himself precariously upon the saddle. The missiles whistled, cutting through the air, with all but one effectively hitting their marks. Even with the minor offensive, the giants stayed on their feet, protruding arrows and all, and lumbered after the horses vigorously. Hanging on the back of Alazar, Cora utilized her crossbow at giant and orc alike, whomever happened to come nearest.

Prince Calien had never been faced against such an overpowering force. He rode with furious haste, eyes round and fearful. The three of them still had a score of ground to travel before they could outdistance the monstrous humanoid's throwing range. Another boulder arched by, landing just in front of Calien's horse. The prince braced for impact, but his stallion showed remarkable agility avoiding the large stone. He breathed a sight of relief and reminded himself to feed his mount well, if they did indeed escape.

Several stray arrows whizzed by, all of them missing badly. After several more unnerving strides, they seemed to have momentarily eluded the giants. The enormous beasts had fallen behind and were taking chase, along with a legion of orcs.

"A miracle will not help us defeat them! We must cling to hope that our horses will hold up and we can outrun our pursuers!" Alazar yelled to Cadwan, who quickly nodded in reply. In silence, they pushed on. In time, the distance between them and their hunters widened considerably. A few orcs riding on mounts hung close for a longer period of time, but they eventually pulled back.

It felt as if the full pursuit had lasted hours. In reality, it had endured for only fifteen minutes or so. Several hills now gaped the two enemies and Cadwan temporarily slowed his party.

"Have we lost them?" Prince Calien asked, wiping the lagoon of sweat that coated his face.

"No," Cadwan tritely answered. "They will keep coming. It will be some time before we can turn toward Oester. We must bridge the gap far enough that they can no longer follow our trail."

"So we continue to ride northwest?" The prince's voice was weak and raspy, not from fatigue, but from the tension of the chase.

Cadwan nodded with a straight face.

"But for how long? These hills are not safe. It is more than possible that we could run into another clan of orcs, or barbarians, or worse."

"Hopefully, not long," Cadwan proffered, shifting back to gaze sightlessly at the beasts they had barely evaded. He could still hear the throng of them coming and he understood that they couldn't dawdle here for long. "We cannot afford to lead an army of orcs and giants into Oester. Certainly, Prince Calien, you must attest that the village has enough problems already without orcs running rampant among the hubbles. If we can widen the gap beyond seeing distance, we can alter our direction without them knowing and then lose them permanently. This ground is not easy to track tread on, so I am fairly confident they will resign their pursuit once we are lost."

The reasoning was sound enough for Calien to discontinue his dispute. With a sigh, he firmly gripped his saddle's pommel and bemoaned quietly. "Why did they even attack us?"

Cadwan heard the self-imposed question and answered anyway, "They are orcs. Do they need a reason?"

*   *   *

"This wood should have already ended," Darin commented, stepping over a loose slab of timber. "Why are we still in them?"

Kyligan peered forward into the endless assortment of trees that skulked the terrain and blocked much of the light from the sky beyond. The dwarf was not mistaken. The small grove they had entered when fleeing the orcs could not possibly have stretched this far. And from the looks of it, it wasn't ending anytime soon. "Perhaps we got turned around?" he speculated aloud.

"Hmph." The dwarf was visibly not pleased. He was having trouble navigating his way through the jagged terrain and wanted nothing more than to return to the level, easily traversed grassland. "Or maybe this wood is magical and has entrapped us for all time within its unrelenting grasp?"

Kyligan couldn't stifle his laugh. Darin's cynicism in such predicaments was priceless. "I think that unlikely." The ranger bent downward and picked up a loose branch. The bark around the short piece was brittle and fell off easily to the touch. "All the same, however, we should remain on our guard. We know not what lurks around these parts."

After treading another half-mile, their surroundings appeared almost identical as before and both men quickly grew dubious.

"We could always turn around and go back the way we came," Darin entreated.

Stopping suddenly, Kyligan crooked his shoulders and gazed backwards at the direction they had come from. For many seconds, he stared, his emerald eyes darting over the area, taking in every detail. Ultimately, his shoulders seemed to stoop slightly and he shook his head. "We cannot even renege a few simple trees. What makes you believe we can retrace the way we came? We have plodded through this gallow for a solid hour and I am not familiar with any of what I have seen."

Darin gripped his waraxe with both hands, his arms flexing in response. Kyligan regarded the dwarf's limbs. He had crossed paths with a handful of dwarves in his lifetime, but none of them had the muscles that Darin displayed so freely. The dwarf was extraordinarily strong and the ranger was thankful he had never been on the opposite end of Darin's weapon.

"Never have I seen you so uncertain within the company of trees," the dwarf remarked. "Be honest with me, friend. What is happening?"

"I . . ." Kyligan hesitated, scratching his brown hair with a baffled expression. "I am not sure. Something is wrong. Every time I turn around and look back, it is as if the world has changed behind our backs." He pointed toward a tree behind them. The trunk was tall and rested innocently, unassuming in the ground. "See that tree there? It appears normal, but I can swear to you that it was not there a moment earlier, before we passed that spot. None of what you see now is exactly as it was mere seconds ago. The forest itself seems to shift."

The dwarf skeptically eyed the ranger. Kyligan wasn't known to exaggerate in the slightest. For that reason, Darin knew his friend was fully convinced of what he was saying. But still, he found such comments hard to believe. *The forest itself shifts? Impossible.* "To be honest, I have noticed nothing," he replied with untailored emotion.

Kyligan postponed his wary observations and slowly met the dwarf's gaze with eyes that exposed no pretenses. "The differences are subtle, but they are there." He gently ran his finger over a plant that reached over, touching his leg. The ranger plucked loose a leaf and brought the thin slice close to his face. "Even the plants have changed. This type did not grow when we first entered the grove."

"I have no reason to distrust you, Kyligan, but this is a matter I am unacquainted with. What are you proposing we do? Shall we change directions?"

The ranger helplessly lifted his shoulders. "I do not think it will matter. We are being led somewhere."

"Come now! Speak logically," Darin chuffed. He was not getting answers that satisfied his queries. "Led somewhere? What nonsense is that?"

Once again, Kyligan peered about, studying the surroundings with sharp awareness. The woods had gotten slightly darker. Although the overhanging trees were blocking sight of the sun, it was apparent that the burning sphere above had begun its daily descent. Their vision was growing more obscure, more arduous. Kyligan strained his eyes to discern the adjacent greenery. "I have no explanation, Darin, but for some reason I believe that whichever way we choose to go, we will only end up in the same place. That is the best rationalization I can give you. Of course, I could still be wrong."

"And what if you are right?"

Kyligan simply smiled and held his hands upward. "Then we see where the forest leads us. Certainly, there must be some reason for what is happening."

"Bah!" Darin grumbled excessively. "What kind of world is this where the trees themselves choose a traveler's path? Let me tell you this, Kyligan, Frundin is the only one who chooses my path."

Kyligan did not respond to the dwarf's outburst. Instead, he gave him an austere look that seemed to silently pronounce; *you can believe whatever you want, but we are here, nonetheless, and Frundin is not going to hoist us up on his godly shoulders and carry us to safety without some effort of our own.*

With that construal, Darin wholeheartedly agreed. "Well," the dwarf coaxed Kyligan, pretending it was the ranger who had been in denial, "standing here will not get us very far. Let us go."

The two plodded through the darkening hedge, while the shadows of the approaching night dangled before them, blurring the path and easily hiding whatever wished not to be seen. It was dreadfully obvious that they were no longer within the cluster of trees they had initially entered. The landscape was changing ever so slightly and the delicate slopes of before, weaving gently upward and downward, had now been replaced by a flat, low-hanging elevation. Strange noises, their sources indiscernible, resounded about them. Ever observant, Kyligan absorbed the environment with intricate detail. But as they progressed, even he succumbed to the notion that he would never knowingly be able to find his own way out. Everything was unknown to him and glancing at Darin, he was certain that the dwarf felt the same. Pools and streams of fetid water began to make their appearance, moving at a crawling pace, and more than once the travelers had to maneuver around such obstacles. The ranger felt uneasy, almost sick, over the dark ambiance of their environment.

Making their way around a group of bushes, torn bits of spider web suddenly netted Kyligan's face and the ranger stopped a moment to wipe it free. As he did so, the dwarf spoke softly. "The brush grows foul," Darin said, pointing toward some shrubbery they had just passed by.

Kyligan nodded in response. The dwarf's analysis couldn't have been more accurate. The trees had turned twisted and dark, slowly giving way to a damp and dreary marsh. The air hung unnaturally thick and heavy, and slow moving lines of mist obscured the area before melting away to expose twisted limbs of stunted black trees that seemed to claw angrily at them. The stagnant bogs only added to the vile nature of the place. Kyligan shuddered, breathing in the stench of damp mud and rotting vegetation. To both men, it was obvious that the deranged woods abounded with creatures of a darker nature.

"And the ground grows excessively soft," Kyligan added, lifting his foot out of a swell of soft mud. "Be careful not to drop anything, or it is lost for good." Noting the dark environs, the ranger pulled a torch from his makeshift pack and set fire to the end. The added light was comforting, but it did little to soothe their sense of apprehension.

Again, they set off, Kyligan leading the way. With the many obstacles, their pace had slowed considerably. Twice, Darin halted his progress momentarily to wedge his stout boot from out of the ductile mud. The latter time, the muck had sucked him up nearly to his knee, and it took much effort from both Darin and Kyligan to free him. The ranger heard Darin curse the way no priest ever should, his face evolving into a perpetual red scowl. It was apparent he was not enjoying himself in the least.

"Try to mimic my steps," Kyligan instructed.

"You speak as if I've been doing otherwise!" the dwarf snapped.

Normally, had their circumstances not been so dire, Kyligan would have found Darin's irritation amusing. As it was, he could only empathize with the dwarf, as even he felt a complete lack of control. Moving again, they went slow, covering little ground but taking extra care to avoid any of the mud pits that seemed heavily abundant within the swamp.

Abruptly, Kyligan froze, causing the dwarf to bump him from behind.

"Why have you stopped?" Darin asked, resecuring his footing.

Kyligan swung his torch about him with his head following, gazing at the squalid greenery and moldy air. "I have just realized something. This is the place of my dreams."

"Dreams?" Darin stared at Kyligan, his forehead crumpled. "You have only told me of one. Have you remembered another?"

"Only a night ago. I had not told anyone for fear it would lessen our already dampened spirits."

"I do not believe our spirits can be lessened any further." Darin began to search around him. In due course, he located an area with a relatively hard surface. Sitting with a fatigued groan, he asked, "And how did this particular dream unfold? I am predicting it did not end well, if you held it from us."

The ranger wiped hair that was sticking to his perspiring face. "I drowned in one of these pools of water." Kyligan paused to consider his words. "It was perplexing, however. I was in a girl's body, a girl I did not recognize."

Darin sat silently for several long seconds, thinking about his friend's revelation. When he did speak, his voice had reverted to that of a priest consoling a sufferer, soft and gentle. "Do these foresights of death bother you?"

Kyligan shrugged, the links of his chain shirt armor shifting slightly. Moving from his current standing position, he sat next to his dwarven friend and gazed at the lighted torch in his hand. "They bother me, as they would anyone. Dreams are funny that way. They give you premonitions, whether truthful or not, and in the end they leave you feeling helpless. I do not know if I should mentally struggle with them, or just submit myself to their whims."

Placing a comforting hand on the ranger's shoulder, Darin encouraged, "Frundin did not grant me aptitude as a seer, so I have few words of wisdom to bestow upon you. But know this, Kyligan, I am here with you now. If something is to happen in these woods, it will have to contend with a disgruntled dwarf first." Darin waved his waraxe with overemphasis, making the ranger smile. When he lowered his weapon, his eyes were honest and sincere. "You have always been a man of honor and of pure heart, through and through. Such men are rare. If I were to die fighting by your side, Frundin could impart me no greater honor."

Kyligan accepted the compliments with outward stoicism, but inwardly he smiled. The dwarf had never before spoken to him with such emotion, such meaning, and the words greatly warmed Kyligan. Ever since joining Cadwan's group, he had always spent most of his time with Alazar and Cora and he never truly discerned how Darin had felt about his company. Now, after such heartfelt words, he would never view Darin as anything less than a close friend. "Have I ever told you of my parents, Darin?" he asked.

The dwarf seemed taken aback. "Your parents? I do not believe you have."

"Your words reminded me of my father. My parents were forest hermits, like me. I was not an intentional birth, a fact they let slip accidentally once, but they still raised me with love and dedication. Throughout my younger years, they taught me everything they possibly could. My mother educated me on how to find the best fruits, vegetables, and nuts, while my father taught me how to hunt and use a sword. They spent much effort on me, more than most parents I would assume. And yet," Kyligan paused for the slightest moment. "in all the years they had me, the one thing they could not teach was how to be sociable. Never once did I meet another soul. Back then, all I had were my parents and the forest."

"What happened to them?" Darin queried.

"When I was thirteen, both of them were struck with a severe case of black-fever. The fever struck them quickly and both were near death before they realized what was happening." Kyligan placed the torch that he was holding to the side. Their surroundings were now completely dark and the torch gave them the only source of light. "They would not let me care for them for fear I would contract the sickness, as well. So, from a distance, I watched my mom die first." The ranger shook his head, sadly. "To this day, I can clearly see my father, only hours from death himself, stroking her hair with tears streaming down his face. Soon afterward, he called me to come within hearing distance. I cried like a small child while he spoke, telling me how proud he was of my growth and how he had never been happier in all his life than when the three of us had been together. He went on to say that I was now on my own, but that I knew everything needed to survive. Not long after, he joined my mother. For a solid week, I mourned before starting life anew."

"Such a sad tale," Darin commented. "It takes great mental resilience to undergo such tragedy at the scanty age of thirteen and then go on and live your life alone."

Reaching into his meager belongings, Kyligan withdrew two apples, handing one to Darin. Taking a bite, he took a moment to chew the moist portion before answering, "At the time, there was little else I could do. If I had just rolled over and died, it would have defeated the purpose of all the teachings my parents had bestowed upon me. I started living for the sake of living, to put to use everything they had instilled in me. Unfortunately," he reflected, "black-fever is not something you can one day take revenge on."

"No, I suppose not." Darin took some time to finish off his apple. The fruit was especially juicy and the dwarf savored it. "It sounds as if you were brought up well and your story gives me even more respect of you."

"I did not reveal my past to gain your respect, Darin. I did it merely to show you how important you and the others are to me. I do not have many friends. Therefore, those I do have, I cherish."

The duo sat for some time longer, gaining essential rest for what would certainly be an unpredictable night. "What is the plan, Kyligan?" Darin wondered aloud.

The ranger had been wondering that very question. "At this point, there are very few plans to be made. We are at the mercy of whatever has led us here. Sleep will not be safe in this place, so if one of us grows weary the other will have to stay on watch, while he gets a couple hours rest."

"That sounds reasonable. Perhaps we should get on the move again?" With a heavy grunt, Darin lifted himself back unto his feet. Kyligan followed and soon the two of them were trudging through the soggy underbrush, taking careful watch of the mud pits. The utter blackness of night nibbled graspingly at the edges of the single torchlight. The noises around them had increased in volume, though what was causing the eccentric sounds was still a mystery to both men. The going was very slow and each had a firm grip on their weapons, deeming such precaution as more than necessary.

Kyligan had lost all sense of bearing. With the sun no longer visible, he could not ascertain whether they traveled north, south, or any other direction. In fact, he mused with morose irony, it was even possible, albeit unlikely, that they were no longer on the surface of the world, but rather on some abyssal plane. The ranger quickly wiped such nonsensical thoughts from his mind, knowing that it wouldn't help with their situation.

Ruffling from a nearby bush, and the snapping of a branch interrupted Kyligan's ruminations. He swiftly whirled the torch in the direction of the sounds, but was only fast enough to witness several leaves shifting back and forth from a recent disturbance. Both men gazed at the scene with morbid entrancement.

"Someone follows us," Darin whispered, not removing his eyes from the sight.

"Stay right behind me," Kyligan replied. He carefully made his way to the bush accountable for the noise, sword in hand. Clearly, whatever had disturbed it was long gone. There was nothing to see but sickly green leaves.

Darin was breathing loudly, every nerve of his body on end. "This is absurd," he hissed. "The night has only just begun and we are already being toyed with."

Kyligan said nothing. He waved the torch around them one last time, hoping to find the culprit, but the darkness was so thick it did very little for their abysmal vision.

"That timberstick is worthless! We might as well just walk with our eyes closed." The dwarf snatched the flare from Kyligan's hand and snuffed out the burning embers. "This is one instance where Frundin comes in a might handy. Hold still moment." Darin held the dead object high in the air and closed his eyes. His prayer was brief and a moment later an unnatural light burst forth from the end of the torch. The luminance was powerful, imbuing the surrounding area with a glow that no natural object could perform. Kyligan stared at the scene, awestruck, then gingerly placed his hand on the source of the light at the tip of the torch. He quickly pulled back, expecting his hand to be burned. Instead, it was cool to the touch, not harming his fingers in the slightest. The ranger looked at the dwarf with questioning eyes.

Darin shrugged off the ranger's enthrallment. "Light is one of the divine favors granted me by Frundin."

"Why did you not do this when it first became dark?" Kyligan asked. "We might have been able to spot whoever follows us."

Darin handed the gleaming torch back to Kyligan and gripped his waraxe with both hands. "First of all, this strong light will make us extremely noticeable by all others within this place. I wanted to wait until I was certain our presence was already detected. Secondly, this light will not last forever. I cannot abuse Frundin's gifts, so I do not wish to call upon his powers repeatedly."

Kyligan waved the radiant torch about, amazed at its brilliance. "How long will it last?"

"It should last for quite some time, though I cannot say exactly how long."

With torch in one hand and sword in the other, Kyligan stepped forward. "Let us not waste it then."

Even with the newfound light, the terrain proved no less difficult. After a few minutes of trekking at a snail's pace, they were fortunate enough to come upon a wide stream. No less fetid than the other pools they passed before, the water carried a slightly quicker current and brought along a brief optimism for the two men.

"We should follow this downstream," Kyligan commented. "It must lead somewhere."

Darin silently agreed. Keeping close to the sodden banks of the brook, they meandered carefully alongside the creek, following the movement of the water. For a time, very little was said. Kyligan made certain he undertook a path that was easy to trail and the dwarf took extra precautions to follow it as flawlessly as his lumbering feet would allow.

"The current shows no sign of gaining speed. I fear it might go on longer than we hope for."

The words had barely left Darin's mouth when two shadowed figures leapt out from the cover of the surrounding brush. The figures appeared tall and sinewy, and when they exited the shadows and emerged within the artificial light both men understood why. "Lizardfolk!" Kyligan spat.

Both men raised their weapons and gazed upon the newcomers. The naked, green-skinned lizard men stood erect at seven feet tall, carrying thin frames that hunched over slightly. A crude wooden spear was held by each one, the only noticeable adornment. As they moved nearer, long tails excitedly tapped the earth behind them, their yellow reptilian eyes eager with anticipation.

"Peace, lizardfolk." Kyligan announced, lowering his weapon. Lizardfolk were an abomination to mankind, the result of some mad mage's experiment ages ago. How appropriate, Kyligan reflected, that such tainted creatures would inhabit this place. The ranger had no love for them or their savage ways, but he knew that it was wise to offer amity before heedlessly throwing oneself into combat. There could be more hidden in the trees. "We wish you no harm."

Both lizardfolk stopped. "Why you here?" one of them asked, surprising both men with its use of the common tongue. Bits of decaying teeth exhibited prominently from the creature in the synthetic radiance granted by Frundin.

"We are nothing more than strangers lost in these woods. We only wish to leave." Kyligan glanced briefly at Darin. The dwarf had not lowered his waraxe and he studied the lizardfolk with eyes that betrayed more than simple suspicion.

"Veptuna not like guests who not expected," the lizard man said through a thick accent. It's tongue flicked outward twice.

"Who is Veptuna?" Kyligan inquired.

The lizard man's mouth turned crooked, a pathetic excuse for a smile. "Veptuna dominant. Lead us with great power. Veptuna help us rule woods."

"*You* rule these woods?" Kyligan shot back, utterly appalled. Is that why the trees and undergrowth were in such a horrid state? It seemed improbable to the ranger, but certainly not impossible. "Bring me to this Veptuna, so that I might speak with him."

A long strand of drool fell from the side of the lizardfolk's large mouth. "Veptuna busy. Grraknack deal with you now. Lizardfolk need meat. Lizardfolk hungry." The reptilian creature raised its spear, and with clawed feet digging into the mud, advanced on the two men. It was followed by the second lizard man.

Apparently our conversation has come to an end, the ranger mused. Kyligan wedged the glowing torch in his tiny backpack, so that the point faced upward, still illuminating the battleground. There was no noticeable difference between the two attackers, so Kyligan simply raised his weapon to the closest one, the one who had called himself Grraknack. He took a fleeting moment to check on Darin. The dwarf was preparing to duel the other opponent, his waraxe lifted high in the air by his powerful arms. Satisfied that his friend would take care of himself, Kyligan refocused on his adversary. A foot taller, the lizard man had the benefit of a longer reach, a fact that was supplemented by the spear it wielded. The weapon might have been rudimentary, but the point was sharp, nonetheless. When the lizard man came near enough, it thrust its weapon at Kyligan's chest.

The ranger easily deflected the blow, his polished steel sword glinting in the god granted light of the torch. Then, he stepped backward out of range, consumed with confidence. The lizardfolk's attack had been reckless and slow. Its skills were poor and the ranger knew he should have no difficulty slaying the beast. Circling to his right, he waited for his opposition to attack a second time. He didn't have to wait long. Again, the spear came streaking toward his torso. Kyligan parried it to the side. With a long stride forward, he was poised to drive his blade through the lizard man's gaunt body, but something grabbed his leg. At least it felt like something had grabbed his leg. In reality, the mud under his right foot had given way and his leg had slipped into the squalid muck all the way to his knee. He was immobile and ensnared in an awkward position. His opponent cackled in delight and sent his spear aiming for Kyligan's face. Still holding his sword, the ranger was able to bat the wooden shaft away. Without movement, though, he could make no counter attack. He was at the mercy of his foe.

"Darin!" Kyligan bellowed. He had to assume the dwarf was close to finishing off the other attacker, and he hoped the dwarf would come to his aid soon. Once more, he blocked a rushing spear and flailed his weapon before him, trying to keep the lizard man away.

Suddenly, a shadow came leaping past him. The next moment was a blur, but when it was over the lizardfolk that called himself Grraknack had been severed in two at the waist. Darin's axe had cut clean through the beast. A sickly red color coated and dripped from the dwarf's weapon.

"Darin, you have to help me out of this." Kyligan squirmed, not yet taking the time to thank the dwarf. "Every time I move, I feel like my leg slips deeper in."

The task was more daunting than either had expected, but after much effort Kyligan's leg was freed. The ranger sat for some time readjusting his mud soaked leggings. "Thank you for your help, friend," he remarked. "Unfortunately, I am going to tell you something neither of us wants to hear."

"Yes?" the dwarf prompted. The situation had gotten bad enough to where he didn't much care what the ranger was about to say.

"Although the ground is not very accommodating, I believe that we will need to quicken our pace, or I fear we will be seeing many more of these lizardfolk." Kyligan then added with a touch of gloom. "Or perhaps even worse beasts."

Darin swigged a large breathe of air, slowly letting it out. "I am beginning to wonder if we are indeed trapped in this pitiable forest. How will we escape?"

Kyligan offered no words of optimism. Silently gripping the torch from his pack, he held it before them and strode forward, the dwarf falling in behind like a shadow.

It is said that when one is exposed to a pervading silence for long periods of time, one begins to hear voices. The source of such voices are often indistinguishable, hiding behind a veil of anonymity, though rarely does that concern those who are spoken to. Truths or falsities, it matters not which, slowly chip away at a sound mind until all that remains is a madness obsessed with grudges and aspirations that time has already passed. These cryptic murmurs energize such irrational desires, and in doing so happily devour what sanity remains. In fact, the voices have ambitions of their own, ambitions that are never understood by the puppet it fuels.

The figure in the shadows heard these voices.

Strolling within its sanctuary, the figure recommenced a conversation it had undergone with itself, or perhaps the wraith-like whisperings, thousands of times prior. Each time was left angrier, more enraged than before. Reaching into the inner recess of its aura, the figure searched anxiously for the locality of the visitors that would soon step foot upon its home. But it received nothing. It hadn't the power to determine exact locations. In truth, it knew no locations. Its world no longer existed beyond the room it stood within. However, it did continue to sense their presence. Stronger, in fact. The speed of their pace was unexpected, but welcome.

Satisfied that the confrontation would come soon, the figure returned to the whispers that spilled dark words upon its mind.

And dark intentions.

XVI

Cadwan led his team northward, parallel to the road but never veering directly toward Oester. As he reached the base of a mound wedged sidelong into a hill, he brought them to a halt and examined his group. They looked weary and rightfully so. They had pushed their mounts hard for the better part of two hours, without respite. The horses themselves were nearly done in from fatigue. Surveying the area, Cadwan nodded in satisfaction and announced, "We will make camp here."

"Are you jesting?" Alazar responded, shifting a little in his saddle which he was now sharing with Cora. "We have lost the orcs. Let us make our way to Oester."

"And what proof have you that we have lost them? Tell me, Alazar, how well do you know these hills?"

Alazar leered at the soldier a moment before answering diffidently, "I know them not."

Cadwan rotated his shoulders and leaned back to dig within his pack. He removed a small yoaw and bit deeply, the fruit crunching noisily in his mouth, as he chewed. "Nor do I, but I'll wager the orcs know them well." He paused to swallow, then take another bite that nearly finished the entire orange fruit altogether. "If we leave east for Oester now, we would arrive in an hour or two, but our condition would be nothing short of pure exhaustion from a full day of riding. If the orcs are still chasing us and follow us to Oester, we are finished. Camping now will allow us to rest our horses and ourselves. We will be alert and prepared, as we arrive in the village tomorrow morning."

"What if the orcs do still follow us and we are ambushed in the night, while we sleep?" It was Prince Calien who asked the question.

Cadwan regarded the prince earnestly. Behind him, dusk had brimmed over the horizon, painting a lavender hue across the Barren Hills and casting strange light upon the four adventurers. The soldier was pleased that Calien had shown no ill effects of his injury in Mullikin during their frantic escape. He had rode with a vivacity that amazed Cadwan and never once spoke a word of complaint, as they relentlessly pushed themselves onward. Indeed, Darin had done fine work healing the prince. Cadwan briefly wondered how his good friend and the ranger were faring. Those trees had been merely a speck upon the landscape and it would have been difficult to evade several orcs from within. Of course, he reminded himself, both Darin and Kyligan can be quite resourceful in a pinch; a fact he had seen several times first hand.

Dismounting, Cadwan eyed the surrounding hills. "While we sleep, we will have to place our belongings in a manner that will allow us to mount our horses and flee in a moment's time. We will also have to split watch tonight, each taking a few hours."

The other three threw glances at each other. Alazar appeared the most skeptical and, indeed, it was the robed enigma who spoke next. "The hills are a dangerous place, Cadwan. Any manner of beast could come upon us tonight. Not just orcs."

"It is a possibility, but I have a feeling we will be safe for one night. If we see nothing of our orc pursuers, we have probably evaded them."

There seemed little point in continuing the debate. Cadwan's mind was firmly made. Soon, the four of them dismounted and arranged a crude campsite. All their possessions were placed within quick and easy access and before long they circled a diminutive fire that scarcely lighted the darkness around them. Nighttime in the Barren Hills was an ominous experience. The lack of trees gave liberty to the expansive sky above which now loomed black, swathing them like a mantle of shadows. Each of them, even Cadwan, felt pangs of uneasiness. They nervously eyed the overhanging gloom, their weapons not far from their reach.

Ultimately, it was Prince Calien, ever fervent in his quest for knowledge, who broke the heavy silence. "Alazar, I have yet to hear your tale. Why have you joined this adventuring party? You seem to have agendas of your own that do not coincide with the others," Calien suddenly sensed an unbidden tension rise among the camp, the eyes of Cadwan and Cora darting scrupulously toward the robed man. The prince was quick to add, "though I am sure they are no less noble."

Alazar was nibbling on some herbs, but the question stopped him dead. He slowly lowered the herbs and peered at the prince through narrow eyelids. His tanned face and thick eyebrows divulged no expression. "I hail from Asharria, the sands of the east."

"I have never heard of Asharria, but I have heard of the 'sands of the east.' From my studies, I remember learning of a great desert far across the Great Divide and deep in the south, well past the Nardûn Sea and the shores beyond." Calien reached his hands forward to warm them by the anemic fire, constructed purposefully in such a manner so as not to give away their position.

Alazar bobbed his head once in affirmation. His hood had been tossed back during the frenzied escape and he had so far neglected to replace it. The black locks atop his head were as thick as his beard, the hair curled this way and that, with no real pattern or purpose, shaggy and neglected. It was a stark contrast to the man's exquisitely maintained facial hair. "That desert was my childhood home," he said, indifferently.

Calien had not realized that Alazar felt uncomfortable speaking about himself, so he pressed on, "What brought you here, so far from home?"

"I know this one," Cora interrupted. The halfling had been waiting for just the precise moment to spring in the conversation. "He seeks the 'The Dragon,' whoever that is. Alazar essentially ignores questions about it, so you can concede any hope that he will tell you something interesting."

Alazar gave the halfling a look of annoyance, but said nothing.

"The Dragon? Surely, you do not mean the tale of Mhenjhor?" Calien asked.

"What tale is that? I have never heard of Mhenjhor." Cora replied, obviously interested in anything that would help her learn more of her secretive comrade. A quick glance at Cadwan suggested that he too had no knowledge of the name.

Calien began untying his boots, pulling each lace from its knothole with a patience that agitated his listeners. When he finally removed his footwear, he sighed contentedly and began. "The tale of Mhenjhor is but one of many tales written within The Fables of Ithidon. It is an ancient work written long before our earliest ancestors that has somehow managed to survive, passed down from generation to generation. It was one of my favorite books growing up, though it has been many years since I read it last." The prince's eyes fell on the fire in concentration, attempting to recall what he once could recite so flawlessly. "Inside is a tale of a great sorcerer known as Mhenjhor. It is said that Mhenjhor was more powerful than any number of sages put together; that he perhaps was not even human, but rather some sort of demi-god walking the earth. He had many followers, people who would do his bidding regardless of the consequences; for his might alone put them in awe and submission. His power was a fundamental sort, fire, ice, rock, and so forth. He controlled such elements on a whim, creating and destroying as he went.

"After centuries upon the world, he sought greater knowledge and desired to take his talents elsewhere, the planes perhaps, but even then he wished to leave a mark in his absence. Choosing his four most favored disciples, he granted each of them a sorcery of a certain force which they would channel from the planes to achieve power of an extraordinary nature. To one, he gave the power of ice, to be called 'The Witch.' To another, the power of the earth and what grows from it; 'The Giant.' Yet another, the power of fire; 'The Dragon.'" Calien glanced passingly at Alazar. "There is another." Pausing, the prince closed his eyes and massaged his temples. "Alas, I cannot remember the last. As I said, it has been long since I read the tale. Before his departure,

Mhenjhor then deemed that there could only be one sorcerer of the four elemental forces, and for another to take his or her place he must defeat the presiding one in a duel."

The prince looked up to see the faces of his companions listening eagerly. Alazar appeared apathetic.

"Of course, all of it is supposedly just fabrication, a story of lore with no truths," the prince stated with a shrug.

"It is no fabrication." Alazar suddenly declared with seriousness, the faint glow of the fire turning his face golden red. "'The Dragon' is somewhere here in Calas."

Cadwan placed a tiny slice of timber into the fire and stared at the robed man. "Are you certain of this, Alazar?"

"I have seen this beast several times in visions. When the time comes, we will duel. Either I will perish at his hands, or I will take his place."

There was a brief silence before Cadwan spoke again. "Apologies, Alazar, but it all seems outlandish to me. Do you know anything of this 'Dragon?' If a beast of such incredible ability lived within the borders of Calas, surely someone would have heard about him."

Several sparks from the campfire flew upward, accompanied by a series of pops. Alazar lowered a small morsel of dried meat onto the ground, near his resting chameleon. Disfrazal scurried to the piece and gulped it down with little hesitation. "I believe 'The Dragon' lives an isolated life, interacting very little with the rest of society."

Cora burst into laughter, startling Disfrazal, who flitted over to hide under Alazar's bent leg. "Is it not always the case! Supposedly, an existing sorcerer of great power lives in isolation, unbeknownst to the rest of civilization. The stuff of barroom tales, indeed!"

"I do not jest," Alazar spat in Cora's direction. "My entire life leads up to the moment we will battle."

"But if he is 'The Dragon,'" Cadwan mentioned, "he must wield forces that are difficult, if not impossible, to defeat. I would not think you prepared to face him."

The robed man scooped up his lizard and placed the alert reptile onto his shoulder. "Perhaps not yet, but I can still learn about him. Once I discover where he resides, I can face him on my own time, after I have sufficiently developed my skills."

"So you are willing to risk your life simply to earn this status unknown to the rest of the world?" Cadwan questioned.

"Is it so hard to believe? As I have said, my life leads to it. I cannot avoid it now."

Cora pulled thick hair from her face and tied it with a band behind her head. "If this elemental power you seek is fire, why do you wear robes of gray?

Why not red?"

Alazar took a sip from his waterskin, swishing the fluid in his mouth and spitting it into the fire. A faint sizzle sounded from the blaze. "I will not adorn the color of red until I have defeated 'The Dragon.' Only then will I have earned the right."

A sound of a twig snapping interrupted them. Everyone whirled to find a figure standing just beyond the light of the small fire, silhouetted by the darkness behind. In an instant, all four were on their feet, weapons in hand.

"Step into the light, so we may see you!" Cadwan commanded, his bowstring pulled rigid and an arrow nocked.

The figure did as it was told, taking three slow steps ahead until the dim light washed over it. Cadwan's eyes opened wide. *A woman*! She was tall and strong looking, with long wavy hair that fell past her shoulders, reaching her back. Her face was more handsome than beautiful, with a prominent jaw line and fierce eyes that showed no sign of fear. With the exception of a leather skirt, her garments were nothing more than animal hides. Fur boots were tied all the way to her knees, showing only glimpses of her powerful legs. Cadwan knew the kind; wildmen, or in this case, a wildwoman. They were a tribe of violent barbarians that roamed the Barren Hills, making the terrain their home with all the other monsters.

The soldier did not lower his bow, nor did the others drop their weapons, but the woman returned their wary stares evenly. Taking her battleaxe and her shield, she tossed them to the person who was nearest, then lifted her flat palms forward in a motion of peaceful intent.

"What do you want?" Cadwan demanded.

The woman pursed her full lips and stretched out an arm that pointed to the south. "Orcs chase you." Her speech was stunted and harsh.

In Cadwan's surprise, he inadvertently lowered his bow. "How do you know of this?"

"Watch chase for long time." The wildwoman swept her hand to encompass each of the party members. "Follow 'til you stop and make fire."

Alazar stepped around the dying blaze and near the woman. "What do you want? Are there more of you hidden in the darkness, ready to ambush us?"

The woman shook her head, her rolling brown hair flopping before her face. "Alone. Help you."

Beyond the wilting embers of the campfire, the night had taken on an eerie silence. To Cadwan, it felt as if the blackness was listening to every word with interest. He found himself whispering, though he knew it shouldn't matter. "I do not know many wildmen that are willing to help people from the towns."

Without an invitation, the woman took a spot around the fire, sitting comfortably. She even smiled for the first time. "No longer with tribe. Exiled."

Cadwan motioned for the others to resume their place, and he did as well, although his bow still rested on his curled legs as he sat. "You have been exiled from the barbarian tribe?"

The woman's head bobbed up and down. Cadwan watched the wildwoman closely. He was intrigued. She seemed quite powerful and fierce. Yet, in her disposition she did not demand to be feared, only respected. He wondered how long ago she had been exiled, and if she merely wished for the gracious company of others.

For a short period, everyone sat quietly, unsure what to say. Cadwan rekindled the minor flames and waited. He knew Alazar had a thousand questions to ask and he could only withhold for so long. The robed man would speak soon enough to break the silence.

"You said you are here to help?" Alazar brazenly stated. "Does that mean the orcs are still chasing us?"

"Yes," she answered. The four listened as the woman, who announced her name as Birna the Brown, went into story of how she witnessed the initial ambush and followed the hunt in its entirety from a distance. Although her rough dialogue was difficult to follow, Birna seemed to realize this and spoke slowly enough for everyone to understand. When she ended, she revealed that she had been alone for a long time and found the chase to be excellent entertainment.

"I am glad our perils can amuse you," Alazar muttered, with a half-grin.

The sarcasm was not lost on Birna and she laughed, jovially.

Cora stood up and shifted her head to the south, gazing into the horizon, as if she could see past the blanket of darkness. "If the orcs are still coming, what should we do?"

"Birna help if orcs come. Sleep now to be ready if orcs find us."

"What reason do you have to help us?" Alazar interrogated.

The woman's face grew repugnant, a look that was unexpected on her bold features. "Birna hate orcs. When child, orcs kill many friends. Birna kill orcs since."

Alazar dolefully swung his head back and forth. "How can we trust her?" he exacted, looking at Cadwan. "She has done nothing to prove her good intent. This whole thing could be a ruse to lull us into a false security. For all we know, the woman will axe us in our sleep."

Cadwan lifted his shoulders, with a steady expression. "I do not believe that to be the case. Besides, we will have someone on watch all through the night. I'll begin. Calien, I'll wake you after a few hours to take my place." The soldier turned to the wildwoman. "Lady Birna, you are welcome to sleep within our camp. But you must acknowledge that you place yourself in danger if you accept our company."

Birna grunted something that Cadwan guessed was some kind of thank you. Within a half hour, the fire had been stifled and only the soldier remained sitting, leaning his back against a rise in the hill watching his companions and Birna. Foreseeing a possible hasty exit, their bedrolls had not been used that night to give them one less object to pack; thus, all of them lay on the dirt ground attempting to find rest. None moved, but due to the situation Cadwan wasn't convinced they were all sleeping, except for Birna. The woman was snoring loudly and showed no signs of unease or ill-comfort within a camp of complete strangers.

Gazing upward, Cadwan could see the moon was nearly full and would be so in a day or two. Its soft glow touched down on the campsite, giving the faintest illumination amid the black surroundings. He perceived his own hope as similar to the moon; just as faint, with something terrible ahead of them and orcs chasing from behind. *But is hope not always bounded by dire circumstances? Maybe a glimmer of hope is all that is needed.*

Just then, Birna rolled over, smacking her lips as she did so, and went still again, sleeping soundly. Cadwan studied the wildwoman. Her entire presence was surreal, as if the hills had pitied them and sent her forth. He didn't blame Alazar for being skeptical of the woman. There was no true reason for her to wish to help them. They certainly hadn't asked her and she owed them nothing. Yet, she was here, touting on about how she would assist them when the time came. The woman showed no hints of trepidation when speaking of a legion of orcs. It seemed nothing more than a game to her. *Perhaps* she doesn't show fear because she *has* nothing to fear? Perhaps she has allegiance with the orcs, helping them find our party and helping to finish us off. Outlandish accusations, no doubt, but viable enough to consider. The more Cadwan deliberated on the subject, the more he agreed with Alazar, her arrival was too strange and coincidental.

He would have to watch her closely tonight.

*   *   *

"Darin, have you ever heard the name Veptuna?" Kyligan asked his dwarven follower. The duo had progressed gradually down the banks of the stream for well over an hour. The tepid water had curled and bowed several times, but had yet to lead them anywhere promising. The night was in full swing, its heavy cloak pushed back by the unnatural light of the torch Kyligan held. The ranger had taken extra measures to ensure that he didn't lead either of the two into a mud pit, or a covered millpond. The only setback they had encountered since the lizardfolk was a trio of small snakes. The snakes had apparently decided the two of them would make a nice meal, but Darin's waraxe and Kyligan's sword made quick work of them.

Darin took a slow step that mirrored the ranger's, as he answered. "Never have I heard such a name."

"The lizardman had said she was helping them rule these woods. I find it difficult to believe that anyone would want the foul lizardfolk to rule a single tree, much less an entire grouping of them."

"You are wrong with that presumption, my friend," the dwarf huffed. "There are plenty of wicked people and creatures about that would gain many benefits in having monsters like lizardfolk control an entire swamp. It surprises me not in the least."

Kyligan halted to examine the ground ahead. When he felt satisfied in his planned course, he persisted through the sickly brush. "Do you think we will come across this Veptuna?"

"Truly, who can say?" Darin slipped, but was able to right his body. Without the hold of Kyligan, he would have tumbled into a small pocket of water on the side. He swore under his breath. "I am more concerned with escaping this bedamned place. I'll never take solid ground for granted again."

The rivulet turned sharply to the left, followed too closely by a thick cluster of overhanging trees for the two men to stay along its banks. Kyligan momentarily led Darin through a notch among the trees, away from the stream. During their journey within the strange marsh, not once had the perils of travel become easy. Even Kyligan grew aggravated at their sluggish progress. He shuddered at the thought of continuing this for days. There *had* to be some way to escape this awful swamp. But how would they find it? Only by staying on the move, he conceded, as arduous as it might be. Amid the enclosure of trees, they had completely lost sight of the stream, though they could still hear the desultory waters churn and swirl. Kyligan continually looked for paths to his left, hoping to return to the water's edge, as quickly as possible, lest they lose contact with it all together. With much urging, he forced Darin to squeeze between the smallest of openings. Once again, the ranger could glimpse the bubbling stream only a short ways ahead.

When Kyligan heard the splash, he immediately looked at Darin to see if the dwarf had heard it, as well. A silent nod from the dwarf confirmed that the ranger was not the only one. Weapons already drawn, both cautiously approached the embankment, their eyes shooting in every perceivable direction.

A second splatter of water, followed by a muffled cry, sounded as they neared the shore. Kyligan could see droplets of water fly upwards and sideways, spraying the brush with moisture. Whatever was causing the splashing was before them, hiding behind a wide, towering tree that grew from the bank itself, its type indistinguishable from the moss and slime that covered the bark and leaves.

Both men froze, open-mouthed and wide-eyed, when they witnessed a beautiful woman bend forward, away from the protection of the tree, and wring water from her jet black hair. She had been swimming and was completely naked, oblivious to the prying eyes that watched her so shamelessly. Kyligan and Darin could only see her upper half, as her lower body was concealed behind the large tree and some bramble that grew at its base. Her dark hair contrasted ivory white skin, skin that covered a voluptuous body with uncanny smoothness. There was no need for Kyligan to admit she was attractive. The word would have almost seemed an insult to her stunning beauty. Every feature, at least every one the ranger could see, was awe-striking, from her face down to her perfectly sculpted waist.

Kyligan knew he needed to say something, but he could find no words. Her beauty had rendered him speechless. Succumbing to a foolish stupor, Darin's silence was confirmation that the dwarf was under the same spell.

The woman finished wringing her hair and turned directly toward the party, her silvery-brown eyes showing in the enhanced torchlight. Immediately, she fell back to conceal herself with an article of clothing that Kyligan could not discern. It was a poor attempt at modesty. Her expression betrayed curiosity, not embarrassment as would be expected.

"I . . .," the ranger stammered, "I am sorry, m'lady. We have just arrived and have seen nothing." Of course he was lying. Her entire rapturous upper body had been in full view, but he had no desire the make the woman more self-conscious than she already was.

The woman, her chest now protected by thin cloth and her lower body still hidden behind bushes, curled her sensuous crimson lips into a smile. "You have not harmed me, so you are forgiven," she purred. "I was only startled by your sudden appearance. But your drawn weapons remain daunting to a defenseless woman."

Suddenly realizing that they still held their weapons outward protectively, the men quickly returned them to their respective holders. Darin stepped forward and politely bowed. "Our apologies again. We had no intentions to intrude upon your swim, but have come here unintentionally – by accident." He motioned his thick arm toward the ranger. "This is Kyligan Ladach and I am Darin of Ludun. We are lost in these woods."

The woman examined the men with intelligent, confident eyes. Her tongue lightly stroked her upper lip. "How unfortunate for you," she remarked seductively, while her alluring eyes fell heavily upon a still shamed Kyligan.

"Yes, quite so," Darin continued, stopping only to clear his throat. "To be honest, we are not certain which forest we are in. We would be grateful if you could inform us."

Peeling her eyes from the ranger and back to the dwarf, the woman coolly replied, "These are the Blackened Woods."

"The Blackened Woods? But that is impossible! That forest is many miles north, beyond Oester!" Darin swept his vision across his surroundings in disbelief. "We could never have traveled such a distance so quickly on foot. Are you certain?"

"These are the Blackened Woods," she repeated, her voice revealing tones of force and intimidation. Her eyes narrowed with an expression that showed she did not take kindly to being questioned. "Perhaps you were brought here intentionally against your will?" She halted briefly, then added, "Though what force would do such a thing, I do not know."

Darin looked at Kyligan, his mouth wide and speechless. The ranger met the dwarf's gaze, but quickly refocused his sight on the woman. Her appearance had not changed, but Kyligan felt nervous now. She was beautiful, almost goddess-like in her prominence. Her gleaming eyes met his and she smiled again. Her expression secreted inexplicable intent that made the ranger unknowingly fidget. He had to force himself to speak. "And who are you, m'lady, to swim willingly in the water of the Blackened Woods?"

"I am Veptuna, goddess of these woods." The woman's answer was short, but a deep yearning expression lingered on her face, as she viewed the two men.

Veptuna! It was the name the lizardfolk had mentioned. Kyligan had expected it to be some foul beast of monstrous appearance. To his surprise, it was a gorgeous woman.

The two men glanced at each other, speaking words of silent warning. Promptly, Darin began another conversation with the woman, but Kyligan was not listening. He heard another splash, stifled and weak, as if something had broken the surface of the waters only to be pulled fiercely back down. He gazed past Veptuna, into the brook behind her, looking for something that might explain the breaking of the water. And then, like a hammer upside his head, another grim realization struck the ranger. The stream was identical to the one from his dream only a night ago. No, not just identical, it *was* the stream from his dream. At once, all the surrounding details came flooding into his mind, as if he had known them his whole life – the thick tree on the embankment, the adjoining foliage, decayed and foul.

The movement was lighting fast, but his eyes caught it before it disappeared and now there was no mistaking his horrible discovery. If only for the briefest of moments, a tentacle had shown itself amidst the brush near Veptuna.

The girl! Was she here? She must be, for every other detail of the visions had come to life. Kyligan unsheathed his blade and held it forward. Taking two determined paces near the woman, he announced boldly, "Step from the bush and show yourself!"

"Kyligan . . ." Darin had begun to protest, but the ranger cut him off with a stern swipe of his hand.

"Show yourself!" Kyligan repeated, warily eyeing the woman.

Veptuna feigned a look of utter astonishment and repulsion. "How dare you speak to a lady in such a way! What have I done to merit this?"

The woman's beauty still weighed upon the ranger, but he angrily pushed it to the back of his mind. "If you do not step out now, I will pull you out myself and I will not be gentle about it!"

Veptuna's innocent features suddenly altered. Her forehead and eyebrows curled down, as her nose and cheeks carved upward into a ferocious scowl. Her eyes bore threateningly into Kyligan with a rage the likes of which the ranger had never seen before. "I do not take commands from mere mortals! But you will know agony!" Her voice seethed with anger, but surprisingly she complied and slowly moved forward, pushing over the feeble bush that had concealed her lower body. What the dwarf and the ranger saw next was a spectacle neither man had ever heard of, much less witnessed first-hand.

Below the waist, the woman was far from human. Just under the midsection, her body transformed grotesquely into writhing, snakelike tentacles, six in all. The thick tendrils weaved back and forth, with twitching, hypnotic movements, extending to eleven feet at full length. Kyligan wondered how she was able to effectively conceal them behind the tree and bushes. In her right hand, she held a trident that gave off a soft red aura. The ranger hadn't remembered seeing the weapon earlier and momentarily wondered where it had come from. Veptuna slid forward, her tendrils pushing her along. Her eyes were like spears, piercing the resolve of both men.

"Fools!" she hissed. "You are but bugs to me, easily squished. Were it not for your wanton stupidity, I might have let you live."

Each man stepped away, cautiously sizing up their abominable new foe. Kyligan gazed upon the gruesome tentacles with an expression of revulsion as they jerked and thrashed about, dripping a sickly greenish fluid. He wondered how he would attack such a monster when he suddenly noticed something else. One of the beasts tentacles lie unmoving, trailing her and falling backwards into the stream.

"Witch! Show your other tentacle!" Kyligan's forthright demands surprised himself more than anyone, but while the octopus-like woman was a dreadful opponent what lay at the end of that tendril frightened him worse, giving him an uncanny resolve.

Infuriated, the monster's once beautiful face turned blood-red. With startling quickness, the tentacle in question snapped upward, tossing a large object through the air. The object, the body of a young girl no more than seven, landed hard on the mucky ground behind the two men. She rolled to a stop, unmoving, her skin casting a blue tint from obvious suffocation. The ranger spun his body intending to run and help the girl, but something hit him across the back of the head sending him into the mud. Another tendril wrapped quickly around his neck, squeezing and cutting off his air supply. With bulging eyes, he reached up and tried to pull the grimy limb off, but it was stronger than he would have ever guessed and held him firmly. His grunts were inaudible, as he struggled futilely against the overpowering grip of the monster.

144

He heard Darin yell, Veptuna scream out, and then the tentacle around his neck suddenly went slack. Kyligan coughed while he rolled to his feet. Glancing at the dwarf, he noted that a sickly green liquid coated the edge of the Darin's waraxe. The dwarf had attacked the tendril that was choking him, causing it to pull away. Veptuna was still before them, cursing in a language the ranger had never heard before. All of her snake-like limbs moved with normalcy and Kyligan assumed the damage Darin inflicted must have been minimal.

The ranger sucked in rapid breaths of air and positioned himself for battle. "Darin, see to the girl!"

"Are you mad? She will destroy you!" the dwarf answered.

"The girl is dying! You must tend to her!" Kyligan felt the dwarf hesitate and shouted with alacrity, "Hurry! Save her, if you can!" This time, he heard Darin's heavy footfalls draw away, toward the girl. Confident that the child would be attended to, the ranger refocused upon the monstrosity before him.

Veptuna slithered closer. Her six ghastly limbs squirmed menacingly, one still carrying Darin's imparted wound. Her face remained a deep crimson as her anger escalated, matching the glow of the trident in her hand. She bared her teeth and jeered, "I could have slaughtered the both of you, effortlessly. And you think you can combat me by yourself! I will take pleasure in butchering you slowly and with great pain!"

Kyligan's positioned himself with his sword at the ready, but his mind was reeling. For a year, all his nightmares, his tortured sleep, his solemn musings; it had all led to this moment. Why? Was he merely a puppet whose strings were held by the cruel whims of some god for amusement alone? What did this all mean? He had unwillingly been led to this swamp, and now faced a grotesque monster. Surely, he was not meant to slay the beast. It was far too powerful for his meager talents. *The girl perhaps?* She would undoubtedly be dead had Darin and him not happened upon this site. *Is this all to save her?* It was the only reasonable explanation the ranger could think of. If the child died, then this would all be for naught. There was but one decision to be made. He had to give Darin time to save the girl, *if* she were still savable, and that meant staying alive long enough for Darin to work whatever healing skills he had.

"What in the black hells are you?" the ranger asked with disgust, as he shifted his body guardedly.

"Do you not know? I am surprised," Veptuna spat. "Your words were so bold moments before. Now you show fear. I find your regret comical."

"I regret nothing, Witch!" the ranger retorted with feigned heroism as he bit back his fear as well as the urge to turn on his heel and flee.

Veptuna suddenly threw back her head and laughed. "If it will appease your curiosity, I will tell you." Her smile returned, her eyes becoming wickedly seductive. "I am born from the unholy coupling of gods, good and evil alike.

And you dare oppose me?"

"You are a demon!" Kyligan screamed and danced away from a tentacle that neared him.

"Perhaps to some," Veptuna admitted, "but to others I am a savior." The Vargenzin tilted her head and squared it evenly with the ranger. Her face reeked of vile hunger. "For you, I am death."

A tendril shot forward at Kyligan. The ranger ducked just in time to avoid the flailing limb. He rushed in, his sword above his head and slashed the blade downward aiming for the Vargenzin's torso. The attack was met by her glimmering trident and parried away. A slimy tentacle wrapped itself around the ranger's waist and raised him off the ground with ease. The ranger felt his body lifted high and then flung recklessly through the air. He came to a halt when his ribs landed hard against a moss covered trunk of a tree. Pain shot through his side. He couldn't tell if one of his ribs was broken, but the throbbing that emanated from the injury made it a pointless matter. Fortunately, he had maintained his grip on his sword, though the bow around his shoulder had snapped in two from the collision.

Gathering up his body, he groggily gazed at the Vargenzin. She was slithering forward with an evil grin, enjoying every moment. Kyligan ignored the aching in his ribs and called out, "What did you want with the girl?" In truth, he was no longer interested. He only hoped to stall the demon, while he formulated some kind of plan, futile as it may be.

"I wanted nothing of the girl," Veptuna hissed. "The pathetic child just showed up moments before you did. I was hungry. I am still hungry." Another green limb veered toward Kyligan. He met the attack with the edge of his blade, cutting into the tendril and causing a spurt of olive liquid to splatter his face. Veptuna grunted and pulled the wounded limb away. She thrust her trident ahead, aiming for the ranger's heart. Again, Kyligan brought up his weapon soon enough to deflect the assault. He quickly backed away to avoid getting snatched by any of her six tentacles.

The ranger gaped at the advancing demon. He could perceive no weaknesses, no way to defeat her. She was too formidable, too powerful. He risked a momentary peek at Darin. The dwarf looked to be in the midst of trying to resuscitate the child. Kyligan prayed he was successful and could flee with the girl soon. He feared that one death was already imminent; his own. Reaching down into his boot, he pulled out a small dagger and flung the weapon at the looming Vargenzin. The demon dodged the spinning blade with a snake-like movement, her torso bobbing to the side. An oily limb reached for his arm. Kyligan stepped away, but another limb wrapped around his leg and tripped him up.

On his back, the ranger cried out and with both hands drove his blade into the responsible tentacle. The skin of the tendril's were thick and chitanous, but his blow was fierce, nearly cutting the limb in two. The tendril pulled away, but another quickly pinned the ranger on the ground across his chest. Kyligan struggled to free himself, but his arms were restrained under the sturdy hold of the grotesque appendage. Veptuna was chuckling malevolently, as she slid close to the helpless ranger. "Your face shows your demise better than I could ever explain. I am certain you will taste exquisite, but I'll not kill you immediately." The Vargenzin lifted her trident high and plunged the forked blade into Kyligan's left shoulder. The pain was excruciating, and though the ranger bit his lip to hold back the cries of agony, he could not. Blood poured freely from his newly acquired injury, sullying the ground beneath him. Veptuna reveled in the ranger's pain and lifted her weapon again with horrid satisfaction, readying for another strike.

"No! Back to the hells with you, demon!" It was not Kyligan who had screamed, but Darin. The dwarf was dashing at Veptuna, his waraxe in the air. The Vargenzin spun to view the oncoming dwarf with scorn. She flung a tendril his way and the limb smacked his face before he could avoid it, spinning him to the ground. With the demon's attention diverted, Kyligan felt the limb around his upper body loosen just slightly. It was enough for him to wriggle free. He slid away from his detractor and with stunning quickness leapt to his feet. Pulling back his sword with his right arm, he plunged the steel into Veptuna's abdomen just as she was returning her interest toward him. A ghastly, spine-numbing howl issued forth from her lips and the demon slithered backwards several feet.

Kyligan gazed upon the Vargenzin's wound. A disgusting greenish fluid oozed slowly from the aperture of her flesh. The ranger couldn't determine if the lesion was fatal; probably not, he guessed. The demon looked down at the opening in her gut and furiously sneered. Darin rolled awkwardly to his feet and also stared at the injured demon.

"Mortals! You have made a horrible, horrible mistake!" Veptuna screeched with rage, but her voice had lost some vigor. Her pain was impossible to conceal. "Pray we never cross paths again!" The Vargenzin moved slowly back into the stream, disappearing beneath the dark waters below.

For several long moments, both men could only stare silently, visibly shocked by the outcome. Kyligan finally looked at Darin. "The girl?"

"Miraculously, she lives," Darin answered, turning back to view the child, who was laying in the fetal position, unconscious on the ground. "A few more seconds and I do not think I could have brought her back." Slowly, Darin viewed Kyligan, a look of wonder in his green eyes. "How did you know?"

Kyligan shrugged. "The dreams."

"Then perhaps you are free from them now?"

"If what I was meant to accomplish has been done, then perhaps." The ranger shook his head, his sweat-drenched hair flopping about his face.

"Strangely, I am not sure if I have achieved what was intended. I do not have that feeling of finality."

The dwarf neared Kyligan and firmly clasped his arm. His red beard looked extra bright in the still powerful light of the torch. "I can say this with certainty. You saved the life of a small child and the life of a grumpy old dwarf. That alone is something remarkable."

Kyligan peered at Darin. "How have I saved your life? If anything, it was the other way around. She had me trapped."

"If you had not forced me into that grove of trees, I would have died at the hands of those filthy orcs. There is no denying that."

Kyligan found himself smiling. "If you had not come willingly, we both would have died at the hands of those filthy orcs."

Darin grinned. "Come, let us take the girl and leave this forsaken place." He gestured at Kyligan's crimson shoulder. "You will need some healing, as well."

The two men reached the girl and the uninjured Darin hoisted the limp child onto his shoulder. They had taken only three steps when a bolt of wrenching pain shot through Kyligan. Dizzy, he fell to his knees and then flopped onto his back. Darin quickly lowered the girl and knelt next to the ranger, examining the open wound. The crimson fluid had begun to cake around the corners, but the center was still damp. Kyligan's entire shoulder was red, the blood sticking his threads of clothing and chain shirt together in a gummed mess. Darin also noticed a puss-like green substance exude from the lesion in small amounts.

"Gods," the dwarf said, shortly.

"What? What is it?" Kyligan asked between a pair of coughs.

Darin closed his eyes briefly and took a heavy breath. "Poison. Her weapon must have poisoned you."

The ranger winced, not at the news, but because he was starting to feel more pain and his breathing becoming less natural. "Can you expel it?"

"I . . ." the dwarf paused, still peering at the nasty wound. He shook his head, "I do not know." His thoughts were interrupted by the sound of bubbling water coming from behind them, back within the stream. Darin looked back and frowned. "Can you walk a little ways?"

"I think so," Kyligan answered.

"We need to get away from this water. That monster could come back anytime. After a short distance, we can stop again and I will tend to you." Darin scrutinized the ranger closely. "Is that reasonable enough?"

Kyligan nodded and slowly rose to his feet, groaning as he did so. He felt nauseous, and his vision was hazy, but he made no complaints. Darin scooped up the child and lumbered away from the stream, with Kyligan stumbling behind.

XVII

Cadwan awoke to a hand on his shoulder, shaking him gently. He rolled over to his back and looked up to discover the hand was Calien's.

"Wake up, Cadwan. The orcs have found us," the prince whispered.

Cadwan was on his feet in an instant, raking over the campsite. It was still nighttime, but small hints of an early sun shown far off. Dawn would come in an hour or two. Cora and Alazar slept soundly, but Birna was standing at the opposite edge of the camp's perimeter, her face pointed toward the hills to the south. With battleaxe in hand, a wooden shield was wrapped around her left forearm. For a moment, Cadwan wondered how she could be awake. She was in a deep sleep when he had called upon Calien to burden his watch. Had the prince waken her first? Surely not. It was peculiar, but a mystery to be mulled over at a later time. More urgent concerns consumed him now.

"Are you certain?" Cadwan asked the prince, shaking off any effects sleep had had upon him.

Calien nodded. "I heard them myself only minutes ago. They are not so far off. We must hurry!"

"Wake the others, then gather your belongings and mount up. We must leave, as soon as possible," Cadwan commanded the prince.

Calien rushed off and Cadwan quickly prepared his own possessions for a hasty exit. When finished, he rushed over to where the barbarian woman stood, still gazing off into the distance. The woman heard his approach and turned to face to him. Her wild hair and untamed features brought the soldier to a premature halt before reaching her. She was intense and battle-hardened. Her face showed no signs of anxiety.

"What do you think?" Cadwan asked, not knowing what else to say.

"Orcs not far. Here soon." She lifted her head to the southern horizon, gesturing to where they were approaching. "Your people ready?" she asked.

"Ready to flee for our lives. We cannot fight them all. Our only hope is escape."

"Not leave yet," the large woman stated. "Wait." She trotted off, leaving an astonished Cadwan behind. Disappearing around a small niche in the hillside to their north, she returned only a moment later riding a great horse. The mare was large and stunning, its brown skin covering a muscular frame and thick, rugged legs.

Cadwan gaped at the fantastic beast. He hadn't expected a barbarian to own such a marvelous steed. "Why have you kept this horse hidden?"

Birna ignored the question. Drawing stern eyes over the encampment, she spoke with unyielding firmness. "Do not go yet. Take horses and hide behind hill." She pointed a strapping arm to a large knoll north of camp.

"Why?" Cadwan asked.

"Birna lead orcs far away." The woman adjusted the animal skins around her waist.

Cadwan was momentarily at a loss. Then, he grasped her meaning. "You are going to divert the orcs away from us?"

The woman barbarian grunted affirmatively.

A puzzled look draped over the face of the soldier. "Why would you do such a thing? We have not helped you in any way. What makes you so willing to help us?"

Birna face lit up, her smile jovial and friendly. "Good people. Birna help good people. Birna hate orcs."

"How do I know this is not some kind of trap? You could easily tell the orcs where we are and then we are finished." A simple look of repugnance from the woman at the mention of helping orcs convinced the soldier, otherwise. "Are you certain you are willing to do this?" he asked, earnestly. Although Cadwan welcomed any help the group could receive, he was hesitant to allow one woman to risk her life for them, especially considering they had done nothing to warrant such assistance. It was a debt he felt he could not repay.

The woman kept her buoyant expression and simply nodded. "Go now. Hide behind hill until you hear orcs no more. Go now!"

Before the solider could say another word, Birna reared her horse southwest, apparently with designs to cut off the beastly army and pilot them away from the adventurers. For a brief moment, Cadwan watched her go, and then the words of his comrades diverted his attention.

"Where is she going?" Alazar asked, still rubbing his sleepy eyes, as he sat upon his steed, Cora's arms wrapped around his body.

Cadwan shook his head. "I can explain in a minute. First, we need to get behind that hill over there and conceal ourselves." The soldier ran to his mount and lifted his body atop the saddle. Urging his mount ahead, he led the group hastily around the eastern flank of the lofty hill. After a brief jaunt, he deemed they were sufficiently blocked from view and called them to halt.

At a standstill, Alazar quickly grew impatient and demanded an explanation. Cadwan regarded his arcane friend, his expression brusque. "Birna is drawing the orcs away from us. We must wait quietly until they pass."

Alazar's eyes went wide. "What? How can . . ."

"Be silent!" Cadwan snapped. "We can discuss this freely later. Now, we must remain quiet and listen." On cue, a crescendo of a thousand legs across hard dirt swelled up, rumbling throughout the hills. It came from the south and drew westward. For many minutes, the ground shook from the footpaths of the horde. The company held their breaths, hoping to see none of the orcs rise above the crest of the hill they hid behind.

Then the sound declined, slowly at first, but soon the thundering was merely an echo from the west until it ultimately vanished altogether. The four of them let the silence enfold upon their ears, a sullen reminder of what they might have faced. Cadwan ruptured the silence by swinging his gelding around to face the eastern sky and announcing, "We are free to go. Let us make haste."

"Why did she do it?" Alazar asked, incredulously. "I never would have trusted her."

Cadwan lifted his shoulders. "Divine intervention, perhaps? Truthfully, I do not know, but we should be thankful for it." Cadwan was relieved and remorseful at the same time. They had escaped an army of orcs that would have slaughtered them mercilessly, and yet something saddened him. He had never expressed his gratitude to the mysterious barbarian and doubted he would ever have the chance again. A shame, he reflected, for her strong resolve and battle presence would have been a welcome addition to their traveling party; although, he admitted regretfully, she likely wouldn't have been accepted by the civilized communities. In such a respect, it was probably for the best she remained in the hills. A wildwoman has no use for *refined* civilization.

With a gesture to the others, he led them eastward to their next goal; the village of Oester.

*   *   *

Kyligan tripped on his own feet and crashed into a puddle of wet mud.

Darin witnessed the ranger keeling on his side, his face wracked with torment. Glancing at the girl who walked with him, he gently whispered to her, "Do not move. I need to help him."

Not long after the foray which had forced the trio to flee from the brook that contained the demon, the girl had wakened. She had declared her name to be Odna, but said little more and had not yet revealed what had brought her into the clutches of Veptuna. Darin was hesitant to bring the dismal subject up. Now, she walked hand-in-hand with the dwarf, while Kyligan stumbled along at the rear. Earlier, the dwarf had tried to purge the poisons that coursed through the ranger, but his attempts yielded no results. The poison was strong, deadly, and far beyond his meager healing abilities. Each passing moment, Kyligan's state worsened and yet the ranger refused to rest, pushing himself on in an attempt to dispel any fears the girl, or Darin for that matter, might have. But now, he could go no further. The poisons had overtaken him and he lay trembling in the muck, his skin sickly pale.

An hour ago, the sun had breeched the skies and Darin was able to determine their direction for the first time. He immediately turned them west, knowing that the road from Mullikin and Oester rested along the western fringes of the Blackened Woods. As precarious as travel was the previous night when Kyligan led them, the dwarf now found their course strangely uncomplicated. The mud pits had thinned out and there were no signs of monsters, so the route of travel had been much less dangerous – though the spattering of trees and millponds still forced an indirect route. Sadly, Darin no longer believed they would reach the road before Kyligan's body surrendered to the foreign toxins within him.

Reaching the ranger's side, Darin spoke softly, with a compassion rarely used. "My friend, how do you feel?"

"I do not feel much of anything," Kyligan gasped, his eyes not focusing squarely on the dwarf's. "Just a little cold, nothing more."

Darin looked over the ailing man. The bloodied wrappings around Kyligan's shoulder had done well to conceal the wound, but the ranger looked no better for wear. Giant beads of perspiration ran down his face and his skin was a colorless, ashen white. Along with the continuous sweat, his body shook incessantly, often rattling his teeth. He was dying. The sight tormented the dwarf mentally, but he would not let the ranger see his anguish. "We have some time to rest. Go to sleep, friend. Rest will improve your state. I'll wake you when we are ready to leave again."

Even in his ill state, Kyligan understood all too well. The dwarf tried to mask his grim thoughts, but he couldn't conceal the solemn look his eyes portrayed. The ranger realized he would not wake again when the next sleep took him. Opening crusted lips, he sucked in some air and spoke weakly. "Darin, let me see the girl."

The dwarf spoke no reply. Curving his lips downward, he nodded once and called the girl. "Odna, sweet child, come her a moment." The girl responded and approached the two men, her eyes falling upon the downed ranger. For a girl of seven, she was pretty in her own right. Innocent eyes shined and curly blond hair fell untamed about her face. "Odna," Darin continued, "I want you to know that this man saved your life."

Odna said nothing, but continued to stare at the ranger. Kyligan returned her gaze with unsteady eyes, his face brightening ever so slightly. His mouth moved briefly in what Darin assumed was an attempted smile, and then the ranger's eyelids closed.

It was a plagued slumber, but the tiny movements of Kyligan's chest assured the dwarf that a flicker of life remained within him, though it too would extinguish shortly. For a lengthy stretch of time, Darin looked upon the unconscious Kyligan. As silence pervaded within the forest, thoughts of disbelief churned inside his mind. *After all this, he is just going to die?* Darin recalled the ranger's dreams that Kyligan had told him of; the first of which Kyligan had died, and the second it was Kyligan, in the girl's body, who had died. But now, in reality, the girl lived. Was the ranger *supposed* to die for this unknown girl? What was so special about her?

Turning pained eyes to Odna, the dwarf spoke, "Child, sit with Kyligan, while he sleeps. You may rest, too, if you like." Darin pointed to a tree across the way. "I am going to spend a short time alone to decide what we are to do, so it is important that you watch over this man for a few minutes. Do you understand?"

Odna nodded slightly and sat down next to the limp ranger, her introspective eyes never leaving his pallid face. Contented that the girl would obey, Darin left her and proceeded to a tree several feet away. He squatted his rotund frame upon the ground and bowed his head, his eyelids closed. Disregarding his physical surroundings, he mentally reached upward, past the sky, and into the planes beyond. He was only one of many working clerics in Frundin's faith, not a high-priest, but he hoped that the deity would answer his summons. The dwarf had called upon the god for an audience only once before and that was many years ago. Extending his mind, he visualized his own perception of Frundin and respectfully pleaded for a consultation.

For many minutes, Darin waited, feeling nothing, and he soon began to worry he had been rebuked. Perhaps Frundin had more pressing matters than to worry about the plight of a simple cleric? His doubts were removed when his body abruptly stiffened and a saintly force imbued him, body and mind. He felt as if he were sharing his soul with another other-worldly being. But the presence was comforting, reassuring, and the priest was consumed with new hope.

My loyal disciple, why have you called to me?

Darin did not hear Frundin's words aloud, but from within. Listening to his master's saintly voice was like a jolt of strength to his weary condition, filling him with renewed vigor and faith. He basked in his god's company, for there was no greater sensation. This is why I chose to serve the clergy, he reminded himself heartily.

"Holy Frundin, my friend Kyligan, he dies and I cannot save him." The dwarf spoke to his god with deep-rooted emotion.

Yes, I have been watching. It is sad and unfortunate.

"But he does not deserve such a fate! He has carried himself with honor and selflessness, sacrificing his life for a child he did not even know."

As you well know, fate is an agony all its own. At least he will die a hero.

Despite the hallowed presence of Frundin, Darin felt a helpless anger well-up from inside. He balled his fists and shook them in frustration. "Master, I cannot let this happen! I cannot let this man die before me, not after he has saved my life and the child's. Is there nothing I, or you, can do for him?" The dwarf felt a touch of sorrow from the ubiquitous voice, as if it feared where the conversation might lead.

Your pain affects me deeply, but even I cannot meddle with the inexorable providence of death. Not without repercussions.

"Repercussions? What repercussions? I will shoulder any blame and responsibility for his returned health. It is my burden to bear." Darin sensed an evasive air in his god.

My devoted follower, do not tread this path. It never leads where you hope it to. You have always been levelheaded and wise. Do not let some momentary sorrow cloud your judgment.

"Master, my judgment has not been clouded. His death is unjust and it is my obligation to do whatever I can to aid him."

Many deaths of the world are unjust. Is it your obligation to make them all right?

Darin halted a moment to consider this. *There is no reasoning with a god,* he realized. But the dwarf would not be dissuaded so easily. If it was somehow possible, Kyligan would live. "What must be done?"

There was a long pause, a silence. Had Darin not still felt the presence of his god, he would have thought him gone, left entirely. But Frundin remained with his priest and Darin felt the deity regard him sullenly.

Death will not release him. Not without compensation.

"The death of another?" Darin asked.

Not necessarily, but a sacrifice of different kind. Most certainly one you will have to make.

"Then tell me the sacrifice that must be made," the cleric urged, his muscles tensed in nervous anticipation.

And how will this man live, bearing such a burden? Will he be pleased knowing his life was spared at the expense of another.

"He will never know."

Then your mind is made, is it? Are you ready to hear what you have afflicted upon yourself? Frundin's voice was sad, regretful.

"I am, Master."

As the words poured from his god into his mind, the dwarf froze, unbelieving, for even he had not expected the new fate he was condemned to.

Perhaps it *had* been a mistake . . .

XVIII

Oester sat along the northeastern border of Calas, resting between the Barren Hills to the west and the thick marshes of the Blackened Woods flanked directly on its east. Established centuries ago, the village was a prime example of royal neglect, showing no sign of military defenses other than a crumbled tower to the north that had been devastated by a war one-hundred and fifty years prior. With a population wavering around four hundred, most of the citizens were either woodsmen or farmers, living a life of toil and perseverance in inhospitable lands, while enduring hardships without self-pity. Life in the small community had always been harsh and the village itself had been forced to resettle more than once on the eve of destructive raids from the fierce Hellar tribes to the north.

As a result of the kingdom's disregard toward Oester, the people showed little loyalty to the Crown. In fact, they saw themselves as an independent part of Calas, demonstrating individuality and self-reliance, despite the fact that through legal jurisdiction they were in fact owned by the Crown.

As Cadwan's company approached the thatch huts and wooden houses of the village, a gentle morning breeze caressed their faces. Their ride from the campsite had only lasted two hours. For much of that time, Cadwan had pondered how the barbarian woman fared against the army of orcs that had chased her away. Although he felt no personal feelings or attachment toward the powerful woman, he was still more than thankful for her inexplicable aide. The whole experience baffled him. But, as Oester rose into view ahead of them, he was forced to alter his attention.

From a distance, the settlement appeared ordinary and unassuming. But as they drew nearer and the clip-clopping of their horse's hooves reached the edge of the village, it became apparent that something terribly tragic had occurred. It was absolutely quiet. Not a single sound could be heard; birds, bugs, nothing. Only their horses disrupted the unsettling silence. Not a single person walked about, and a sour stench hung heavily in the air. Cadwan wrinkled his nose and his stomach twisted from the rank odor. With a glance at Alazar, he realized the others had also noticed. Alazar returned his look with concern draped across his face, the robed man's lips curved downward, frowning.

"Gods, what is that?" Calien cried out, pointing to a shape on the ground. Twisted in the grass alongside the road, the horrid contour of a man lay motionless.

Alazar rode near the figure and examined it closely. After a short time, he looked back. "His skin is rotted. He has been dead for many days."

"What?" Prince Calien responded, his voice displaying liberal revulsion. "How can this be?"

"Look at the buildings," Cadwan mentioned, his eyes sweeping across the nearest houses. "The windows are shattered and the doors bashed. It is as we feared."

As the four made their way toward the center of the town, more bodies displayed themselves along the ground, each in similar state as the first. But something even more horrific became evident. "The bodies," Alazar commented, "some have been fed upon, and not by crows, methinks." Many of the grotesque carcasses had small parts, or even entire sections of their flesh and body torn away by a means indiscernible. The prudence of Alazar's statement only seemed to cast more trepidation upon the others. Throughout their discovery, Cora had remained utterly silent, her face nothing short of sheer terror. Her arms tightened around Alazar and he thought he could hear small sobs from her face that was buried in the folds of his robe.

The air had grown heavy with the thick smell of decaying flesh and Cadwan had to concentrate to keep himself from gagging. The scene became gristly, as more dead bodies appeared, their warped remains strewn about heedlessly. Only the morning sun above gave the four any recourse from the scene, but it was little remedy. Each had their weapons prepared and their senses heightened. Whatever had caused this was probably still around, Cadwan guessed, and he had no desire to join the perverse corpses that littered the earth.

The soldier cautiously led them onward, studying the area, until they witnessed a man walking among the macabre scene. Clearly alive, the man turned to view them with astonishment. Cadwan called the party to a halt and they returned the stranger's stare, equally stunned and speechless. A plain-looking man of modest dress and stature, the stranger was holding a broom in one hand, as he gazed at the party in disbelief. Then, an expression of pleasant surprise overtook his calloused features. "Oh, hello there! Forgive me for staring, but it is strange to see visitors in this place now." The man's voice was calm. He casually gestured to the unsightly scene surrounding him. "Everyone here is dead, or has fled the plague."

The sight of a living man, casually making his way through a refuse of corpses seemed bizarre. In took extra seconds for Cadwan to bring himself to speak. "What . . . what are you doing?"

The man smiled. "I am just sweeping up the street a little. It is an easy job nowadays, as no one is around to litter them."

"You are sweeping the streets, but leaving corpses on the ground all around you?" Cadwan asked, baffled.

"Oh, well," the man scratched his cleanly shaven chin, "there are just too many to clear away."

Prince Calien led his horse even with Cadwan. His face was aghast at the gruesome setting. "What has happened here? This town is a graveyard!"

"Yes, and I am the undertaker," the man joked with a chuckle, though he quickly straightened his face when the others showed no amusement to his grim humor. Lowering his voice, he spoke softly, "A horror has crept upon our village. As I have already told you, all have fled or died. I blame it on the curse."

"Curse? What curse do you speak of?" Calien asked.

"The curse. It is something not to be spoken of outside." The stranger's eyes suddenly narrowed, suspiciously. "If I may ask, what are you doing here?"

"We have been sent by King Anuron himself to investigate the condition of Oester," Prince Calien forcefully announced. "As we are now witnessing, there was good reason to do so."

The man toyed with the broom in his hand and shook his head. "So the king has abruptly taken interest in our humble village? A little late for us, would you not say?" He paused to lament his own words, his face forlorn. "Ah well, I do not believe there is much else you can do."

"Are you the only survivor?" Cadwan asked, beating the prince to the word.

"Myself, and my wife and son. They have gone foraging for food in the woods and will be back later to eat."

"Perhaps, while you wait for them you can tell us more of this 'curse' you have mentioned?" Cadwan said. "We would like to learn more of what happened here."

The stranger regarded the proposal, then nonchalantly shrugged. "Well, if you would like you are welcome to stay at my inn at no charge. I do not have much to offer, as there is not much food left, but I do have plenty of clean rooms available."

Cadwan tilted his head. "Your generous offer is appreciated. We will endeavor not to take up too much of your time."

The man seemed to find Cadwan's last statement amusing. "Time is the one thing I have plenty of."

The man introduced himself as Fargus and led the group to the western edge of town, back the way they had originally come. Fargus's modest inn sat alongside the main traveling road that led north and south. The building was wooden, double-storied, and solidly built, appearing to have been well used in its day. Cadwan noted that one of the front windows was smashed, and the door, while still on its hinges, was dented and heavily splintered.

Fargus brought them inside and sat them around a large dining table in the center of the inn. Cadwan was impressed by the charming subtleties of the décor. He had expected a rundown, wood thatched interior, but the inside was well maintained and cozily adorned. The table of the main dining room was constructed of smooth glazed oak and showed few hints of use, though the soldier was certain it was used often. A small doorway led into the kitchen, where Fargus exited after seating his guests. Although he had little means, Fargus did his best to be a gracious host. He brought them turnip soup and stale bread, all-the-while muttering his apologies about his meager offerings. The party accepted the hospitality, with much gratitude. Fargus joined them at the table and the five fell into discussion.

At first, the conversation was light and full of simple discourse. Fargus exclaimed he had moved to Oester as a teenager and married a local woman. When he was old enough, he adopted the local inn from a retiring old man and took to restoring it. Apparently, the inn did quite well, as nearly every traveler that journeyed north to Helleras or south to Mullikin made a stop there.

Eventually, through much effort, Cadwan was able to turn the dialogue back toward the plight at hand. "How is it that you and your family have survived and yet everyone else is gone?"

"We simply locked ourselves in the basement of this place until the worst had passed. We should have fled with the others, but my wife did not wish to leave our property. What can I do?"

Alazar glanced at Cora. The halfling seemed more at ease now that she was indoors and away from the sickening carnage outside. Although the robed man didn't want to admit it, he was relieved to see Cora handling herself better. *Why this strange new concern for her?* Shifting his sight to Fargus, he asked, "You mentioned something about a curse?"

Fargus wrinkled his face, then dropped his elbows on the table and buried his head in his hands. The man took several large muffled breaths before composing himself. "Do any of you know of the battle that took place in Oester a century and a half ago?"

Every head shifted to Prince Calien. The scholar seemed to know everything about the history of the kingdom and this instance was no different. Calien nodded his handsome face. "Of course. The Hellar barbarians raided the village from the north, overrunning the town and eventually sacking the northern tower. The tower is still in ruin today."

"Is that it? That is all you can say of it?" Fargus asked.

"Did I forget something?" Calien seemed taken aback. "I know that the Hellar barbarians eventually settled farther north, allowing the village to repopulate."

The innkeeper scoffed. "Your history teacher overlooked some details, my educated friend. Let me give you a different account, one that holds more

158

truths than the Crown is willing to admit. A few years before the raid of the Hellar, the ruling monarch at the time, King Lodan, bestowed the land to a chivalrous knight by the name of Sir Vernest. Vernest vowed his allegiance to the Crown and was deemed a vassal. He was a powerful knight. Legend has it that he wielded a mighty greatsword that had no equal. For a short time, Vernest worked diligently as the vassal and Oester lived in peace under the shadow of his newly constructed tower. But the partnership did not thrive for long and soon things went awry."

Fargus paused to regard his audience. He was pleased to observe that they were all listening intently, rapt on his every word. When he continued, he lowered his tone to put more emphasis on his tale. "For some reason, a reason that has never been revealed, Baron Vernest began remitting fewer taxes to the king. No one has ever discovered the true reason for this lack of judgment, but for himself and the people of Oester it proved to be a grave mistake. Not long afterwards, the Hellar barbarians breached the shores north of the village and threatened Oester. Though capable, Vernest's troops were small in number and the baron quickly sent word south to Calas demanding reinforcements. A month later, the barbarians reached Oester, and though the outnumbered warriors of the village fought with courage and valor, they were overtaken. Yet, amidst the assault, the tower still stood defending the survivors. During this siege, Vernest continued to hold hope that reinforcements from Calas would come and save them.

"But King Lodan had been angered by the baron's meager tax offerings and he never planned to send the aid required. Instead, he prepared a counter-offensive in Mullikin to drive the invaders back north. It is said that Vernest slowly went mad, as a result of the king's betrayal. Ultimately, the tower was overtaken and everyone inside slaughtered. But the tale does not end there, for rumor has it that Vernest, in his raging madness, had cursed the tower and all within. That is why the structure has never been reconstructed. In fact, the building has been avoided ever since that battle."

"A fabulous tale, Sir, but how can you be sure that it is nothing more than myth?" Calien asked.

"Perhaps some is myth," Fargus replied. "Nothing is for certain. But as I said earlier, I believe there are more truths to that tale than the Crown will ever admit to, or even acknowledge."

Cadwan lowered a glass of water he had been sipping. "That was one hundred and fifty years ago. What connection does it have with what has happened to your village now?"

Fargus stood from his chair and exited the room. He came back a minute later with another bowl of soup for himself. Easing into his chair, he scooped up the red broth and took a long sip before lowering his spoon and peering at Cadwan. "I believe that the baron's tragedy has somehow caused a plague to overcome the residents. A couple weeks ago, that damnable tower was embraced by a disturbing blue glow the likes of which I have never witnessed before. Then, a day later, Harstak fell gravely ill."

"Harstak?" Cadwan inquired.

"He is, or was, just a simple citizen of the village, a woodsman. His house was the closest building to the tower. Anyway, he got real sick, sweating and shaking terribly, and mumbling incoherently. We all feared contagion, so we left him in his house and boarded up the place, leaving only a small crack in a window to provide him food and drink. Our hope was that he would overcome whatever ailed him and we could let him out. Then, two nights afterwards, a woman named Laela was shrieking in terror. We found her fainted in the middle of town, a terrible wound across her neck. When she awoke, she exclaimed that she was attacked by a horribly deformed man with frightening, devilish eyes and skin drawn gripping to the bone. She was adamant it was Harstak, but that he was only a hideous shadow of his former self.

"We rushed to Harstak's house and found the boarded door broken down, and the piles of food given him left spoiling. But there was no sign of Harstak anywhere; vanished with no trace. It was hours later that Laela began showing the same symptoms as Harstak, and soon she disappeared in the middle of the night, as well. Over the next few days, more disappearances occurred and the people all feared they would be the next." Fargus looked up to make eye contact with each of his listeners. "And then it happened."

"What happened?" Calien urged, gripped by every word. "Go on!"

"One night, horrifying creatures emerged from the shadows of the Blackened Woods, attacking us with no mercy. They were," Fargus suddenly stopped, checking his words. He whispered something under his breath that the others couldn't hear. A moment later, he appeared to regain his senses and moved on with his narrative. "They were like men, but not. It . . . it was the villagers who had disappeared, but they were now just sick atrocities of their former selves. They killed and fed upon the living until the brink of sun-up, then retreated back into the forest. They would only show up during the hours of darkness. The living all fled Oester, though some remained to fight a hopeless battle in which they eventually succumbed and became the unnatural and gruesome beings. The plague, or sickness, if you will, consumed the entire village until all were dead, or had escaped. What you have seen outside is the remnants of this horrible tragedy."

"They *fed* upon the living?" the prince asked, every fiber of his voice exuding repulsion. His hands quivered, as he gripped his mug of water, the cup lightly tapping the wooden table. Fargus only nodded a reply. There seemed no statement worth reinforcing such an awful vision.

"Chilling," Cadwan muttered earnestly, his head shaking, "but if I may ask, how has your family been spared of this 'sickness'? It would seem to me that you should have gone mad like the others."

"Luck perhaps?" the innkeeper guessed. "How can I truthfully say? I can only give my account of what I have witnessed. I have no answers when it comes to reason, for how can one rationalize what has occurred?"

Cadwan drew invisible lines with his fingers upon the table, his mind entrenched within the tale presented. His thoughts swirled recklessly upon various possibilities and explanations. Unfortunately, Fargus was correct, rationalization was impossible. "Are you safe now?" the soldier asked.

"Safe?" Fargus squinted his eyes, questioningly.

"I mean, are you still in danger from these . . . things? Will they continue to come out at night from the woods?"

The innkeeper opened his mouth, about to answer, then abruptly closed it. As the others watched, he stood from his chair, while mumbling something about needing more water. He quickly exited the room without another word.

Cadwan stared at the man's back until he had disappeared past a door. Turning, he found Alazar looking directly at him, the robed man's face showing more concern than the soldier had ever seen him convey.

The tension within the room had grown sharp, cutting each of them with a bitter disquiet that matched the foul stench of the dead beyond the walls of the inn.

*   *   *

It was late afternoon when Kyligan opened his eyes. They were blurred from his slumber. At first, he wondered if he had passed beyond death's gate. After the ceaseless nightmare of the venture he had gone through, he almost welcomed such a thought. But then the world came into focus and he realized he was lying in the very same place he had fallen asleep earlier; the place he had formerly believed would be his death bed. Yet, somehow, someway, he was alive.

Gingerly, he sat up, rubbed his head, and made an internal inspection. He didn't feel sick and though his wound still pained him slightly, he no longer suffered the biting sting of the poison. He reached up to his shoulder and felt the slickness of the bandages wrapped around it. Delicately, he tore them loose and viewed the injury beneath. It was healing fast, *amazingly* fast. Kyligan lifted his arm to test the range of motion in the joint. He discovered it was nearly complete. Strange, he thought. How could I have healed so suddenly? I was certain my time was up.

Pleased at his progress, he cast about to find the others.

Darin was lounging against a tree, nonchalantly sharpening his waraxe on a whetstone. The girl sat next to him. She looked relaxed, but not quite comfortable in the presence of the dwarf. Kyligan pushed himself to his feet and ambled slowly to his friend.

The dwarf looked up from his task and regarded the ranger with a slight grin. "Well, it seems our companion has awoken from his nap."

"Yes," Kyligan answered, disbelievingly, "and I find I am not walking some plane of the afterlife." Drawing near the others, he instantly noticed a difference about the dwarf, something he couldn't plainly see, but rather sensed. It wasn't obvious, but it was there nonetheless, something peculiar the ranger couldn't place.

Darin returned to sharpening his waraxe. The scraping sound of the steel blade rubbing on the whetstone resounded through the trees.

"What happened, Darin?" Kyligan asked. "I should be dead. That poison was killing me."

Not meeting the ranger's eyes, Darin shrugged. "While you slept, your body somehow overcame the poison. I was as surprised as you are now. Remarkable, would you not say?"

Kyligan walked over to the girl. She gazed up at him and smiled. He sat next to her and returned her affable guise, but his focus was still on the dwarf. "How? Not that I am complaining, but how could my body, so close to the end, suddenly prevail over such a potent toxin? It does not seem possible."

Placing the whetstone in his pack, Darin rose to his haunches and notched his waraxe to the leather holder on his back. "Why question such a mystery? Why not be thankful for it?"

"I am thankful," Kyligan muttered. "I just find it odd. I had resigned myself to death and now that I am not, I feel strange – like I have cheated fate."

The ranger's last statement caused the dwarf to take a stumble backwards, his guise appearing defensive. Blood rushed to his face. "Must you examine this so fervently?" Darin shouted, with unexpected vehemence. "Why not accept this for what it is; a miraculous stroke of luck! Do not second guess good fortune so readily!"

Kyligan stared back at the dwarf, speechless. Darin's bizarre outburst had left the ranger at a complete loss for words. It was unlike to dwarf to act so ardently, as he was judicious with his thinking and normally analyzed happenings in a rational manner. Kyligan found this latest exploit out of character and he shifted uneasily in place wondering what had caused it.

The alien features that exuded from the dwarf lasted for several seconds, while the ranger searched for something to break the deviant silence. Then, Darin broke from his daze as if a dark shadow escaped his body. His features softened and he lowered his head, dropping pained eyes to the ground. "Forgive me, my friend." The dwarf's voice was sad and apologetic. "The latest events have caused me undue anxiety." He reached his arm to Kyligan, palm open. Kyligan took the dwarf's hand in his own and let the dwarf hoist him to his feet. "It is good to see you well. I had worried heavily. Your friendship in this last

162

day alone has meant much to me and your new health gives me hope. Come, let us leave this cursed place."

"No apology is needed," Kyligan answered. "An encounter with a demon can test one's resolve. We should both be thankful to merely be alive." The ranger smiled at his friend reassuringly and patted his shoulder. Turning to the girl, Kyligan helped her to her feet and firmly grasped her hand. "Come child, the sooner we leave this forest, the better."

The trio pushed on through the bramble for several hours. If the Vargenzin had been correct and they were indeed in the Blackened Woods, navigation wouldn't be simple. Kyligan nor Darin were familiar with the strange woodland swamp, so neither could distinguish their exact whereabouts. The only plan was to continue westward until they reached the edge. But as the sun dropped lower in the sky and the dying rays of light cascaded off the treetops, the three of them were still trodding among the undergrowth of the foul wood.

"Perhaps whatever force brought us here will not let us leave?" Kyligan mentioned, feeling his injured shoulder. He was astounded at how quickly the wound had healed. During their jaunt, his skin had grown over the laceration, closing the gash and leaving only a small red mark in its wake. His range of motion had fully returned and he no longer felt the jabs of pain from movement.

"Eh," Darin grumbled. "That is an outcome I will not accept." The dwarf's retort was terse and fleeting.

Again, Kyligan noticed something unusual about Darin. His eyes pointed forward, but it seemed he was looking blindly, as if deep in his own thoughts and oblivious of his surroundings. Kyligan envisioned a man who was bearing a heavy affliction and would not speak of it. What could have caused him to suddenly be like this? Darin was not a man of secrets, nor did he show weaknesses.

The ranger sucked in his breath and spoke. "Darin, you look troubled. Does something ail you?"

The dwarf gave his friend a calm expression, but he couldn't veil the sorrow in his eyes. "It is nothing, Kyligan. Just these damned woods. I yearn to be free of them once and for all."

The answer was valid enough, but it didn't quell the concerns the ranger held for his dwarven friend. There was more than he was letting on. Pressing his fingers to his temples, Kyligan checked on the girl, Odna. He had felt an immediate connection to her ever since they had begun walking together. He wasn't sure if it was because he had saved her life once already, or if there were something else to her quiet persona. Either way, a closeness was present that caused him to watch over her like a cautious father would a daughter. On several occasions, he caught himself ruffling her hair, or smiling at her. She seemed to enjoy the attention and grasped his hand ever more tightly, as they walked along.

With dusk approaching, very few sunbeams slipped past the crest of the trees above and the wood had grown exceedingly dark.

"We need to get out of this place soon. I loathe the thought of spending yet another night in this horrid bog." Darin did not bother looking to the others when he spoke. He hand was gripped firmly on his waraxe and he made no effort to avoid obstacles, preferring to go over or through them, as was necessary.

Kyligan glumly shook his head. "Though we arrived here unnaturally, I have a feeling we are nearing the . . ."

The ranger's words were cut off by a howling that caused all three of them to freeze in their tracks. A born woodsman and ranger, Kyligan knew most animals that lived in forests and had spent much of his life with them. The sounds that animals made were easily recognized, but the wailing that persisted now was something he had never heard before. It was no wolf or wild dog. Rather, it was some kind of mournful cry that was quickly joined by others of the same sort. For nearly a full minute, though it felt like several, the trio listened to the wind carry a crescendo of deep moaning that imbued them with unknown dread.

When they stopped altogether, the utter silence that followed was just as frightening. Odna clasped to Kyligan, her little arms shaking.

"That was no animal," Kyligan lamented, his hand fallen to the hilt of his blade.

Darin finally took the opportunity to gaze over at Kyligan. He face showed a multitude of expressions; anger, frustration, exhaustion, and fear among them. "What in the hells of Nazgoth have we brought ourselves upon?"

*   *   *

Fargus, innkeeper of the Oester Inn and apparent survivor of a horrifying plague, proved himself a cordial host and a pleasant man. As the day passed along, however, his company grew increasingly lackluster. With the passing of each hour, he appeared more and more distracted and less talkative. Even though he had insisted the four of them stay at the inn for the remainder of the day and for the night ahead, his thoughts continually seemed to drift elsewhere. For Cadwan, it was completely understandable. Losing one friend is hard enough. He couldn't imagine losing an entire village full of them. Calien and Cora had been in similar sorts all day, speaking very little. Each had a difficult time overcoming what they had witnessed outside.

Beyond the window, the great orb of light was just beginning to dip below the horizon. A sudden thought occurred to the soldier. "The day is nearly at an end and your wife and son have not yet returned. Are you not concerned about this?"

Wrenched from his own thoughts, Fargus snapped his head up suddenly. "What? Oh, yes, it is late. I shall go look for them."

"Perhaps we should go with you," Cadwan added. "It has grown dark and it could be dangerous out there. It is the least we can do after you have been so kind."

The innkeeper lifted a defiant hand. "Your offer is charitable, but you do not know your way around. The woods are so twisted a stranger could become easily lost. It is better if you stay here and rest."

"You show admirable concern for your guests," Cadwan replied, as he tapped his hand upon the pressed oak of the table. "However, it is hard for me to let you go alone. My offer is not one of charity, but one of concern. After what has happened here, it would be safer for someone to accompany you."

"No!" Fargus shot back, with sudden fury. He quickly composed himself and coolly soothed out his shirt, but it was too late for everyone not to take notice. They passed silent glances toward each other. The innkeeper continued, far calmer. "Please, I insist you stay. My conscience will not allow me to put you in danger, and my wife and child do not know you and may not trust you, if you call to them. I shall find them. Do not worry."

There was no immediate reply. Puzzled looks were thrown back and forth among the others. Eventually, Cadwan deemed he must say something. "Well, if that is truly how you feel, then we will stay."

Fargus vainly attempted a smile. "Thank you. I cannot in good conscience allow any more deaths in this place. I should not be gone long. If," the innkeeper paused and cast one last peculiar glance at each guest seated at the table. "if you will excuse me, I am going to get my overcoat and leave. I'll return soon."

The innkeeper departed, the sound of his footsteps descending stairs rose to meet them. Cadwan found it unusual for a man to keep his coat in the cellar. Moments later, the same steps resounded again, this time climbing the stairs hurriedly. Fargus reappeared into the dining room, embarrassed.

"I must have left my coat upstairs." He crossed the room and marched through a door on the opposite side. The four listened to the man pace up a different stairway and reach the floor above. The pounding of his steps echoed through the ceiling, and then a door slammed shut. Everyone remained silent, each electing to wait with their questions and reservations until the man had left the building and could no longer hear them. For a prolonged period they lingered, but no more noises were heard above.

"That must be one elusive coat," Alazar ribbed, with a smirk of his hairy lips.

Cadwan looked warily at the robed man. "Something is wrong. I wonder if the . . ."

A low, guttural moan intruded the soldier's comment.

"What in the name of great Calas is that sound?" Calien asked, shaking.

Slow, meticulous steps could be heard scaling the cellar stairs, and as they came higher the volume of the moaning increased.

"It is coming up the stairs," Cadwan spurted. Four pairs of eyes watched the door in rapt horror as footsteps and rasping vocals gradually climaxed, reaching the main floor. The door flung open and the party's panicked fear was nearly tripled by reality.

Jaws dropped as two humans, no, not quite humans, pushed their way into the room, a female and a child. The figures were repulsively disfigured, twisted and hunched over. The skin of the abominations was purplish-green and rotting over the bones of their deformed, emaciated bodies, while red eyes glowed with an awful madness. The room exploded into a frenzy of horror stricken activity. All four members of the party stumbled to their feet in haste, cursing unintelligible words and knocking the table over in a resounding crash.

"Gods alive! What . . ." Calien was trying to back away from the smaller figure, which came at him with uninhibited, evil intentions.

"Ghouls!" Alazar shouted.

"Ghouls? But what . . ." Calien started to answer, then stopped himself to concentrate on the monster that neared him. His jeweled sword was unsheathed and brandished before him, yet even then he was hesitant to attack the small childish figure.

"Walking dead! Do not let them touch you!" Alazar informed the prince. The robed man and Cadwan stood before the other ghoul, the female. She lumbered toward them with unthinking determination, as Cora scurried to the back, her screams forcing the others to shout above her cries.

Calien gaped at the ghastly shape before him. *Walking dead? How does one kill the dead?*

"You must dismember it, Prince!" Cadwan yelled. The prince's question had not been spoken aloud, but apparently Cadwan understood his next logical doubt.

Prince Calien nearly wretched at the thought of dismembering the form that loomed near. "This thing is but a child! I cannot do it!" He moved a chair before himself and the monster to impede its progress. The child-like ghoul mindlessly bumped into the obstacle several times, then proceeded to climb over until it could continue after its target.

"There is no hope for it, Prince!" Cadwan yelled above Cora's screaming. "You must end its tortured unlife! There is no other way!"

Cringing at what he was about to do, Calien lifted his sword and swept it hard. The small ghoul made little movement to avoid the attack and the blade cut cleanly through its neck, lopping the head clean off. The rotting skull bounced on the paneled flooring and rolled away. Decapitated, the ghoul took another step before falling to its knees, then its stomach. Its arms continued to flail for a short time before finally coming still. Calien closed his eyes like a child would do to make something scary disappear, but when he opened them the grotesque body still lay before him. He looked away and witnessed his comrades battling the woman ghoul.

Cadwan had his mace out and Alazar his staff. Simultaneously, Cadwan slammed his spiked weapon across the head of his foe while Alazar took out its legs with one swipe. Once on the ground, the two continued to pummel the writhing creature until its worm-ridden entrails dappled the area. The brief skirmish was over and the men gazed at their work, ruefully.

"This cannot be real!" Calien bemoaned. "What is happening? It is like the chilling stories my friends and I would tell as a child."

Alazar heard himself laughing. "Yes, life outside the cozy palace has its surprises. This is real enough, Prince."

Cadwan spat at the carnage, the spittle landing amid the bowels of what was once a woman. "This has to be Fargus's wife and child. They were ghouls. He must have kept them in his cellar and released them to feed on us, while he was safely hidden upstairs. Let us go pay this innkeeper a visit."

Seconds later, the four of them were upstairs standing in front of a closed door. Cadwan tried the knob, but found it locked.

"Fargus! Open the door!" the soldier yelled.

A muffled whimpering came from behind the door. "Please forgive me. I had no choice!"

"Let us in, or we will kick it down!"

After a slight hesitation, a scraping sound was heard, a couple steps, and then the latch released. Cadwan reached his arm forward and forcefully pushed the door back, throwing the man behind it to the floor. Fargus's room was simple and unadorned. The only contents were a bed, an old dresser, and a small rack where a handful of plain outfits hung. As they entered, the innkeeper cowered at their feet.

"Please spare me! There was nothing else I could do I only wished to be with my wife and child!" Tears of imminent death clouded the man's eyes.

Cadwan lifted his mace just above the head of the trembling man. "Explain yourself, now!"

"Did," Fargus paused. His face showed the signs of a man who already knew the painful answer to a dreaded question. "Did you kill them? My wife and child?"

"It was in self-defense and they were already dead. You set them upon us!" Cadwan's rare anger was rising at the innkeeper's useless responses.

Fargus placed trembling hands to his face and wept. "Eostra, Wilfrid, I am so sorry."

Alazar stepped over to the man and pulled his hands from his face. He bore a scowl that was twice as intimidating behind his facial hair and the hood of his robe. "You will join them, if you do not give us answers. Why did you loose them upon us?"

Fargus lifted watery eyes to the robed man. "I, they, need to eat."

"So you would rather have four peaceful, innocent guests killed at the hands of your wife and child, even though they are already dead? Insanity!" Alazar hissed.

Tears continued to stream down the innkeeper's face. "I did not wish for you to die, but I was bound to them and was ready to do whatever I must to keep them."

"They were already dead!" Cadwan shouted with rage.

"No, not dead. Just diseased. I was going to cure them . . . somehow." Fargus sadly shook his head.

"Ghouls cannot be cured!" the soldier retorted, pushing his mace up against the innkeeper's chin. The cold spikes of the weapon scratched thin lines of red in the man's stubbled jaw. "You were willing to sacrifice our lives for the sake of two beings of tormented evil. Give me a reason why we should spare you?"

Fargus lowered his head. When he spoke, his tone was slow and doom laden. "I could not leave them." He gazed at the floor, as if reliving the dreadful experience again. "The disease spread so quickly. When an infected person physically harmed another, they too would become ghouls shortly after and disappear into the night with their newly dead companions. When enough had vanished, they began to attack the village at night. Any survivors that had been injured were left to the same fate, while others were killed outright and eaten. The bodies outside," Fargus gestured to the window, "are the ones that the ghouls have killed and eaten. The smart people fled the village. One night, as my family prepared to escape Oester, my wife and son were attacked by those hideous monsters. I was able to rescue them, but not after they each bore awful gashes from the attack. I knew what their fate would be, so I locked them in the cellar before they showed the symptoms. I could not part with them. From the other side of the door I listened to them change, become undead. There was nothing I could do to stop it.

"Each night, I undergo the routine of releasing them to feed upon the corpses outside, while I hide under the bed. As daybreak nears, they return to the cellar and I lock them in. That is how I have kept some semblance of them with me." Fargus halted to look up at the faces of the four adventurers. "I am sorry. My love for my family clouded any thoughts of reason."

Glass shattering on the floor below caused everyone to freeze.

"Oh, no!" Fargus cried. "They have heard us. They are coming in! We must escape!"

"Who is coming?" Cadwan asked.

"Them! The ghouls! When it gets dark, they come from the woods to feed upon the dead! Or the living, if they can find them." The innkeeper stood and herded the party toward the door.

The five of them raced down the stairs and discovered glass covering the floor by a window. A ghoulish creature was attempting to crawl through the pane and enter the inn. The front door was banging, and the low, lifeless moans from behind suggested that more ghouls were trying to break it down.

"How many of these things are there?" Prince Calien shrieked.

"Too many," Fargus replied, leading the party into the back of the building. "We can flee through the back door. Come!" The innkeeper hastily guided them through two hallways until they reached a small wooden door. Before he opened it, he pivoted to view each of the others. "Listen carefully! When we are outside, you must run to the temple. It is but a short ways down the road. You will be safe within. Just run east along the road. The temple is easily recognizable. The undead will not enter its confines."

"What of our horses?" Calien asked.

Fargus made a face that portrayed half-amusement, half-revulsion. "Forget your horses. They are dead. Think only of your safety. The temple."

Cadwan grabbed the man's shoulder. "Wait. Are you not coming with us?"

Fargus shook his head. "No. I will lead the creatures away from you. I tried to kill you once and now I repay the debt. With Eostra and Wilfrid dead, there is nothing left for me anyway."

Before anyone could argue with the man, he flung open the door and ran off, heading toward the nearest ghouls. As the ghastly figures reached for him, he shouted back to the party. "Hurry! Go to the temple, or you will all die!"

The sight of Fargus encircled by several ghouls gave Cadwan enough motivation to heed the man's words. He bolted forward, opposite the way of the innkeeper. The others filed out behind him. A sickening carrion stench filled the air and the four were greeted with a scene that none could have ever imagined, not willingly. The ghouls roamed about, some aiming their sluggish gait toward the party, while others feasted upon the corpses of the dead that littered the ground. Even more gristly was that these same dead bodies, half-eaten, were attempting to rise, despite the fact that most were missing limbs or other body parts. One figure hobbled toward them on a crooked leg, its right arm torn off at the bicep and its jaw missing.

"What nightmarish hell have we come upon?" Prince Calien cried between rushed breaths. In respite, he looked away from the scene to the sky. It was starless this night. To the prince, it looked like swirling black ink, ready to fall upon them and wash them away.

Cadwan ignored the prince. "Do not stop to fight unless they directly impede our path! They are slower and cannot keep our pace unless we allow them. We go straight to the temple!"

The soldier led his party down the street Fargus had instructed them to use. Their path proved unimpeded until two shambling shapes emerged from the darkness ahead and staggered directly into their path. Not slowing down, Cadwan raised his mace and bashed one upside the skull. The ghoul's head exploded into an array of disgusting green viscera, as it crumpled to the ground. Calien sliced the other form in the chest, not killing it entirely, but knocking it effectively to the side as they continued on.

"There is the temple! Quickly!" Cadwan yelled. Ahead, the structure that Fargus spoke of, the temple, showed itself amid the carnage. The building was not as majestic as the soldier would have predicted. It was wooden and square, roughly the same size as its surrounding counterparts, with only a large holy symbol and a wooden sword looming above the roof to cause the small building to stand apart.

The four of them had nearly reached the door when Alazar shouted above the fray. "Cadwan, to the north!"

The soldier, and the others, instinctively twisted their necks the direction the robed man had stated. Each found themselves stopping in place, momentarily mesmerized by a sinister blue glow that emanated from the north. Cadwan quickly realized it was coming from the abandoned tower, the tower Fargus had depicted.

"What is it?" Cora asked, her eyes fixed on the azure glimmer.

"Something bad," Cadwan answered. He spun his body around and witnessed a half-dozen ghouls slogging toward them. "Inside the temple, now!"

The temple door opened easily. After the party successfully piled inside, Cadwan slammed the door and bolted the latch. The slow footsteps of their pursuers could be heard outside, but no contact was made against the door, even after several minutes. Perhaps Fargus had been right and they were indeed safe within the temple?

Cadwan leaned against the door and slid to the ground, his breathing heavy from the effects of their race. The others were in a similar condition and each took the necessary time to recover, both physically and mentally.

Outside, the wailing of the dead chilled their spirit and their resolve.

Darin was tired. As Kyligan watched the dwarf stumble through the flora, he found it impossible not to take pity on him. After being poisoned, the ranger had been gifted nearly a half-day's worth of sleep and the effects had been noticeable beyond his expectations. He was alert and watchful, willing to persist though a journey that had already become far greater than he could have ever envisioned.

Unfortunately, the dwarf's forlorn visage was a stark contrast to the vivacity of his companion. Kyligan guessed he probably hadn't slept in days. That, coupled with the recent events, was taking its toll upon the cleric. He had hardly spoken in the last hour and his pace scarcely altered from the rhythmic trot that carried him dispiritingly along. The ranger wanted to speak to him, wanted to encourage his friend to persevere through this bizarre journey they had taken, but presently Darin didn't seem open to any kind of persuasion. The stout dwarf just stalked ahead, with head bowed. Kyligan was convinced that there was something wrong. True, the dwarf had always had his moods, but this was different. Before, he would be openly irritable, pushing his moods on others with rash complaints and grievances until *everyone* knew he was in a foul mood. But now, it seemed like he had shrunken in on himself, taking his torment internally and giving nothing. It was not the same Darin that Kyligan had spent the last two days with and the ranger found himself worrying tremendously for his friend.

With the passing of dusk, the world of darkness and obscurity returned. Unwilling to ask the brooding Darin to call upon Frundin again, Kyligan had lighted one of his torches naturally, but the dim flame only partially kept back the shadows that pressed upon the three of them. Fortunately, there was some good news. The trees appeared to be tapering and the ranger was certain they would soon be free of the nightmarish soon.

Gathering himself, Kyligan spoke to Darin for the first time in a half-hour. "Take heed, Darin, the trees are thinning. We grow close."

Surprisingly, Darin stopped and swiveled to look back at Kyligan. He said nothing, but the tiniest air of hopefulness brushed across the dwarf's round face before he resumed his steady pace through the undergrowth. Kyligan found the expression, brief as it was, as a heartening sign. Perhaps the ranger was overreacting and the dwarf would be fine once they were freed of the Blackened Woods.

Squeezing Odna's hand, the ranger led the child forward and followed the blazing trail that the dwarf made through the brush. Then the air was once again alive with the awful clamor of uncanny howls, the same howls they had heard earlier. Darin's waraxe was instantly readied, as was Kyligan's sword. Odna clung to the ranger tight and they waited, casting helpless glances at the darkness around them until the shrieks slowly dissipated and they were once again engulfed in an uncomfortable, foreboding silence.

"It was louder that time," Kyligan muttered, stating the obvious.

Darin spat onto the ground. "And closer. I have a feeling that whatever is making those sounds does not possess noble intent."

"Quite perceptive, my friend," Kyligan's joke fell flat, as the dwarf gave him no reaction. The ranger inspected their immediate surroundings closely, but it was too dark to notice anything beyond the torrential gloom that hung over them. "Let us keep moving."

Nothing more was said and again Darin thrashed a trail west. All at once, the group stepped past the last tree and were suddenly in an open space, their feet falling atop soft grass and leaving a solid line of flora and trees in their wake. The black sky opened above them and the world took a different perspective. All three were taken aback, and Darin's legs actually bucked at the shock of it.

"I cannot believe it!" the dwarf stuttered, his face full of astonishment. "We are out of that hell! I had nearly given up hope!"

"And look!" Kyligan pointed a triumphant finger. Just to the north, not two-hundred feet away, sat a collection of small buildings. Even with night in full swing, Kyligan could make them out. "Oester! We have made it."

Darin gave the ranger a hearty slap on the back and chuckled, as renewed vigor and optimism imbued him. "I wonder if our friends have made it?"

Kyligan returned the dwarf's hopefulness. "They are probably waiting for us. We should not waste more time." He took a step forward, but something held him; Odna. Kyligan looked back at the girl. She had dug her heels into the soft ground and was staring ahead at the village, while she pulled on his arm, a look of panic draped across her soft features.

"What is it, Odna?" Kyligan asked.

The girl didn't answer. She shook her head fearfully for a moment and then looked into the ranger's eyes. Her expression was clear; *I am not going over there.*

Kyligan took several seconds to eye the girl. She was afraid, no doubt. Afraid of what? Kyligan had gotten the girl to speak a little during their walk through the Blackened Woods, but she still hadn't revealed how she found herself in the hands of a demon, so her story had remained a mystery. Obviously, the experience had scarred her tremendously and he didn't want to push her to divulge it too soon. Regardless, something spooked her. The ranger kneeled down to eye-level with the girl, meeting her with an overly calm, though concerned look. "Have you been there before, Odna?"

The girl nodded, slowly.

Kyligan glanced at Darin, who was watching with interest. Bringing his eyes back to the child, Kyligan asked, "Is there something bad there?"

The girl nodded again. Her petite figure trembled.

Darin walked up beside the two of them. He leaned close to Kyligan's ear and whispered quietly enough that Odna was unable to hear. "We have to go there, Kyligan, regardless of how the girl feels. It is why we came."

Kyligan nodded. Of course they had to go on. The problem was; what to do with the child? He hated the thought of forcing her back into a place that terrified her witless, but he couldn't very well leave her here; not alone. She had to come. *What a painful choice to make*, Kyligan admonished himself, though he knew there was no alternative. Brushing hair from his eyes, he gave Odna a fatherly look. "Listen, child, I know you are scared, but I will protect you. I *promise* you, I will not let anything hurt you. You have to trust me."

The girl fidgeted anxiously in place, as a lone tear fell from her eye. The sight of the tear running down her cheek nearly tore the ranger apart, but he remained resolute.

"Trust me. Are you ready to come?"

The girl seemed ready to burst into tears, but she managed to nod in confirmation. Kyligan took a firm grip of her hand and walked with Darin toward the assortment of ramshackle buildings ahead of them. As they drew nearer, Kyligan found it somewhat strange that no lights shown. Of course, it was the middle of the night. *Perhaps the whole village has already gone to sleep?* That was one possibility, though not a valid one. He knew of few towns or villages where there wasn't at least *someone* awake at all hours. The ranger kept his weapon at the ready.

The crunching sound of heavy footsteps on dried grass were suddenly heard. A moment later, the vague outline of a person shown ahead, walking their way. Kyligan held his torch to the fore, but the figure was too far away to be clearly seen.

"Hold there, friend. Who approaches us?" Darin, whose thoughts had run parallel with the ranger, spoke with calm authority.

There was no answer. The figure continued its gradual approach, ever so slowly coming into view. Kyligan felt Odna clutch him with frightful fervor, and he realized that whoever approached was likely a threat. "Darin, be . . ."

Kyligan's whispering was cut off by a sonorous, guttural noise that sounded like a cross between a moan and a hiss. When the dreadful sound stopped a few seconds later, the figure stepped into full view of the ranger's torch. Stunned, both Darin and Kyligan's eyes opened like large round coins. Odna screamed.

Before them stood a creature that was nothing short of nightmarish. The thing was once a man, Kyligan knew, but it was nothing but a monster now. Tattered and torn clothes hung from an emaciated body of bluish-purple skin. It's face was feral, with yellowed eyes that hungrily darted back and forth between Kyligan and Darin. Strips of dried flesh hung from its hands, hands that now sported fingernails twice as long as any man should ever allow. The most grotesque feature was the beast's tongue. The cord of flesh hung loosely from the opening of its mouth and dangled all the way to the base of its chin.

"What in the name of the gods?" Kyligan pushed Odna, who was still screaming, behind his back and lifted his sword.

"It is a ghoul," Darin stated with abhorrence. "An undead."

As the dwarf finished speaking, four more of the same monsters, in various conditions, emerged from the darkness, surrounding them. They eyed the group with evil intentions. Odna went hysterical, screaming at the top of her lungs. as she buried her face into the back of Kyligan's cloak.

"Gods! There is more!" Kyligan pivoted his body and waved his weapon outward.

Darin had his waraxe in both hands and was prepared to drive it into any ghoul that neared. The ranger shifted his body, so that he was back-to-back with the dwarf, Odna wedged between them.

"Darin!" Kyligan shouted. "Call on Frundin's might to turn these undead away. His holy power should overcome them, should it not?" Most clerics had a god-given ability to destroy or turn away creatures that lived an unlife and the ranger was more than ready for the dwarf to put such a talent to use.

Darin did not immediately respond. Finally he muttered softly, "I . . . I cannot."

"What do you mean? Why not?" Kyligan's eyes had not left the ghouls that encircled them, but he was intent to discover what ailed the priest of Frundin.

Before Darin could reply, the five ghouls gave a simultaneous low growl; a sound that bit sharply at the ears of Kyligan. Then, as if commanded by some unseen force, they moved in together.

*   *   *

"I do not understand," Calien spoke, pacing the meager confines of the temple. The building was little more than a small praying room, with a few wooden benches lining each side. Before the benches was a small water basin raised on a dais, it contents still full of holy water. On the walls hung religious symbols, as well as various weapons including battleaxes, swords and spears. Well schooled in religious matters, Calien had already determined the temple as a shrine to Thrygen. At first, Calien was surprised to see a temple dedicated to Thrygen, as he was an older deity that was rarely worshipped in the present generation. A god of conquest, Thrygen's followers were typically limited to warriors and marauders. Considering Oester was originally founded centuries ago by raiding barbarians, the placement of a shrine to Thrygen made sense to the prince.

"What do you not understand?" Cadwan asked. The soldier, along with the others, had spent the last hour hiding from the ghouls within the sanctuary of the temple. The undead monsters seemed aware that their quarry was inside Occasionally, they would stand outside the door and moan hungrily. However, none of the ghouls would touch the door, much less bash it in. Apparently, Cadwan surmised, the holiness of the temple kept their vileness at bay.

"These monsters, these . . ." Prince Calien paused, trying to articulate the proper word in order to fully express his disgust.

"As I said earlier, they are called ghouls." Alazar was sitting in one of the rickety pews next to Cora. The innocent, lighthearted halfling had experienced more in the last year of adventure than in all her previous years combined, but nothing could have prepared her for the utter gruesomeness of the undead. She was very shaken, and strangely Alazar had taken it upon himself to comfort her. He couldn't explain why he was bothering with her. He wasn't a compassionate person, nor particularly thoughtful. But something, he had to admit, was drawing him to her. He could think of no way to refuse it.

Calien scoffed at Alazar's arrogant correction. "Fine then. These *ghouls*," the prince's face showed obvious revulsion at using the word, "only come out at night? That is what the innkeeper said."

"True," Alazar replied, patting Cora's back. The woman merely stared at the floor, shaking her head. In her hands was Disfrazal. The tiny lizard also seemed to be trying to comfort her.

Calien walked over to one of the walls and studied a pair of ancient decorative swords hanging across each other. Archaic runes and symbols graced the steel of the weapons, giving them a sort of primordial appeal. Had the prince been a thief with no morals, he would have stolen the swords, as they surely would have brought a fine sum from any merchant. Fortunately, Calien was no such thing. Absently tracing a rune with his finger, he spoke. "Is there a reason they only stalk at night? Surely, they are not intelligent enough to realize that the cover of darkness will make an easier kill."

Alazar stood from his bench and patted the folds of his robes. "You would be surprised how clever some ghouls can be. Many retain various levels of intelligence. Regardless, the reason they come out at night is because ghouls are susceptible to sunlight. It burns their skin and causes them great pain. Extended exposure can even kill them." When Alazar noticed the look of surprise draped over the prince's face, he added, "Yes, ghouls can still feel pain, believe it or not."

Growing up, Calien had been educated by the finest instructors Calas had to offer. To complement that, he was a very eager and willing student. Knowledge in general fascinated him and he took it upon himself to learn as much as possible. That being said, he knew nothing of undead monsters. True, he had heard of such things growing up, but only in tales and stories spoken by peers and the like. Although he found it odd, and curious, that Alazar knew so much on the subject, he could not withhold his interest. The topic repulsed him, but his ingrained desire for knowledge won him over. "Are there other types of undead?"

"Many," the robed man answered. "Hopefully, you will never come across them. Most undead are entities of evil." Alazar smirked. "Thankfully, all are rare and some are merely lore taken out of context. The line of truth and embellishment is thin, indeed."

Calien absorbed his companion's words and considered them for several moments. "So how do . . ."

A shrill scream, a human scream, lanced its way through the silence outside. Shortly thereafter, it was followed by another.

Cadwan, who had been on the floor resting, jumped to his feet. "Someone is out there!"

The other three silently stared at their leader.

Cadwan met each gaze, with stoic determination. "If someone is alive out there, we have to help them!"

No one moved. Defiance etched their faces, a defiance stemming from fear and dread over what they had already witnessed.

"Damn you people!" Cadwan called out. "I am as scared as you are, but there is a *person* out there. Can you live with a death on your hands; especially a death of that nature?"

The scream rang out again.

Abruptly, Calien unsheathed his ornate blade and stepped near Cadwan. "I will go."

The soldier nodded and prepared his bow and mace. "Let us move." The two of them stepped to the door.

"Wait!"

Cadwan and the prince turned back in surprise. It was Cora who had called them. She handed Disfrazal back to Alazar. "I am going. Those things scare me to death, but that could easily have been me out there and I'd want as much help as I could get. Besides," the halfling cast a quick glance at Alazar and elbowed him gently in the ribs, "Alazar will watch my back."

The robed man only shook his head placed Disfrazal in a pocket of his robes, and readied his staff.

Cadwan looked over the group. "Then we are all going." The solider flung the door open and burst out, the other three on his heels. The scene was much the same as before. Bodies were strewn about in the darkness and randomly placed undead corpses sauntered among the carnage. The human screaming still persisted, much more clearly now that they were outside the walls of the temple. The solider took a moment to listen to the high-pitched resonance. "It is coming from the south. Move swiftly. We are quicker than the ghouls, so we can to stay out of their grasp. Follow me!"

The four of them ran with speed that Cadwan did not think was possible, especially Calien, who still wore his thick platemail. The nighttime air around them was heavy and foul, and the sordid stench of death permeated like buckets of human waste. Cadwan breathed through his mouth and pushed his legs to the limit. He didn't take the time to turn around and see if the others were coming. The sound of their cursory footsteps assured him they were.

Mercifully, there was little obtrusion from the wandering ghouls, as they raced along. Those that did notice the group were too slow to catch them. In no time, Cadwan had brought his followers to the southern border of town. The soldier could now hear shouts; shouts that seemed to be coming from living men, as indicated by the low pitch and lively manner. He strained to see ahead, but the encompassing darkness prevented any substantial visibility. Still, he knew they were getting closer because the screams had gotten far louder.

"Look! Over there!"

Cadwan swung his body to see Calien pointing diagonally to their left. The soldier could see it now. Several ghouls had surrounded a pair of victims, relentlessly hounding them. He couldn't distinguish how many people were being attacked, but he wasn't going to waste time counting. "On them! Kill the ghouls!" he ordered, slinging his bow from his shoulder and pulling taught the bowstring. His skill in archery was well established. Even on a dead run, he let one loose and watched the projectile plant itself firmly into the back of a ghoul. The monster howled in pain, but Cadwan didn't bask in the glory of his accuracy. Casting his bow aside, he unhooked his mace from his belt and ran to the fray.

Arrow still lodged in its back, the ghoul turned around just soon enough to witness the faintest glint of Cadwan's mace before the weapon caved in its face. The result was an explosion of purple blood and stinking gore, as the ghoul, its head now torn asunder, fell to its knees and was still.

Calien and Alazar had quickly taken another one down by surprise. Prince Calien sliced the unknowing ghoul cleanly through its misshapen spine, as Alazar bludgeoned the perverted head with his staff. Cora had successfully fired three crossbow bolts into yet another ghoul before the foul beasts realized they had been ambushed from behind. The three remaining ghouls, one showing a deep wound in its chest while another carried Cora's bolts in its side, took several steps back to survey their new opponents.

It was then that Cadwan recognized who the ghouls had been converging on. "Darin! Gods man, am I glad to see you!"

The dwarf forced his attention away from the undead monsters and over to the soldier. On Darin's neck were a series of claw marks that had drawn blood. Otherwise, he seemed unharmed. Standing next to him was Kyligan who also exhibited minor wounds on his arms, but nothing of critical nature. Huddled at the ranger's feet was a small child that Cadwan did not recognize. The dwarf's face brightened with elated wonder when he gazed upon the soldier. "I must say you came at an opportune time! Praises for that!" Darin proclaimed. He refaced the ghouls and snarled, "We can get caught up on old times after we send these monsters back to the world of the dead where they belong."

Darts of flame cast by Alazar whizzed past Cadwan and burst into the chest one of the ghouls. Set afire, the monster wheeled backward and tumbled into the grass, squealing painfully as it rolled to unsuccessfully kill the flames. The other two ghouls momentarily turned to look upon their burning comrade, and Darin used the brief moment to lunge an attack of his own. The beast saw him approach and swiveled to face him, but the dwarf was surprisingly quick and he lopped off the monster's right leg at the upper thigh. The ghoul fell, but even then, it did not stop. Its long, mutated tongue lapped eagerly as it crawled on its arms toward Darin's feet. Even from a few paces away, Darin could smell its fetid breath and he suppressed a gag. The dwarf yelled a battle-cry, as he raised his waraxe upward and lowered a killing blow down on the monster's shoulder blades. The sound of bones breaking and flesh tearing were heard as the large weapon tore brutally through the ghoul's body, severing the beast from shoulder to abdomen.

Cadwan and his own entourage finished off the last ghoul. The beast didn't stand a chance against four opponents. He dropped amidst his own rotted entrails and viscera to a handful of deadly hits. When the battle ceased, Cadwan quickly checked the others for injury. Alazar and Cora were unharmed, and Calien, save for the fact that he hadn't been able to hold back his nausea from the scene and was vomiting fiercely on the fresh grass, was also uninjured. Darin had the scratches on his neck, which the soldier knew would need to be looked at immediately. But Kyligan; strangely, the ranger hadn't moved since Cadwan had arrived. In fact, he was in the exact same battle stance.

"What is wrong with Kyligan? He is not moving," Cadwan asked the dwarf, while retrieving his bow.

Darin was busy wiping his waraxe on the grass to rid it of ghoul innards. At his friend's question, he sighed, frustration evident is his tone. "Because of their inhuman icy cold touch, ghouls can sometimes paralyze their pray upon contact. It does something to the nerves. Rest assured, it is only temporary. He should be fine in an hour, unless," he paused and ran his finger through his dense beard, "he has also been diseased."

"You have scratches as well," Cadwan commented, pointing to the dwarf's claw marks on his thick neck.

Feeling his neck, Darin grunted. "So, I do."

Cadwan lifted his eyebrows thoughtfully at the dwarf, and then he suddenly remembered the child, who was still cowering at the frozen ranger's feet. "And what of this child?"

"It is a long story," Darin answered.

"Well, we have time, but let us get somewhere safe first. There are more ghouls about and the temple is our only refuge. We can talk more and take a look at those wounds once there."

Cadwan hoisted the motionless ranger onto his shoulder. Moments later, one frightened child and six adventurers, each of them no less shaken than the girl, rushed back to the shelter of the temple. Just before they had made it to the door, Darin froze. "What is that?"

Cadwan swore under his breath, displeased at having to stop outdoors. Straining under the weight of Kyligan to see what Darin was talking about, he realized it was the blue radiance coming from the north. "We do not know, but it is coming from a tower. Come inside, I can tell you about it in the temple." Holding open the door, he quickly prodded everyone through the entryway. There was a successive sigh of relief from each person, as they entered the holy sanctity of the building and temporarily escaped what lie beyond.

Once inside, Cadwan immediately set to the task of helping Darin tend his wounds. Four long, parallel scratch marks lined the right side of the dwarf's neck. The edges of each cut were swelling noticeably and had altered into a bluish-purple color, while the surrounding skin was turning red with rash. The soldier frowned as he examined the shallow lacerations. Prodding them gingerly with his finger, he mumbled, "I am no healer, but I can see that disease is just starting to proliferate. I have some herbs and tonics in my pack that should prevent it from expanding in your body." Cadwan looked up at his shorter friend and twisted his lips sideways. "You are fortunate to be getting treated so quickly. Had we waited longer, even an hour from now, it would have been too late. You would have been one of those." He gestured with his hand, as if pointing past the wall and into the night beyond.

"Then waste no time," grumbled the dwarf. "I do not wish to spend the rest of my life as an undead horror."

Everyone rested, while Cadwan retrieved several dried leaves and two small vials from his pack. As he arranged the materials, he began to ponder something that had struck him as odd. Darin had healing abilities, yet the priest made no mention of asking his god to cure the disease. Why not? Perhaps he has already called upon Frundin several times recently and did not want to nuisance the deity? Even so, he was putting an awful lot of faith in Cadwan for something so critical. The soldier could administer the medicines adequately, but he didn't have the curative knowledge of Darin.

Finishing with his preparations, Cadwan spread a clear liquid over the slashes, then topped it with a white, velvety ointment. "Here, eat these." The soldier handed Darin three small leaves. The dried folio nearly crumbled in the dwarf's hand when he took them, but he quickly sucked each one down without a wince. "That is all I can do." Cadwan added. "We will find out soon enough if it works." He moved on to Kyligan's scratches and repeated the process, going as far as forcing the leaves down his throat and getting the ranger to swallow reflexively.

Within an hour, Kyligan's nerve-endings and bodily control had finally overcome his unnatural paralysis. When he was able to respond well enough, the others greeted him as cheerfully as was possible. He responded in kind, thanking them for his rescue. Odna sat next to him and he immediately clasped her head under his arm, keeping her close. He still couldn't explain why he was so protective of the young child, other than as her rescuer he felt an obligation to keep her safe. But there was something more. His thoughts were drawn back to his parents and the loneliness he had felt when they died. He wondered if he was subconsciously relating the girl to his own life, to the abandonment that he coped with for the better part of his youth. Although, he admitted, he had never undergone such a traumatic experience as being drowned by a demon-monster as she was, or witnessing horrible undead creatures at such an early age. Yet another reason to be protective of her, he supposed. The poor child has already gone through a lifetime of terror.

When all seemed calm, the party gathered to discuss the incidents that occurred while they had been separated. Darin and Kyligan went first. They thoroughly described the events once they entered the small grove of trees, from their unfathomable trip through the Blackened Woods to the battle with the Vargenzin. No details were left unsaid, at least not to Kyligan's knowledge. Unbeknownst to the ranger, Darin held back one very important event. Kyligan's recovery from the water-demon's poison was explained as a miracle of fate. Darin knew that not to be true.

The others listened with intent, their eyes going back and forth from Kyligan and Darin, occasionally falling on the girl. None interrupted. When the tale was complete they sat for a moment, unmoving. Alazar's sinewy voice finally broke the stillness. "Have you any explanation as to how you ended up in the Blackened Woods?"

Kyligan shook his head. "None. I know it sounds impossible, but that small grove of trees led us to the Blackened Woods. We never left the forest."

"Curious, indeed," Alazar muttered, though only to himself. Sitting on one of the pews, the robed man held his staff vertically into the air, Disfrazal balancing at the very top. It looked as if the lizard was playing some sort of game that no one paid attention to. "I wonder if it has anything to do with your dreams?" he added, wistfully.

"It must," the ranger answered. "Everything that I remember from my dreams came to fruition . . .," Kyligan's speech stunted abruptly, and then he added with a hint of suspicion, "except my death."

"Yes, you certainly are not dead. For that, we can be thankful," Cadwan added with a smile.

"Then your dreams are over?" Alazar asked, his curiosity peaked. He had seen his friend tortured with recurring nightmares far too many times and he hoped it had finally come to an end.

The ranger shrugged. "Who can say? I'll find out eventually, I suppose."

"But what of your story?" Darin butted in suddenly, looking at Cadwan. The soldier noted that Darin seemed overly anxious to change the subject, improbable as it was. "What happened to you after we parted ways?"

It was Cadwan's turn to recount everything, relating the incident in the Barren Hills with the strange barbarian woman, Birna. He then moved on to the core of the story, their encounter with Fargus, the discussion they had undertaken, and how the man had left the party as bait for his ghoulish wife and son. However, Cadwan made it a point to not exclude Fargus's redemption; how the innkeeper had informed them of the location of the temple before leading the ghouls away, so they could reach it safely. Lastly, he spoke of the peculiar blue aura coming from the tower on the northern edge of town.

"So, you believe this tower has something to do with the plague of ghouls?" Darin wondered aloud.

Cadwan nodded. "I do. What else have we to go on? The innkeeper said that the ghoulish sicknesses started just after the blue glow shown from the tower." Cadwan viewed the others and noted their grim visages. "We must at least explore it to be sure."

"None of the villagers explored it?" Darin asked.

"It was prohibited. The townsfolk believed it to be cursed."

The dwarf crooked his head in bewilderment. "Cursed?"

"If I may." Prince Calien asserted, looking at Cadwan. When the solider nodded in approval, the prince cleared his throat and continued. "I will make this brief. The north tower was the sight of the Hellar barbarian raid a century and a half ago. At the time, the baron of the village was Vernest, a warrior of great renown. Though his loyal troops were vastly outnumbered, he did well to hold off the fierce assault. During the attack, a small part of the tower collapsed, and eventually Vernest's forces were overcome. Though victorious, the Hellar never did populate the area. They were pushed back north by a great force in Mullikin. In time, the village was resettled by other locals and some who had originally fled the battle. The tower, however, was never reclaimed. As the years past, word of mouth spread that the building was haunted. Of course, there is, nor has there ever been, proof to back up any such rumors. Regardless, the tower is avoided."

The dwarf stood and rubbed his tired eyes. "Hmm, I need to spend more time learning the history of this kingdom," he remarked and then stretched out his arms in acquiescence. "I suppose there are few other choices. But if we are to search this tower, we must do so in the morning. I can hardly stand and I need rest."

"As do all of us," Cadwan confirmed. "We will sleep. Sometime tomorrow, when we are fully revived and the ghouls have all fled from the sunlight, we will investigate the tower."

"What about Odna?" Kyligan interposed. "It is not safe to bring her."

"I can stay here with her," Cora volunteered, hopeful. The woman had been sitting on the opposite side of the small girl and had spent the better part of the last half-hour playfully teasing her. It had helped the halfling almost forget about the frightening events outside.

Cadwan smiled, but to Cora's grief, he shook his head adamantly. "Your offer is considerate and thoughtful, Cora, but you know that we need you. Your thieving skills are indispensable. If there are locked doors to be picked, or traps to be disarmed, who else can we turn to besides you?"

The halfling frowned and said no more. It had been worth a try, at least. Though she was normally up for any death-defying escapade, she had little enthusiasm for battling the dead. She could think of few things less enticing. Unfortunately, Cadwan was right. No one else could rival her pilfering skills, so she was vital to the party.

"Then, I am staying," Kyligan announced.

Cadwan walked to the ranger and patted his shoulder. "You know we cannot do this without you, Kyligan. If there is truly something evil in that tower, *everyone* will be needed."

"So we just leave her here, alone?" The ranger's response was outwardly divergent.

"Kyligan," Cadwan offered before pausing a moment to gather the correct words, "it should not take us much more than an hour, two at the most, to investigate that place. The ghouls will not even be out during the day. She will be fine here in the temple and we will be back in no time. We can leave her some food and water to help her get by until we return."

Kyligan's face grew very serious, his green eyes driving into Cadwan. "And what if we do not return? What will she do then?"

The soldier didn't flinch at the question. "We will return. We have not come all this way to fail now. Surely, you feel that as well?"

Internally, the ranger admitted that he was confident in their success. As a group, they had overcome so much. Running his hand through his matted, loose hanging hair, he withdrew a long sustaining breath and whispered only to Cadwan. "She will not be happy about it."

Cadwan winked. "She gravitates to you. Your job is to assure her that she will be safe in our absence. I realize it is not an easy task, but I have seen you tackle responsibilities far more imposing than that of a small child."

"Come on, Kyl," Cora added, poking the ranger in the ribs. "None of us would leave her behind, if we did not think she would be fine."

Nodding slowly, Kyligan gave a faint grin. "I will tell her. But first, I can see we all need sleep. I was lucky enough to get a nap earlier, so I will stay on watch."

Not one person argued that point. In a short amount of time, the candles were snuffed and each individual had found a spot to rest their weary heads. Kyligan had unfurled his bedroll for Odna to sleep on. Within seconds, the exhausted girl was inhaling and exhaling in the deep comatose of sleep. Satisfied, Kyligan paced the chamber, searching the party for a particular individual. When he spotted Darin turning about as he lay, the ranger quietly skulked to him. He knelt down and spoke softly. "Darin, are you asleep?"

"Very nearly," came an irritated mumble. "What do you want?"

"Something has been on my mind. When we fought the ghouls, why did you not call on Frundin to turn them away? I thought priests had such power over the undead?"

Darin rolled his head sideways to look at the ranger. His answer was laconic and evasive. "They do."

"Then why did you not use that power?"

Quickly drawing his eyes away from the ranger, Darin grimaced. His tone was sad and weary. "Kyligan, we have been though much together in the past few days, but this is a conversation for another time. I am tired and need sleep."

Kyligan's reply wasn't immediate. He studied Darin's somnolent features and pondered his words. As he had suspected ever since waking from his poison induced slumber, there was something different about the dwarf. He had changed. "Another day, then. Sleep well, Darin." Kyligan stood and took position in a chair near the temple doors.

Soon, the entire party was asleep, the murmur of delicate breaths filling the room. Gazing at the party, Kyligan was left alone to his thoughts.

* * *

Dawn was just a hint in the hazy lavender clouds. The air was still, no wind, no sounds, only the calm tranquility of the approaching morning. *If only that were so,* Kyligan pondered, quietly closing the doors to the temple and returning to his chair. He had seen no sign of the ghouls that had run rampant throughout the night. Obviously, they had retreated to the cover of the Blackened Woods for the daylight hours. Unfortunately, the bodies of the dead remained sprawled over the ground, as did the sickening stench that emanated from their rotting corpses; a grim reminder of the previous night.

The ranger had been on guard duty all night and he remained every bit awake as the day before. Perhaps it was the anticipation of the tower excavation that gave him no yearning for sleep? Or perhaps, he reflected dourly, he was afraid to sleep for fear he might rediscover his nightmares had not abandoned him. Whatever the reason, he was eager to go. The others were still sleeping soundly and though he was anxious, Kyligan decided to give them as much respite as possible. What lie ahead would almost certainly present a challenging task and everyone needed to be at peak alertness.

He still needed to make his peace with Odna. She wouldn't take kindly to being left by herself, but he hoped she would come around with enough persuasion. Right now, she slept like an angel. His eyes fell on her. The girl was on her stomach, her blond hair draped messily over her face and her thin arms wrapped around the underside of the bedroll. The steady lifting and lowering of her shoulders ensured Kyligan that she was breathing just fine. Even while a peaceful smile grew across his face, he couldn't help but worry over her. She was in a place, a circumstance, never meant for a child of any kind. He silently vowed to do whatever necessary to free her of this undeserved fate. He didn't know if he could take care of her himself, but if not he was certain he could find a family willing to care for an angel.

If only he could stay alive tomorrow.

184

With the coming of sunlight, the darkness was dispelled, only to be replaced by a thick, swirling haze that seemed bent of engulfing them into obscurity.

The party stood on the uprise of a small hill, just before the daunting Tower of Vernest. Cadwan peered through the overhanging mist toward the dark, circular structure. A chill crept up his spine and he shuddered. As if the large white *X's* painted all over the sides of the rounded walls weren't enough of a warning, something deep within the soldier told him to turn back. Yet, Cadwan knew that turning back was no longer an option. As a whole, the tower was not overly impressive. It was no more than three stories high, with a parapet atop. The round greystone walls had aged terribly, turning an ash color and growing raw and jagged. From his perspective, a fourth of the tower, the front left portion, had crumbled to the ground. Rubble filtered from the collapsed portion like the purging of a malady and was strewn across the grass.

With modest concern, Cadwan shot inconspicuous glances at Darin and Kyligan. Thankfully, neither of them showed any signs of developing the ghoulish disease that had stricken Oester and turned the village into a living graveyard. The soldier privately smiled, grateful that the remedy he had administered was working.

"It is said that no one has stepped inside since the siege," Calien breathed in undertones, peering unabashedly at the tower.

"Then we will be the first." Darin offered. The dwarf bravely strode forward to the double iron doors that marked the entrance. The others cautiously followed on his coattails, throwing nervous looks back and forth. Taking a firm hold of the door handle, Darin gripped his waraxe and turned back to view the others.

Putting on their bravest faces, the company prepared their weapons and gave the dwarf successive nods. Darin pulled, but the door did not budge. With a cantankerous grunt, he pulled again, harder this time. Again, the door gave no ground.

"Get up here, Cora," Darin shouted. "I think it is locked."

The halfling weaved her way through the others and reached Darin's side. Leaning in, she meticulously examined the door for one full minute, then abruptly shook her head. "It is not locked. I think it has been welded shut, probably by the villagers. It will have to be forced."

"Step back," the dwarf muttered, pushing the frail halfling aside. He gave the doors a mighty kick. The iron slabs caved slightly, but did not part. "Someone get up here and help me knock this open."

Not wanting to look emasculate, every male in the party quickly stepped to the dwarf.

"I do not need all of ya!" he snapped and grabbed Cadwan by the arm, turning the solider to face the door. "Here we go. One, two, three . . ." The two men kicked the iron doors, simultaneously. A loud *crack* was heard and the doors burst open.

"Ha!" Darin proudly proclaimed. "That is how ya . . ." His victory speech was interrupted when his senses were invaded by a stale, musky odor that oozed from the recesses of the tower.

"Gods!" Prince Calien hissed, covering his face. "It is as bad as the smell from the ghouls."

Between coughs, Alazar added, "Obviously, the tower has not been well ventilated. Let us wait a moment for our noses to grow accustomed."

Little persuasion was needed for the others and several minutes passed before the party felt they could handle the heavy stench.

When Cadwan deemed everyone ready, he spoke up. "Alright. Get your weapons prepared and get a couple torches lighted. It looks dark in there." The soldier was in possession of the torches and he pulled two of the final three from his pack. After taking a moment to light them, he handed one of the burning sticks to Kyligan. "I want you bringing up the rear," he told the ranger. Kyligan nodded and moved to the back. With mace in hand, Cadwan proceeded forward into the shadows of the tower.

Although gloomy, the entrance room proved less ominous than Cadwan anticipated. A few vagrant beams of sunlight escaped the cracked exterior and dimly illuminated the inner walls. The torches assisted the faint light to give the party ample range of vision. The party stood in the tower foyer, which was nothing more than a humble looking hallway in the shape of a *T* that turned left and right further ahead. The passage would have seemed inconsequential had it not been for the striking appearance of the one hundred and fifty year old remains of a ferocious battle.

The floor was littered with bones. Some were still attached fully to the skeleton that had once supported a living body, while others were scattered and indiscernible to where they once had belonged. A rectangular fifteen-foot long table had been upturned, many of its chairs smashed and broken. Evidently, much of the fighting had taken place in this very room. Countless objects of war were scattered about the bones; swords, shields, and the like.

Cadwan noted that a very faint blue aura, the same aura that was seen from the night before, hung lazily about them. Strangely, as if it were an entity in itself, the glow provided no illumination.

"What a mess!" Prince Calien stated the obvious, kicking a broken candle that was resting near his feet. A tiny cloud of dust wafted upward from the action.

"Watch your step everyone," Cadwan warned. "A sprained ankle is not what we need now."

The scraping sound that followed his words resounded clearly about the foyer. It lasted for only a second, but every person took notice.

"Did you hear that?" Cora mouthed, her eyes darting in every direction.

"It came from up ahead," Kyligan said, "from the floor I think. A mouse, perhaps?"

The scraping returned, but this time the origin of the noise became plainly, and dreadfully, clear. The party watched in horror as several bones scuttled across the floor, ultimately joining others of the same ilk. At the far end of the hall, a figure rose up among the wreckage and scrutinized the party. It held a well crafted shield in one hand and a sword in the other. Tattered and frayed chainmail draped its frame. When the realization pummeled Cadwan, he sucked in a quick breath. The figure was no person! It was a fully formed skeleton! A battle helmet sat upon its bony skull, while vacant eye-sockets viewed the intruders unemotionally.

"Our bedamned luck! This is absurd!" Darin spat. "More undead! What is happening here?" The dwarf took one step forward and called to the figure, "What is your purpose, tortured one?"

The figure remained silent and motionless, its unreceptive skull twisted to the side, as if waiting for something. Then several more skeletons emerged from the stone floor, all in various states of completion. Some bore weapons, others none at all. A few were even missing limbs and ribs. The leader seemed content at the advent of his outlandish army. His impassive stare returned to the party. With slow, deliberate steps, he approached them, while his cohorts mindlessly followed.

"They are attacking!" Cadwan yelled. "Defend yourselves!" The solider counted nine advancing skeletons. It could be worse, he decided, preparing himself. With full force he slammed his mace into the chest of one particularly eager foe who had gotten ahead of the rest. With a resounding clatter, the ribs of the skeleton shattered. At the same moment, Alazar extended his arms and from open hands a ray of white light sprung forth. The beam flew directly into another skeleton's spine and the undead form exploded into several hundred fragments.

Prince Calien looked at his robed companion with baffled eyes. "I thought you only knew flame attacks," he said.

Alazar grinned. "Not all my arcane knowledge is fire related. Although fire is often the most effective, this is not one of those times."

The skeleton enemies were direct and fearless in their attack, but save for their leader the party made quick work of them. With powerful attacks, their frail bodies were shattered about the foyer, making a worse mess than one would have thought possible. Only the leader still stood, his prowess obviously a cut above the others.

Kyligan and Cadwan were in a dead-lock with the undead warrior. It held their attacks at bay, without giving ground. At one point, it bashed his sturdy shield into Cadwan's forehead, causing a small cut. As they battled, Alazar crept quietly behind the fierce undead adversary and with the bluntness of his staff, whacked off its sword arm. Left with no real offensive capabilities, the persistent skeletal warrior soon fell to the brute force of his opponents.

When the battle was completed, the party looked over the carnage. The hall looked much the same as before, except the bones were now even more spread apart and splintered.

Darin gazed at the destruction, his face full of disgust. He ruefully shook his head. "These long dead corpses are not rising willingly," he stated. "Something horrible is causing this."

Kyligan pulled the skeleton leader's shield from the rubble and turned it over in his hands, studying it. The steel shield was constructed exceptionally well. It looked as if it hadn't aged a day, much less used in a battle nearly two-hundred years prior. The silver polished edges still held their gleam. On its face was an intricate design of a bull holding a sword and inscripted along the top was the word *Mordan*.

"Take a look at this, Darin. You needed a shield."

Darin took the disc from the ranger and hefted it. It was lighter than he expected. "Not bad. It is not as large as my old one, but it will do." The dwarf swung the shield about him in mock battle. He felt a faint pulsation beneath his fingertips, as if the object were alive. "It feels enchanted. I will have to get it examined by a smith when we return to Calas." The dwarf paused when he saw the inscription. "Mordan? Who is that?"

Every head turned to Prince Calien, who always seemed to know obscure historical facts. The prince brushed blond locks from his forehead. "Mordan . . ." he mouthed, tapping his chin, "the name sounds familiar, but I cannot place it."

"He was probably one of Vernest's warriors," Cadwan furthered. "It looks like more than a few died in this room."

Darin angrily huffed. "Yes, and now they are coming back alive. We must end whatever curse is causing such atrocities."

The party nodded their agreements and took to searching the first floor in its entirety. They discovered that the main floor was mainly used to house soldiers of the tower. They came upon an old guard room, a barracks and the officer's quarters. It was evident that no fighting took place in these rooms, as each proved void of any more long dead corpses. Cora, who was rummaging through cabinets and drawers, was able to pick the lock of an old oak chest in the barracks. Inside the container were several silver pieces and an old dagger. She tossed the dagger away, but quickly pocketed the coins without a second thought. Ultimately, the company found themselves reunited in the lobby and looking at a pair of staircases, one leading down, the other upwards.

"Which way?" Alazar asked.

"Perhaps we should split up?" Prince Calien offered. "It would cut down time in our search."

Darin emphatically shook his large head. "No. It is never wise to split a party up. We stay together."

"Then let us investigate the top portion first. If we are still unsuccessful, we can delve below the ground." To Cadwan, the idea of descending into the underground bowels of the tower was not on the top of his list. He had heard of warriors that made a living by searching ancient dungeons and caves, battling monsters that never reached the surface, but he was not one that yearned for such a life. He secretly hoped that whatever they sought was somewhere above them. Lifting his torch, he led the party to the eroded stairway that ascended to the next level.

In décor, the second floor hallway was very similar to the first. No adornments or fixtures, save for empty sconces, lined the rough walls. However, the hall itself ran straight across, never turning. On the opposite end was yet another set of stairs, obviously rising to the top level of the building. Flanking the hall were two doors on the right and a solo door on the left. Had there not been a skeleton sprawled on the floor before of them, the corridor would have been completely empty. As Kyligan, bringing up the rear of the line, emerged onto the upper landing, the skeleton mindlessly lifted up and stalked them, its bones rattling and scraping each other. Cursing, Darin quickly sent the tormented atrocity back to the abyss by bashing his newly gotten shield upon its head. Bones scattered across the floor in all directions. Shaking his head, the dwarf muttered, "Quickly, let us get these rooms checked. Kyligan, Alazar, and Cora, you check the doors on the right side. The rest of us will search this door."

"But you said we should not split up," Calien sputtered.

"Not on separate floors. Here, we are but a shout away from rejoining. Let us be on with this."

Kyligan, Alazar, and the halfling broke from the others and neared the first door. Alazar reached for the rusted knob and gave a satisfied smirk when it proved unlocked. When he pulled open the door, he nearly stepped onto a floor that wasn't there. Alazar teetered forward, certain he would fall, but Kyligan's strong arm grabbed the man's robe and yanked him back.

"Good job, Alazar, you sharp-eyed mastermind," Cora mocked. "Nothing gets past you!"

The robed man profited no retort for the halfling. Instead, he gave Kyligan a look of *thank you* for pulling him away from certain injury and possible death.

Kyligan dismissed the gratitude and moved to the edge of the broken floor. The halfling and Alazar crammed into the space to look on as well. Surrounding the sides of the room, breached only by a massive break in the wall that opened into the light of day, were several shelves. Books that had managed to avoid falling were strewn about haphazardly. A two-foot length of flooring, littered with rubble, ran along one side of the room.

"This is the section of the tower that collapsed," Kyligan stated.

Alazar sighed. "A library. Such grand knowledge wasting away. If we had time, I would salvage as many of these tomes as I could."

"Perhaps you can return after our success," offered the ranger.

A familiar rattle sounded in their ears. On the far side of the damaged room, a skeleton, who had been balancing on the edge of the floor, began to animate. As it nearly stood to full length, its left leg discovered the missing floor. While the adventurers watched, the skeleton tumbled comically over the edge, shattering as it crashed onto the jagged rubble below.

"That was easy," Cora ribbed with a smile, and the three companions moved to the second door. Again, Alazar found the portal unlocked, but this time he made certain there was floor beneath him when he stepped inside. The room was cluttered with badly burnt books and scraps of paper. A desk to their left was overturned, leaning crookedly on a torn bed. A fireplace rested in the corner, ashes lining the underside.

Kyligan and Alazar flipped over the desk, standing it up on wobbly legs before searching its inners.

"Empty," Alazar mused audibly, with a tinge of disappointment.

"Hold on," Cora muttered, pushing past the two men. Her small arm reached into one of the drawers, prodding around until an ever so gentle *snap* resonated. She then removed her arm from the open drawer and reached around to the side of the desk. It looked as if she were pulling on solid wood. Instead, a secret compartment released.

"How did you know?" Kyligan asked, fascinated by the halfling's work.

Cora shrugged, meekly. "The desk is far too large for only a single drawer in the front. It was obvious." The woman pulled out two single leaf sheets of parchment and studied them. Sparse writing covered the flaccid leafs. "It looks like simple notes, or reminders." She began to read them aloud.

As Alazar and Kyligan listened, a few passages captured their attention above all else.

. . . *Today, Baron Vernest passingly mentioned how much he fears growing old. As is my job, I advised and comforted him, saying age is not a bane in all ways. Age grants us wisdom and a moral-fiber that nothing else can develop. And of course, age is also inevitable and therefore not worth agonizing over. He walked away from me. As he left, he called back, "Must death loom so heavily at the end of such wisdom?"*

I was speechless . . .

. . . Baron Vernest is again using my tomes of demonic energies and has locked himself in the laboratory below. I must remember to ask him why he insists on researching such dark scriptures and then record my findings within my journal . . .

. . . Yesterday, I advised the baron that these books he manipulates should not be handled unless the possessor is fully aware of their dark power. He shouted furiously, claiming I should mind my own affairs. Fearing the worst, I hid the books today where he would not find them. Upon such a discovery, the man near went mad with rage, threatening me with harm if I did not relent and give him the books. A curse upon me . . . I relented . . .

As Cora finished her full recitation, the two listeners remained thoughtfully silent. Alazar scratched this tousled beard, eyeing the delicate ink lines. "This was obviously the room of the baron's advisor," the robed man remarked. "These papers the halfling girl has discovered might have provided us important information."

Alazar's usage of the phrase 'halfling girl' was an obvious slur thrown in Cora's direction. She scowled at him irritably, mentally recording that she owed him an insult.

"The writings also mentioned a journal," he continued. "I wonder where it is?"

"It might be around here somewhere," Kyligan said, driving his sword through the bed mattress to check the insides.

The remainder of the room was scoured, but little else was discovered. Cora found only a trio of silver pieces, which she hastily kept. Only Alazar found something useful. Laying near the fireplace was an old spellbook that apparently once belonged to the former resident of the chamber, its corners singed only slightly. Alazar eagerly lifted it and flipped through the pages. "This is marvelous!" he stated, excitedly.

"Do you ever get tired of that stuff?" Cora muttered.

Alazar dropped smug eyes on Cora. "My child, one can never get enough knowledge, especially of the arcane." He reached inside his robes and pulled Disfrazal from an inner pocket, placed the lizard on his shoulder, then inserted the book into the very same pocket.

"I am no child," Cora shot back, squaring her petite shoulders on the robed man, "and I am about ready to shove that book of yours up your underside!"

Alazar viewed the mischievous wrath in Cora's sharp eyes for several seconds. Abruptly, his thick lips curled into a smile of resignation. "Understood."

Hoping the feud was arrested temporarily, Kyligan announced, "Let us bring our discovery to the others."

They found them in what looked to be a bedroom for a small child. The room was well-furnished, with a couple of expertly-woven tapestries hanging on the walls. A small table with two tiny chairs sat in the middle of the room, and a bed was pushed against the wall to the right. Next to the window was still another chair, and what sat in the chair was a saddening reminder of the cruel realism of the tragedy. The skeletal remains of a small child, wearing the moldy remnant of a pale blue dress, gazed out into the azure sky beyond the tower.

"The baron had a daughter," Prince Calien lamented. "Even the young are not spared from the evils of war."

Cora's eyes fell to the skeleton's neck. Wrapped around the small neckbone was a sparkling silver necklace with an exquisite moonstone charm. The halfling knew such a prize would most certainly bring nearly two-hundred gold from a merchant. Yet, when clarity overcame her sense of greed, she quickly turned away her eyes and cursed herself. Stealing from the corpse of an innocent child was one action she would not succumb to.

Kyligan had almost brought up the subject of the discovered papers when the skeleton began to shift and slowly reanimate.

"No! This is enough!" Darin screamed. "Must this curse warp even the helpless?"

Everyone stepped back and cast aggrieved looks at one another. None were certain if they were actually supposed to smash the diminutive bones of the now rising skeleton, as they had done all the others. The shape eventually stood from the chair and awkwardly turned their direction. Cadwan turned his head to the side, closed his eyes as if the action pained him, and sent his mace through the feeble ribcage. The bones splayed in every direction.

"You can rest forever now, child," Darin forlornly said.

Cora located the silver necklace, which had skidded under the table. Grasping it firmly, she walked over to the bed and dropped the treasure atop the pillow. This was one room she would leave untouched.

*　　　*　　　*

The party stood within the hall of the third floor, each with weapons drawn and fully alert. One wooden door flanked them on the right and two on the left. A ruined staircase that once led to the roof sat at the far end. From the visible trappings, it was clearly evident that this floor was primarily used by the baron and his wife. Lavish paintings draped the walls on each side. Striding leisurely across the hall, Cadwan examined the pictures closely.

"This must be the baroness's side." The solider gestured toward the various images of flowers and meadows. Conversely, the opposite side contained images of glorious battles and heroic warriors. "Their tastes were certainly different."

Prince Calien ran his finger along the picture of a knight slaying a mighty winged panther. "Baron Vernest took great pride in his war prowess. From the looks of it, he thought of little else."

"We can confer over the intricacies of art later," Darin grumbled. "Let us finish these rooms."

Cadwan opened the door to the baroness's side, but when he witnessed the interior he did not step within. Along with the rest of the tower that paralleled this section, the baroness's antechamber had collapsed. Except for a small slab of wooden flooring along the right corner and a five foot space in front of a separate door to the left, the ground was almost entirely destroyed. A fine looking jewelry box was situated on the isolated slab and it immediately grasped Cora's attention when she peeked into the room.

"We cannot reach her bedroom. The jump is too dangerous." Cadwan shook his head.

"I can make it," Cora fervently announced.

Cadwan frowned. "Possibly, but the risk is not worth it. We do not need you falling to your death unnecessarily. We can always come back later."

"But I can make it. I promise I can."

"Cora . . ."

Before Cadwan could argue, the halfling had pushed him away from the doorframe and was preparing to leap across the gap, aiming for the slab of flooring in the right corner; the jewelry box. With stealthy efficiency, she flew over the drop and landed both feet with perfect balance upon the segment of floor. Lifting the container, she shook it, pleased to hear the muffled sound of jewels bounce within the wooden interior. Tossing the container over to Cadwan, she proceeded to make her return leap. Cadwan grabbed her firmly when she seemed to waver along the edge.

"That is good enough, Cora. We . . ."

"I can make the door, as well," The halfling interrupted, energized by her first triumphant foray.

Cadwan wasn't thrilled by Cora's risk taking, but he also knew that once the halfling had made up her mind, there was little persuading her otherwise. "Are you certain, Cora? This jump is further."

The halfling gave herself room and then flung her body airborne. Her eyes widened when she realized she had misjudged the distance and found herself coming dangerously close to the serrated edge. She reached up with her arms and caught the top of the flooring, as her legs fell beneath. Adrenaline surged through her limbs and everything seemed to fall to slow motion as she struggled to keep herself from slipping and falling to a certain death below. With one forceful heave, she managed to pull her legs up and over the wooden plank. Curling her body against the closed door, she took several calming breaths and wiped instant sweat from her brow, while her onlookers finally managed to exhale.

"That was too damn close, Cora!" Cadwan admonished from the other doorway.

"Sorry about that," the halfling replied, still gathering herself. She stood and viewed the door to the baroness's room. It was well fitted and sturdy, and wouldn't budge when Cora pulled on it. "Hold on, it is locked." The halfling withdrew a small lockpick from her pocket and set to work. A minute later, the bolt released, unlocking the door. Cora replaced her tool and turned back to smile triumphantly at the others.

"Cora! Take this with you." Cadwan tossed a torch across the miniature chasm. The halfling caught it easily. With a resolute breath, she pulled a dagger from her boot to carry in the other hand and opened the door.

Cora immediately felt a shiver run up her spine. The baroness's bedroom chamber was unnaturally cold, dilapidated, and yet, hauntingly beautiful. Fixtures of all variety adorned the elegant space, but the centerpiece was a spectacular satin-covered bed. The marvelous divan, with its spiraling posts and hand-carved headboard put the rest of the décor to shame. Within the room, not a sound could be heard, nor movement of any kind. Cora found the utter stillness oddly disturbing. As she brought the full torchlight onto the bed, something even more unsettling gripped her. Someone appeared to be sleeping in it.

Nervously adjusting the grip of her dagger, she crept silently forward. Drawing near enough, she found it was not a person, but a horrific corpse, apparently that of Baroness Anisa. Unlike the skeletal remains they had previously encountered, Anisa's corpse remained strangely well-preserved. Gray and purple skin gripped tightly against her facial bones, and thin strands of hair, now gray, tumbled lazily to the side of the pillow. Her mouth gaped open, showing clear agony before whatever death had taken her. The baroness's passing must not have been a peaceful one, Cora reflected. Spider-webs clung to the cadaver, undisturbed for decades. The halfling had to momentarily turn away from the sight to recover her resolve. After several self-inflicted words of encouragement, she returned to view the ghastly sight.

The halfling gazed at the corpse's arms, purposely avoiding a glance at the tortured face. A pen and a small leather-bound green journal sat cradled within the arms of the deceased. Around the corpse's neck was a chain holding an iron key. Cora glumly shook her head. She understood that both objects could be important, but she trembled at the idea of touching the cadaver in order to attain them. Squinting her eyes, she slipped the blade of the dagger under the chain and pulled it over the baroness's head. As the chain slipped free, the lifeless head lolled sideways, a stretching noise coming forth as the skin moved for the first time in years. An involuntary shudder gripped the halfling at the sight and sound of the hideous corpse in movement. Although it filled her with revulsion, she slipped the chain over her own neck for easy carrying.

She knew the journal would not be so easy. Both arms were draped firmly over the top of the volume and Cora would have to pull it loose. Sheathing her dagger in her boot, she wedged her hand beneath the book and pulled.

A bone-chilling shriek came forth.

Cora swung her frame around to see a translucent form soar through the air toward her. Instinctively, the halfling dove to the ground. The ghostly apparition swooped overhead, barely missing her as it continued to squeal loudly. Terror consumed the halfling. She went faint, feeling a calming darkness seep its way over her. *No! I cannot faint now!* Forcefully, she shook away the dizziness. Leaping to her feet, she pulled the journal free and bolted in sheer terror for the door, not bothering to look back.

In the hallway, the others heard the dreadful noise and began shouting Cora's name. The halfling appeared through the door frame, her blue eyes stricken with panic. She tossed the book and torch to Cadwan, then leapt wildly across. This time, she had no trouble reaching the other side as her fear-driven adrenaline gave her an extra boost. She went crashing into Cadwan, knocking him and any others in their path backwards into the hall.

"What is going on?" Cadwan screamed, clamoring to his feet.

Cora never had the opportunity to reply. Right through the wall, still shrieking madly, coalesced the ethereal phantasm. The entire party gaped at the spectacle, rendered speechless in awe. The hideous form swayed in the air, its shape vaguely humanoid, but without clear features and sifting to nothingness below the waist. Its face was gaunt and frenzied, as if something had driven it mad. Suddenly, the spectral shape shot toward Prince Calien with amazing speed, screaming as it came.

Calien never had time to raise his weapon. He merely curled in with closed eyes and prepared himself for whatever incorporeal damage the monster would inflict. But seconds passed by and after feeling nothing, he reopened his eyes. The apparition was still upon him, flailing away, but he felt no damage from her attack.

"I do not believe it can harm us," Alazar pronounced.

"Well, as great as that is, how do we get rid of it?" Cora had no intention of having this maddening ghost follow them everywhere they went.

The spirit continued its futile attack on Calien, swinging ethereal arms across his body in a depressing act of vain belligerence. The prince raised his sword and slashed it sideways through the phantasm. Although the weapon passed through the attacker as though striking only air, the sallow form seemed to fade ever so slightly.

"Again, Calien!" Darin called. The dwarf had shifted his heavy physique next to the prince.

Calien swiped his blade again. As before, the apparition faded. Darin joined in and the two men ultimately forced the ghostlike monster to disappear altogether, leaving only faint streaks of white vapor behind. Soon, even the vaporous material dissipated.

His task completed, Prince Calien fell against the wall in a troubled blend of fear and bewilderment. "What is happening here? None of this is natural!" He lifted his arms over his blond hair, covering his quivering face. "Am I even awake? This place is nothing but a hellish nightmare!"

"Keep your wits, my Prince," Darin retorted, placing a steady hand over Calien's shoulder. "You are still alive, are you not? We will survive this. Cora," the dwarf turned to view the halfling, "what happened in there?"

Cora described what she had seen in the baroness's bedroom, as well as her actions up until the point of the apparition's attack. "I do not know why her body had retained its skin. Even thinking of her face makes my skin crawl." She then pointed to the small journal, still in Cadwan's hand. "Perhaps there is something revealing inside."

On command, Cadwan opened the tome and studied the pages meticulously. Only a few entries proved legible, but he read what he could.

. . . *My husband, Vernest, has become anguished. He feels terribly betrayed and has acted furiously toward me and Clorisa. I am fearful of his rage . . .*

. . . The siege continues. We cannot hold much longer. My love wishes for us to retreat in the dungeon, but I beg him otherwise. I would rather stand here and perish nobly than exile myself to a dark and miserable end . . .

. . . My daughter has been shot by an invader's arrow. One of the servants found her this morning. Despite her father's order to have all openings to the tower shuttered, her window was opened. She always loved to look at the night sky. I did not even hear her cry. My sorrow overwhelms me now and my husband is detached from me even more. There is no place to bury her . . .

. . . I now see everything clearly. We are doomed. Soon, I will bring this to an end myself, for I should not have to suffer any longer . . .

Cadwan stopped his reading and slowly closed the tome. "You do not think she meant . . ." the soldier let the rest of his question trail off.

"It would explain the specter and the preserved corpse." Alazar thoughtfully eyed the journal in Cadwan's hand. "Often one's spirit cannot pass beyond if it had taken its own life while consumed with madness. Its existence is far too tormented and it will not let go of the reason it was driven to death. Now that we have destroyed the baroness's maddened spirit, her body should decay naturally."

Cora slapped Alazar on the thigh. "I am shocked. Your collection of useless knowledge is actually paying off."

The robed man looked down at the halfling, prepared for a suitable retort, but his intentions were halted by Darin's deep falsetto. "We have the baron's room to search yet. Come, let us finish up here. The dungeons below await." With no hesitation, the dwarf pushed open the door on the baron's side and confidently strode in. The others brought up his heels.

To the relief of many, the sitting room proved void of undead and was very nearly empty. Although more war-wrought paintings lined the walls, the stone statue in the center forced everyone's attention. The elaborate sculpture depicted a large man holding a great two-handed sword, a fierce and battle-worn scowl across its proud face.

"Baron Vernest, no doubt," Cadwan remarked.

"I think so. Take a look at this." Kyligan was examining a mural that deviated from the common theme of war. It was a portrait of the baron's family. Vernest appeared as a robust, dashing young man, with a black mustache. The apparent plainness of his wife, the baroness, was belied by her beautiful brown hair and wide, green eyes. The daughter looked about five years of age, her face timid and introspective. None of them looked happy posing for the picture. Kyligan frowned. "I would say 'happier times,' but perhaps that is not the case."

Prince Calien drew close, rapt by the portrayal, particularly the image of Vernest. After several long moments, he muttered, "Even the most powerful are not immune to misfortune."

"Sometimes I think the powerful are *more* susceptible to misfortune," Cadwan offered.

"The door is open to the baron's chamber." Darin stepped around the statue and guided his burly physique to the door. Breaking away from their examination of the portrait, Calien and Cadwan quickly joined him.

The room of Baron Vernest left no doubts to the party that this was his domain. Extravagant tapestries, no less vibrant than when the room was occupied, hung on all sides, and the high walls were lined with the mounted heads of several beasts. Among the gruesome trophies, Cadwan could discern a basilisk, an owlbear, and two wyverns along with several other monsters he had never seen before. In the corner was the baron's bed. Next to it was a fine cherry armoire. Across the room sat an oak desk flanked by a chest. A fireplace, destroyed from the outside by the siege, carried a strong draft, as well as light into the bedchamber.

Upon the desk was a single piece of parchment. Prince Calien moved close and lifted the paper, blowing off the layers of dust that covered the letters.

"What does it say, Prince?" Cadwan asked, noting Calien's expression after reading the words.

Calien said nothing, the hand holding the parchment trembled slightly.

"Prince?" Cadwan ran over and witnessed the evident pain in Calien's eyes. Taking the paper from his hand, Cadwan read the words:

Hold steady now and your bravery shall be rewarded. Assistance shall arrive in due time. – His Royal Highness, King Lodan of Calas.

Calien was still speechless, his teeth gritted. Utterly baffled, Cadwan threw a questioning look at Darin, but received only a puzzled shrug in return. "What is it, Prince?" Cadwan asked.

"Do you not see? The former king, *my* ancestor, forsake Oester! The innkeeper was right. We let the tower fall to its doom, even though we could have prevented it." Calien banged his fist onto the desk, which held firm despite the force.

Cadwan placed a hand on Calien's shoulder. "It was one-hundred and fifty years ago. There was nothing you, or your father, could have done."

"A shameful thing, nonetheless!" Calien spat. "And to promise aid, knowing full well he would not send it."

"Perhaps that is why you came, to make things right for your bloodline." Cadwan didn't know if there was any validity to the statement, but it sounded good. Truthfully, over the course of their adventure, he had grown quite impressed with the young noble and his sense of justice. It was no mystery why Calien would be aggrieved over such news. He was young and idealistic, envisioning the world in only two colors, black and white. Treachery to him was a despicable act, and yet his own father had most likely succumbed to such acts more than once. Most leaders, even respectable ones, often did. It saddened Cadwan to think that one day when Calien was king, he too would probably yield to acts of injustice, if it meant the survival of the kingdom. Young and idealistic evolves into shrewdness, cunning, and necessity; the way of the world.

Calien tore up the parchment. "I only hope my father knows nothing of this."

"What does it change if he did? He could have done nothing."

"I got it!" Cora suddenly screamed. During the moral reflections of the prince and Cadwan, the halfling had been busy working the lock on the chest near the desk. Upon her success, she eagerly pushed open the lid and smiled at her fortune. Inside, shining at the open air, was a pile of gold and silver, along with some red garnet gems and a rolled up scroll. She snatched the scroll and handed it to Cadwan before delving into the gold.

The soldier grasped the scroll, slid free the ribbon and methodically unfurled it. He shot a look at Darin.

The dwarf was aware of Cadwan's various expressions and this particular one alarmed him. "Read, friend."

My greatest enemy has reared its head upon me and my sword is useless against it. It is age, it is death. It stalks me like a cloud of darkness, waiting in baleful anticipation. I am still healthy, yet I see it in the distance, smiling at me. Whispering to me. Goading me closer with each passing day.

I will not surrender, I will not fall. I will conquer death.

I will live forever.

XXI

The darkness of the basement churned before them, the flow of immersed shadows pulling at every fiber of their being. Cadwan could not discern if it was a warning to force them away, or a calling to draw them nearer. Either way, it left him with a dreadful sense of unease. Even standing before the stair that would lead them into the basement of the tower, he could feel evil wrap its invisible tendrils around the party. What they sought was below, awaiting them. One way or the other, their expedition was soon coming to an end.

As before, the soldier took the lead position of the group, with Kyligan and his torch acting as rear guard. Pushing his fears to the side, Cadwan led them into the lasting blackness. With each step, his muscles tensed. He felt as if he were being slowly swallowed by an eternal malevolence. The stairs seemed to last forever, but ultimately he reached the landing and paused to allow his vision to amend itself to the dying luminance. Unlike the tower above, no light existed within the confines of the dungeon. Even his torch's efforts seemed obstructed, somehow. More inexplicable, the mysterious blue glow that had surrounded them since they entered this accursed place had thickened, growing ever more prominent, yet still giving them no additional illumination for their vision.

Unwilling to spend eternity in the bowels of earth, the party swept through the top level of the dungeon. To a mixture of relief and disappointment, they found very little. Among the several rooms, including a kitchen and various storage spaces, all of which showed the obvious scars of disuse, the only threat had been a half-dozen dire rats that hungrily attacked the party. With little effort, the overlarge rodents were cut down.

An iron trap door, clearly visible amid the stone-tiled ground, marked the path that would take them deeper still. Cadwan stepped ahead and pulled on the handle, but found the portal did not budge. "Darin, give me a hand. This damn thing is heavy."

Darin situated himself next to the soldier and both pulled with every ounce of force they could muster. The door lifted ever so slightly before hitting what sounded like a bolt.

Cadwan nodded. "It is locked. Cora, can you . . ." As Cadwan turned to speak to the halfling, he suddenly remembered the key that was still hanging from her neck. "Cora, do you have any idea what that key is for?"

The halfling wrapped her hand around the iron key, feeling its weight. "Are you thinking it might open the trap door?"

The soldier shrugged. "Why not? It has to open something."

Cora slung the chain over her head and placed the thick instrument into a keyhole situated just above the handle. She tried to turn it, but her diminutive strength was unsuccessful.

Cadwan moved her aside and tried his own hand. With great effort, the key budged. A moment later, the click of a bolt unfastening sounded off. Cadwan stood and wiped sweat from his brow with an already dirt-stained hand. Looking at the others, he asked aloud, "Now, why would the key to this trap-door be around the neck of the baroness?"

Though his voice was emotionless, Darin chuffed at the question. "Has anything we have encountered thus far made sense?"

"I suppose not, but perhaps we will get our answers below."

The two men bent over the cover and grasped the handle of the heavy iron door. With great gnashing of teeth and bulging of muscles, the door raised, accompanied by loud creaking. The lid had nearly swung open entirely when Cadwan cried out in agony. The solider was staring at his feet with a look of horror stricken pain.

On the ground, next to the opening of the trap door, two iron spikes with steel tips had shot up from the ground. One had missed the unaware solider, but the second had driven itself through Cadwan's boot and into his heel, pushing four inches up his leg. Already the floor had started a small crimson puddle.

With a show of remarkable strength, supplemented by his immediate concern for his friend, Darin shouldered the cover fully open by himself and rushed to Cadwan. The soldier had not moved from the spot, he legs still holding him in a standing position.

"A spike trap. Gods, Darin, it is way up there." Cadwan spoke through trembling lips and a quivering body. He leaned on his square-bodied friend.

"Listen, Cadwan." Instantly, Darin's tone had altered from his irritable mood to that of a calming priest. Sadly that is no longer the case, he lamented to himself. But this was no time for self-pity. Pushing the depressing thought away, he said to Cadwan, "I have to lift you up. It will hurt, but you cannot remain in this spot. Do you understand?"

Cadwan said nothing. It was not difficult to discern that the soldier was in severe pain and scared for his life. Normally, the dwarf knew Cadwan as the consummate leader, one who rarely showed fear or pain for the sake of the others. Yet now, he was clearly distraught. His eyes were shut tight and both hands pressed tightly on Darin's shoulders. The dwarf realized it made no sense to wait on his actions. Not giving Cadwan more time to think about the process, he dropped low and wrapped his arms around the knees of his limp friend. With one singular heave, he propelled the body upward and off the iron barb. Although Cadwan gritted his teeth to keep himself from screaming, Darin could plainly hear the grunts and curses escape his pursed lips.

The dwarf placed his body in a sitting position along the wall and went about removing the man's ruined boot. The rest of the party watched the procedure without a sound, a clear mixture of shock and panic veiling their features. Darin took one glace at the object responsible and nearly wretched. The iron spike was longer than he had guessed, almost a half-foot long and blanketed by Cadwan's blood. The soldier's wound was no less grisly. A gaping hole was nestled in the center of the man's heel, turned red and black from blood that was caked around the edges and working its way toward the center.

Kyligan stepped forward from the onlookers and spoke aloud. "Darin, you need to heal him now."

The dwarf paused a moment and glowered. He knew that eventually this time would come, yet he was no more prepared than had it come earlier. Perhaps he could bluff his way beyond revealing what had become his anguished secret for over a day now. "Maybe not," he stated, trying to sound authoritative, though it came out as weak and unconvincing. "If I can . . ."

"No, Darin." Kyligan was in no mood to prolong the conversation. "You must call upon your god and heal him now! He is losing much blood and the wound might become infectious."

Lowering his head, the dwarf let out an elongated breath of air. With a shake of his head, he simply stated, "I cannot."

"Why? What do you mean?"

Darin lifted his eyes and met Kyligan's evenly. "I can no longer call upon Frundin."

Kyligan was taken aback. Never did he expect to hear such a thing from Darin, a man who had always proclaimed each of his deeds as dedication for the glory of Frundin. It seemed a farce, a jest. Yet, from the dwarf's countenance alone, Kyligan could see he spoke the truth. "How can this be?"

Darin groaned, making no efforts to mask his grief. Even Cadwan, wounded leg and all, had become enthralled by the dwarf's revelation and temporarily forgot his terrible pain. Darin removed Cadwan's pack from the soldier's waist and untied it. Pulling out a rolled bandage, he dressed the injury, as he continued to speak. "I have never abandoned Frundin, nor would I ever, if that is what you are wondering."

The chamber was deathly quiet. Every member of the company waited for the dwarf's rationalization for his inexplicable separation from his deity. Darin could not bear himself to meet their eyes, but he knew their thoughts. Inexplicable. That's what they would think. A man that has devoted his entire life to the faith has unaccountably pronounced that he can no longer do so. As he considered it, it seemed inexplicable to himself. Pangs of regret coursed his body. And yet, looking at Kyligan's face, a strange sense of overwhelming pride filled him, as well. *Have I truly given the ultimate sacrifice to save a life?*

"Remember," Darin said, his discourse intended solely for Kyligan, "when you were infected with poison by the water fiend?"

"Of course I remember. I nearly passed beyond the gates of death."

The dwarf shook his head in correction. "No. You *would* have passed beyond the gates. There was no uncertainty in the matter."

Kyligan pitched dubious glances at the remainder of the party, then again fixed them on Darin. "I do not understand."

"You were going to die. You had, in fact, nearly done so." Darin's expression went reflective and pensive, as if reliving the experience. "Our journey through those blighted woods had given me a sense of admiration for your courage and fortitude, as if Frundin himself had touched you with his strength. Not only had you saved my life, but that of an innocent child. Though I knew I should have let you die a hero, your valor touched me and I could not. I pleaded to Frundin, begged him to spare you. But of course, there are prices to be paid for such colossal actions. And my price was a hefty one, for I have lost my connection to my god."

As the confession penetrated Kyligan, he was simultaneously honored by Darin's sacrifice and appalled at his detachment from a faith he had given so much to. "So you can no longer call upon Frundin?"

"It is as if an unbreakable wall has been placed between us. I no longer hear his assurances and commands, and no more can I speak to him." The dwarf tore away a second bandage and continued his work. "That is why I did not turn away the undead in the village. That is why I cannot heal Cadwan now."

Kyligan furrowed his brow, creases of bewilderment forming around his eyes. How could he respond to that? He was alive because of his sacrifice, and yet the weight it had placed on him was unbearable to witness. Kyligan found he could not speak.

"There is nothing that you need to say," Darin proclaimed, almost reading the ranger's mind. "You do not owe me your life, nor would I ever wish it that way. It was a conscious decision I made. I alone bear the guilt and satisfaction of my choice." Even the dwarf was not convinced of his own words, as he realized that Kyligan would never, not in a million lifetimes, forget such a sacrifice made for his life. He only hoped the ranger would not be guilt-ridden.

A thousand questions bounded though Kyligan's mind, but he understood that this was not the time, nor the place to perpetuate the discussion. The man's sorrowful revelation had been made, and if Kyligan felt beckoned to continue his queries it would be at a later time. For now, they would have to make the best of the circumstance laid before them. Looking over Cadwan's wound,

Kyligan stated, "He cannot continue like this. For him, it would be unhealthy. And for us, a hindrance."

In consent, Darin nodded. "Agreed, but we cannot just leave him here alone. We should take him down with us and leave him near the stairs with someone else."

At this, Cadwan objected, albeit weakly. "I need not for someone to watch over me like a child. I will be fine on my own."

"You have no say in this," Darin contended, emphatically, as if he were speaking to an underling. He had sufficiently wrapped the man's lower leg, but that didn't prevent the soldier from weakening. Darin needed someone to stay with the man, to speak to him and keep him conscious and aware in such dreary surroundings. *No man should die in a place like this.* Yet, if he passed out now, there might be no bringing him back.

"How is your leg, Cadwan?" Kyligan asked the soldier.

Cadwan grimaced, not from pain, but in an attempt to keep himself cognizant. He was light-headed, like someone who had consumed too much ale. "I cannot feel the lower half of my leg, so there is little pain to feel."

Kyligan threw Darin a worried look. The news could have been better.

"Come, Kyligan, help me carry him below." The dwarf gestured the ranger near the man's head. Together, they hoisted up the limp form of Cadwan and descended the steps that lay beyond the trapdoor.

*   *   *

"Can you feel the evil of this place?" Cora voiced with concern. "It chokes me."

The company was situated at the base of the stairs that led back up through the trapdoor. The room was wide and spacious. Empty braziers lined the walls and a single square table was pushed to one side, its aged woodwork cracked and frayed. No chairs surrounded it. Along with the occasional weapon, a smattering of bones lay dotting the cold limestone floor and the party instantly grew attentive at the appearance of the skeletal remains.

Cadwan leaned back against the wall, very near the bottom step, with eyes closed and muscles relaxed. The rhythmic motion of his chest and occasional movement of his head insured the others he was conscious.

"It chokes the light, as well." Kyligan muttered, holding up his torch. The illumination from the stick was practically non-existent, giving only a small percentage of the light it should have. "Something horrid lurks here."

Darin lighted the last of the torches, giving them an additional source, but the radiance remained minimal. The dwarf gruffly adjusted the suit of plate over his bulky frame.

The clatter of bones sounded about the room like a premonitory omen. As the party unfavorably expected, the bones were shifting to form the grotesque lifelike apparitions of their former selves. When the corpses fully rose, Darin made a quick count. Nearly ten full, one brandishing a monstrous two-handed axe. The bizarre army advanced with mechanical determination. The dwarf caught himself momentarily regretting his newly established inability to turn undead.

"Make a line!" Darin commanded. The four men formed a row of defense, while Cora, her crossbow and dagger of little use against chintinous bone, fell behind to cover Cadwan. Before the two units clashed, Alazar sent forth another ray of white light that quickly inaugurated one unfortunate skeleton as the first victim of the battle. The remaining corpses pressed forward, hacking away with their weapons, or if no weapons were available, simply grabbing at their adversaries. Darin met the charge of the most formidable foe, the wielder of the axe. Using one of his patented low blows, he slashed at the femur. The skeleton collapsed under the attack and Darin dropped his shield across the skull, smashing it to bits. The dwarf allowed himself a brief smile of satisfaction. He was continually astounded at the prowess of his newly gotten shield. It was an impressive instrument of combat.

Next to him, Prince Calien had already amassed a large number of skeletal parts around his feet. With each subsequent encounter during the journey, the prince had grown ever more confident and aggressive in his inborn sword wielding abilities. The adjustment from sparring with other soldiers to the reality of true combat no longer existed, and the mindless skeletons stood little chance against his efficient attacks. He shattered one after another, with his ornate blade.

With the battle soon over, the four men dourly appraised their work. Each of them were injury free and a little surprised at how quickly they had dispatched their larger numbered foes without Cadwan's help.

Darin returned to the resting soldier's side. "Cadwan?"

"Yes?" The answer came through closed eyelids.

The dwarf reached into his pack and withdrew a tiny vial filled with a thick blue fluid. "Here, drink this. It will not fully heal you, but it will give your body added strength, as it mends the wound." He popped off the cork and drew the vial to the soldier's lips. Wordlessly, Cadwan bent and swallowed the liquid, then returned his back against the wall. Darin glowered, an expression all too familiar as of late. His features radiated concern for his friend. "Cora, you will have to stay here with him."

The halfling's eyebrows curled downward. "Why, because I am the only woman?"

"No," Alazar chimed in, "because your exasperating banter will surely keep him awake."

Cora stalked toward the robed man with ill intent, but she was grabbed from behind by Darin. The former priest whispered gently, "Child, you have a caring presence. Cadwan will be comforted and calmed by your disposition." The dwarf peeked at the soldier, then the other men of the party before lowering his voice even more, so that only Cora could hear. "And also, I cannot spare the abilities of the others. If what we face is as formidable as I believe, we will need all the offensive power we can muster."

"And what if you need a lock picked?"

"We will be on the same floor, so it will be easy enough to come back and get you. Cora, you must agree to this." Darin softly pleaded. "We simply cannot leave him here alone."

Cora exhaled, then nodded in concession. "I know. But if you hear me screaming for help, you had better be here fast!"

Darin smiled. "Even faster."

The halfling took a spot next to Cadwan, while the four other men readied their arms and moved off, disappearing within the cloak of blackness that hung like a void over the walls and floor.

It became apparent that the size of this area was much larger than the previous levels of the tower. The men moved through two connecting corridors, a deafening quiet stalking them with each step. For Kyligan, it was like a pocket of silence had ensorcelled the party. Even the sounds of their boots upon the cold stone appeared muted in the dank, dreary atmosphere. Eventually, they came upon two rows of prison cells, one lining each side of the hall. Noiselessly, they inspected each hold, but discovered each of them empty – until they came to the last. Sitting alone, inconspicuous atop a stone bier, was a thin manuscript. Kyligan stepped ahead and lifted the loosely bound papers, opening the cover. "It is the journal of Welnor, advisor to the baron. Strange that it would be in a prison chamber."

"Strange, indeed," Alazar confirmed. "Please, friend, enlighten us with its content."

The ranger rested himself on the bier and began to recite the last several entries of the journal penned by the baron's advisor. The script was more attune to that of a story than most journals and Kyligan, not the most fluent of readers, did his best to ebb his voice to match the sentiment of the writing. Everyone was engrossed in the tragic tale of Welnor and though perceptive glances were cast at each other, nothing was said until the ranger finished.

"The baron had truly gone mad," Darin spat.

"But what madness forces a man to imprison and torture his own men?" Prince Calien incredulously stammered. The prince was horrified by the account, continually shaking his head in disbelief.

Darin could only shrug. "A sane mind can never make sense of madness."

Alazar scratched his coarse chin hair. "Perhaps this Welnor was correct and Baron Vernest was indeed seeking some form of eternal life?"

"And willing to sacrifice all his friends to achieve it," Darin added. "One thing confuses me, though. The journal states that the baroness killed herself down here after the siege took place, yet Cora found her corpse high in the tower. How could it have gotten up there?"

Alazar considered the question. "The only assumption I can make is that if something does truly lurk down here, it might have carried her body above. For what reason, I cannot say."

Darin gripped his waraxe tight. "Well, there is more yet to discover, so let us be about it."

The four continued their excursion, delving deeper into the shadows that would lead them to an undesired, yet necessary destination. Though it seemed impossible, the sheer force of malevolence that pervaded about them grew more threatening with each step and it took all the determination the four men could muster to carry on, pitting their mental fortitude against an ominous evil. The lack of luminosity, swallowed up by the overpowering darkness, did nothing to help matters. Their stoic expressions were only a mask to the trepidation each man suffered beneath.

The corridor turned sharply and was followed by a door to their left that caused the party to halt its progress. Darin checked the knob and found it unlocked. With a subtle glance at the others, he strode within, his weapon raised. The others followed in similar state. To their relief, they discovered the room void of threatening enemies. It was a small chamber, but the walls contained shelves that were lined with books. Surrounded by four chairs, a table sat in the center of the room, a lone tome atop the wooden slab. Alazar went to the book and curiously examined it. It was extremely thick, bound in black, with large red lettering.

"The Tome of Necromancy," Alazar announced. "There is no longer any doubt. The baron was seeking unlife." He lifted the volume and fingered the soft binding, but the others noticed that he made no effort to open it and view the pages within. "I have heard of such a book. It deals with various ways to raise the dead, or sustain an unnatural life. If the baron has used this book, it is no surprise what has happened to the people of Oester, for using such methods often have other undesired effects. Essentially, you are making a deal with evil itself."

"But that was over a century ago." the prince stated. "Why would Oester become plagued only now?"

The robed man lifted his eyebrows. "Perhaps it took time for the evil to seep beyond the tower walls?" Alazar lowered his eyes, as if he were speaking to the floor. "We must find whatever is down here and destroy it now."

"I think we are all in agreement about that," Darin added. The dwarf then caught site of Alazar placing the tome in his robes. "You are keeping that demon possessed thing?"

"For now, yes. It is safer in my hands until I can determine how to rid the world of it."

"It does not bother you to have it?" the dwarf asked, incredulously.

Alazar gave a sly smile. "Very little bothers me, my dwarven friend."

Darin only shook his head. He knew Alazar was not a man to be understood easily, but he didn't much like having the dark tome accompany them wherever they went. Though he wasn't going to object now, it was something he would have to keep in the back of his mind. He hoped Alazar wasn't foolish enough to keep the book in his possession for very long.

The corridor they followed came to an abrupt end with one final door. The portal itself looked no different from the previous ones they had encountered, yet each man paused before it, as if they all had heard the same voiceless warning. The air turned noticeably cooler.

"I have an eerie feeling that beyond this door lies the conclusion of our journey," Alazar said.

Kyligan looked at the robed man. His face ever composed and unemotional, Alazar was a man who rarely showed evidence of tension or strain. Yet now, just before they faced an unknown, but obviously powerful enemy, the ranger could discern the faint signs of nervousness creep upon his face. Alazar tapped his fingers uneasily on his staff, his eyes darting back and forth. Even Disfrazal wasn't himself. The lizard had fled into a pocket, only to emerge seconds later. This process was repeated two or three times. It seemed the reptile could sense his master's dithering.

"I will not let my fears do me in," Darin proclaimed, forcing the door open before he could stop himself. He strode within, trailed cautiously by his comrades.

"A laboratory," Alazar commented, a tinge of relief in his voice.

Two long tables flanked the walls of the square room, each holding glass flasks and other delicate alchemy equipment. Various glass vials were shattered about the floor. The men stepped carefully around the jagged shards. Across the room was a bizarre looking steel door, with strange inscriptions covering every inch. The blue glow, brighter than ever, and some kind of mist or smoke seeped slowly from the bottom. Darin moved forward to view the inscriptions on the portal. Runes and signa were etched along every available space, forming patterns and designs the former priest could not decipher. He felt pain, the pain of knowing that once he could have asked Frundin to help him understand the writing. Now, he was helpless. If he asked for help, he would get nothing but a black void. Why must life come to such decisions? But truly, what noble man could have willingly let a friend die? *My hand was forced!* The dwarf sighed and traced several lines with his stubby finger before calling to Alazar.

"Come, look at this."

Alazar left alone the alchemy tools he was studying and neared the dwarf, following his gaze. "It is a glyph of warding."

"Can you read it?" Darin asked.

The robed man continued his stare at the deep lines, mouthing something under his breath that the former priest could not hear. Abruptly, he shook his head. "Very little. The number five and six are used a lot and it says something about a demon. That is all I can understand."

Darin turned sharp eyes to Kyligan. The two of them had already dealt one time too many with a demon, costing the dwarf his priesthood. He was not thrilled with the prospect of battling another.

The ranger could read Darin's expression. Instead of affirming his suspicion, Kyligan gave the dwarf an encouraging grin.

"We have done it before, my friend. And now two formidable allies stand with us."

Darin frowned, but said nothing. Returning his attention to Alazar, he asked, "Does the glyph have to be removed in order to open the door?"

"I do not think so. It only appears to be a warning to keep others away."

"Then let us enter and end this abomination once and for all." Darin gave his comrades a stern look. "Are you ready for this, friends?" Concurrent nods, tentative as they were, answered the dwarf. Content with their resilience, he took one prolonged breath, then reached out and felt the door. It was icy cold to the touch. He nudged it only slightly before pulling back his hand. The steel portal swung inward and creaked loudly on its hinges, the sound echoing in the room before them. A rush of ice cold air accosted the adventurers, setting their nerves on end. The entire room was filled with a hazy mist that was set off by an odd, diffuse blue glow. The mixture cast insubstantial shadows and reflections to sporadically jump about the room. The strange sapphire glow served as the only source of light in the room. Each man found it nearly impossible to see beyond ten feet, as their torches had suddenly been snuffed out.

His heart beating heavily, Kyligan squinted to see into the blue, misty film. "Can you see anything?"

"Nay," Darin replied. "This strange blue darkness is . . ."

At that moment, an eerily wicked, mechanical-sounding voice echoed forth from the recesses of the haze.

"Lodan, is that you? Come forth, for I have waited many years for this day."

*   *   *

A slender hand reached out and shook his shoulder. Gently the first time, then more roughly. "Cadwan. Cadwan!"

"Worry not, Cora, I am not dead," the soldier said, with a soft voice, though he made no move to open his eyes. His arms were folded across his chest, his legs sprawled forward.

Cora sat beside him, simultaneously watching her charge and the surrounding shadows. "How do you feel?"

Cadwan bent the knee of his good leg to adjust to a more comfortable position. "I do not feel pain. I just feel tired and weak." He stopped talking and the deathly silence of the surrounding area took the forefront. With his eyes closed, the effect seemed lessened. He could not see the plainly evident look of concern draped across Cora's face.

"This place is awful, Cadwan! I can hardly stand it." The halfling's crossbow rested on the ground next to her, a bolt nocked and ready. "If you die, I could not bear it alone."

"I will not die." His slow metrical breathing, lifting and lowering the arms on his chest ever so slightly, did some good to ease her anxiety. "My wound is grievous, but Darin was quick to act and stopped the bleeding. Though he could not heal me properly, his bandage work was sufficient. I am more concerned with losing the use of my leg after this is over."

"But what happens, Cadwan? What happens, if the others do not succeed? What if they are slain?" Cora scooted her body closer to Cadwan for reassurance. "If they cannot defeat the evil, surely we would make quick work for the enemy. What can we do if the others do not come back?"

Cadwan opened his eyes for the first time since sitting down. He fixed them on the halfling female, his visage grave and serious. "If after some time the others do not return, we will get the hell out of here."

XXII

The mists parted.

Appearing beyond the murk, approaching slowly, was a figure shaped vaguely like a man. But it was no man and the four companions each took a step backwards at the horrifying apparition before them.

A thin veil of grayish pale blue flesh gripped exposed bones, several of the skeletal parts protruding from the skin. Around the head, which bore only remnants of gray and shriveled hair, sat a silver and moonstone coronet. A dark jeweled necklace hung around the bony neck and glowed ominously, highlighting the shiny suit of silver mail worn over the monstrosity's body. Within its skeletal hands was a very large and formidable sword. Its eyes, two electrifying balls of blue light, flashed at the party with a penetrating gaze.

With the mist dissipated, Darin was able to look past the terror before them. In the back of the room sat an iron chest and a bizarre looking steel and gem-encrusted apparatus. The object appeared to be the source of the eerie blue glow that had followed the group throughout their excursion inside the tower. Simply viewing the apparatus sent shivers down the dwarf's back. He had no doubt that whatever the object was, it furthered the evil of the tower.

The abyssal knight stopped several feet before the party, its gaze terrifying and saddening all at once. "Thou art not Lodan! Dare a soul unknown come to disturb me now?" As it spoke, its jaw moved up and down like that of a puppet.

"What have you done, demon?" Darin shouted at the creature. "The dead rise and innocent people turn to ghouls because of you!"

The creature took one step forward, but did not raise its sword. It made no acknowledgement of Darin's words. "Leave me. Return only when you have brought forth Lodan, for I await his apology. Only then may my soul finally rest and depart this unrelenting existence."

"But Lodan has long passed on, creature of darkness! Centuries ago. Your apology cannot come from the dead." Darin suffered a twinge of nauseousness from the sheer evil of the monster. Quickly, he subdued it and maintained his bold air.

"Such avowals cannot be true." The abyssal knight was undeterred. "He simply refuses to admit his transgression upon me. Lodan has forsaken his people. Bring him to me."

The dwarf raised his waraxe and contemplated a different approach to parlay, but a hand on his shoulder stayed him. It was Prince Calien. The prince gently motioned for the others to stay back before he moved close to the armored horror that was once Baron Vernest.

"Vernest! It is I, Calien, son of Anuron, whose father's forefather was your king, Lodan." The other three men were taken aback by the strength and conviction in the young prince's words.

The abyssal knight seemed to consider the proclamation. Its blue orbs glowed brightly, scrutinizing the prince. After several long lasting moments, it said, "Yes . . . I sense Lodan's blood in you, young one. Then it is true? Lodan is gone? Has it been so long?"

"Longer," Calien stated. "He has rested in eternal peace for many years. I am heir to the throne and am here to deliver an apology long overdue." The prince drew even closer, so that the cerulean luster that sparked from the undead baron's eyes reflected directly off his fair skin. "But before this happens, you must first tell me what you did to your people. What absurd lengths did you take to further your illicit obsessions?"

Although the abyssal knight could make no facial expressions, it somehow portrayed a manner of someone wrongly accused. "I did nothing to wrong my people."

"Surely, you remember the horrible experiments you did upon them! Killing people who served you faithfully, without question, right until the moment you deceived them. Torturing them, without remorse. Only a monster does such things. What of your daughter and your wife? Do you remember them?"

"I ask for my apology, descendant of Lodan." The skeletal face was still fixed squarely on Calien. It was impossible to determine if the undead knight had even heard, or had simply ignored the accusations the prince had thrown its way.

Remaining remarkably calm in the presence of such a daunting foe, Calien slowly nodded. "Very well, Baron Vernest. Once upon a time, you were King Lodan's vassal and you served faithfully. I come here now to apologize, for you indeed have been wronged." Calien brought his hand to his chin, reflecting over his own words. "Let it be known, though, you have also turned your eyes toward unnatural preservation. You hoarded items that did not belong to you, only to extend your own selfish existence. Thus, it is not only Lodan who betrayed you, Baron Vernest, for you betrayed your lord, yourself, your family, and your people."

The other three men were stunned by Calien's bravado. They gripped their weapons tightly, prepared for whatever would follow.

The blue eyes of Vernest flared, and an angry, painful moan hissed forth.

"Thou dare speak to me with such lies and falsities? Calien, spawn of Anuron, outgrowth of a sickly worm know as Lodan, I strike thee down now!" The giant sword was lifted and brought down in a diagonal slash that would have taken Calien's head off had the prince not ducked in time.

"Spread out! Surround it!" Darin yelled, charging in with his weapon raised, defending the prince. His heavy stroke was parried easily by the dark knight, who then calmly retreated several steps to assess his opponents. The former baron observed Kyligan and Alazar shift around his flanks, surrounding him.

"What dishonorable lackey's have you brought to aid you, descendent of Lodan?" Vernest called, the stale voice ever stoic and unnerving.

"They are men of justice. They have come to help me rid the world of your evil." Calien swept his ornate sword forward in three consecutive attacks, each one blocked successfully by the knight.

The blue luminance within the eyes of the dark champion seemed to alter ever so slightly. "Then they are no more worthy to live than you!" Feigning a swipe at Calien, Vernest abruptly turned to his left, arching his greatsword toward Kyligan. The ranger was momentarily caught off-guard and barely lifted his sword enough to defend the strike. The sharp clang of steel on steel resounded, as Kyligan was knocked several feet backwards into the wall by the sheer force of the abyssal knight's attack. The dark entity pressed forward, swinging again with unhindered ferocity. Kyligan threw his body to the side and let the greatsword smash into the wall, a spray of sparks jumping away from the collision.

A flash of orange-red blurred the scene, followed instantaneously by a ball of fire that slammed against the back of the dark warrior. The impact caused the skeletal figure to tumble forward a step, while flames engulfed it. But to the surprise of the onlookers, the fire quickly extinguished, as if stifled by an invisible blanket. Vernest swung his shoulders to view the architect of the magical attack, tiny pockets of flame still smoldering over the grotesque baron's body. Across the room, Alazar's eyes met the glowing eye-sockets of his foe, sockets that secreted nothing short of wicked fury. "Sorcery!" its hollow voice screamed. "The art of the disgraceful! You shall come to know it well!" Vernest lifted a blackened gauntlet and from his hand a blue ray shot forth into the chest of Alazar. The robed man dropped his staff and fell to his knees, clutching himself tightly with both arms draped across his chest.

"Alazar!" Darin screamed and rushed to his companion.

The robed man had balled himself into the fetal position. With great effort, he lifted his head to the dwarf, his voice was coarse and feeble. "I am fine. His magic has only zapped by strength. I am not wounded, only weakened."

"Can you keep fighting?"

"It will take some time for me to regain my energy."

"There is no time! The fight rages now!" Darin scolded impatiently. Behind him, he could hear the ring of steel.

"Then do not waste it worrying over me," Alazar mumbled before his head dropped to the cold stone.

The flurry of swords had resumed between Calien and the abyssal knight. The duel was a stunning display of swordsmanship, the two blades wheeling through the air in perpetual motion. To the prince's credit, he revealed no panic. Time and again, he snaked forward, throwing calculated attacks and gauging for weaknesses or holes in the seemingly impenetrable defense of the dark knight. Moments later Kyligan joined his comrade, and the two warriors pressed their foe backward. Outnumbered, Vernest gave little impression of concern. With unnatural strength, he kept his greatsword in ceaseless movement, sweeping it back and forth to ward off incoming attacks.

Then, the abyssal knight seized an opportunity. Kyligan had made a clumsy stab attempt that brought him too near his enemy. In one continuous motion, Vernest knocked the ranger's sword away and offered him a backhanded fist with his heavy gauntlet across Kyligan's face. The blow was fierce and the ranger's head snapped to the side, his body reeling away and collapsing while blood spilled from a deep gash in his face and a busted nose.

A moment before, Darin had left the side of Alazar and returned to the fight just soon enough to witness Kyligan's body go flailing across the floor. Lifting his waraxe overhead, he rushed Vernest's flank, hoping the undead warrior was too focused on Calien to see him coming.

With quickness uncanny for a body that had been dead for almost two-hundred years, Vernest side-stepped the axe and slashed his blade across the dwarf's back, tearing armor and skin. Darin cried out, forcing Calien to pause momentarily to view the wound of his friend. The hesitation cost him. Vernest had already whirled his greatsword back around, aiming for the prince's throat. Calien could only shift his upper body enough to prevent his neck from being sliced cleanly in two. Instead, the large weapon bit into his left shoulder. The prince immediately felt the warm flow of his own blood spilling freely beneath his platemail. The sting of the wound caused him to buckle and fall to the ground.

The abyssal knight gazed at the four writhing bodies upon the cold stone floor, its impassive features concealing the satisfaction it felt within. For years, the only emotion the former baron had experienced was a burning anger; an anger that had consumed him to the point of madness. But this new feeling, this grim delight in manhandling its self-proclaimed betrayers, was different – and more than welcome. It basked in the sensation, allowing it to imbue every fiber of its being. After decades of idleness, the undead figure was recharged with a sense of eager urgency; the kind of urgency bent on destroying the blasphemers without mercy.

"We cannot defeat it. It is too powerful." Darin muttered the words, trying to stand. The dwarf's back had been laid open, but somehow no vitals were harmed. His thick spine had remained intact despite the fact that at two-foot long gash was laid horizontally across his back. The injury was painful, but not so much that the dwarf couldn't function. With a deep-throated grunt he pushed himself onto his legs and gripped his waraxe.

"If we die, may it be in defiance!" Calien answered, intrepidly. His own resolve was clearly diluted after witnessing the prowess of the dark champion, but he was the kind of man who knew nothing of the word submission. Lifting himself next to the dwarf, he ignored the wounds already acquired from the battle and viewed the scene. Alazar was laying motionless on the far side of the room and Calien was uncertain if the man was alive or dead. Behind the prince was Kyligan. Contrary to Alazar, the ranger was most certainly alive. He even looked tolerable, if one ignored the puddle of blood that had amassed on the ground where his head had landed moments earlier. The left side of his face was crimson from the blow he suffered, but the ranger had somehow forced himself to his feet and was scanning the stone floor for his sword.

Calien could give no more attention to his surroundings. The monstrosity that was once Baron Vernest resumed its affront. The prince lifted his sword and managed to deflect a roundhouse swipe, but his shoulder, still bleeding, protested the aggressive movements with a steady aching.

Knowing he couldn't match the baron skill for skill, Darin lifted his new shield and ran full brunt into the dark warrior. Vernest slammed his greatsword into the steel barrier moments before getting bowled over by the dwarf. The two combatants tumbled sideways upon the floor and jockeyed for a prevailing position atop the other. More often than not, a dwarf, with its short stocky frame, would triumph in such contests of physical prowess, but the abyssal knight was shockingly overpowering. Soon, Darin was pinned to the ground, his arms trapped under the shield that separated the two. He could feel his waraxe wedged behind his back, with no way for him to apply it. He suddenly realized he was at his foe's mercy. He watched with disdain as a black gauntleted hand reached down and grabbed a handful of his thick beard, lifting his large head off the floor. With a violent thrust, his head was forced back down and the last thing the dwarf heard was a loud *crack* before he lost consciousness.

The abyssal knight had no time to revel in its minor victory, as Prince Calien was upon him. With its other hand still gripping the greatsword, the undead monster flung the blade upward and deflected an attack from the prince that surely would have carved off an arm. In one motion, the former baron rolled away from the unmoving dwarf and regained his feet, eyeing Calien with piercing blue sockets.

"End this madness, Vernest!" Calien shouted. His voice had altered, no longer sounding like a young man full of naïveté, but like a wise king for which he would become someday; or so he hoped. "What benefit is gained from our deaths?"

"Your deaths are all the reward I need," the mechanical speech of the abyssal knight answered, obvious disdain soaking each word. "Your line betrayed me, and your people, as well."

The prince circled his opponent, sword at the ready. "Indeed, they did betray you. But have you not done the same thing? Your evil has already spread and destroyed a village. What is next?"

The undead baron did not respond with words, but with a shrill ear-piercing scream as he plunged his sword ahead. Again, the two blades clashed, casting glorious sparks from the deadly embrace of steel.

Near the fighters, Kyligan had retrieved his sword. The ranger was light-headed and woozy. He had difficulty seeing out of his left eye, as blood from both his wounds, his nose and cheek, had gummed within it and blurred his vision. Pausing a moment to regain his bearings, he observed the duel between the prince and the dark knight, admiring the sheer skill of the two combatants. Their arms and legs moved in synchronization, each move countering the other's death stroke. It was like some kind of macabre dance. Then from the corner of his eye, the ranger caught sight of Darin, a score of feet away, laying on the ground. He hurried to the dwarf's side and hastily examined him. He was alive, thankfully, though he had been knocked out quite forcefully, as evident by the swelling on the back of his head.

I can tend to him later, Kyligan decided. Shaking the fuzziness from his mind, he gripped the pommel of his sword and rushed over to aid Calien in the battle.

The prince saw Kyligan coming and called to him. "Stay on his flank and keep your distance. Let him come to you."

The duel evolved from a duo to a trio. A minute later Calien scored his first victory. As the abyssal knight swiped its greatsword at Kyligan, Calien was able to sneak his blade under the dark warrior's guard. The sword struck the hip of Vernest, tearing dead gray skin and cracking bone.

The former baron seethed in a combination of anger and pain before flailing its weapon in a figure-eight pattern toward Calien, intending to butcher the prince a thousand times over. There was a noticeable limp in its movement, though the grievance did little to hinder the effectiveness of the monster's savage barrage. Calien ducked and backed away, trying to put space between himself and his attacker, but Vernest moved rapidly and forced the prince against the wall.

The abyssal knight suddenly arched its back and howled in agony,

Kyligan's sword lodged deep in its back. The monster whirled around so quickly that Kyligan let slip his sword, the blade remaining fixed in place within the dark champion. Weaponless, Kyligan froze before the enraged knight. Vernest slashed his greatsword horizontally and the ranger ducked just in time to keep his head upon his shoulders, but not quick enough to prevent a powerful hand from gripping his neck and slinging him like a doll across the room. Kyligan bounded and rolled across the stone before smashing into a corner table and then the wall, his body laying in a tangled heap.

Laying alone on the far side of the room next to a large blue-glowing object, Alazar watched as the ranger plummeted through the thin legs of the table before knocking his body on the unforgiving stone wall. The robed man shook his head. His strength was returning, slowly. He sat up, gingerly moving his arms and fingers. He was familiar with the spell the abyssal knight had cast on him. A simple enfeeblement spell, an enchantment that most young mages learned early in their arcane career. It was not a powerful enchantment, but it had certainly been effective in keeping Alazar out of the battle. He looked at his hands and clenched his fists as tight as he could. Did he have the strength to throw a spell at the dark warrior? He had tried it earlier, with little success. *Perhaps Baron Vernest is immune to my magical attacks?* he mused. Turning his head, he noticed his staff resting near him. Another grim thought crossed his mind. Surely, he shouldn't confront the beast in melee! His meager skills with a staff would be easy pray for such a master of the sword.

Something moved inside Alazar's robes. Reaching inside, he pulled out a flaccid Disfrazal. For a moment, he thought the chameleon was dead, but then he realized that it had merely been affected by the same enfeeblement spell, as he had. The lizard looked up at his master with faint, weakened eyes, as if asking; *Why have you allowed this to happen to me?* The robed man brought Disfrazal up and kissed him on the back of the head, then returned the limp reptile to the comfort of his robes. With a look of sturdy determination, Alazar grasped his staff and rose off the ground. At first, his legs felt shaky and anemic beneath him, but only a few seconds passed before he grew more comfortable putting his full weight upon them. With an additional deep breath, meant only to bestow himself resolve, Alazar stepped toward the conflict.

Prince Calien was displaying a new wound. Kyligan's sword still wedged firmly in his back, Vernest had found a breach in the underside of Calien's belly and his sword had snuck under the thick platemail of the prince, piercing his abdomen. Calien pulled away before Vernest could run him completely through, but the blow had further zapped Calien's health and his gritty doggedness. He was now fully on the defensive, using every maneuver in his repertoire to merely stay alive.

The blue orbs in Vernest's sockets blazed with fury, each stroke of the large weapon seemingly harder than the last. Calien was tiring and he realized that soon his defenses would no longer hold up to the savage onslaught of the dark champion. It was then, from the corner of his eye, he caught a glimpse of Alazar nearing them, staff in hand. He knew that if Vernest also saw the robed man, Alazar's help would make little difference in the fight, so the prince quickly spun opposite the direction of his companion, turning the abyssal knight's back to the new threat.

Alazar stepped forward, seeing only the backside of the baron and the sword of Kyligan stuck within. Vernest was unaware of his presence. Alazar reared back his staff, took a running start and slammed the pole with every once of his strength into the crown of the dark knight's head.

Calien had just blocked a dangerous thrust when, suddenly, the abyssal knight's head rocked violently. The azure glow in the monster's eyes blinked out for a moment and then it abruptly dropped its weapon. Both hands grabbed its head as if attempting to hold its wavering skull firmly upon its shoulders.

Calien's opportunity had come.

With both hands squeezing his ornate sword, Calien swung with all his might. The blade sliced cleanly through the abyssal knight's wrists and neck. The ghastly skull bounced to the floor, the blue glimmer gone from its eyes. Then, the rest of the body collapsed before the prince.

For several seconds, there was nothing but silence. Alazar and Calien stared motionless at the lifeless form of the dark knight.

"Remarkable," Alazar finally said, breaking the eerie silence.

Calien had no reply until he noticed that the strange mechanism in one corner of the room was still emitting its blue light. Then, there was movement at the prince's feet. He looked down and his eyes grew wide. "What?" he screamed, horrified.

The head was inching its way back to the body, as were the hands. "It is reassembling!" Alazar shouted.

"How can we stop it?" A panicked Calien had backed away, his sword held up.

Alazar gazed about the room, his eyes finally locking on the blue glowing apparatus. He ran to it. The device was covered in strange runes and gems that the robed sage had never seen before. Behind it, against the wall, there was a strange two-foot wide swirling mist. Beyond the mist, Alazar could see visions of another world. He gazed at black mountains, seas of red and strange horned creatures that could only be demonic in nature. "I believe this apparatus has linked Baron Vernest to the abyss! Perhaps this is what has tainted the tower and the village of Oester?"

"What should we do?" Calien answered, watching the hands of the dark knight reconnect to its severed wrists. The head would soon follow.

"Help me destroy this thing!" Alazar shouted back. He began smashing the mechanism with his staff.

Calien ran to his side and joined in, hammering his sword into the peculiar metal of the device. The apparatus was not as sturdy as either man had guessed. As it fell to pieces, there was a great flash of blue-white light.

When both men opened their eyes, only darkness remained.

Feeling his way to the doorway, Calien retrieved a torch and lit the end, holding it up to view the room. The device had been smashed into a hundred pieces and there was no swirling mist to another world. Even the air in the room was different, as if some great poison had been cleaned away.

"Baron Vernest," Alazar said, pointing to a spot on the floor.

Calien looked, but the abyssal knight had disappeared. Utterly. Nothing remained from the former baron, save for one object, laying innocently on the ground and looking as if it had been sitting there for years.

The baron's sword.

XXIII

A beautiful pastel pink had covered the early morning sky. Thin, delicate clouds gave the impression of gentle strokes of fine art adorning the sparkling horizon, an effect that soothed the seven people standing amidst the deserted village of Oester.

It was the second morning since the party's incursion into the old tower. Each member still showed the effects, physical or otherwise, of the dark encounter. Yet, remarkably, every one of them escaped with their lives, and the previous day had been spent in serene tranquility, tending any wounds that needed attention. Cadwan's foot received the most treatment. Even now, he could put no weight upon it, but there was newfound hope that the appendage could be saved after Darin and Kyligan were successful in keeping the infection down after they departed the tower. Other wounds were also cared for and bandaged, though they were less serious than the fighters. Darin had a painful gash across his back, a massive bump on his head and a pounding headache. Kyligan and Calien sported injuries that would heal fully in time.

Holding Kyligan's hand and gazing at the sky was Odna. The ranger had never been tackled harder than when he returned to the temple. The girl nearly bowled him over in her joy and relief of his return.

Taking in a fresh morning breath, Kyligan looked at the child. His face was bandaged, but he didn't seem to care, as he smiled down at her. The seven-year old smiled back and squeezed his hand, warmly.

The mass bodies of the dead were still strewn about the village in a grotesque matter, but no longer were they tormented with unlife. For the first time during the past two nights, all was calm as the bodies remained still on the earth. Even the atmosphere of the village had changed, as if an evil cloud had been lifted from the place and freed. Unfortunately, Kyligan mused, it was too late for the villagers. But perhaps someday the village could be resettled, as it had once before.

"Well, it will be a long walk back to Mullikin to purchase horses." Darin muttered, breaking everyone's silent revere. "Especially with you," the dwarf gestured at Cadwan, "leaning on me the entire way."

Cadwan grinned and slapped his friend heartily on the back. In his hands was Alazar's quarterstaff, for which the robed man grudgingly lended to the soldier on the strict condition it would be returned as soon as another suitable walking stick was found along the way. "I suppose we can always hope to hitch a ride from travelers." His mind suddenly drew back to the strange barbarian woman that had helped them in the Barren Hills. *Would they ever see her again?*

Prince Calien stepped near the two men, a proud expression draped over his features. "You will deem the walk well worth the time after you receive your due rewards when we reach Calas."

"I suppose. Your father *will* pay up, yes?" Alazar, ever the skeptic, asked. Standing atop his master's head, Disfrazal flicked his tongue, emphasizing the man's concern.

"Trust me, friends, after I explain what occurred the old man will be more than happy to reward all of you. He will be happy enough just to see my safe return."

Darin peered at the prince. The adventure had changed him significantly. His innocent eyes were gone forever, replaced with a visage of a man who had seen the worst that evil had to offer. He had proved himself in both combat and in his tenacity. Darin wondered if the party's association with the prince would come to an end when they returned to Calas. Another look at Calien assured the dwarf that it wouldn't. The prince looked at the others as true friends and companions, and the party did the same.

After several more quiet moments, Cadwan turned back to Darin, his voice soft. "Frundin?"

A desolate sigh emitted from the dwarf. "I am incomplete without my lord and I must dedicate my life to reuniting with him. If," he paused, "it can be done at all."

"You will have my help, old friend," Cadwan stated, plainly.

"You will have help from all of us." Kyligan added, knowing he wouldn't be alive without the separation between Darin and Frundin. Similar grunts of affirmation came from the other members of the company, even Prince Calien, and Darin felt a warmth inside that almost made him smile – almost.

Darin reached behind and fingered the greatsword slung over his back, the only physical reminder of their battle with Baron Vernest. The blade had peculiar magical properties, though none of the party could decipher what they were. Darin had decided to bring it along and have it examined by one of the smiths or wisemen in Calas.

In a moment of playfulness, Cora poked the back of Kyligan. "Kyl, what of the girl? Are you keeping her?"

The ranger looked down at the girl again. Truthfully, he didn't know. "I guess I will see what happens when we reach Calas."

"Well then, off to Mullikin?" Darin announced.

Yes, thought Kyligan, off to Mullikin. *There is someone I would like to see at the Iron Hill.*

EPILOGUE

"Your brother and his companions are regarded as heroes."

Prince Hetnar flinched, as if the comment were a knife that jabbed his side. "I am aware of this, Geran."

Prince Calien, along with Cadwan's party had arrived at the palace early in the morning. Now, barely past noon of the same day, the tales of their heroics, whether accurate or not, were spreading like wildfire throughout the homes of the nobles and onto the streets.

"Your assassins failed," Geran stated.

"Damn you, Geran!" Hetnar spat, holding himself back from strangling the older man. "Have you come only to harass me?"

The two men were standing inside Hetnar's private chamber, a well garlanded room that was distinctive because of the sheer amount of womanly murals hanging upon the walls. After the revelry created by Calien's victorious return, Hetnar, petulant for having to feign happiness all morning, had retreated to his quarters. Geran had shown up soon afterwards, uninvited.

"Fear not, my young prince, not all is lost." The king's advisor circled around the prince and over to a small display. With long, thin fingers, he lifted a small figurine depicting an attractive, scarcely-clad woman with ample bosoms. The wiseman involuntarily rotated the object in his hand, his mind on other matters. "It appears that our king-to-be is unaware of your plot to kill him."

"*Your* plot, Geran," Hetnar corrected, irritably. "I merely carried it out."

Geran shrugged nonchalantly, as he replaced the figurine in the exact position it had rested before. "Nevertheless, we are fortunate he knows nothing. Of course, we must eliminate any loose ends to keep it that way."

That much Hetnar agreed with. The orc tribe from the Barren Hills gave him little worries. Reasons were never truly required to hunt down orcs and no provocation would be needed to hire huntsmen, soldiers of fortune, or even the Calas army to slaughter the filthy beasts that held the prince's secret.

But then there was Ayna, the female assassin. No doubt she would prove far more difficult. First off, she would have to be located. The woman could literally be anywhere. Killing her would prove hardest of all. She was a cunning and ruthless mercenary, and Hetnar would need the proper *assistance* to finish her off, if it could be done at all. *What have I gotten myself into?* the prince wondered, regretfully.

"After that, is this farce over?" Hetnar asked.

"Over?" Geran threw back his head and laughed. "You speak as if you no longer wish to be king."

Hetnar raised an eyebrow. "And after this, why would I wish to be king? I am lucky not to be hanging from a rope!"

"Dear prince, why would you not?" Geran's voice was enticing, seductive. "Princes are forgotten, but *kings* are legends. You have the mettle to become a ruler. Even you cannot deny this." The older man paused to shake his head. "I wish nothing more than to one day serve you."

The prince peered into the deep eyes of the king's advisor. With a scowl, he remarked, "You are shrewd, Geran. I have a feeling my ascension to the throne would be more to your liking than mine."

Geran creased his brow. "I would like your ascension very much, Hetnar, but only because it would benefit Calas."

Hetnar scoffed. "And I am guessing you already have a new scheme to rid us of my beloved brother?"

The advisor stepped to a padded chair and slowly sat, a smirk crossing his lips. "Let Calien enjoy his little celebration, for such revelry must ultimately come to an end."

about the author

William A. Kooiker lives in central Virginia with his wife and daughter. *Tower of Ruin* is his second published work. Visit him at: http://www.williamkooiker.com

Printed in the United States
66748LVS00001B/166-195